PENGUIN BOOKS

Clive Cussler's
Fire Strike

Clive Cussler was the author and co-author of a great number of international bestsellers. His series include the famous Dirk Pitt® adventures, such as *The Devil's Sea*; the NUMA® Files adventures, most recently *Dark Vector*; the *Oregon* Files, such as *Hellburner*; the Isaac Bell historical thrillers, which began with *The Chase*; and the recent Fargo Adventures, which lastly included *Wrath of Poseidon*. Cussler passed away in 2020.

Mike Maden is the author of *Clive Cussler's Hellburner*, the critically acclaimed Drone series, and four novels in Tom Clancy's #1 *New York Times* bestselling Jack Ryan Jr series. He holds both a master's and PhD in political science from the University of California at Davis, specializing in international relations and comparative politics. He has lectured and consulted on the topics of war and the Middle East, among others. Maden has served as a political consultant and campaign manager in state and national elections, and hosted his own local weekly radio show.

TITLES BY CLIVE CUSSLER

DIRK PITT ADVENTURES®

Clive Cussler's The Devil's Sea
  (by Dirk Cussler)
Celtic Empire (with Dirk Cussler)
Odessa Sea (with Dirk Cussler)
Havana Storm (with Dirk Cussler)
Poseidon's Arrow (with Dirk Cussler)
Crescent Dawn (with Dirk Cussler)
Arctic Drift (with Dirk Cussler)
Treasure of Khan (with Dirk Cussler)
Black Wind (with Dirk Cussler)
Trojan Odyssey
Valhalla Rising
Atlantis Found
Flood Tide
Shock Wave
Inca Gold
Sahara
Dragon
Treasure
Cyclops
Deep Six
Pacific Vortex!
Night Probe!
Vixen 03
Raise the Titanic!
Iceberg
The Mediterranean Caper

SAM AND REMI FARGO ADVENTURES®

The Wrath of Poseidon
  (with Robin Burcell)
The Oracle (with Robin Burcell)
The Gray Ghost (with Robin Burcell)
The Romanov Ransom
  (with Robin Burcell)
Pirate (with Robin Burcell)
The Solomon Curse (with Russell Blake)
The Eye of Heaven (with Russell Blake)
The Mayan Secrets (with Thomas Perry)
The Tombs (with Thomas Perry)
The Kingdom (with Grant Blackwood)
Lost Empire (with Grant Blackwood)
Spartan Gold (with Grant Blackwood)

ISAAC BELL ADVENTURES®

Clive Cussler's The Sea Wolves
  (by Jack Du Brul)
The Saboteurs (with Jack Du Brul)
The Titanic Secret (with Jack Du Brul)
The Cutthroat (with Justin Scott)
The Gangster (with Justin Scott)
The Assassin (with Justin Scott)
The Bootlegger (with Justin Scott)
The Striker (with Justin Scott)
The Thief (with Justin Scott)
The Race (with Justin Scott)
The Spy (with Justin Scott)
The Wrecker (with Justin Scott)
The Chase

Clive Cussler's
Fire Strike

MIKE MADEN

PENGUIN BOOKS

PENGUIN BOOKS

UK | USA | Canada | Ireland | Australia
India | New Zealand | South Africa

Penguin Books is part of the Penguin Random House group of companies
whose addresses can be found at global.penguinrandomhouse.com

First published in the United States of America by G. P. Putnam's Sons,
an imprint of Penguin Random House LLC 2023
First published in Great Britain by Penguin Michael Joseph 2023
Published in Penguin Books 2024

001

Set in 12.5/14.75pt Garamond MT Std
Typeset by Jouve (UK), Milton Keynes
Printed and bound in Great Britain by Clays Ltd, Elcograf S.p.A.

The authorized representative in the EEA is Penguin Random House Ireland,
Morrison Chambers, 32 Nassau Street, Dublin D02 YH68

A CIP catalogue record for this book is available from the British Library

ISBN: 978-1-405-95878-3

www.greenpenguin.co.uk

Cast of Characters

The Corporation

Juan Cabrillo Chairman of the Corporation and captain of the *Oregon*.

Max Hanley President of the Corporation, Juan's second-in-command, and the *Oregon*'s chief engineer. US Navy and Vietnam swift boat veteran.

Linda Ross Vice President, Operations. Retired US Navy intelligence officer.

Eddie Seng Director, Shore Operations. Former CIA agent.

Franklin 'Linc' Lincoln Operations. Former US Navy SEAL sniper.

Marion MacDougal 'MacD' Lawless Operations. Former US Army Ranger.

Raven Malloy Operations. Former US Army Military Police investigator.

Eric Stone Chief helmsman on the *Oregon*. Former US Navy officer, weapons research and development.

Dr Mark 'Murph' Murphy Chief weapons officer on the *Oregon*. Former civilian weapons designer.

Russ Kefauver Intelligence analyst. Former CIA forensic accountant.

Dr Eric Littleton Director of the *Oregon*'s biophysical laboratory.

Mike Lavin Chief armorer on the *Oregon*. Retired US Army armament/fire control maintenance supervisor.

Bill McDonald Senior armorer on the *Oregon*. Former CIA paramilitary operator.

George 'Gomez' Adams Helicopter pilot and chief aerial drone operator on the *Oregon*. US Army veteran.

Hali Kasim Chief communications officer on the *Oregon*.

Dr Julia Huxley Chief medical officer on the *Oregon*. US Navy veteran.

Amy Forrester Physician's assistant on the *Oregon*. Former Navy combat medic.

Kevin Nixon Chief of the *Oregon*'s Magic Shop.

Maurice Chief steward on the *Oregon*. British Royal Navy veteran.

United States Government

Langston Overholt IV The Corporation's CIA liaison.

Captain Kim Dudash Commanding officer, USS *Gerald R. Ford* (CVN 78).

Robin Stansberry US senator.

Saudi Arabia

Abdullah bin Abdulaziz Crown Prince.

Muqrin bin Khalid Deputy crown prince and Royal Saudi Air Force colonel.

Khalid bin Salman Former deputy crown prince and former head of the General Intelligence Presidency (GIP).

Israel

Sarai Massala Former Mossad agent.
Asher Massala/Duke Matasi Sarai Massala's brother.
Shlomo Gottlieb Shin Bet senior executive.

Surchev (Private Military Company)

Jean-Paul Salan President of SurChev and former French 1st Marine Infantry Parachute Regiment captain.
Moulin Salan's number two and old comrade from the French Marine paratroopers.
Sergeant Angus Fellowes Salan's training supervisor and former British Special Air Service sergeant.
Risto Macedonian SurChev operative deployed to Dr Hightower.
Mat Malaysian SurChev operative deployed to Dr Hightower.
Samson Nigerian SurChev operative deployed to Dr Hightower.

The Hightower Organization (HH+)

Dr Heather Hightower CEO and founder of HH+.
Dr Jing Yanwen Amazon collection team member.
Dr Brigit Schweers Amazon collection team member.
Karl Krasner Hightower's security chief, former Stasi officer.

'History began when humans invented gods, and will end when humans become gods.'

— Yuval Noah Harari

Prologue

Borneo, 1963

A drenching rain in the moonless night was perfect cover for the three Special Boat Section operatives.

The 'wet cousins' of the better-known Special Air Service, the SBS was a commando unit of the Royal Marines specializing in coastal insertions – hence the mission tonight running a Zodiac deep upriver.

A stubborn British national named Rawlinson desperately needed an emergency exfil from his family's rubber plantation. The communist Indonesian insurgents raiding across the region were hell-bent on killing all foreigners and seizing their properties. A Dutch family just eight kilometers away had been decimated by the bandy-legged Marxists the night before and Rawlinson and his wife suddenly realized they were next on their list.

Private Desmond 'Wraith' Vickers killed the Zodiac's big outboard Evinrude and the three men paddled the last five hundred meters in practiced synchronicity. They were grateful for the splattering downpour that soaked their kits but silenced their efforts. All three men scanned the dim shoreline for any sign of movement – of rebels, certainly, but also for Bornean crocodiles, thick as flies in this part of the country. So far, lady luck had paddled along with them.

The lieutenant gestured with his free hand and the men angled the rubber-hulled boat toward the shore. They slipped noiselessly out of the Zodiac and dragged it into the cover of thick brush. Each man unslung their 'Silent Sten' submachine guns and checked their mags by feel. Vickers slipped his hand to his hip and patted the holster of his .38 Webley revolver, then he snaked his fingers down his thigh to the hilt of his razor-sharp Fairbairn-Sykes dagger in its well-oiled leather scabbard.

Good to go.

The lieutenant nodded in the direction of the plantation. Vickers, just eighteen years old and the youngest operator in the entire squadron, took the point, threading his way through the leaves and brush beneath the orderly rows of rubber trees. On base he carried himself with the self-possessed dignity of a landed earl, but in the field he moved with the preternatural grace and cunning of a jungle cat. His inaudible movements and sudden appearances had earned him the moniker 'Wraith.'

Vickers halted at the edge of the clearing that led to the darkened plantation house looming in the distance and scanned the perimeter yet again. The lights were off as per the lieutenant's instructions. So far, so good.

Confident that the way was clear, Vickers dashed for the house in a crouching run, his Sten up and his finger on the trigger guard. He silently prayed that Rawlinson remembered the lieutenant's order not to fire on them as they approached the house. A nervous British civilian armed with a loaded Lee-Enfield No. 1 could prove as lethal as any Indonesian killer.

Vickers leaped onto the porch with quiet ease and gazed into the front window. The rain hammered the sheet metal roofing like a mad drummer. He saw no signs of movement inside as the lieutenant and Corporal Sterling, a hulking Scotsman, thundered up next to him.

Vickers shook his head.

The lieutenant's eyes swept the shadowy perimeter once again before he crossed over to the front door and kicked it open with his muddy boot.

Vickers charged in first, gun up, with Sterling – his closest friend – hard on his heels, and the lieutenant right behind them.

'Rawlinson!' the lieutenant called out. 'It's the Queen's own come to get you out of here!'

Nothing.

'Sterling, head upstairs. Wraith, check the back.'

The two men sped away as the lieutenant pushed open the basement door. He pulled the light chain and called out again. 'Rawlinson! Don't shoot. We're here to get you out. Are you there?' He jogged down the wooden staircase and scanned the dank room. All he found were undisturbed storage shelves laden with canned goods and household sundries.

The lieutenant climbed back upstairs into the kitchen. Vickers and Sterling shook their heads.

Nothing.

'Rawlinson may have already bugged out without telling us,' the lieutenant said. 'But we can't take any chances he's still on the property. Sterling, check the storage shed out back. Wraith, head over to the machine shop. I'll sweep the perimeter. We'll meet back at the drop-off point in fifteen minutes, no exceptions. And give it some rice. Understood?'

Heads nodded. Sterling added, 'Sure, boss.'

The suffocating heat came on as suddenly as the pounding rain had stopped and raised a shroud of fog from the waterlogged ground.

The lieutenant's eyes strained in the dark as he crouched at the drop-off point near the boat. No sign of his two men. He checked his watch. Where were they?

'Boss.'

The lieutenant flinched, startled by Vickers's sudden appearance behind him, seemingly out of nowhere. The boy really was a ghost.

'Any sign of the Rawlinsons?' the lieutenant asked, his whisper masked by the din of chirring insects and croaking frogs.

'Behind the machine shop. Throats slashed ear to ear.'

'Dear God. And Sterling?'

Both men heard the crash of leaves ahead of them, but didn't see the –

Thump!

A Chinese-made 'potato masher' hand grenade splattered in the mud at their feet.

Wraith shoved the lieutenant aside and threw himself on the explosive.

'Vickers!' The lieutenant reached down to grab him, but a bullet plowed through his skull.

His corpse thudded into the mud next to Vickers.

'Boss!'

Vickers crawled to his knees and scrambled over to the

4

lieutenant's corpse. The Chinese grenade was a dud, but the bullets zipping overhead were very much alive and threatened to cut him down, too. No matter.

Vickers slipped away as the Indonesians advanced through the rows of rubber trees. The air echoed with the ripsaw staccato of their automatic-rifle fire as rounds splintered the bark and branches.

Vickers raced perpendicular to their advance, silent as a shadow, then turned north.

Emboldened by the lack of British resistance, the Indonesians shouted and laughed as they emptied their magazines into the bush where the lieutenant had fallen. Moments later, they stood over the commando's shattered corpse.

They had no idea that Wraith had completely flanked them from behind.

Vickers fired his silenced machine gun at the shadowy figures. His bullets found their marks as he emptied the thirty-round mag, stitching across the backs of the Indonesians from left to right, felling them like bowling pins into the mud. Two were left.

Vickers reloaded and angled his gun at the last two rebels ducking behind a tree – one a head taller than the other – and suddenly froze.

Sterling!

Vickers could now see the tall Scotsman was gagged and his arms bound behind his back, pushed along by the shorter communist, who held a pistol to the base of Sterling's spine. The smaller Indonesian hid behind the big Scot, using him as a human shield as he maneuvered between the trees.

Bastard.

Vickers circled through the trees, using the trunks for cover as he closed the distance between them, trying to flank him yet again.

Panicked, the Indonesian spun in circles, keeping Sterling close in front of him, one hand around the Scotsman's neck, uncertain where the next gunshot would come from.

Vickers rested the barrel of his Sten on the side of a tree for stability and sighted his weapon at the spinning figures, waiting for the chance –

Pop!

A single 9mm bullet tore into the Indonesian's chest and dropped him to the ground.

Vickers raced out from behind the tree and straight for Sterling.

His mouth still gagged and his hands still bound, Sterling saw Vickers emerge from the trees and shouted a muffled scream.

And then he turned, and ran.

'Sterling! It's me!'

The Scotsman took three long strides before the British L2 grenade – tied around the back of his neck – exploded.

The Indonesian had booby-trapped him. By looping his finger through the grenade pin, the Indonesian's corpse pulled it when he fell away, just as he had planned.

Vickers stopped dead in his tracks, the air ringing with the rising cacophony of insects and the distant, angry shouts of more rebels in the forest beyond.

What had he done?

*

With the bodies of Sterling and the lieutenant safely secured in the Zodiac, Vickers gunned the throttle, not caring about the roar of the big Evinrude motor nor the splash of bullets geysering the water around him. The boat rose high out of the water as it rocketed away, his tear-streaked face cooled by the warm air beating against it.

Her Majesty's Naval Base, Singapore
Two weeks later

Admiral Bromley glanced up from the file folder on his burnished teakwood desk and crushed out his cigarette in a silver art nouveau ashtray.

Vickers sat upright in his crisply ironed Royal Marine uniform, its creases sharp enough to shave with. His shoes were polished to a gleaming mirrored gloss in stark contrast to the blank expression on his handsome face.

'I refuse to sign this,' Bromley said, stabbing a letter in the file. 'You're one of our finest soldiers and a tremendous asset in Her Majesty's service. We can't afford to lose you.'

'I believe I've made my reasons clear, sir.'

'Nonsense. The board of inquiry found you completely innocent of any wrongdoing whatsoever. No one holds you accountable in the least – except yourself.'

'My best friend is dead because of my actions.'

'Your best friend is dead because a fiendish communist cutthroat killed him. I urge you to see things as they truly are.'

'I've tried, sir.'

'Tell me, Vickers. Do you like military service?'

'All I ever wanted to do since I was a young schoolboy was to serve my country. The day I earned the Bootneck green beret was the greatest day of my life.'

'Your uncle, Sir Edmund Vickers-Hart, was the finest officer I ever had the privilege to serve with. Judging by your exemplary service record, it's clear you and he were cut from the same jib.'

'I take that as the highest compliment, sir, though I doubt I deserve it.'

'Would you consider a transfer away from your beloved Bootnecks and into the Royal Navy?'

Vickers frowned. 'I could never allow myself to be put in a position where I might risk the lives of my comrades ever again.'

'I quite understand.' The admiral held up his pack of cigarettes. 'Care for one?'

'No, thank you, sir.'

'Good for you. Filthy habit.'

The admiral lifted a silver Dunhill lighter and lit another cigarette. He blew a cloud of blue smoke as he studied Vickers's file again.

'I noticed here a number of letters of support from your commanding officers and enlisted comrades.' He held one up for closer inspection. 'This one says you are "well liked, and highly commended for his manners, deportment, and diction."'

'A reflection of my Eton education, I'm afraid.'

'It also seems as if you have quite a flair for the finer

8

things in life.' Bromley held up another letter. '"Something of an amateur sommelier," this officer states.'

'One of the many privileges of my upbringing as the son of a landed viscount.'

'Frankly, I could use someone like you on my personal staff.'

The admiral came out from behind his desk.

'Sir?'

'It's a position as far away from close-quarters combat as I can imagine. But it is honorable service in Her Majesty's Navy. It's a position that requires discretion, tact, and taste. I think you'd be perfect for it. Shall I tell you about it?'

'Please do.'

Vickers's eyes narrowed as he listened to the job description. It only took him a moment to decide.

'Honorable service, indeed, sir. I had never considered it before.'

'I only foresee one difficulty.'

'Sir?'

'You served with one of the finest commando units in the service, and participated in several top secret missions. Missions that were, shall we say, off the books?'

'Yes, sir.'

'Well, when you transfer to another branch, so will your records, and we can't have unauthorized eyes raking over them. To avoid that, we'll have to seal your records permanently so that no one may know of your service with the SBS. In fact, we'll have to terminate the service of Private Desmond Vickers. He'll disappear to "parts unknown," so long as you're in uniform. After you retire, you may resurrect him if you wish.'

'I understand.'

'That means, of course, we'll have to create an entirely new service record for you. A new name, background, everything. How do you feel about all of that?'

'If it gives me the freedom to serve Queen and country, I'm all for it.'

'Excellent. I'll have my adjutant make the necessary arrangements. In the meantime, take a few days off and enjoy Singapore. It's a truly marvelous city.'

Vickers stood, a smile creasing his face for the first time in weeks.

'Thank you, sir.'

The admiral extended his hand. Vickers shook it.

'I look forward to our relationship, Vickers – Oh, say. While you're gallivanting about for the next few days, you will need to conjure up a new name for yourself. A nom de plume, as it were. Something quite the opposite of your given name.'

Vickers frowned, his mind racing for an answer.

'I believe I have it.'

The admiral beamed. 'Excellent. Tell me, then, with whom shall I be working?'

'Last name "Chavasse," after an uncle on my mother's side. Killed at El Alamein.'

'My condolences. Excellent choice.'

'For a middle name I'll go with "Morley" for a cousin I lost in Korea.'

'We lost too many good men in those godforsaken hills. And the first?'

Vickers smiled. 'My father's manservant was buried in our family plot last year. I admired him greatly. Terribly wounded at the Battle of the Somme in 1916. He was awarded a Croix de Guerre with an *étoile d'argent* for valorous service.'

'A hero by any measure. His name?'

'Maurice.'

I

Present Day

Gorno-Badakhshan
Autonomous Region, Tajikistan

The vintage Soviet-era snowcat crested the final rise on the steep climb. Its big diesel engine belched a plume of oily smoke as it roared with the effort. It had taken three hours clanking through a narrow pass high in the towering Pamir Mountains through the swirling snow to reach the ancient Tibetan fortress. It loomed above the forested valley floor, perched on the edge of an insurmountable cliff. Its sturdy walls could resist the siege weapons of its day, but the fort's remoteness and sheer inaccessibility had always been its primary defense. All but the most determined visitors were deterred from even venturing here. How the mighty stone edifice had ever been built by ancient hands in this location several hundred years ago remained a mystery.

The snowcat finally ground to a halt just opposite the short drawbridge crossing the abyssal chasm. The cab door opened and a sturdy Chechen in a sheepskin coat and boots leaped out, then opened the rear doors for the seven esteemed guests.

The passengers – six men and one woman – stretched out knotted muscles and aching backs from the long, monotonous ride. They had sat in silence for the entire

13

trip, sizing each other up with sidelong glances in the snowcat's spacious but utilitarian cabin. Outside in the frigid air, their breaths jetted out of their mouths, but the vapors were quickly swept away by the biting wind.

The morbidly obese Venezuelan, Yeferson Osorio, was the head of security for South America's largest drug cartel. His red-rimmed nostrils and eyes suggested he was addicted to his own product. Despite the temperature, he didn't button up his gaudy, full-length ermine coat and his shoulder-length hair danced in the snowy breeze.

Osorio was familiar with the elegant Russian, Yakov Mityaev, and the bespectacled Chinese woman, Wu Shanshan, from the reports he'd read. Like him, they were the functional equivalents of security chiefs for their respective criminal enterprises, heading up organizations with intelligence-gathering assets that equaled or exceeded the capabilities of most nations. Had Osorio known these two world-class dirtbags were attending today's gathering he would have made other arrangements entirely.

The Venezuelan couldn't identify the others, but he assumed they were high-ranking members of their respective security departments as well. The tattoos peeking beyond the collar and sleeves of the Japanese man identified him as a yakuza even without the missing finger. A portly, clean-shaven Indian; a silver-toed, cowboy-booted Mexican; and a Thai highlander wearing a bright yellow ski parka that reached to his knees rounded out the rest of the passengers.

Osorio wondered if there had ever been a gathering of this level of criminal technical talent before. Police organizations around the world would salivate at the opportunity to gather them all up in one fell swoop.

The Chechen called into his walkie-talkie and a moment later the fort's portcullis rose on its chains. He pointed the seven visitors toward the cavernous entrance, where a tall soldier in a civilian snowsuit waited for them, a rifle slung over one shoulder. A third, shorter man stood by his side with a wand to check for weapons and other contraband items.

The seven invited shuffled toward the gate, their apprehension rising with each step. What lay beyond could change their lives forever.

Or end them.

Osorio silently fumed at the importunity of yet another weapons check as he stood inside the airport-styled millimeter wave scanner. He raised his arms above his massive head for the third time that day. These people were taking their security precautions seriously. He'd counted at least fifty armed guards as he made his way through the ancient castle. It would have been impossible to assault the fortress with any hope of success.

The former Cuban intelligence officer monitoring the wave scanner fought back a smile as he examined the digital readout of the rotund gangster. Osorio's thick beard couldn't fully hide the double chin waddling beneath his jawline. At just over six feet tall with a size sixty-four waist, the Venezuelan crime boss was built like an enormous avocado. His designer-label green velvet tracksuit, though quite expensive, only added to the comic effect.

Despite his poor physique and even poorer health, the

crime boss came fully vetted and possessed more than sufficient funds to qualify for today's auction. The unfortunate man had to climb five flights of stairs because the ancient fortress had no elevator. Sweat beaded his forehead. The Cuban was surprised the Venezuelan hadn't dropped dead of a heart attack with the exertion. How they would have ever managed to move his four-hundred-pound carcass from the narrow stairwell without a forklift would have been anyone's guess.

The Cuban signaled for Osorio to quit the booth as he whispered in his comms, 'All clear.' He nodded at the smaller bins on the table. 'Your jewelry and watch will be returned to you after you finish your business with Mr Martin,' he said in Spanish.

Osorio answered him in the same language. 'Make sure they are, *pendejo*.'

The insult wiped the solicitous smile off the Cuban's face. His eyes narrowed as a voice command reverberated in his earpiece. He turned toward the guests.

'*Señora y señores*, we have one last stop. Please follow me.'

Osorio snatched up his ermine coat from the bin on the nearby table and followed the Russian and the Chinese into another room, where a portable retinal scanning station had been installed. The ex-intelligence officer pointed at the seat just vacated by the Indian.

'Ms Wu' – not her real name, of course – 'if you please.'

Wu nodded and took the seat, and the technician gave her instructions. She leaned forward and placed her chin on the machine's chin rest. Moments later, the retina of Wu's right eye had been scanned and her identity validated. Mityaev followed suit, as did Osorio, who grunted with the effort of mounting the small plastic chair and rising from it.

'Time for business.' The smiling Cuban escorted the seven invitees to a final waiting room. It was well appointed with luxurious, locally crafted furniture. Bottles of wine and iced tins of beluga caviar sat on a long table, along with a silver samovar, bottles of water, glasses, eating utensils, and the like.

'Please help yourselves to refreshments. Señor Martin will be with you momentarily.'

The Russian and Chinese helped themselves to cups of steaming hot tea from the samovar while Osorio cracked open a bottle of water. The others picked at the slabs of goat and sheep cheeses, or tore off hunks from the giant wheels of colorful tandoor-baked flatbreads. Nobody wanted their thoughts clouded by alcohol. They all took a seat in comfortable chairs.

They drank in silence as they watched the large LCD television display. On it, a tall, raven-haired woman in baggy gray prison coveralls paced the floor, her thick-soled running shoes squeaking on the worn stones at each turn. Occasionally she would stop and stare up at the high-def CCTV camera recording her every move. One of her sparkling green eyes was blackened above her high cheekbone, and her lower lip slightly swollen. She looked like a runway model who had taken a nasty spill in a bicycle crash. She'd obviously had a rough time of it somewhere along the line.

Osorio recognized the face. He wondered if the others did as well. He hoped not.

Things could go very sideways if they did.

2

A lean, angular man with wide cheekbones and a long face stepped through a doorway. His silver hair was short and precisely combed. He wore a smartly cut Savile Row suit, handcrafted Paolo Scafora leather shoes, and a Jaeger-LeCoultre wristwatch. He looked every inch the well-heeled European corporate executive that he was, of a sort.

'Madam, sirs. Thank you for coming, and thank you for your patience. I know it's been an arduous journey and our security precautions extraordinary. All of that has been for your protection as much as ours.'

The man's English was faultless, but Osorio detected a slight Eastern European accent. Bulgarian, if he wasn't mistaken. He doubted Martin was his real name.

'My family has been in the kidnapping game since before the fall of Constantinople. I will be so bold as to say we not only invented the business model, but have perfected it. Our auctioning service delivers the highest-quality assets in a manner designed to protect each of the participating parties, including ourselves. Tonight is no exception.

'Your respective organizations were contacted because you alone are able to afford the payment we require. As previously communicated to each of you, all bids will be made and paid for in undiluted isotonitazene, known by its street name, ISO.'

Osorio hid his disgust. ISO was nasty stuff. The latest DEA studies concluded that the synthetic opioid was up to one hundred times more powerful than fentanyl. It was so new to the market that drug enforcement laws and agencies were having a hard time even keeping up with it. The highly addictive and lethal concoction was rare and difficult to produce, which made it all the more valuable.

Martin continued. 'As you are well aware, the asset we have up for auction is the senior systems engineer for the American DEA's Intelligence Program. As previously communicated to you, she has the ability to grant you access to all DEA databases and any other police and intelligence organizations they are connected with, including Interpol, the National Counterterrorism Center, and the FSB, to name a few. Undercover operations, their agents, informants, home addresses, bank accounts – the list of actionable intelligence is endless. Consider what value such information would add to the success of your organizations. Equally important, consider the advantages such information would give you over your competitors.'

Martin didn't bother adding the phrase *Including those gathered in this room*, because he didn't need to.

The seven heads nodded. Suddenly their fatigue and irritation disappeared and they sat up in their chairs.

'The added value we've brought to this transaction is our own impeccable service. As previously communicated to you, we arranged for our asset's untimely death in an all-consuming fire. As far as the DEA is concerned, her remains were unrecoverable. Therefore, no one is looking for her. She is yours to use as you see fit with no fear of authorities searching for her or seeking retribution against you.'

'Is she cooperative?' Mityaev asked.

'Exceedingly so, though of course she initially resisted. But now that she has been fully apprised of her hopeless situation she has become quite compliant. We also briefly employed our own time-proven methods of persuasion.'

A few knowing chuckles burbled around the room.

Martin smiled. 'All of you received supporting documentation and video evidence to validate the asset's bona fides. I assume you verified them independently or you wouldn't be here this evening. Am I correct?'

'Why state the obvious?' Osorio grunted in his thick Spanish accent.

'Then I shall proceed. You have all received prior written instructions, but let me repeat them here.

'First, each bidder will be allowed five minutes alone with the asset. You are not permitted to touch the asset or offer her any form of food, beverage, or technology. In short, you are not permitted physical contact of any kind. Doing so immediately disqualifies you from the bidding process. Any attempt to harm her in order to deprive others of her value will be dealt with most harshly.' Martin nodded to one of his grinning Chechen goons standing in the corner. He wore an enormous blade on one hip and an even larger semi-auto pistol on the other.

'However, you are allowed to ask as many questions as you like to satisfy any other concerns you may have. She understands the penalty for noncooperation, so I believe you will find her quite forthcoming. However, make the best of your limited time.

'Second, your session will be neither broadcast nor recorded for utmost privacy.' Martin pulled a remote out of his pocket and killed the CCTV camera feed. 'We understand that questions you may ask of the asset could have implications for the other bidders present and so we respect your privacy and security. Even in the event you don't win the bid, you may gain some valuable intelligence that would have made your inconvenient travels worthwhile. I should also note that we ourselves have no interest in the asset's information nor its importance to any of you. All we care about is your final bid. Any questions?'

There were none.

'Third, each bidder will only be allowed to submit one bid. The highest bid wins and is final, so make sure you offer your highest possible bid. There will be no post-bid negotiations or offers accepted.

'Fourth, after each bidder meets with the asset they will submit their written bid within five minutes and then retire to the guest lounge. The next bidder will then be allowed to enter the cell for five minutes, and then have an additional five minutes afterward to submit their bid. The third will have the same opportunity. After all seven of you have submitted your bids, you will leave the premises and be transported back to the airport. Each of you will then be contacted by text exactly twelve hours later. The winner will then indicate where the asset is to be delivered and we shall make immediate delivery in good faith. We understand the challenge you face acquiring and transporting such large amounts of ISO. Nevertheless, we require payment within thirty days of delivery.'

Martin's friendly demeanor suddenly darkened. 'Anyone who betrays our faith will suffer accordingly. The so-called untimely death of the prime minister of Zanzibar and his entire family last year is just one such example, rare as they are.'

Osorio remembered reading about the fatal plane crash. Authorities ruled it was the result of a pilot error. Apparently, they were wrong.

'Finally, for the security of the winner, the winning bidder will not be identified nor the amount of the winning bid announced. Any questions?'

The room fell silent as a heavy hand of expectation hung in the air.

'Then *vámonos*,' Osorio grunted. 'Let's get started.'

Martin flashed an oily smile.

'I should also add that there is a minimum bid. I refuse to name that amount because bidding will cluster around that number. We want to maximize our profits. You need to bid the largest possible amount that you can provide within thirty days. If no bidder meets our minimum price, the asset will be terminated along with the possibility of her future auction. Shall we begin?'

'Who goes first?' the Russian asked.

Martin stepped over to the long table. He reached into his pocket and pulled out seven white poker chips marked with the numerals *1* through *7* and dropped them tinkling into a ceramic vase. He gestured toward the vase with his hand.

'Please hold your chip until the last is drawn. Ms Wu, you're first.'

Wu stood and crossed over to the vase and drew a chip.

Martin directed the other bidders in turn. Osorio was the last to draw. The bidders all stood in a loose circle.

Martin placed the vase up in front of Wu first, then Mityaev and finally Osorio.

'Please show your chip to the other bidders.'

They did.

Wu was pleased. She would go last.

Mityaev was even more pleased. He was first.

Osorio hid his discomfort. Number two.

Not good.

Osorio was counting on being the first interrogator in order to give his plan the best chance to work. But he could only play the cards he was dealt.

Exactly five minutes after he crossed the hall and entered the asset's cell, Mityaev reappeared, his handsome faced dimmed by a blank poker face, a skill he no doubt cultivated as a former colonel in the GRU, Russia's military intelligence agency. Osorio knew the very lack of any kind of emotion meant that the Russian liked what he heard and would no doubt be putting in a significant bid. Mityaev had been in charge of the GRU's infamous Unit 74455, the spear tip of Russia's cyber warfare operations. It would be a disaster if he took the woman back to Moscow – though not for the reasons the Russian could imagine as yet.

Osorio cast a quick glance at Wu. She was a cool customer for sure. She reacted to Mityaev's poker face the same way Osorio did, but pretended not to. But the subtle shift in her breathing told the Venezuelan that her own ferocious curiosity regarding the asset had been piqued.

That was bad. If anything, she was even more dangerous than the Russian. She was a former People's Liberation Army intelligence officer now working for China's largest criminal triad.

Osorio drained the rest of his water and crushed the bottle in his meaty fist before letting out a belch that would have impressed a bull elephant seal. It had the intended effect of breaking the concentration of the other bidders. Mityaev used up his entire five minutes in a mock display of indecision and annoyance, but it was clear he had made up his mind before he left the cell. In order to avoid appearing too anxious, he waited until his allowed five minutes were up.

'Mr Mityaev, your bid?'

Mityaev scratched a number on the provided pad, then dropped the folded paper in the same cup as the others. He nodded at Martin and headed back to the banquet table, making a beeline for the beluga caviar.

'Mr Osorio, I believe you're next.'

The Venezuelan turned toward Wu. 'Ladies first?'

The Chinese snorted and shook her head. 'I think not.'

Osorio nodded dejectedly, then raised himself up, leveraging his enormous weight with his hands against his jiggly thighs.

A surly, almond-eyed Turkman with a Tokarev pistol on his hip opened the heavy steel cell door.

'Your five minutes begins the moment the door is shut,' Martin said.

'*Comprendo.*' Osorio stepped through the door and it shut behind him with a clang of ominous finality.

Here goes nothin'.

3

The woman looked up from her cot. She was clearly surprised to see the Weeble-shaped crime lord. She looked haggard but defiant. Osorio was grateful for that.

Osorio bit down hard on the false cap on his left rear molar. This activated a tiny jammer that would block any audio and video signals. Martin may have killed the CCTV feed to the outer room, but there was no guarantee he still wasn't monitoring what was going on in the cell. They were safe now.

'Good evening, Mrs Cabrillo.'

The woman's eyes narrowed with confusion as a smile creased her mouth. 'Cabrillo?'

'Juan and the same.'

'Like I've never heard that one before.' She looked him up and down, incredulous. 'You've gained a few pounds since I last saw you.'

'Livin' la vida loca. We've got less than five minutes to bust you out of Bram Stoker's castle before the vampires come to get you.'

'If you'll look around, I believe you're stuck in the same rat trap. Any ideas?'

'A few.'

'A few?'

'Okay, one.'

'It had better be a doozy.'

Juan Cabrillo stripped off his green tracksuit, exposing his enormous body carpeted back to front in curly black hair.

Gretchen Wagner turned up her nose. 'I don't remember you needing to shave your back. Or all of the other parts. Gross.'

'So judgy. Why did I ever marry you? Four minutes, thirty seconds, by the way.'

'You didn't. That was just our cover in Nicaragua, remember?'

'Guess we dodged a bullet, eh?'

'The night isn't over yet.'

Juan Cabrillo slipped a finger into a carefully concealed joint fold beneath one of his rolls of latex blubber. He found the Velcro fastener and zipped open his enormous belly. Inside it contained everything he needed for the escape – except for the time they didn't have. He was wearing a bodysuit comprised entirely of thick latex, designed and built by Kevin Nixon and his Magic Shop aboard Cabrillo's ship, the *Oregon*, along with facial prosthetics, wig, and even body hair. The heavy rubber suit was of sufficient density to defeat any wave millimeter or other probing devices, including most metal detectors. Even Juan's artificial foot and leg were built with acrylic bones, and covered with the hairy skin-colored latex to appear completely lifelike. As an additional precaution, his technicians equipped him with the fewest metallic materials possible in the unlikely case a more advanced detection device was deployed.

'Here, help me with this stuff,' Juan said as he pulled out prepackaged items from his rubber gut. The largest ones were vacuum sealed and compressed to fit inside the belly compartment. The suit and its contents added nearly two hundred pounds of weight to Juan's body frame.

Though he was an excellent undercover actor, all of his straining and grunting had been for real. Fortunately, he was an expert swimmer and could handle the load, but the exertion had caused him to sweat like a Cajun at an RV show.

'Take this.' Juan shoved an oversize plastic needle dispenser into her hand. 'And hurry. Just three minutes and twenty-two seconds left.' He was confident of the number. His mental stopwatch was as accurate as a Thomas Mercer marine chronometer.

'What is it?' Wagner asked.

'Cyanoacrylate on steroids, the ultimate superglue. Hit the doorjamb with this, especially around the locking mechanism, and it'll weld it shut. Don't get any on you. And hurry.'

'Got it.' Gretchen bolted past Juan and got to work, squirting as much of the stuff as she could deep into the cracks.

It took another forty seconds for Juan to climb out of the sweat-drenched latex bodysuit. The rubber Osorio fell to the floor in a heap of hairy, skin-toned Jell-O like a boneless corpse.

'I think I saw that scene in *The Thing*,' Wagner said as she dashed back over, nodding at the monstrosity on the ground at Juan's feet. 'Only, you're no Kurt Russell.'

Juan then peeled off a pair of synthetic long johns, also dripping with moisture, and tossed them aside. He stood naked as a jaybird. He'd sweated off at least ten pounds of weight with all of the effort he'd exerted carrying the heavy load for the last several hours. His already ripped muscular physique was even more well-defined and glistening with sweat. His musky body odor suddenly filled the room.

Wagner let out a little whistle as she eyed him up and down. 'That's the fake husband I remember. Door's finished. What do you need me to do next?'

'Two minutes until they start pounding on that door,' Juan said as he picked up the heaviest package, waiting for the perspiration to evaporate from his skin.

'Didn't you bring a "Do Not Disturb" sign with you?'

'I asked for the honeymoon suite. I assumed it came with the package. Help me with these.'

Juan pulled out the ceramic knife and cut open the heaviest package. It was comprised of shaped directional charges – blocks of C4 plastic explosive with thick Kevlar plates for backing. He slapped the self-adhesive brick onto the thick stone wall, the first of several that could blast a doorway-sized hole.

'I thought I saw a retinal scanner out there when they brought me to this cell,' Wagner said. 'How'd you get past that?'

'My man Murph swapped the files of Osorio's retinal scans for mine.' Juan slapped another directional charge into place. *'No problemo.'* He handed Wagner a block of C4.

'How did you manage to pull *that* off?' She fixed the explosive brick onto the wall and grabbed another one.

'Long story.'

In fact, Osorio was currently in American custody in a

secret offshore facility. His capture was the only reason any of Juan's crazy plan was even possible.

Gretchen Wagner was a senior CIA field operative posing as the DEA intelligence executive. Her mission was to find and identify the members of the mysterious organization run by Martin, whose real name was Count Ludovico da Porto, the head of a family crime syndicate dating from the time of the Borgias. Their current base of operations was in Bulgaria, but they were a worldwide network.

The good news was that Wagner had successfully contacted the da Porto organization two weeks ago. The bad news was that the kidnapping syndicate was far more efficient and clever than Langley had supposed. Though her cover hadn't been blown – in fact, it had been *too* good – she was whisked away and her death convincingly faked. The CIA panicked because they had no idea where she was or what had really happened to her.

Juan's CIA contact informed him of Wagner's kidnapping. He'd immediately reached out to his nefarious underworld and dark web contacts, whom he worked with on occasion. It was from them he learned about a mysterious upcoming 'auction' of an important DEA asset taking place in seven days and further discovered that the Venezuelan Osorio was invited.

What da Porto's organization didn't realize was that Osorio had been coincidentally swept up in a CIA operation just hours after his invitation. Osorio's outfit couldn't inform da Porto of the development because they had no way of reaching out to 'Mr Martin,' who had a specially encrypted cell phone delivered to Osorio. All communication was strictly sent by da Porto and only received by Osorio. The CIA had recovered the phone when they picked up Osorio and now it was in Juan's possession.

Just thirty-six hours ago, Juan – now posing as the corpulent crime lord – got the call to be at a remote location outside of Karachi, Pakistan, where he was loaded into a private plane and flown to Tajikistan.

And now he was here.

As Gretchen slapped the last C4 brick into position, Juan opened up another package and tossed the rolled garment to her.

'Pull that on.'

'What is it?' Wagner asked as she shook it out.

Juan grinned as he unfurled his with a snap.

'A wingsuit.'

4

Juan pulled on the forty-pound parachute harness as Wagner did the same. She was better parachute-jump qualified than he was. More important, she had spent more time in a wingsuit than he had. That wasn't saying much. She had done it only once and hated every second of it. Tonight was Juan's first attempt at navigating one.

'Thirty seconds,' Juan said. He tossed her a pair of ski goggles. 'Hurry.'

Juan had already pulled on a pair of cold-weather pants and a shirt, and another artificial carbon-fiber leg, along with a pair of boots and a Bivouac 9000 mechanical altimeter he'd had stashed in his big Venezuelan gut. As he snapped on his own pair of goggles he pointed Gretchen toward the far corner along the exterior wall. Staying parallel to the explosion was their best chance of avoiding the blast radius.

'Ten seconds,' he said as they both crouched down. 'Get behind me. Open your mouth, plug your ears, and shut your eyes.'

Juan unfolded a collapsible multi-threat Kevlar ballistic shield and held it up in front of him. It wasn't much protection from the blast and concussion, but it was all they had. The place would be humming with stone shrapnel in seconds.

'One escape route, coming up.' Juan punched the remote wire detonator.

The C4 bricks blew in sync. The blast rang in Juan's ears like a siren and vacuumed the air out of his lungs faster than a Hoover upright. He felt chunks of rock pummeling the Kevlar shield where he held it with his hands.

He turned toward Wagner. 'You good?'

'What? I can't hear you!'

'You're good. Let's go!'

Juan dropped the shield and leaped to his feet. A gaping hole was ripped out of the wall. The room was choked with dusty smoke that smelled like burnt diesel. The acrid cloud was already being dissipated by the swirling snowstorm now licking inside their shattered cell. He heard distant thumping behind him. His brain registered fists beating on a faraway steel door – probably the one just behind him.

Juan dashed across the rock-littered floor to the jagged doorway framed by stones that looked like broken teeth. There was just enough room for him to stand in it. The slashing air caught his fake beard and slapped it around like the hair extensions floating above his head.

He turned to Gretchen, whose ears and nose were leaking blood.

'On me.'

She nodded.

Without another word Juan turned and leaped into the snowy void.

The eye goggles helped, but icy snowflakes in subzero wind hitting his face at a hundred and seventy kilometers per hour scoured his skin like a Brillo pad. Not exactly a day at the spa.

But that was hardly Juan's biggest problem.

He had gotten a quick demo on how to fly the wingsuit from Eric Stone back on the *Oregon*, though 'demo' was probably too generous of a term. It was more like Eric showing him a video game simulating a wingsuit flight and Eddie Seng, an experienced wingsuit jumper, walking him through the process of suiting up and actually flying the thing. Eddie volunteered to take Juan's place, but since there was a high probability of capture or worse, Juan took the mission for himself, despite his total lack of experience in a 'flying squirrel' suit. Gretchen Wagner was an old friend. His only real fear was failing her.

'The biggest thing you need to watch out for is gusting wind,' Eddie said with a final warning. 'It can kill you.'

His words were prophetic, Juan thought, as he battled the gusting winds pummeling him from all directions.

The snowstorm had picked up in intensity since he'd arrived at the fortress over an hour ago. He had no idea it had gotten so bad until he stood in the hole in the blasted wall and felt the wind battering him. But there was no going back.

Juan had checked the weather reports when they were putting together the plan for this op. There was always some kind of wind whistling through the mountains in this region, which contained some of the highest peaks on the planet. It was because of those winds that a straight parachute jump from the top of the fortress had been ruled out. The wingsuit idea was their best and only option.

The initial dive into the snowy night felt like every other night jump he'd ever done. The difference was that he wasn't falling straight down. He and Wagner had to cross over twelve kilometers of rough mountain terrain to reach the clearing down on the forested valley floor. That's where George 'Gomez' Adams would pick them up in the AgustaWestland AW609 tilt-rotor.

In order to cover that distance, Juan had to slow his descent as much as possible and that meant stretching out his hands and legs in order to maximize the aerodynamic qualities of the wingsuit. That changed his geometric profile to something akin to a maple leaf and the turbulent wind was playing havoc with his stability. He felt like he was trying to hold on to a sheet of plywood in a hurricane. It didn't help that his entire body was numbing from the freezing temps.

The only way to avoid the turbulence was to draw his arms to his sides and close his legs and form an arrow, minimizing his wing surface. But as soon as he did this his speed accelerated to over two hundred and forty kilometers per hour – and so did his descent. His only hope was to feel his way between the two extremes, alternately surfing the breaking waves of air or plunging through them like a spear, the noise of the rushing wind roaring in his ears.

He didn't have any way to communicate with Gretchen and he couldn't turn around to check her progress. Chances were that she was doing a lot better than he was. If she survived the ordeal she would be able to notify Juan's next of kin – except he didn't have any.

Through the swirling flakes clouding his vision he

could barely make out the forest clearing far up ahead. There was no sign of the tilt-rotor and he was losing too much altitude too fast. The automatic aviation device in his parachute pack would fire off his canopy as soon as he hit two hundred and fifty meters, and according to his altimeter that was going to happen any second –

Fwop!

Juan's parachute deployed. Too soon, he thought.

There was still a long way to go.

5

Juan's ram-air parachute deployed perfectly, jerking his frame as it snapped open. He gripped the leather loops of his steering toggles with his nearly frozen fingers, alternately cupping and flaring the canopy, trying to keep it on course through the buffeting winds. He was having about as much success as a plastic shopping bag fighting a leaf blower.

And the trees were coming up fast.

Spinning around in a haphazard loop, he managed a glance up and saw Wagner several hundred meters above him, dancing the same aerial dance beneath her black canopy, and struggling as much as he was with the wind.

Suddenly he felt his body drop as a violent downdraft collapsed his chute like an invisible fist pushing down on a pillow. Just as quickly as it hit it disappeared and the canopy reinflated, but not quick enough to keep him from crashing into the trees.

Pine needles scraped his face as he plummeted through the branches until his silks finally snagged on one. He jerked to a hard stop and found himself dangling five meters above the snowy forest floor. The freight train noise of rushing wind ceased in an instant, all sound absorbed by the blanket of snow and trees. The utter sensory stillness was instantly calming until he heard the faint, mosquito-like whining of engines in the distance.

Was it the AW's twin Pratt & Whitney turboshafts?

No, he decided. Those were thunderously loud.

Snowmobiles.

He counted two. Even if all they carried were a couple of slingshots he was in big trouble. Stuck up here he was helpless as a kitten. He hoped Wagner had fared better.

As if on cue, Juan heard her crash into the trees a hundred meters behind him. She cried out in pain as she snapped to a halt. He turned around in his harness, but he couldn't see her.

'Gretch! You okay?'

'I think my wrist is busted. Where are you? You good?'

'All good. Just hanging out. We have company on the way.'

'I hear it. Can you get me down? I'm stuck.'

'Let me see what I can do.'

The two former Russian mercenaries had received the prisoner escape message from their commander. They could hardly believe his description of the incredible wingsuit stunt. Minutes later they both saw two parachutes struggling in the high winds above the forest.

It was an insanely brave move to try and wingsuit their way out of the fortress, they agreed, though insanity was the better explanation than bravery. Their orders were to recover the woman unharmed, but to kill the man they called the Venezuelan if he offered any resistance.

They gunned their turbocharged four-stroke Yamaha Sidewinders and raced across an open area toward the chutes falling in the distance. Snow rooster-tailed behind their fast machines. They reached the edge of the forest nearest where they thought the parachutists had landed and dove into the tree line. It took another ten minutes slaloming through the sturdy pines to reach the area where they thought the asset and her rescuer had descended.

'There!' one of them said in his helmet comms, pointing high in the branches just up ahead. Gretchen Wagner hung helplessly in her harness several meters above them, suspended by a ripped chute perilously clinging to a single branch. Suddenly the air began to beat with the heavy chop of big rotor blades.

'That's a helicopter,' the first merc, a former Army sergeant, said. 'One of ours?'

'In this weather? Must be a rescue mission.' The second merc had been a corporal in the same Army unit.

'Go check it out. Shoot it down if you have to. I'll take care of the woman.'

'What about the Venezuelan?'

'Shoot him if you see him. Otherwise, I'll find him. Go!'

The Russian nodded, cranked his throttle, and sped back toward the sound approaching the clearing.

The other Russian killed his engine and got off his sled. His boots sunk down into a foot of soft snow. He opened up his face mask as he trudged over to Wagner's tree and called up to her.

'That was a very stupid thing you did,' he said in labored English. 'Mr Martin is very angry with you.'

Gretchen answered him in Russian. The mercenary laughed.

'You kiss your mother with a mouth like that?'

'Who do you think I learned it from?' she replied. 'Make yourself useful and get me down from here.'

The former sergeant pulled his sidearm and glanced around, searching the trees.

'Where is your Venezuelan friend? I'd like to ask him a few questions.'

Gretchen pointed in the direction of Juan's tree. 'He's over that way, about thirty meters. Stuck in the branches like me. Don't hurt him. He's not such a bad fella, even if he is my ex-husband.'

'I won't hurt him . . . much,' the Russian said, laughing, as he climbed back onto the Yamaha. The rotor sounds were louder now.

'Definitely a helicopter . . . but one I've never seen before,' his friend reported over the comms. 'Civilian, no guns.'

'Then take him out!'

'Will do, Sarge.'

Moments later, automatic-rifle fire echoed in the valley and the roar of the turbines changed as the helicopter began evasive maneuvers.

The ex-sergeant goosed the throttle and wended his way through the trees, his eyes scanning the treetops in search of the Venezuelan's parachute.

That was a mistake.

The Russian picked his way forward at a crawl until he saw the flapping shroud high in the branches up ahead. He killed the engine and jumped off his sled as he drew his Archon Type B pistol. Dashing behind a tree for cover, he gripped the gun in both hands and pointed it at the parachute. His eyes narrowed as he tried to get a better view.

Just as he realized the harness was empty, Juan exploded up out of the snow at the mercenary's feet and drove a ceramic-bladed knife into his groin. The Russian cried out as he dropped his gun.

Cabrillo finished the job with a couple of quick thrusts and left the man in the snow.

The other mercenary gunned his engine and chased the AW609 for several hundred meters, firing at the tilt-rotor with one hand and his other on the throttle. Despite the snowstorm, he could see his rounds sparking against the aircraft's metal skin.

He heard the big Yamaha turbo engine screaming out of the woods before he saw it. He turned around to see his helmeted comrade racing straight at him.

'Grab your rifle, Sarge! I've already hit him once! We can take him down!'

'Hold your fire! But stay with him!'

The corporal didn't understand the order, but he knew to obey it. The *podonok* probably wanted the pleasure of shooting down the helicopter himself.

He slowed enough to shove the rifle back into its plastic scabbard, then slammed the throttle again, turning the snowmobile to match the AW's turn. The odd-looking machine was circling the clearing, waiting for something to happen. But what?

The AW continued to turn and his sergeant's Yamaha was coming up fast. Out of the corner of his eye he saw the big machine screaming through the snowstorm and coming right at him.

Before he realized what was happening, the sergeant's

snowmobile slammed into his rig with a roaring crash. The merc was tossed hard out of his seat, which probably saved his life because the other Yamaha climbed right over it, the ripsaw track tearing up the saddle and everything else underneath it.

Buried in snow, the stunned merc reached for the pistol in his leg harness, but the helmeted figure leaped off his sled and crashed into him, driving his knees into the Russian's gut and knocking the wind out of him. The Russian felt his helmet ripping off his head just as the giant rotors of the descending AW appeared right above them, the rising sound of the blades nearly deafening. The rotors kicked up so much snow that the Russian could hardly make out the helmeted man standing over him, holding the corporal's own pistol in his hand and pointing it at his face.

Cabrillo pulled off his helmet and tossed it aside.

Before the AW even touched down, two *Oregon* operators – Eddie Seng and Raven Malloy – leaped out of the cabin door with rifles drawn and stormed over.

'It's your lucky day, Ivan,' Juan said in excellent Russian, one of three foreign languages he spoke fluently. 'We're going to go for a little ride in my tilt-rotor. You're going to tell me everything I want to know and then I'll drop you off. How high that drop is will depend on how quickly and how well you answer me. *Ponyatno?*'

'*Da, ponyatno!*'

'Where's our package?' Seng asked Cabrillo.

'She's in the trees. We'll have to rope her out.'

Malloy nodded at the Russian. 'What happened to his friend?'

'He won't be joining us.'

Juan never flinched from taking a life when it meant protecting the lives of his people, but he took no pleasure in it, either, and avoided killing whenever possible.

'Let's vamoose. His other friends will be coming along any minute now.'

'Aye, Chairman.'

Juan grabbed the Russian by the nape of his neck, hauled him over to the tilt-rotor cabin door, and tossed him in. Moments later they were all airborne, the sound of more snowmobiles roaring in the distance far below them.

6

Dr Jing Yanwen was in charge of her first mission, but she wasn't in control of it. At least, it didn't feel like it.

Part of her feared the head of her security detachment, a Macedonian named Risto. It wasn't just his physically imposing presence. Yanwen was a trained martial artist, but she was under no illusion as to her relative capabilities. Risto was shredded like an Olympic gymnast, and there was no doubt in her mind he could beat any man to death with his lightning-quick boxer's hands. She'd also seen a demonstration of his preternatural speed and accuracy with his weapons. It shouldn't have frightened her. After all, that was his job. But it did.

It also didn't help that Risto exuded an unspoken arrogance that was unintentionally dismissive and demeaning. She knew it was a natural by-product of his superior conditioning.

No, what unnerved her most was his general demeanor. She couldn't quite name it. All of his explosive energy was just waiting to unleash itself, like a grenade with the pin already pulled out and rolling around on the floor at her feet.

Her sense of a loss of control was more than a clash of personalities. She and her medical technician, Dr Brigit

43

Schweers, had trudged through the dark canopied jungle for days, escorted by Risto and his two men, a bearded Nigerian named Samson and Mat, a Malaysian with a braided ponytail thick as a rope, both eager as Rottweilers straining at the leash. 'Escorted' hardly seemed the right term, Yanwen thought. More like driven.

Risto, Samson, and Mat were products of the same conditioning program. The men never seemed to fatigue despite the heat and jungle terrain, even with their hundred-and-twenty-pound packs stuffed with ammunition, medical gear, food, and water rations. They would disappear on far-ranging forays in search of their targets and then circle back, urging Yanwen and Schweers to hurry along with indignant sneers and curt commands. To Risto's credit, he kept the other two under tight control. They'd both been casting hungry looks at the two women, who neither wanted nor encouraged their libidinous intentions in the flickering firelight of their nightly camps.

Despite the sweat, swarming insects, and utter exhaustion, Yanwen rejoiced when they finally managed to locate one of the small bands of 'Poison Arrow' people they'd been searching for. They were one of the last Indigenous tribes in the Amazon who remained untainted by modern civilization and its ills. Their extreme isolation made them one of the most genetically pure people on the planet. That made them extremely valuable to the project.

Yanwen was an expert on the subject of human genetics. 'Genetic entropy' was an incontrovertible fact and a troubling reality that the scientific community had failed to address for reasons unrelated to the actual science involved. But it was precisely this phenomenon and the

44

rigors of the scientific method that brought her to the Amazon.

Yanwen's own research had substantiated the observation that, contrary to the theories of Darwinian evolution, the human genome – that complex chain of nucleotides that defined the human organism – wasn't improving over time, but actually devolving. It was a startling revelation with wide-ranging implications for science and society. Her published findings, though meticulously researched and mathematically precise, resulted in her being fired from her first postdoctoral assignment.

Her dismissal from a prestigious institute was the most humiliating experience of her life. She had been punished for following the science she understood far better than her so-called peers. Yanwen had once explained the concept of genetic entropy to her mother, an uneducated seamstress, and even she could grasp the reality of it.

'Nucleotides are the molecules that make up DNA, the way that letters make up words. And if DNA constitutes words,' Yanwen explained, 'then genes are sentences. And all of the sentences put together form a single document called the human genome.'

Like a photocopier, cells are designed to maintain perfect copies of each nucleotide within the body over generations. Scientists even called this process 'DNA replication fidelity.'

But biological cells, like mechanical photocopiers, break down over time.

If the ink cartridge on a copier runs low, subsequent copies will fade and not print evenly, and even drop letters or portions of images. The next generation of copier will take that degraded copy and reproduce it along with those additional errors and then add more degradation errors and so on down the line, generation after generation.

Besides cellular degradation, it was also well documented that the human genome was under environmental attack. All kinds of natural extraneous factors were causing mutations, including excessive sunlight and viruses. Even more damaging were the harmful civilizational inputs of chemical pollution in the food, soil, air, and water, along with electromagnetic radiation. Self-inflicted contamination included socially acceptable variables such as smoking, recreational and pharmaceutical drugs, and alcohol.

All this added up to what some scientists estimated were over three billion mutations that the human genome had accumulated over the millennia, and that each new generation was acquiring three thousand mutations more. In fact, the number of mutations was accelerating.

Most of those mutations were benign – like specks of dust or ink on a photocopy that gets passed along in later copies. But some mutations were degenerative, like dropping or corrupting lines of code in a complicated software program. At some point, the software will cease to function and the human genome – the very essence of what it means to be a human being – will be degraded beyond recognition.

Given the current accelerating trends, Yanwen estimated that the human genome would collapse entirely within the next three hundred generations, if not sooner.

Her published research brought her to the attention of Dr Heather Hightower, who hired Yanwen and tasked her with finding the earth's purest, most undiluted strands of human DNA untainted by environmental mutations. Yanwen was proud to head up Hightower's field collection team searching for the Poison Arrow people, whom she believed to be the most primal and untainted population on the planet. They drew their name from their use of poisonous frog venom and the deadly sharp-barbed arrows they used to hunt with – fish, frogs, monkeys, and peccaries – small pigs that half resembled tiny hairy hippos.

The highly mobile bands of Indigenous folk were referred to as 'spirits of the forest' by other tribes because they were nearly invisible, capable of disappearing into the bush without a trace. But still they had found them.

Despite her misgivings about Risto's terrifying demeanor, he had proven to be a world-class tracker with hearing and eyesight that far exceeded her own capabilities. When she first heard of the genetic therapeutics Dr Hightower had pioneered, she was skeptical. But now seeing her work literally in the flesh, Yanwen had become a true believer. Dr Hightower's pioneering work would change human history.

Dr Yanwen was proud to play her own small part in that vision, even if that meant working shoulder to shoulder with a human hand grenade like Risto, who suddenly burst out of the bush, a rare smile plastered on his lantern jaw.

'We counted sixteen adult fighting males, fourteen breeding females, eight infants and toddlers, and six old people,' Risto reported. 'They're just up ahead, and settling in for a big meal. This is the perfect time to make contact.'

Yanwen brushed a lick of matted hair off her sweating face. She agreed. If the Indians slipped away, they might never find them again.

'Let's do it.'

7

Dr Brigit Schweers spoke flawless Portuguese and Spanish, but neither language was of any use here in the remote wilderness. She was nonetheless a talented linguist and, more important, a sincerely warm and kind spirit. After Risto had located the band of some forty people, Yanwen chose Schweers to make first contact.

The stunning blond researcher no doubt drew the Indians' curiosity. The small children stared in wild-eyed, rapturous wonder at the German scientist's golden mane of hair and luminous blue eyes.

Schweers was surprised at their response. She thought they would bolt at the sight of a stranger. Instead, they seemed oddly curious. Even friendly.

Schweers generously allowed the children and women to paw at her hair and skin, which created an immediate intimacy and bond between them. The sharp-eyed men, however, kept their distance, constantly scanning the forest for signs of threat or entrapment. But after a few minutes, even they began to soften and their stoic features turned to warm smiles and even laughter.

When she felt the time was right, Schweers gestured that she had more friends that wanted to visit, and signaled for Yanwen to appear. She did so slowly, but with a wide smile. The men stiffened at the sudden intrusion of yet another stranger, but the women and children were equally enthralled by the Chinese American's appearance, with her sharp cheekbones and glossy black hair, and ran to embrace her.

'I don't understand,' Yanwen said. 'I thought they were frightened of strangers.'

'They should be,' Schweers agreed.

Once Yanwen was accepted into the group, Schweers reluctantly signaled for Risto to appear.

He stepped carefully out of the jungle. His imposing form sent a shock wave of concern through the tribal men, whose hands instantly fell to their bone knives and longbows.

Risto had the presence of mind to hold up his hands in a gesture of peace and surrender. He went even further to sniff the air and rub his belly, signaling his desire to taste some of the pork roasting on the fire.

An exchange of glances by the men resulted in the largest one of them stepping forward, though even he was a foot shorter and a hundred pounds lighter than the Macedonian. The Indian sliced off a hunk of crackling pig flesh and handed a piece to Risto, while he devoured the other steaming half. Risto made a big show of his pleasure and let out a raucous belly laugh that set the rest of the tribe laughing along with him.

So far, so good, Yanwen thought. Maybe Risto wasn't so bad after all. Now she had to get to work collecting blood and DNA samples. She'd have to rely on Schweers to pull that off.

Risto kept his position by the fire, letting the sweet smoke of the roasting pig wash over him, his eyes constantly scanning the tribal members. The women and children were still fixated on the two women, but the men kept a careful watch over him as each approached and cut off slices from the peccary.

Schweers unpacked containers of *maracuya*, *camu camu*, and other fruits and berries that were common to the region, but not always easily acquired. The last thing she wanted to do was contaminate their pristine physiologies with corn-syruped snacks or GMO-tainted grain bars. She passed out her indigenous food gifts to the delight of the women and children, and soon endeared herself to the group.

She suddenly noticed that one of the young girls wore a thin beaded bracelet, the only one of its kind in sight. Schweers swore it had been manufactured – the beads were too perfect and symmetrical – but as far as she knew these gentle souls had no outside contact with the modern world. She held up the little girl's arm. 'Dr Yanwen, look at this.'

Yanwen had the same reaction. 'That's not native jewelry. They've had outside contact.'

'With whom?'

'How should I know?'

The German frowned. 'What does that mean for the purity of their DNA?'

'There's no way to know. We'll still take samples, but we'll put notes in the log for Dr Hightower.'

Yanwen removed her backpack and began setting up her miniature collection station for blood, saliva, and skin cell samples. After collection, everything would have to be carefully stored in the portable solar-powered refrigeration unit, all of which Mat carried on his broad back somewhere out in the forest.

When everything was finally prepared, Yanwen and Schweers played a spirited game full of laughter and smiles as they swabbed and spat in order to demonstrate how they would begin collecting DNA samples. Once the Natives' confidence had been won, the two scientists would advance to the more difficult challenge of drawing blood samples.

The Indians were mesmerized by the display, including the ever-watchful men, who turned all of their attention to the strange women. The hyperalert Poison Arrow men were so captivated by the spectacle they failed to notice the shadows of Samson and Mat looming in the forest just beyond the camp.

When Yanwen thought it was time, she chose a healthy young girl who couldn't have been more than five years old and reached out to her. The shy girl resisted and clung to her mother.

It was at that moment that Samson chose to step silently into the clearing like an apparition. His giant frame was terrifying. The tribal warriors all turned in unison, their eyes widened with terror and their limbs quickened for a fight.

'You're both idiots!' Risto said as he charged over to the reluctant girl and grabbed her thin little arm in his massive paw. 'Just jab the kid! She'll get over it. Do it!'

But the moment Risto grabbed the child, the mother shrieked and tried to pull her daughter away from the giant white man. The other mothers hissed and muttered angrily as the girl's father pushed his way through, shouting at Risto and wielding a bone knife in his hand.

Yanwen was shocked at the speed with which Risto's

thick-knuckled hand backslapped the Indian father, flinging him into the leafy dirt, knocked out cold.

The women and children scattered noiselessly like quail into the bush, disappearing into the thick leaves like ghosts as the warriors pulled their bows.

Before the first arrow was nocked, Risto and Samson were firing their pistols, emptying their magazines into the warriors as fast as they could pull their triggers. Screeching birds bolted out of the trees in a blast of colorful feathers and monkeys screamed as they raced through the branches in terror.

All of the Poison Arrow men lay dead on the ground beneath a haze of gun smoke, their skulls and torsos riddled with bullets. Not a single shot missed.

Utterly shocked by the earsplitting noise and overwhelming carnage, Yanwen barely managed to shout for Samson to stop as he turned and raced back into the forest. She glanced at Schweers, whose mouth was still agape at the horror she had just witnessed.

Though Yanwen's ears were still ringing from the noise, she could hear gunshots blasting in the forest all around her.

'Tell your men to stop! There's no need for any more killing!' Yanwen shouted.

Risto swapped mags and reloaded his weapon before holstering it.

'We can't leave any witnesses behind.'

'You had no right –'

'Those men were going to attack us.'

'Only because you –'

'I'm here for your security. Your job is to collect DNA. I did my job. Now do yours.'

'You can't be serious,' Schweers said, pointing at the butchery all around them. 'Not after this.'

'Grab your samples from them. They won't care. Or wait until my boys drag back the others. Shooter's choice.'

'This was so unnecessary,' Yanwen said, her voice cracking.

'Our instructions are to get in and get out without detection. Any survivors are potential witnesses.'

'How can they be witnesses? Look how long it took for us to find them.'

'I can't take that chance. Besides, they are no doubt in contact with the other bands. Thanks to us, those bands won't be warned and scared away. That means you can get samples from them as well.'

Schweers reddened with rage. 'And then you'll just kill them, too.'

Yanwen began to protest as well, but Risto held up his palm to silence them both as he touched his earbud.

'Say again?' Risto said, frowning. He glanced over to Yanwen, utterly confused. 'Bring her to the camp.'

Now it was Yanwen's turn to frown. 'What was that all about?'

Thick leaves parted as Mat stormed into the clearing, his iron-hard hand wrapped around the forearm of a dark-haired Indian woman dressed in cargo pants and boots. She was clearly terrified. Mat tossed her to the ground like a rag doll.

Yanwen dashed over to her and knelt down. 'Who are you?'

'Dr Aline Izidoro. I care for these people. You're not allowed to be here.'

Yanwen's eyes widened. She lowered her voice. 'You need to keep quiet. Or you'll get in big trouble.'

Risto shoved Yanwen aside as he pulled his specialized Russian pistol, a Yarygin, chambered in 9×21mm.

'She already is.'

8

Riyadh, Saudi Arabia

The party guests were in a jubilant mood, which made the food service all the more efficient. The courses passed without incident and the chefs received high praise. The convivial host, Prince Khalid, was in his early sixties, sported a thick painter's brush mustache and fine steel-rimmed glasses. He seemed to be quite pleased with the whole affair.

Khalid's luxurious home in the exclusive western suburbs featured the Italian marbles, silk carpets, and gilded fixtures that the older Saudi princes preferred. Their ostentatious displays of wealth harkened to an earlier, less restrained era. The younger generation was no less profligate, only less garish.

There were literally thousands of Saudi princes – all blood descendants of Muhammad bin Saud, the founder of the first Saudi state. Most royals were content to live off the generous monthly allowances the kingdom distributed to the family. Some actually accepted 'make work' government and business positions to justify their lavish incomes. Most simply chose to live like, well, princes. Their ambitions were limited to their appetites.

However, there was a core of a few hundred Saudi royals who vied for serious political power. The ultimate prize was the royal throne itself and the near absolute power it possessed. The kingdom had always been a monarchy governed by the privileged sons of the House of Saud with the blessing of the ultraconservative salafist clergy, and always would be, if managed wisely.

But what did 'wisely' mean in the twenty-first century? This was the schism that divided the family. In recent years, the power and wisdom of the older generation was giving way to the ambitions of the young. It was as yet unclear what the future held.

Khalid was sympathetic to the younger generation. In his youth he had spent some time in London, where he had fallen in love with both English theater and a beguiling West End actress. He had even taken to the stage briefly in a production of *Macbeth*. It was a time of youthful madness cut short by his father's intervention, thanks be to Allah. He had seen the error of his ways and now his slippered feet trod the sacred path.

Saudi Arabia's current king – his actual royal title was 'the Custodian of the Two Holy Mosques,' not 'king' – had thirteen brothers, each of whom had several sons, and the king himself had eleven sons. But with recent reforms, the selection of the heir apparent, known as the crown prince, was made not by the king but the Allegiance Council, a group of royal princes determined not to allow one narrow branch of the family to own the throne in perpetuity.

At the present time, the king's youngest son, and arguably the most talented of the young royals, was Prince Abdullah, a radical reformer. By the will of Allah, and a narrow partisan vote greased with baksheesh, the Allegiance Council had chosen him as crown prince.

The council in its wisdom also chose Abdullah's best friend and cousin, Prince Muqrin, to be the deputy crown prince, the next in the line of succession. Muqrin was a man of rare substance, and a highly decorated officer in the Royal Saudi Air Force. He shared Abdullah's views on rapid modernization.

Clearly, the young royals were winning the balance of power against the older conservatives at the present time, and they were determined to drag the kingdom into the Western world. But the older generation feared these turns of events and were equally determined to save the House of Saud from its reckless heirs.

Given the king's rapidly fading health, the status of both Abdullah and Muqrin had elevated considerably in the last few weeks. Of the thousands of Saudi royal princes, none were more important than these two men.

This evening's attendees were the familiar faces of the traditional Saudi power elite – royals, generals, and high-ranking business and government officials. Several trusted foreign dignitaries were also there, including a senior British diplomat and an American congressman. It was unsurprising that Khalid, the former head of the General Intelligence Presidency (GIP), Saudi Arabia's version of the CIA, could assemble such an impressive guest list. Khalid's own royal ambitions, like his intelligence career, had been shoved aside by Abdullah's rise to power.

Missing from the ranks was the elderly Saudi king himself, though that was hardly unexpected. Not only had the king's mental condition degenerated considerably over the last year, he was now under hospice care in his palace with only days to live.

The king's son, Crown Prince Abdullah, wasn't there, either. He was rumored to be encamped on his personal pleasure island with a bevy of swimsuit models somewhere in the Maldives.

But it was Khalid's son, Deputy Crown Prince Muqrin, the highly decorated Air Force colonel, whom everyone had come to see.

An accomplished fighter pilot, the roguishly handsome Muqrin was seen as a brave and serious member of the royal family who gave up many of the privileges of his rank in order to serve his nation. His devotion to duty, military accomplishments, natural diplomatic skills and, most important, his close friendship with Abdullah – the man next in line to be king – had fueled his rise to the near pinnacle of Saudi royal power.

Khalid spent the evening stealing glances at his son as he worked the room. Muqrin's natural charisma and force of character had easily won over the power brokers clamoring for his attention. Without a doubt, the kingdom's future was inextricably bound to Muqrin's fate, whatever that might be.

Inshallah.

Cesar Patrimonio carried himself with an unassuming yet elegant dignity. He was impeccably groomed, and his starched white uniform was perfectly fitted to his iron-hard body. The winsome Filipino was only one of dozens of foreign nationals serving up the lavish meals in the Saudi royal household today.

The house steward called Cesar over to his station with an exaggerated hand gesture from across the room. Cesar finished delivering a platter of poached quail eggs and sped effortlessly over to his boss. The steward, a white-haired Pakistani national, gave Cesar the once-over yet again, his cautious eyes darting between Cesar's face and his QR-coded name tag for the third time. Prince Khalid employed over a hundred servants between his five palatial residences, and new ones were being added all the time, even as others quit for better opportunities or were deported home. Cesar's personnel records indicated he was the newest member of the household staff at Khalid's beachfront home north of Jeddah. Tonight was his first service at the Riyadh estate.

'It's time to serve the peach tea. You will begin, of course, with Colonel Muqrin. It's his favorite. Do you understand the privilege I am offering you with this assignment?'

'Yes, sir.' Cesar well understood that the lecherous old fool expected to be reciprocated in either cash or an immoral assignation with him. What the steward didn't understand was that Cesar intended to repay him neither.

'Be sure that you do. Now go. I'm keeping my eye on you.'

'Thank you, sir.'

Cesar was careful to duck behind the corner of the pantry closet before touching the back of his left ear with his index finger, which, if seen, would have violated the sanitary standards of the kitchen. But it wasn't filth he touched.

A biological microdot was now affixed to his fingertip.

Cesar instantly reappeared and fetched the chilled crystal serving pitcher under the Pakistani's watchful gaze.

Cesar brought it to the beverage station, where a cute young Filipina sous-chef smiled at him as she poured the specially prepared peach tea into it. He held her gaze. She blushed, and nearly spilled the tea. The chef in charge of the tea preparation scolded her from across the kitchen. She darkened with embarrassment, never noticing that Cesar had touched the inside of the crystal pitcher with his left index finger.

As soon as the microdot touched the sweet tea, several hundred thousand nanobots were released into the fluid.

'Don't worry about the chef. He's all gas,' Cesar told the girl.

'I can't lose my job. My family back home depends on me.'

'You deserve better than this,' he said, nodding at the crowded kitchen.

'You better hurry,' she said, feeling the burn of the chef's steady gaze on the back of her neck. She lowered her voice. 'But thank you.'

Cesar winked and nodded with a confident smile. 'I'll be back.' He lifted the serving pitcher and headed for the dining room.

'Wait,' a voice said. Cesar stopped and turned around.

An imperious Egyptian in a pencil-thin mustache glared at him. 'Where do you think you're going?'

'The deputy crown prince is waiting for his tea, sir,' Cesar said.

'Don't you think I know that?'

'Sorry, sir.'

'Do you know who I am?'

'No, sir.'

The Egyptian nodded at the pitcher. 'Bring that with you. Now.'

The Egyptian – the 'taster' for the royal household – led Cesar over to an empty serving station and gestured for him to set the pitcher down. The Egyptian poured an ounce of the tea into a shot-glass-sized container and then removed a poison detection kit from his suit pocket. The detection device itself was merely a strip of specially treated paper that could instantly detect thallium, cyanide, atropine, and other deadly water-soluble toxins. He dipped the paper into the glass and held it there for a moment.

Cesar focused on his breathing to calm his racing heart, as he was taught to do. There was no discussion of a food inspector in his brief. No matter, he told himself. He was following his orders perfectly.

'You may serve now,' the Egyptian said, tossing the strip into the trash container. 'Next time, don't make me find you.'

'Yes, sir.'

The peach tea was a big hit. The deputy crown prince praised it effusively. It had been carefully crafted with the juice of fresh Georgia peaches, flown in especially for the occasion just that morning, and Sri Lankan loose-leaf black tea sweetened with Madagascar vanilla-bean-infused honey. A second waiter close on Cesar's heels garnished each glass with a sprig of mint, and a third added a fresh slice of succulent, white-fleshed peach, also from Georgia.

Colonel Muqrin took just a moment to explain his love of peach tea. Directing his comment toward the American congressman from Texas, the deputy crown prince told how he had acquired his affection for the delightful concoction while he was stationed in Texas for fighter pilot training with the United States Air Force.

'Americans are the friendliest people in the world, and Texans are the friendliest Americans,' he said to the congressman before turning to Prince Khalid. 'And thank you, Father, for this wonderful celebration.'

Khalid nodded as he laid one hand over his heart.

'My pleasure.'

Cesar had performed his services admirably, even earning a small compliment from Prince Khalid himself, which was communicated to the steward. The well-groomed Pakistani laid a manicured hand on the small of Cesar's back when the other kitchen staff weren't paying attention, signaling his desire to receive compensation.

'I'll be in touch soon,' Cesar said as he turned aside.

The steward frowned with irritation and dismissed him with a wave. 'Be sure that you do.'

Cesar stole a quick glance from the Filipina sous-chef who had poured his tea. For a moment he thought about getting her number and clearly she wanted to give it to him, judging by the come-hither look in her pretty dark eyes. But his training pushed the thought away. There was no point to it.

He changed clothes in the servants' locker room, then hailed an Uber on his burner phone. Forty-five minutes later he arrived at the apartment and slipped inside with his copied key. He checked his watch. It was just after 2 a.m. Time was getting short.

He did a quick check of the apartment one last time. He'd already done a thorough sweep of the place, searching for any evidence that he might have left behind, but it never hurt to be overly cautious. His commander had arranged for his uniform, and acquired his ID badge, work permit, and passport by hacking into the prince's personnel records and the Saudi national databases. All the assassin had to do was show up and do the job.

Confident the place was clean, Cesar snatched up an oversize duffel bag and sped into the bathroom.

The real Cesar Patrimonio lay in the ceramic tub, his neck broken cleanly, his throat collared with a purpling bruise. His impersonator and killer was Ismael Akbar, from Mindanao, the hotbed of Islamic extremism in the Philippines. Ismael pulled out a pair of zip ties and bound Cesar's wrists and ankles together for ease of lifting. With seemingly superhuman strength, he quickly stuffed the corpse into the duffel and pulled it up onto his shoulders effortlessly, gave the apartment one last look, then headed out the door.

Ismael sped down the apartment steps and checked for prying eyes. The sprawling apartment complex warehoused the working-class menials who serviced the gleaming city in the sand. Someone was always coming and going, but he caught a break and no one was around.

Ismael tightened the duffel's straps and jogged into the desert with Cesar on his back. He'd bury the unfortunate waiter in the sand five kilometers out beneath the blanket of stars, then rendezvous at the pickup point via GPS. It had been a good mission. His commander would be pleased.

His only regret was not killing the filthy *kafir* Pakistani with his bare hands.

9

On Board the Oregon

Earlier that evening, Juan had climbed into his custom cabin shower and cranked the spigots to full blast. He was bone-tired and filthy after Gretchen's rescue. The nearly scalding-hot water from the multidirectional showerheads pounded his skin until it pinked him up like a newborn baby. He lathered up with his favorite bar of soap, Dr Squatch's Pine Tar 'Heavy Grit.' The black block of oatmeal, shea butter, sand, and pine tar not only smelled like an old-growth forest but exfoliated his skin like soft sandpaper.

Finally clean from the day's work, he slipped beneath his set of Egyptian cotton sheets and passed out from exhaustion.

But a few hours later, vivid dreams and the relentless throbbing of phantom pain beneath the stump of his leg woke him up and wouldn't let him go back to sleep. He knew not to fight it. The phantom pain haunted him on a regular basis, though thankfully it had lessened over the years. Dr Huxley had done extensive testing for underlying physical causes like neuromas, but never could identify anything.

Cabrillo read the old-school mariner's clock on his lamp stand, a 1940s antique befitting the decor of his cabin. It read four a.m. He yawned. There was only one thing he could ever do to take his mind off the phantom pain.

He yanked off his twisted sheets and sat up, fighting another yawn.

Cabrillo jerked open the door to the Olympic-size swimming pool housed in one of the *Oregon*'s ballast tanks. It was one of his favorite places on the ship.

Nobody would be here at this hour. It was a familiar haunt for him; he swam here almost every day and tried to pick times when no one was about, when he could find silent refuge in the shimmering pool lights and rippling waters reflecting in the Carrara tiles artfully laid to the rounded surfaces.

But apparently he'd miscalculated.

Maurice, the *Oregon*'s chief steward, stood on the far side of the darkened facility, his outstretched hands and lean body moving in the slow, graceful motions of a tai chi routine. He was dripping wet and bare-skinned, save for his red Speedo.

In all his years of service, Juan had never seen Maurice half naked before, let alone working out. The former Royal Navy steward was in his late seventies. He was always impeccably dressed in his serving uniform of sharply creased black slacks, crisp white collared shirt, and gleaming leather oxfords. In fact, that's all Maurice ever wore, even on shore leave, though he sometimes carried an old military rucksack when he traveled off by himself.

Maurice had always appeared younger than his years with his spry, soundless steps, smooth skin, a full head of silver hair, and bright eyes. But now stripped down to almost nothing, Juan saw the fine, rippling muscles activating in his long, powerful arms and well-developed legs.

'Captain Cabrillo. What are you doing up at this ungodly hour?' Maurice didn't break his stride, driving his clawed hands through the air with praying mantis-like precision as he spoke, his voice echoing off the tiles. The former Royal Navy steward refused to address Cabrillo by anything other than his appropriate seafaring rank.

'I might ask the same of you.'

'Five hundred push-ups, five hundred squats, and two miles in the pool. My regular routine.'

Juan stepped out of his terry cloth robe and hung it on a hook.

'I had no idea that Royal Navy stewards were so tough.'

Maurice dropped suddenly into a low-lunging Snake Creeps Through the Grass pose.

'*Mens sana in corpore sano.*'

'"A healthy mind in a healthy body,"' Juan translated as he pulled off the slipper from his specially designed diver's leg. It was partially weighted to compensate for unnecessary buoyancy that would hamper his swimming above or below the surface of the water.

Maurice rose slowly to a standing position, crossing his arms in front of him.

'I should have known you spoke Latin.'

Juan stepped over to the pool.

'Hardly. But I remember the phrase from a class I took years ago. A line from Juvenal. I think it says something like "Pray for a healthy mind in a healthy body, and ask for a stout heart that has no fear of death, and deems length of days the least of Nature's gifts . . ."'

Maurice lowered his crossed arms and extended his open hands waist-high, as if gently pushing against an invisible wall, ending his routine.

'Just so, Captain. Just so.'

Showered for a second time, fed and refreshed after an hour in the pool, Juan Rodriguez Cabrillo strode into the *Oregon*'s conference room in a casual linen shirt and slacks. Free of the Osorio bodysuit, wig, and contacts, he now appeared every inch the Southern California surfer he had been in his carefree youth. Just over six feet tall and built like a competitive swimmer, he had his mother's clear blue eyes and cut his sandy-blond hair spiky and short.

A natural thespian, Cabrillo had first learned the dangerous business of undercover work as a CIA operative decades earlier. Over the years he had perfected the art form with his linguistic talent, dauntless sangfroid, and now the technical support of the *Oregon* crew.

Similarly, the *Oregon* wore its own undercover attire. Outwardly she appeared to be a 590-foot tramp steamer, rusted, wrecked, and ruined by near-criminal neglect. But hiding underneath the faux salt grime and simulated chipped paint was one of the most advanced combat and intelligence-gathering ships in the world. The *Oregon* was the operational platform for the Corporation, Cabrillo's private security firm. And because Juan ran his ship and crew like a corporation, he called himself the Chairman, and his senior staff bore corporate titles as well.

Juan approached the memorial wall in the *Oregon*'s

conference room, a higher-tech version of the White House Situation Room. He studied the framed photo of Tom Reyes, the third and latest *Oregon* crew member to die in the line of duty. His picture hung alongside photos of Mike Trono and Jerry Pulaski. They were all good men, and good soldiers. Juan deeply missed their comradeship. He hated the fact they had died under his command, but death was part of the business.

Every member of the *Oregon*'s valiant crew knew what they had signed on for when they joined the Corporation. It was dangerous work, each assignment seemingly more perilous than the previous one. Each man and woman on board the clandestine vessel was a patriot to the core and embodied the values of duty, honor, and country, though none of them, including Juan, served under the color of uniformed authority these days.

In a word, they were mercenaries.

For risking their lives and sacrificing their time away from home, family, and friends, each crew member received a generous share in the Corporation's profits from the security work it carried out around the world. Often that work was commissioned off the books for the American government, but the Corporation also contracted with other governments and private entities as the opportunity arose. They could take those lucrative assignments with a clear conscience because they never accepted a contract that compromised the security interests of the United States.

Juan straightened Jerry Pulaski's picture. Cabrillo and his crew believed the greatest honor they could pay to the memories of their fallen comrades was to serve with the same distinction and self-sacrifice these men had shown. Their photos were the crew's reminder of that unspoken commitment.

Juan's eyes fell on the golden Roman *aquila* also hanging on the wall, symbolizing the gallantry of his crew, a gift from the Italian government. The ancient battle standard had become the unofficial symbol of the *Oregon*.

Below the *aquila* hung the bejeweled yataghan sword once wielded by Suleiman the Magnificent five hundred years ago, the lavish gift from a grateful Turkish government for the *Oregon*'s resolution of the Kanyon affair. The *Oregon*'s crew had saved the lives of millions of Turks.

Both trophies were reminders of the important work they did year in and year out, thwarting evil and saving lives on missions the American government couldn't or wouldn't undertake. They may have been mercenaries, but it was an honorable duty, and exceptionally well rewarded. Each crewman's percentage of the take was determined by rank and time of service, but even the lowliest deckhand could expect to retire a multimillionaire.

'Chairman, you have a call from Mr Overholt.' Hali Kasim's voice boomed over the intercom. The third-generation Lebanese American was the *Oregon*'s communications director. He was the only crewman of Middle Eastern descent, but he couldn't speak enough Arabic to order a bowl of *balila* in Beirut.

Juan headed over to the nearby conference table.

'I'll take it down here.'

'Aye, Chairman.'

Juan didn't bother picking up the remote for the

videoconferencing camera and big-screen LCD panel on the far wall. Langston Overholt IV hated videoconferencing and Juan wasn't particularly fond of it himself. He took a seat in one of the high-backed executive leather chairs and parked his Sebago leather moccasins on the long mahogany table.

A moment later, Hali's voice came over the intercom.

'Langston Overholt is on the line.'

'Patch him through.'

'My dear boy, I'm so pleased you're still alive,' Overholt said. His octogenarian voice, still clear and strong, reverberated in the surround-sound speakers.

Overholt had recruited Juan directly out of Caltech undergrad and into CIA field operations, mentoring him through dozens of hazardous missions over the years. The famed spymaster was about as old-school as they got, and a dyed-in-the-wool patriot – just two of the many traits they both held in common, and why they had such affection for each other.

'Not half so pleased as I am, Lang. But thanks.'

'I heard your wingsuit escapade was a bit touch and go.'

'Less touch, more go.'

'I can't thank you enough for Miss Wagner's last-minute rescue. Her cover wouldn't have lasted much longer. If she had fallen into the wrong hands, CIA operations worldwide would have been completely jeopardized, to say nothing of the suffering she would have endured at the hands of those degenerate hoodlums.'

'No need to thank me. There isn't anything I wouldn't do for Gretchen.'

'Oh? So, I needn't wire your customarily exorbitant fee?'

'I said, "No need to *thank* me," not "No need to *pay* me." I've got a crew that likes to eat every day, sometimes more than once a day. Navy beans and hardtack aren't as cheap as they used to be.'

Overholt laughed. He knew that Juan was something of a gourmand and only fed his crew the most sumptuous meals prepared by Cordon Bleu-trained chefs, one of the many perks of living and working on the *Oregon*.

'The electronic check is already in the mail, so to speak.'

'How is Gretchen doing?' Cabrillo was worried about her. Wagner had been through a long and grueling under-cover assignment. Amy Forrester, a former Navy combat medic and physician's assistant, had given Wagner the once-over on the AW flight back from Tajikistan, splint-ing her broken wrist and cleaning and bandaging several minor wounds. After a quick exam in the *Oregon*'s med-ical clinic, Wagner had been cleared for the long flight back to the US for a comprehensive physical at Walter Reed.

'Already discharged from Bethesda with a wrist cast and a clean bill of health. She had high praise for your team, and a few choice words for you and that wingsuit stunt you pulled on her.'

Juan chuckled. 'Can't say that I blame her. Not the best idea I ever had. It was sort of like bungee jumping, only without a bungee.'

'All that matters is that you both survived the ordeal.'

'So why the call?'

'I have a favor to ask. I know it's something of an importunity given the fact you've barely had time to recover from your recent adventure.'

'Name it.'

'Do you know the name Shlomo Gottlieb?'

'Shin Bet. Israel's version of the FBI. He's pretty high up the food chain as I recall.'

'He called me with a problem. Two, actually.'

'The first?'

'He has an asset named Asher Massala. He was recruited for undercover work with the Sons of Jacob, an Israeli-Russian mob organization operating in Israel and around the world. Their particular focus at the moment is Africa. Unfortunately, he's gone missing.'

'If he hasn't reported in, he's most likely dead.'

'A fair assumption, given that they found the body of Massala's handler. He'd been tortured and killed.'

'By whom?'

'It's unclear,' Overholt said. 'One scenario is that the Sons of Jacob discovered the true identity of the handler, and under torture, blew Massala's cover.'

'So Asher is either dead or on the run.'

'True . . .' Overholt said, his voice trailing off.

'But another possibility is one that might really scare Shin Bet – that Asher went rogue and killed his handler either before or after the handler discovered something Asher wanted hidden. Any idea what it could be?'

'This Asher fellow was recruited out of prison. Apparently he had ties to the Sons of Jacob before his arrest. Supposedly, he was trying to make amends for his past crimes by serving his country.'

'So Shin Bet thought they found the perfect candidate to infiltrate the Sons of Jacob. But maybe it was the Sons of Jacob that found the perfect candidate to infiltrate Shin Bet.'

'That's the worst-case scenario as far as Shin Bet is concerned,' Overholt said. 'His murder is a close second.'

'But Asher Massala could still be alive, either held against his will or hiding to protect himself. If he is still a Shin Bet operative and the Sons of Jacob know it, they'll want to get their hands on him.'

'And so would a dozen other malefactors. Shlomo is keen on finding Asher and retrieving him, whether or not he's gone rogue.'

'Can't say that I blame him,' Juan said. 'What's holding up Shin Bet or even Mossad from grabbing him up?'

'Lack of resources in the region. The Israelis have their hands full right now – Gaza, Syria, Lebanon. The pot's boiling over and the few cooks they have can't afford to leave the kitchen.'

'So that's where you come in.'

'In more ways than one,' Overholt said.

'How so?'

'Shlomo's call was something of a courtesy. I have a connection to Asher Massala. His sister, Sarai Massala, is a former Mossad agent. At my request, she once did the Company a good turn. A *very* good turn. Unfortunately, it was perceived as against Israeli interests. It cost her her career, but it saved several American lives. She is officially persona non grata with the Israeli government, and in particular, the Israeli intelligence community.'

'And here's where you tell me that you feel like you owe her a favor and you want to find her brother.'

'Yes, of course. But it's more than that. It seems Sarai has been rather aggressive trying to find out information about Asher. Neither Shin Bet nor Mossad are happy about it.'

'And they haven't told her he's undercover because she's out in the cold.'

'Even if they did tell her, she'd still want to know where Asher is. If they tell her they don't know, she'll accuse them of incompetence. She could go to the press or turn up the heat some other way.'

'And if they tell her he's gone rogue, she might not believe that, either,' Cabrillo said. 'She'd probably accuse them of stonewalling.'

'She's not backing off. Shlomo said in not so many words that her persistence is not only threatening ongoing operations but possibly her own brother's mission – if it's still intact.'

'I wouldn't back off, either, if it were my brother.'

Overholt's tone turned ominous. 'Nothing good will come of it for Asher – or for her.'

'Then you need to deploy CIA assets to find her brother.'

'The favor she did for me that terminated her employment with Mossad created a significant crisis between our two agencies that wasn't easily resolved. It also resulted in a letter of reprimand for me. The CIA can't be seen as doing anything connected with her, out of fear of alienating our most important Mideast partner.'

'So it's not just that the Israelis are shorthanded. She pushed too hard, and turned *his* case into *her* case.'

'As always, you see the bigger picture. Shlomo called me as a friend, not as a Shin Bet officer.'

'So I'm guessing that's where I come in. What can I do?'

'I want you to reach out to her and see what services, if any, you can provide to her. I would of course pay you for your expenses – off the books.'

'You always pay me "off the books."'

'I stand corrected. Off-off the books. And I should add, there is some urgency.'

'Unfortunately, we're already scheduled for a contract with a berobed gentleman in Bahrain. We're on our way there now.'

'Is there any chance you can delay that contract? As a personal favor?'

When Juan quit the CIA, it was Overholt who encouraged him to start his own private security business and it was Overholt who stood him up on his feet by giving the Corporation its first contract at a very lucrative government rate. Since then, Overholt – on the undocumented behalf of the CIA – had been Juan's most regular client. Juan really did owe him everything. More important, he was a friend.

'If it's that important to you, I'll make other arrangements with the Sheik of Araby.'

'My fear is that Sarai is about to launch out on her own and put her life at risk. Given her status as a former Mossad field operative, she'd prove quite the catch for foreign intelligence agencies – or worse, the terrorist thugs she used to hunt.'

'Sounds like another Gretchen situation.'

'Ironically, yes.'

'My wingsuit is still at the dry cleaner's, but I'll see what I can do.'

'I've already spoken to Sarai. She needs someone she can trust. That's why I've referred her to you.'

'Text me her number so I can give her a shout.'

'She prefers to meet you in person. Tomorrow, if at all possible.'

'Like you said, she has trust issues. I'll need an address and a photo so I can recognize who I'm meeting with.'

'I'm sending them over shortly and forwarding your number to her in case she decides to reach out beforehand. And please remember that our conversation is top secret. Sarai can't know that Asher is working undercover for Shin Bet.'

'If not for her sake, then yours. Shin Bet would know you were her source for that information.'

'I'm in your debt.'

'Not until I send you the bill.'

Overholt rang off with a chuckle.

Juan sighed as he stood. There was something about this meetup that bothered him, but he couldn't figure out exactly what it was. His private cell phone dinged with a text from Overholt. He opened it. The text included an address for the meeting and a picture of Sarai Massala.

What a knockout.

Whatever misgivings Juan had about the mission suddenly evaporated. He headed over to the intercom.

'Hali, patch me in to Gomez. I need to catch a ride.'

'Aye, Chairman.'

Juan started to sign off and then remembered something.

'Any word from Dr Huxley?'

'No radio contact in the last five hours.'

That wasn't good, Juan thought. The *Oregon*'s chief medical officer was on the other side of the planet and if she got in trouble he'd have a heck of a time pulling her iron out of the fire.

Hali read his mind. 'I wouldn't be too concerned. Sat phones are notoriously unreliable in bad weather conditions. I'm sure she's fine. After all, look who she took along with her.'

Juan smiled. Hali was right. She was in good hands, wherever she was.

I I

Vale Do Javari, Brazil

Dr Julia Huxley, the *Oregon*'s chief medical officer, was turning a shade of green. She was riding in the cramped backseat of the ancient Cessna 172 Skyhawk as it bounced and slewed in the thermals. As a former naval officer, she'd sailed some of the roughest seas on the planet and had never tossed her cookies. She chalked up her current queasiness to the consumption of a tasty roadside *pamonha* – the Brazilian version of a tamale – comprised of unspecified ingredients. *Probably the ground-up body parts of the local health inspector*, she'd decided after her first nauseated burp.

It also didn't help that she couldn't see out the plane's front windscreen, making her a little claustrophobic. Her forward view was blocked by the shoulder-to-shoulder wall of muscle crammed into the front seats.

Chuck 'Tiny' Gunderson was a contract pilot for the Corporation. He didn't serve on board the *Oregon*, but he was the organization's primary fixed-wing pilot for operations beyond the ship. A stint with the Defense Intelligence Agency honed the flying skills he took into the private sector. He could fly anything from a hang glider to a Boeing 747 and everything in between.

His massive six-foot-four, two-hundred-and-eighty-pound frame filled up half of the front cabin. The man was so big he practically had to wedge himself into the diminutive rental aircraft when they loaded up at the airfield hours earlier. Hunched over his yoke and crouching to keep his head from rubbing against the overhead, the former University of Wisconsin tackle looked like a Harlem Globetrotter riding a child's tricycle.

The other half of the windscreen was blocked by the other giant in the front seat, Franklin 'Linc' Lincoln. With his weight lifter's muscular physique and shaved skull, he was the Black version of Mr Clean. He was a member of the *Oregon*'s security operatives affectionally referred to as the 'Gundogs.' The former Navy SEAL sniper was a massive unit, but he was famously agile on his feet like a ballroom dancer, and despite his massive fingers, was easily the *Oregon*'s best lock picker. He loved riding his custom Harley he kept stored aboard ship. Another of his favorite hobbies was reading aviation magazines. He'd spent the last few hours picking Tiny's seasoned aviator brain.

Despite the obstructed front windscreen, the view outside of Huxley's passenger window was breathtaking, especially now that they were flying just three hundred meters above the canopy. The Amazon rainforest was a sea of green – in fact, many greens. 'Just like me,' Huxley whispered to herself. She had no idea there could be so many variations of a single color. Every tree, bush, leaf, and vine had its own shade of green, amplified by the variegating light through the low-hanging clouds of a gathering storm.

The plane took another roller coaster dip that nearly crashed her skull into the low overhead.

'Sorry about that, Doc,' Tiny said with an accent straight

out of the movie *Fargo*. His deep voice crackled in the wonky headsets they wore. 'Another thermal.'

Huxley's tummy gurgled. 'No worries. Any idea how much farther?'

Linc held up an iPad he'd brought along with the GPS coordinates.

'The landing strip should be just up ahead. Ten minutes, max.'

'Straight ahead I can handle. It's the up and down that's giving me fits back here.'

'I'll try and smooth it out,' Tiny said.

Huxley patted his broad shoulder. 'Your flying's not the problem.'

She was grateful for their company. Anyone needing a definition of manhood only had to look at her two friends, the epitome of masculine virtues. Their massive torsos played havoc with her aerial sightseeing, but it was pretty cool to have nearly six hundred pounds of pure muscle escorting her on this foray into the remotest part of the Amazon. None of them were carrying weapons. They were on a medical mission, not a combat operation. And the hassles of trying to transport guns across international borders, particularly in Brazil, wasn't worth the trouble. She knew their intimidating size would deter any knucklehead thinking about causing a problem.

At first she had objected to disrupting Tiny's and Linc's work schedules, but the Chairman insisted they tag along. Huxley was technically on vacation and wanted to use the time to deliver much-needed supplies to a dear friend from medical school. But when Juan found out where she was headed, he decided to pull rank and call this an official

Corporation charitable donation so that he could assign her protection and cover her expenses. She was grateful for his generosity and concern.

The three of them had made quite a spectacle when they transferred planes at the local airport. Tiny and Linc towered over Huxley's diminutive five-foot, three-inch frame. She looked like a Chihuahua being escorted by two bullmastiffs. It was hard to believe she belonged to the same species.

Huxley's stature didn't pose a threat to anyone, but her exceptionally curvaceous figure often drew unwanted attention. God help the idiot who made any kind of unto-ward suggestion – she'd dressed down more than one hapless fool who dared cross the line. The *Oregon* crew was never a problem in that regard, but even on her stor-ied decks Huxley muted her Jayne Mansfield body beneath baggy clothes, wore very little makeup, and kept her dark hair in a simple ponytail. Her current uniform of cargo pants and matching shirt was equally concealing.

The customs officials they encountered in their cross-globe adventure assumed she was a movie star dressed down to hide her celebrity. They knew only someone ter-ribly important or famous would be in the company of such large and intimidating bodyguards. Of course, Hux-ley was neither.

They'd been traveling for twenty-one hours, three of those stuck in border control and customs checks. Huxley had all of the legal and medical documentation she needed to transport the non-refrigerated antibiotics and other med-ical supplies she was bringing to her friend, Aline Izidoro, a Brazilian missionary doctor. Huxley had previously joined her in her work in Africa, but Aline had just begun serving the Indigenous people of the Amazon in her native country. Her mother was from a rainforest tribe and her father was of Portuguese stock. With her long thick hair and shorter stature, Izidoro fit right in with most tribal peoples throughout the Amazon basin.

Huxley had never been to the deep interior and was looking forward to the adventure. Like most Americans, she had seen television documentaries and photographs of the Amazon. But to actually experience its immensity was something else entirely. She'd also read about the illegal farming and gold-mining operations in the area that threatened the habitat of the Indigenous people. The numerous fires and strip mines that dotted the horizon were sad testaments to that reality.

'Got it,' Tiny said in his microphone as he pointed through the windscreen. A patch of cleared jungle lay far below, a hundred meters or so beyond a wide meandering tributary of the Amazon River. His massive paws eased the yoke forward.

They all breathed a sigh of relief. A tropical storm had sprung up unannounced in the last hour and was blanketing the region. By some miracle they had stayed in a window of turbulent sunlight. As long as that storm was smashing the area, there was really nowhere else for them to land and it was impossible for them to turn back around.

Huxley's squeamish stomach felt the gentle descent. She'd be glad to get her feet on solid ground again. Patches of low-lying fog gathered like spider silk in the treetops below.

'How's your visibility?' she asked.

'Spotty, but not bad. You sure about this landing strip?'

'Only what Aline told me. Her team used it last month. I don't think there's going to be a Starbucks down there.'

'A double caramel macchiato with extra whip sounds pretty good to me right about now,' Linc said.

Huxley's stomach curdled at the thought of the hot, sweet, caramelly goo.

'I'll pass.'

Gunderson aimed the high-winged aircraft at the postage-stamp-sized clearing in the distance, adjusting his flaps and throttle on the approach. It was a narrow strip of clear-cut forest. Hardly an asphalt runway, but at least it appeared to be free of obstructions.

Huxley watched the treetops rise in her little side window as the plane descended, and the change of perspective gave the illusion they were speeding up as tree trunks sped past like freeway signs.

'Whoa!' Tiny shouted as he yanked back on the yoke. The plane's nose lurched into the sky as he slammed the throttle home.

Huxley thought she was going to blow chunks as her stomach sank into her feet. She clutched her seat belt as Tiny made a steep turn.

'A herd of pigs,' Linc said. He turned around and saw Hux's distress. He offered a comforting smile, flashing his enormous white teeth. 'Ran right out where we were going to land. We scared them off.'

'Circling around. We'll be fine,' Tiny said.

'No doubt,' was all Huxley could offer.

Moments later, Tiny began his second descent.

'Pig free!' Linc shouted. He turned around and threw a thumbs-up at Hux.

She felt the fat rubber bush tires touch down. The Cessna shuttered and bounced on the uneven ground, hitting every low stump and shallow ditch, but they were doing fine.

Until they crashed.

12

Tiny Gunderson had once executed an emergency landing with a C-130 Hercules transport plane on the pitching deck of an American aircraft carrier in the middle of the Indian Ocean. No easy feat, especially without the benefit of an arresting hook. People who witnessed the event described it as watching a drunk trying to park a Buick on a picnic bench. After that stunt, his money was no good at the Officers' Club at Diego Garcia. Free drinks for life.

Tiny could have used a slug of booze right about now.

Landing the Cessna 172 in a jungle clearing should have been a whole lot easier than touching down on a bucking tarmac at sea, and technically it was. He'd deftly landed the Skyhawk on the ground and kept her on a steady course with the rudder pedals and yoke as the tires bounced along the uneven terrain.

But suddenly a five-hundred-pound tapir – appropriately called a 'bush cow' by the locals – charged across his path.

Tiny stomped the pedals and twisted the yoke to turn the plane and avoid hitting the long-snouted beast. A full-on collision with the propeller would have turned the animal into ribbons of pork sushi, but it might have destroyed the blades and maybe even the airframe. The sharp turn avoided the crash with the tapir, but it drove the Cessna off the narrow airstrip. A moment later, they collided into a vine-covered log.

Linc's head thudded against the passenger window and Huxley's face mashed into the back of Tiny's headrest, but otherwise they were all unharmed.

The plane, not so much.

The nose wheel strut collapsed under the impact.

The crunching metal sound elicited a blue streak from Tiny that shocked even the two salty Navy veterans. He killed the engine and yanked off his headset as the prop slowed its rotations.

'Everybody good?' the big pilot asked as he unbuckled his harness.

Linc pulled off his headset. 'Still waiting for that double caramel macchiato.'

Tiny grinned. 'Extra whip, right?'

'Chocolate sprinkles, too, if you got 'em.'

'I'd like to get my boots on the ground, fellas,' Huxley said. 'The sooner, the better.'

Tiny pushed open his small cabin door and began the process of extricating himself from the cramped cabin like a giant clown climbing out of a mini circus car.

He stepped outside and planted his big boot onto a rotted branch that cracked under his enormous weight. The big man went down with a shout, his ankle badly twisted.

He suddenly wished he were back at the O Club on Diego Garcia.

Huxley examined Gunderson's twisted ankle. Nothing broken, as far as she could tell. Just a nasty sprain. No need for a splint. But he wasn't going anywhere, either.

'You need to RICE this ankle. Rest, ice, compress, and elevate.'

She pulled an instant cold pack from her kit, broke it, placed it on his ankle, then secured it with an Ace bandage – snug but not tight.

'How am I supposed to wear my boot with that rig?'

'Not my problem. Just make sure you keep your leg elevated above your heart whenever you lie down. We've got plenty of ice packs. Thirty minutes every three hours. Mostly I want you to stay off that ankle to give it a chance to heal up.'

'The plane's not going to fix itself,' Tiny said.

Huxley pointed at the busted nose strut. The front of the plane knelt down as if in penitence. 'How are we going to fix that?'

Gunderson winced with pain. 'Baling wire, chewing gum, and a hunk of good old-fashioned American ingenuity.'

'Is that all?'

'In my preflight, I found a pretty decent tool kit in the belly storage compartment. Everything I need for a fix. It won't be pretty to look at, but it'll get the job done.' He turned to Linc. 'Find me a stick I can use as a crutch, will ya?'

'Sure, pal.' Linc headed for the trees nearby. A few drops of rain began falling, pelting the Cessna's aluminum airframe and the leaves.

'Seriously, you can fix this?' Huxley asked. She handed him a canteen and a couple ibuprofen tablets.

'I think we just blew a gasket. That's why you see all that hydraulic fluid on the piston. I can make it good enough to get us off the ground.'

Linc marched back with a sturdy branch thick enough

to support the weight of the big Swede. Linc extended one of his frying pan-sized hands and helped Tiny to his unsteady feet while holding the crutch firmly in place. Huxley eased in beside the towering slab of Nordic beef and helped him up as best she could.

They were all getting wet as the rainfall surged.

'What are our options?' Huxley asked.

'There were no storms on the long-range radar track before we left. Whatever this is' – Tiny held out his palm to catch a few drops of rain – 'it should pass before too long. Might be ten minutes, might be ten hours. Even if the plane was good to go we'd have to sit tight until the weather clears.'

'We have to get you back,' Huxley said. 'You're pretty banged up. I'd like to get you x-rayed to make sure there's nothing else going on.'

'Don't worry about me. I'll stay here and work on the plane while the two of you get those supplies to your friend.' Tiny balanced himself on one leg and the crutch with ease to prove his point. He turned to Linc. 'You good with that?' Technically, the former sniper was in charge of security, but as the plane's captain Tiny was responsible for his passengers' safety.

Linc pulled a map from his pocket and checked it.

'We still have an eight-hour hike ahead of us. We're getting a late start, but we'll still get there before dark – assuming, of course, your friend's coordinates are correct.'

'Aline was right about the airstrip.'

Linc fought back a smirk as he glanced at the busted-up airplane. 'Yeah, I guess so. The extra gear won't be that heavy and I don't see any serious obstacles in our path.'

'You going to be okay here by yourself until tomorrow?' Huxley asked Tiny.

'It'll take me that long to get the Skyhawk sorted out. It'll give me something to do.'

Huxley was torn. There was a chance Tiny had suffered some other internal injury that wasn't presenting itself right now, as unlikely as that was. She was more concerned about him being out here all by himself. The jungle seemed to be designed to kill and eat whatever happened to be hanging around uninvited, humans included. Gunderson might get bit or clawed or poisoned by any number of critters. Or he could get banged up working on the plane by himself.

But then again, she wasn't Tiny's mother. And her friend Aline was counting on their supplies.

Huxley stepped over to the luggage hatch in the plane's fuselage and fished out a small emergency medical kit from her gear and handed it to him.

'You know how to use one of these?' Huxley asked. She held annual emergency and practical medical trainings for the *Oregon* crew, but Tiny wasn't a crewman.

'I can work a Band-Aid pretty good.'

The doctor turned to the big sniper. 'Stay or go?'

Linc glanced around the clearing. He nodded at a path cutting through the trees. He was torn.

'I hate to come all this way just to fail the mission.' He looked back at Tiny. 'You sure you're good to go?'

'If there's a problem, I'll radio you on the sat phone, soon as the storm clears. Piece of cake.'

Linc nodded. 'Okay then, we'll saddle up and get this show on the road.'

13

The Cessna 172 Skyhawk airframe, first produced in 1956 and still in production, was originally designed for civilian commuter flights for asphalt runways in the more civilized parts of the world. But the tiny workhorse was so reliable and easy to fly that enterprising bush pilots simply upgraded it with bigger 'tundra' tires front and back for unpaved surface landings, and in this particular case, an extra storage compartment slung beneath the fuselage.

Tiny's preflight inspection included a look-see into that belly compartment. There was plenty of room for baggage storage, but it also contained an exceptionally well-thought-out toolbox for bush repairs. It was practically a miniature mechanic's garage pared down for weight.

Before Linc and Dr Huxley marched into the jungle, he had them hook up a small, hand-powered portable winch – what his grandpa used to call a 'come-a-long' – to a distant tree with a couple lengths of lightweight tree-saver tow straps. Within a few minutes the three of them had wrangled the lightweight aircraft back onto the field, just as a cloud burst overhead and drenched the trio in a warm rain. They all pulled on their ponchos.

Linc hauled a couple of heavy logs and laid them carefully against the top of the tail section near the rudder. The weight of the logs easily lifted the nose gear clear off the ground and gave Tiny plenty of room to work.

As Linc and Huxley divvied up Tiny's portion of medical supplies and hiking gear, the big Swede maneuvered around on his throbbing ankle to inspect the nose gear, while pulling the toolbox with him. By the time they shook hands and parted ways, Tiny had made his assessment of the actual damage.

As near as he could tell, it looked as if the crash wasn't structural. He wouldn't know until he pulled everything apart, but his best guess was that when the nose gear hit the log, the hydraulic fluid blasted past the O-ring assembly and dislodged the rings. At least he hoped that was the case because he didn't see any spare parts lying around.

The worst-case scenario was if he couldn't effect a minimal repair they wouldn't be able to take off, given the unevenness of the airstrip. He needed to be able to get the Skyhawk up to speed in order for the plane to generate lift – like a high jumper needing a distance of track to run before making the leap. Some of the really tricked-out bush planes could practically take off without much forward movement, but this old bird wasn't one of those, especially with a full passenger and baggage load.

As Tiny opened up the toolbox he suddenly wished he was with Linc and Dr Huxley. It wasn't fair they had to pack in his heavy load through miles of jungle, but there wasn't much he could do about that with his twisted ankle. He pushed the guilt out of his mind. His goal now was to get this plane fixed up.

Failing his friends wasn't an option.

Gunderson spent most of his adult life in the cabins of modern aircraft, surrounded by the glow of LED screens, the aroma of plush leather seats, and the comfort of air-conditioning.

But he couldn't have been happier sweating beneath the Cessna and slapping away the mosquitoes. His nose was filled with the sweet smell of hydraulic fluid, his thick fingers were slicked with grease, and his knuckles got scraped up as he wrestled with the bolts, roll pins, and snap rings he had to loosen or remove in order to pull the nose gear assembly apart.

All of it brought back great memories of his youth spent at his grandfather's airfield in Wisconsin. 'Farfar' Gunderson was a working crop-duster pilot, but also ran a small rural flight school. It was literally a one-man operation, from pilot to grease monkey, until Tiny, still in grade school, took his first airplane ride. After that, he wanted to learn everything there was to learn about flying. His grandfather only owned one trainer: a Cessna Skyhawk, the plane Tiny first learned to fly, and fix.

Before Tiny had finished high school he had manufactured, rebuilt, or replaced just about every single part on the venerable 172. Some of his happiest childhood moments were learning basic mechanical skills at his grandfather's elbow, a teacher as patient as he was skilled on the ground and in the air.

Tiny shared his grandfather's respect for the practical genius of the Cessna's design. For all the revolutionary whiz-bang gadgetry aboard modern aircraft, Tiny preferred the Skyhawk's analog simplicity. All he needed in order to complete today's repairs was a hammer, a couple of wrenches, a flathead screwdriver, and a bicycle pump, which would not only fill the air in the tires but also the air in the nose gear piston. There wasn't any spare hydraulic fluid for the fluid-air mixture the piston preferred, but he could pump enough air into it so that the piston would give plenty of cushion for takeoff. It would be a little spongy, but he wasn't angling for style points.

Tiny held the two rubber concave backup rings and the main O-ring in his fingers and inspected them closely. They were completely undamaged, just as he had hoped. He needed to wipe off the stainless steel ring pack support with a rag and relubricate it with a little engine oil before he could set the rings back inside of it, just the way his grandfather had taught him.

If his luck held, and if his throbbing ankle would allow it, he might even have everything reassembled before dark. If not, he could finish things up first thing in the morning before Linc and Dr Huxley returned. He'd use whatever time he had left before their arrival to do a walk-around – or at least a hobble-around – to make sure there weren't any other problems, and do a preflight check of basic components, fuel, and fluids. Though he was completely lost in the art and joy of the repair process, a tingling feeling crawled up the back of his neck. It was the same kind of feeling he had gotten when approaching the pitching flight deck of that aircraft carrier, or one of a hundred airfields he'd flown into at night without lights. He glanced around, scanning the tree line for trouble. His uncorrected twenty-twenty eyesight revealed nothing. But he knew he was being watched.

14

Gash-Barka Region, Eritrea

The abandoned monastery had stood for centuries at the foot of an arid plateau worthy of a John Ford Western landscape. Eritrea had made Christianity its state religion back in the fourth century, the first African nation to do so, and the Nine Saints monastery had been one of the faith's earliest beachheads among the pagan tribes.

Ruined by earthquakes and wars over the centuries, the venerated institution had been rebuilt and enlarged numerous times. Its primary virtue was a natural spring water well. But Eritrea's harsh political and economic climate had withered away the last remnants of forestation in the region along with the monastery's faithful purpose a decade earlier.

Its original mission forsaken, the monastery found rebirth as the headquarters of SurChev, a mercenary organization. Jean-Paul Salan had spared no expense for the reconstruction project. SurChev had made Salan more money than he could possibly spend in a lifetime.

The sudden notice from President Tedros Keflezighi of his imminent arrival by helicopter hadn't caused Salan any particular concern. The military-style facility was always in good order and its operations in full swing.

'Looking forward to it,' Salan had said on the phone.

Fortunately, it wasn't a video call. Otherwise, Keflezighi would have detected Salan's flexed jaw and narrowing eyes. He bore no resentment paying his ongoing bribes to the President. Salan simply calculated them as another maintenance expense. But part of what that money was supposed to buy was his privacy. In the three years Salan had been in operation, Keflezighi never expressed any interest in his operation.

Why now?

The President's desert-camouflaged Soviet-era M-24 Hind attack helicopter circled the compound twice, its blades drumming the air so hard Salan could feel the pressure beating against his chest as it descended in a cyclone of stinging sand particles. The Hind was the bane of Afghani tribesmen in their war with the Soviet Union decades ago. It looked like a heavily armored dragonfly to Salan's eye with the rocket pods under its stubby wings and the Gatling guns in its rotating nose.

President Keflezighi, tall by Eritrean standards and much better fed, exited the helicopter in a crouch, followed by his six-man security entourage. Salan had done his homework and knew the background of the President's trained killers. Two were members of the infamous Eritrean National Security Office. The other four were foreigners and ex-service members of their respective countries – a Ukrainian, a Dutchman, and two Nigerians.

Salan raced over to the President and extended a hand.

The President took the measure of the man standing in front of him. Salan was casually dressed in cargo shorts, desert boots, and a collared pocket shirt. He looked more like a French movie producer on location than a captain of mercenaries. He stood at just five foot seven, but the bearded forty-five-year-old carried himself with the energy and strength of a much younger man. He possessed an undeniable military bearing that belied the mischievous eyes and winning smile. Salan had previously informed the President that he had served as a captain in France's elite 1st Marine Infantry Parachute Regiment, though why he had separated from service was unclear.

Keflezighi, an otherwise imperious and dignified figure, warmly shook Salan's hand, his confidence bolstered by the watchful eyes of his six gunmen.

Salan had been careful not to bring along his own people to avoid any kind of unnecessary confrontation. He knew well from experience that mercs working for a petty dictator like Keflezighi were constantly vying for his favor to secure promotions and bonuses. The best way to earn such favor was to prove themselves more violent than any potential threat.

'Mr President, welcome to Nine Saints,' Salan said in his native French, his father's language. He knew the President had studied at Saint-Cyr – France's version of West Point – for his military education. Though his grades didn't reflect it, the President must have been a good student. He had led rebel forces in the final years of the bloody revolution against Ethiopia and won independence for his nation in 1993. A constitution was written and a grateful legislature elected him President.

But Keflezighi's professed commitment to universal human rights and self-determination evaporated soon after he assumed office. He was now the head of a uni-party state without a functioning legislature or a judicial branch that could check his ambitions. With absolutely no freedom of the press, lifelong universal military conscription – essentially, battalions of slave labor – and absolute police power, it was with good reason that Eritrea under Keflezighi's ruthless dictatorship had been labeled the North Korea of Africa.

All of which made it the perfect location for Salan's mercenary organization.

Keflezighi gestured toward the compound beyond the revitalized monastery.

'I could barely see any of this from the air. It's very well hidden.'

'We've learned a few tricks over the years, Your Excellency.'

Besides the refurbished monastery complex, Salan had expanded the base's infrastructure. It now included several large area maintenance shelters (LAMS) – huge portable fabric buildings used by military units around the world. Salan deployed them to create barracks, a helicopter hangar, maintenance and repair shops, and training facilities. Each of the LAMS was tan, which blended in perfectly with the landscape. Anything else in the compound that would appear as angles or straight lines in overhead surveillance was covered with camouflage netting to keep prying satellite eyes occluded. The entire complex was heated and cooled by underground geothermal coils and powered by a hidden supply of hydrogen fuel cells.

Salan watched the President studying the compound with a banker's eye.

'Quite impressive.'

'It's adequate, certainly.'

'I should like to see more of it.'

'I've had my chef prepare lunch for you and your team.'

'Later.' Keflezighi nodded toward the compound. 'Lead the way.'

Salan cast an eye at the bodyguards in their Kevlar vests and holstered sidearms. They all seemed to want Salan to resist.

'Of course, Your Excellency. Follow me.'

15

'This way, Your Excellency,' Salan said as he steered him toward the air-conditioned gymnasium housed in one of the giant tentlike structures.

Salan opened the door. The President's bodyguards went in first. The President followed right behind them. As soon as Keflezighi entered the doorway, a whistle blew and thirty-eight of Salan's trainees – 'boots' – leaped to rigid attention, facing the doorway.

Keflezighi scanned the room of young, hardened faces. None older than thirty-five, the President guessed. There were white-skinned Europeans of various ethnicities, but even more Africans and Middle Easterners. Several Asians were in the mix along with a handful of women. The boots were all dressed in gym shorts and T-shirts. Every thigh, arm, and chest was heavily muscled, and not an ounce of fat was on display.

Satisfied, the President nodded curtly. 'As you were.'

'You heard the President! Back to work!' the booming voice bellowed in a Scottish brogue.

Keflezighi turned and saw the sandy-haired commander storming around the room, his cabled arms covered in tattoo sleeves, yelling more instructions.

Salan nodded in the Scotsman's direction. 'My training supervisor, Sergeant Angus Fellowes. Special Air Service. Tough as they come.'

The President turned to his giant Ukrainian bodyguard, a former operator with the infamous Azov Regiment. Keflezighi asked him in English, 'Have you ever worked with the SAS? Are they as good as they say?'

The Ukrainian nodded. 'Yeah. They trained us. Good fighters, for sure. And smart.'

'Shall we?' Salan asked.

Salan led Keflezighi around the spartan facility, the President's entourage in tow and on guard passing through a room full of soldiers in training – all potential threats. There were several stations of hanging bars, ropes, rings, and free weights. Each station was occupied.

Keflezighi stopped at a pull-up station. Two men were hanging full length on one bar, and two women on another next to it, motionless.

Fellowes stormed up. 'Let's go and count 'em out! Fifty!'

'Yes, Sergeant Fellowes!'

The two men and two women began their pull-ups. Their forms were slow and letter-perfect – toes pointed down, no swinging, chins touching the bars.

'Eighteen . . . nineteen . . . twenty . . .' they sounded out in unison.

Keflezighi watched with amusement. They rose and fell like perfectly timed pistons pumping on a fine German engine.

'Forty-one, forty-two, forty-three . . .'

The boots never slowed, and moved as one unit.

The President exchanged an incredulous glance with one of the Nigerians. He looked around the room. Every one of Salan's boot camp trainees was equally engaged in their respective exercises, each moving in effortless, synchronized perfection.

'Fifty!' the four finally called out and dropped to the ground as Fellowes blew his whistle twice. Every boot rotated to the next station. A moment later, Fellowes whistled thrice and the recruits resumed their workouts.

'They're like robots,' Keflezighi said. 'Automatons.'

'Not exactly. Our rigorous training program merely conditions them to act as one and to obey orders instantly, two essential qualities in combat operations.'

'How do you find such recruits?'

Salan hesitated to answer him. Whether by accident or intuition, Keflezighi had asked the single most important question. Recruiting was key to building his mercenary program – but it was only the beginning.

'We have a network of relationships that help us locate men and women with the particular set of physical and psychological characteristics we require.'

Which was completely true – just not the whole truth.

Salan had grown up a street fighter in the worst ghettos in Marseilles. But it was beneath the cold stone walls of the prison yard where he learned that men were not naturally pacifists. It was so-called civilization that blunted a man's innate brawling instincts and tamped down his evolutionary compulsion to control others through force. Only prison or war could ultimately free a 'civilized' man to be his true self by stripping away the outward restraints society imposed upon the born savagery of *Homo sapiens*.

That was why he culled men and women from the worst prisons in the world to become his soldiers and honed them for combat here at his desert training camp.

And there was so much more to Salan's program. He was building an army of super mercenaries the likes of which the world had never seen. Human history turned on the actions of the heroic few. In the hands of his created killers it would turn again very soon.

But all of that was information the Eritrean President didn't need to know, now or ever.

'They are obviously in fantastic physical condition. What's your secret?'

Salan smiled. Keflezighi wouldn't believe it even if he told him about the revolutionary science behind the program. A lie would be easier for him to digest.

'Nutritional supplements, and a little bit of sweat.'

Salan led the President and his security team through the indoor pistol range, where the boots demonstrated their incredible marksmanship skills, before taking them back to the monastery for the meal prepared for them.

The entourage took up security positions outside the building as Salan and Keflezighi dined on fresh swordfish hauled from the waters of the Red Sea just that morning. The wide variety of fruits and leafy greens on the table were flown in from Israel and stored in the monastery's commercial refrigerators.

After finishing up their meal, Salan and Keflezighi lit fat Cuban cigars as they sipped their icy mojitos, the President's favorite adult beverage.

'I have to say, you have a most impressive operation

here,' Keflezighi said, blowing out a cloud of blue smoke. 'You must have spent millions.'

'Hardly, Your Excellency. Most of what you see was already in our storage facilities or transferred from other locations. And, of course, we have an abundant source of cheap labor.'

The President pointed at Salan with his cigar. 'I think you are too modest.'

'I don't deny I'm paid a handsome fee for my services, of course,' Salan admitted. He couldn't risk stoking the President's greed by telling him of the vast amount of money he was being paid by his Saudi employer. 'But the costs of doing business are extraordinary. Foreign governments are well equipped and always on high alert.'

'Tell me, Salan. You were born in France and fought under Le Tricolor. Would you ever take an assignment against your home country?'

'SurChev is my home now, and my nationality is money. In my experience, avarice proves more constant than patriotism.'

'And you have no moral qualms about killing for money?'

'I would wage peace if it were profitable.'

Keflezighi laughed. 'You are too cynical. I suspect you have no religion, either.'

'Money is the purest medium of human interaction. It is the hatred of money that is the root of all stupidity. A holy man can easily lie, but price only tells the truth.' Salan shrugged. 'But my amateur philosophizing is hardly interesting. Tell me, Your Excellency, what is on your mind today?'

'Eritrea is a poor country with few resources, and ravaged by drought. More Eritreans are fleeing for Europe than any other African nation.'

Salan held his tongue. It was true. Without jobs, freedom, or opportunities to better themselves, young people were getting out as quickly as they could. But it was Keflezighi's Marxist collectivism and poor central planning that had driven his nation to the brink, not global warming.

'I'm already paying you a generous fee, Mr President.'

'Perhaps there are services you can render as further recompense.'

'Such as?'

'There are traitors and malcontents living abroad who need to be silenced.'

'For hire?'

'You are a guest in my country because I allow it. I would think you would do everything within your power to maintain our relationship.'

'I know that you come from a socialist perspective, so let me remind you how entrepreneurial capitalism works. I only make money when you pay me for my services. I don't make money when I pay you to provide those services.'

Keflezighi stiffened, and stabbed his cigar into the yellow crystal ashtray.

Salan had hit a nerve. The President was clearly unused to people denying him what he desired. But Salan had no intention of becoming a puppet on his string. Still, he hated to lose Eritrea as his base of operations. It had proven quite useful. And there was an elegant solution to the problem at hand.

'I have another suggestion, if I may.'

Keflezighi folded his hands. 'I'm listening.'

'Your security team seems quite competent. I suggest allowing me to put them through my conditioning regimen. They will experience everything you saw today, and more. I can bring them up to standard, and then return them to you and you can deploy them as you wish.'

'And what will that cost me?'

Salan took another puff of his cigar. 'The cost per specimen is exorbitant. But since we're friends, I'd consider it a favor if you would allow me to donate my services for all six of your bodyguards.'

A smile crept across the dictator's narrow face.

'Favor granted.'

Salan lifted his mojito and they toasted their agreement. The smile on his face was genuine. Keflezighi had played right into his hands.

The presidential helicopter lifted off the pad, spattering sand and dirt in Salan's face. Fellowes held up his hands to shield his eyes.

The Scotsman shouted over the thunderous roar of the two turboshaft engines.

'And what did His Excellency Lord Bawbag want?'

'What else? More money. And perhaps worse.'

The two men watched the Hind turn and arc away back toward the capital, Asmara. The rotor noise began to fade.

'You think he wants to take over the operation?'

'I wouldn't put it past him.'

'What do you intend to do about it?'

'I made him a counteroffer, which he graciously accepted.'

'Which is?'

'We're going to run his bodyguards through our program.'

Fellowes laughed. 'What a bloody *eejit*. He'll rue the day, that's for sure.'

Salan nodded. Fellowes was sharp as a knife. By running Keflezighi's bodyguards through his physical- and mental-conditioning program, Salan would gain control of them. He could then easily pick the most opportune time to assassinate the murderous autocrat and gain control of the entire country for himself.

'What time is the mission brief tomorrow?' Salan asked. The India mission was the most complex operation SurChev had ever undertaken. The Saudi was paying him a royal fortune to carry it out, which made it well worth the high risk. This would be the greatest test yet of his super mercenary army.

'Five a.m. All senior hands will be on deck.'

'You know that while we're gone, you'll be running these boots.'

'Not a problem, I assure you. This batch will be finished with their final evolution in two weeks. When is the next batch coming in?'

'Dr Hightower estimates within the next week.'

Fellowes nodded. 'Good. Seems we're losing them faster than we can make them.'

'Like my mother always said, "You can't make a soufflé without breaking a few eggs."'

'Your mother never made a soufflé in her life. Couscous, maybe.'

'No, not even that.'

In truth, Salan hadn't seen his mother since the day he turned fifteen, the same day a French magistrate sentenced him to prison for manslaughter.

Salan threw an arm over his old friend's shoulder.

'Let's grab a drink. We have a lot to celebrate.'

16

'I think I hate green,' Huxley said as she mopped the sweat from her eyes. The wide varieties of the emerald color had enthralled her earlier that morning when she was in the comfort of an air-conditioned aircraft cabin high above the jungle canopy.

Now, some four hours later, the Amazon felt like a hot, sweaty, itchy, bug-infested army blanket draped around her shoulders that she couldn't shrug off. The soaking rain that fell on them back on the airstrip had passed an hour before. She and Linc couldn't pull their plastic ponchos off fast enough before the sweat began to run in rivulets. What little relief from the heat the storm had given had long since passed.

Though they were both Navy veterans, Huxley had spent most of her career in the enclosed environmental comforts of naval medical facilities either on board ships or dry land. She had ended her naval career as the chief medical officer at the San Diego Naval Base, one of the nicest duty stations around and the best weather in the continental United States. But Linc had spent nearly his entire Navy career as a frogman scrambling by foot over and through some of the harshest terrains on the planet, hunting dangerous killers with extraordinarily bad intentions. He seemed impervious to every discomfort they had encountered so far. She was more than happy to follow his lead on this expedition into the deep interior, even though he was technically there as her bodyguard.

The temporary lull in the storm allowed Huxley to report in to the *Oregon*. She told them that they had a successful landing and were on their way in to drop off the medical supplies. She also thought it prudent to not define the term 'successful' nor that the medical supplies slung across her shoulders were likely to drop her in this heat. She didn't see any point in worrying them, since the *Oregon* could do nothing for them this far away.

Huxley had also checked in on Tiny. Despite his obvious physical distress, he sounded genuinely happy to be busy with his repair work and reported that it was going well.

Huxley closed the comms wondering if Tiny was as good of a liar as she was.

Linc held up a big right fist to signal a stop, as if on patrol. In his left hand he held a cheap Chinese-made machete. After clearing customs, they'd picked up three of them at a little bodega near the airport along with some other camping supplies. Huxley trudged up quietly behind him. She estimated they were only about four hours away from their rendezvous point with her friend Dr Aline Izidoro.

'Hear that?' Linc asked.

'A river.' She had been lost in thought and missed the sound of the rushing water as they approached.

Linc stuck the blade of the machete into the wet ground, pulled his waterproof map out of a pocket, and showed her their location.

'We're right about here.'

'About halfway.' Hux was surprised how tired her voice sounded.

'Hang in there, Doc. Won't be long now,' Linc said, his bald head dripping with sweat like a rain gutter spout. The straps of his heavy rucksack strained against his broad shoulders. Because Tiny couldn't make the trek, Linc was carrying over a hundred and fifteen pounds of medical supplies, along with over half of their personal gear and food. Huxley was carrying just under sixty. Right now, she thought it felt like six hundred.

'Do I look that miserable?' Huxley asked. She hadn't said a word, but she'd been grumbling in her mind for hours. 'Sorry.'

'It's not you I'm worried about. It's all of those poor mosquitoes you're overfeeding.'

'I'm fine, really. More annoyed with myself than anything.' She shifted the weight of her pack where she stood. 'I spend a lot of time in the gym doing Pilates. But now that I'm out here I suddenly realize I need to change up my routine and start focusing on functional fitness.'

'You're doing fine, Doc.'

'That's only because you're the one who's carrying the heavy load.'

'I was built for that sort of work, don't you think?'

'No doubt. But you've taken what God gave you and added to it with a lot of hard work and training.'

Linc was about to compliment her for being a skilled combat surgeon when suddenly they heard shouts in the distance over the noise of the river. They both ducked down as Linc shed his massive ruck.

'That's Portuguese I'm hearing,' Huxley whispered. 'What are they doing here?'

The Vale do Javari was a region of the Amazon under the protection of the Brazilian government to prevent the destruction of the rainforest and preserve the habitat of the Indigenous tribes. The only outsiders allowed to travel there had to acquire government permits to do so. Huxley, Linc, and Tiny had secured their permits with Dr Izidoro's guidance and carried them in waterproof sleeves.

'I don't speak Portuguese, but from the tone of their voices, I don't think it's an anthropology convention,' Linc said. Proving his point, a shovel clanged against a rock in the distance.

'Wait here,' he whispered.

Before Hux could say a word, Linc disappeared into the bush.

Linc lay on his belly under the cover of a red flowering shrub on the edge of the wooded riverbank.

On the other side of the fast-moving river, several trees had been cut down and the vegetation cleared away. But this wasn't a logging operation. The primary activity of the men opposite him was directed at the dirt they were stripping away and dropping into rough-hewn sluices fed by hand-carried river water.

A gold-mining operation. And totally illegal.

Most of the men were carrying buckets of either dirt or river water in each hand; others were shoveling. One man picked up a chain saw and yanked the starter cord. Its motor roared to life in a haze of oily smoke. He laid the spinning chain to the base of a nearby tree, gunning the engine as he began cutting through it, spraying wood chips.

But what caught Linc's eye most of all were the half dozen gunmen milling around the perimeter in muddy jeans, tennis shoes, and T-shirts. They each carried an AK-47 or a variant, with an extra mag or two tucked in their belts. Some rifles were slung over shoulders, others held loosely at their sides. The youngest shooter, a teenager, lit a cigarette, one of the few men not already smoking, including the laborers sweating in the heat.

Definitely not a disciplined outfit, Linc told himself. But he still wouldn't want to be on the other end of the 'spray and pray' volley those pistoleros could throw at him. His hand involuntary reached for a nonexistent holster. He and Juan had talked about trying to either smuggle in a few guns or secure them on the ground through local contacts. But gun smuggling and possession were illegal and would have put Dr Izidoro's work in jeopardy. It was supposed to be an easy, one day, in-and-out mission and Dr Izidoro promised them it was safe.

Linc had seen enough. Time to get back to Dr Huxley with the bad news.

Hux sighed, angry and frustrated. 'Gold miners?'

'I counted fifty-three men in total, seven carrying weapons,' Linc said. 'If they're working in shifts, there might be even more back at their camp – somewhere close by, I'm guessing.'

'They're right in our way. Not exactly what we need right now.'

'Like a pimple on prom night.'

'How far around do we need to go?'

Linc pulled out his map and traced a line with his finger.

'To play it safe, I'd say at least a half mile past wherever this goldfield ends. If we're lucky, we'll be able to cross there. If not, we'll push on until we can find a spot. I want to stay back from the river, too, just in case they're running patrols. Once I think we're clear of them, we'll walk the riverbank. It's easier than trying to work our way through that brush.'

'We're looking at adding a couple of hours to our trip.'

'Each way.'

'Think we'll still make it by dark?'

'Depends on the terrain. We'll have to get after it. But I don't want to push you over your limits.'

'If we don't get there in time, there's a chance the Poison Arrow band will move on, and then there won't be any point to hauling any of this stuff.'

'True. But that's not what I said.'

'I'm fine.'

'My mama taught me that lying was a sin.'

Huxley shrugged. '"The only easy day was yesterday," right?'

Linc smiled. She was quoting the famous SEAL team motto.

'So I've heard.'

'Lead the way.'

17

On Board the Sekhmet

The mercy ship *Sekhmet* split the cerulean waters of the Arabian Sea. The ancient vessel, a Greek passenger liner, had been completely refurbished and repurposed for its current mission with laboratories, surgical suites, and accommodations for staff and patients. It wore the symbols of both the Islamic Red Crescent and the Christian Red Cross.

Dr Heather Hightower, an avowed atheist, winced the first time she saw the *Sekhmet*'s white-painted hull and its two bright red religious emblems.

'It looks like a giant "C+" from a distance,' she'd told the captain. Hightower was the CEO of the Micah Foundation, the nonprofit organization that operated the *Sekhmet*. She'd never earned less than an A in any course of her studies all the way through her PhD/MD doctoral program in genetic engineering at Yale.

Now sailing in the heart of the Arabian Sea, she felt a long way from New Haven, Connecticut – and happily so.

Hightower stood in the animal lab with one of her assistants, a veterinary technician. The secured facility was located on the lowest deck, in part to shield the passengers and crew from the noise and smell of the kennels, but mostly to hide their existence.

A wall of cages on the far side of the room each held a single juvenile Malinois, a cousin of the Belgian sheepdog.

'Which one?' Hightower asked.

The young Spaniard, Eva Quezada, consulted her tablet. 'Number four. Female.'

'Let's do it.' The former Olympic volleyball captain towered over the diminutive technician.

Tall and broad-shouldered, the forty-four-year-old Hightower was in the best physical condition of her life, which she considered both a perk and an obligation in her line of research. Her size had always intimidated most men, but her Nordic good looks, full lips, and penetrating green eyes were irresistibly attractive. The few men who were physically confident enough to approach her inevitably withered under the intensity of her extraordinary intellect. Only one man had ever truly won her heart, her late husband, Dr Jonathan Hightower, twenty years her senior. He called her his king-sized version of Scarlett Johansson, a nickname she never cared for.

Quezada tapped a virtual toggle on her tablet and the electronic lock on cage number four ticked open.

Hightower opened the door. A bright-eyed, short-haired puppy with a smooth tawny coat and dark muzzle smiled at her with sharp white teeth and a lolling pink tongue. Massive for its young age, it weighed nearly sixty pounds.

'Hello, beautiful,' Hightower said as she deftly lifted the hefty dog into her arms. She turned to Quezada. 'Lead the way – and don't forget your gloves.'

'Yes, ma'am.'

*

A single-story wall of cages on the far side of the next room each held a wide variety of mature, mixed-breed dogs.

As soon as the two humans entered, the caged canines jumped to their feet and barked, betraying their vicious natures. Seeing the puppy in Hightower's arms only increased their frenzy. Their barks sounded like gunshots echoing off the steel bulkheads. The two women had to shout above the noise.

The Malinois pup trembled in Hightower's arms. She set the dog down in the center of a low-walled circular cage in the middle of the deck. The vet techs called the circular cage the Colosseum, for obvious reasons.

The trembling puppy sat on its golden haunches, staring up with soft brown eyes at the tall scientist.

'This is your first time in the lead, isn't it?' Hightower asked.

Quezada's voice quavered. 'I've assisted Dr Dominguez twice before.'

'So you know what to expect.'

'Yes, ma'am.'

'Good. You take it from here.'

'Yes, ma'am.'

'Then let's get to it. I'm on a tight schedule.'

'Do you have a preference?' Quezada asked.

'It's your test. You decide.'

Quezada nodded. She consulted the tablet in her hand and selected one of the smaller dogs and tapped the virtual toggle next to its cage number. The electronic lock clicked open.

'Not that one. Larger. And male.'

'Yes, ma'am.'

'And you don't have to call me "ma'am." Heather is fine.'

'Yes, ma – Of course. I mean, yes, too small. Sorry.'

Quezada tapped the virtual toggle again and the cage relocked. Then she hit another toggle for a different cage. Inside was a muscular animal with a broad chest, a squarish head, and massive jaws. His examination records identified him as a pit bull terrier mix of unspecified genetic origin. His short hair was the color of cigarette ash and his bulging bloodshot eyes indicated a state of high agitation. Like the Malinois puppy, it was unusually massive.

Quezada pulled on her pair of heavy leather gloves and approached the cage with trepidation. The pit bull's snout was pressed against the cage door and shoved it open when Quezada released the latch. It took all of her strength to keep the ninety-pound animal from charging out toward the Colosseum. She blocked its progress with her legs and one gloved hand as she slipped the other beneath the dog's thick collar.

The infuriated beast growled as its nails skittered on the steel deck, trying to get at the trembling puppy. Quezada held on tight as the pit bull mix whimpered and snarled, rising up on its powerful hind legs against the force of her grip.

'Better not let go,' Hightower said, bemused. The pit bull could easily turn on the small woman and tear her apart. Its already violent disposition was further trained to increase its ferocity for the sake of the testing protocols.

Quezada barely managed to get her other hand underneath the pit bull's collar, but with the two-handed purchase she was finally able to control the enthusiastic street killer and maneuvered him toward the Colosseum entrance.

'Here, let me help,' Hightower offered as she tapped a button on her digital watch. She opened up the arena door and Quezada let the animal go.

The snarling beast lunged through the open Colosseum door to the chorus of caged dogs howling with bloodlust.

It took only seconds for the brutal murder. The kennel rang with the din of the other dogs snarling, yelping, and whining in their cages, all triggered by what they had just witnessed.

Hightower tapped her digital watch again. She picked up the Malinois puppy, but held it away from her body so that its paws and muzzle couldn't touch her. By the miracle of her genetic manipulation, it was the small dog that had won the fight.

She handed the dog to Quezada, who took the animal into her arms. The puppy licked the Spaniard's face as its paws crimsoned her lab coat.

Hightower's digital watch alarmed. She pulled off her gloves and tossed them on a nearby exam table.

'I need to get going.' Hightower nodded at the pit bull's bloody corpse in the ring. 'Get a deckhand to help you clear this mess.'

Quezada struggled to carry the Belgian puppy toward the cleaning station.

'Will do.'

'And get me your report by end of business today.'

Hightower didn't wait for a response as she turned and hurried out of the lab.

She had humans to attend to.

18

Hightower noticed a speck of blood on her lab coat as she entered the evaluation lab, but decided it wasn't worth taking the time to change out of it. She couldn't tolerate tardiness in others and simply couldn't allow it for herself. The incompetent always made excuses, but nothing was more easily accomplished than punctuality.

She tapped in the code to the electronic door lock, stepped inside the spacious facility, and shut the door behind her. Ten new recruits, all men, huddled together in self-defined groups of race or nationality on the rubber-matted gym floor. Some were large and muscular; others small and wiry. Most were in between. None were obese or shorter than five foot seven.

They all wore matching gym shorts, running shoes, and T-shirts. Portable heart monitors were attached to their wrists like watches, and small Band-Aids marked their blood draws from earlier that morning. Their shaved heads improved connectivity to their wireless electro-encephalogram monitors that looked like high-tech swim caps affixed to their skulls.

When Hightower entered, every eye turned toward her. They had all met with her previously, but in entirely different circumstances.

Hightower read the room instantly. She saw a potential

behavioral problem with one of the recruits, but ignored him for the moment.

Facing the far wall was a row of twenty treadmills and above them were large LCD monitors corresponding to each treadmill. Another wall was lined with stacks of rubber hex dumbbells of various weights up to one hundred and twenty pounds. Hack squat machines, dip stations, pull-up bars, and a jump rope station made up the rest of the fitness equipment.

There was also an empty cage, six meters across, located near the back bulkhead.

The tech, a slim Estonian, stood behind a laptop. He glanced up at Hightower's entrance and smiled his acknowledgment.

'Subjects are ready, Dr Hightower.'

'Excellent. Let's begin.'

The Estonian tapped a key on his laptop and ten of the treadmill LCD monitors flashed on. Each displayed a discrete identification number along with live feeds of brain waves and heartbeats. The prisoners quickly caught sight of the displays and were amused. They tried to figure out who belonged to which monitor because names were not listed.

'Gentlemen, eyes on me, please,' Hightower said in a commanding voice. The recruits all turned around.

'Each of you has volunteered to undergo our conditioning program and that program for your cohort officially begins today. We have a strict regimen that each of you will follow in order for us to establish your individual performance baselines. Once those baselines are established, we will tailor a program to your specific deficiencies. Everybody following me?'

Heads nodded, shoulders shrugged.

'We will compensate for your deficiencies by hacking your biological software through gene editing.'

Several of the recruits exchanged nervous glances.

Hightower had seen the same reaction countless times.

'No worries. There's no surgery involved. It's all quite painless. We're going to make each of you better, faster, stronger. Your physical performance will be greater than any professional athlete or Special Forces operator. Better yet, you will feel no pain and experience no fear.'

'Like X-Men!' one of the men cried out. The room rippled with nervous laughter.

'Something like that,' Hightower said. The tension had broken. That was good and bad. Hightower had to be careful. These men were nothing more than meat bags stuffed with volatile chemicals that had yet to be controlled.

'What happens after we leave here?' another recruit asked.

'You will be sent to a training camp run by my colleague, Jean-Paul Salan. There you will be taught combat fundamentals.'

'Guns?' one of the recruits asked hopefully.

'Rifles, pistols, grenades, knives, martial arts, even drones. The whole nine yards.'

'And then what?'

'Then you'll go out on missions of Salan's choosing.'

'And if we refuse?'

'You will be returned to prison to serve out the rest of your sentence.'

'How much will we get paid?'

'More than you can spend in a lifetime.'

This was technically true. What she didn't tell them was that as a result of their physical conditioning their life spans would be cut drastically short. They would last two years, at most.

The room warmed quickly as the men laughed and jostled with each other, each caught up in fantasies of untold wealth and the pleasures it secured.

Hightower smiled. What these men also didn't realize is that their memories would soon be wiped away. Not only would they not recall their past lives or the conditioning process they were about to go through, they wouldn't even remember this conversation.

'Anybody want to quit? Now's the time.'

An Asian male named Hao stood with his arms crossed to enlarge the size of his well-developed biceps. His left arm flashed a dragon tattoo and the logo for the 14K Triad, his former criminal organization.

'Why quit? Beats the hell out of sitting in the can,' Hao said. Like the other men in the room, he spoke English, though heavily accented. Minimal English-language proficiency was another recruiting guideline for the program.

The other men laughed.

Hightower ignored them. 'Any questions?'

A Ghanian with his hands on his hips demanded, 'Where is Sulemana?'

'Your cousin is in the ship's hospital. We found a nasty bacteriological infection in his blood when we ran his physical this morning. He's on a heavy dose of antibiotics and other medications. He'll join the next cohort if he recovers.'

'And if he doesn't?'

Hightower flashed her first smile. 'Then he'll miss out on the opportunity of a lifetime. Anybody else?'

There were no more questions.

Hightower knew she wasn't addressing a room full of Rhodes scholars, but all of them had scored well on the IQ tests and two were exceptionally intelligent. She wasn't expecting questions about scientific method or program design. Despite their displays of bravado and stoicism, she knew they were apprehensive, even scared. Experience, though, had taught her that at least one of them was already contemplating an escape or even organizing a resistance.

And she had a pretty good idea who it was.

Hao eyed her up and down, an act of defiance and intimidation all at once.

Hightower ignored him. 'Okay then, we'll begin on the treadmills. We'll start you on an easy walking pace to warm up, and then my assistant, Dr Sorga, will speed you up gradually. The purpose of this test is to measure your cardiovascular health and overall level of stamina.'

Hao turned his head slightly toward another Chinese standing next to him and whispered something.

The two men snickered at their private joke.

Thanks to her own conditioning, Hightower was able to hear every word. She also understood Mandarin. In the course of her genetics studies, she'd had to read and speak the language in order to access Chinese scientific journals and scholars, some of whom were the best in the world.

Roughly translated, Hao had said he'd show her how

good his cardiovascular health was by an all-night session of heart-pounding carnal relations.

'I don't think you could keep up with me,' Hightower said in faultless Mandarin.

Most of the other recruits didn't speak Chinese, but they could all tell by the tone of her voice she'd just put the muscular gangster down. They laughed.

Hightower cast a glance at the LCD screens. Their heartbeats were all accelerating as brain waves jittered and danced.

Hao smiled and stepped forward, lowering his thick-knuckled hands to his sides. His heartbeat was the slowest of them all.

A real cool customer, Hightower thought.

Hao glanced around at the other men, then over at Sorga, and back to Hightower.

'You know, lady, you have a real pretty mouth, even if it talks too much.'

The other men oohed or laughed. The energy in the room suddenly changed.

Sorga glanced up from his laptop, concerned.

Hao saw the man's weakness. So did the others. Hao glanced at the Ghanian, then pointed an index finger at the technician. The big Ghanian obeyed the unspoken command and stepped toward Sorga's laptop station.

The other recruits whispered excitedly to each other. A feral energy shot through them like a bolt of electricity – a wolf pack on the verge of an attack.

There were ten of them, and only one of her.

And she was one hell of a good-looking woman.

Hao stepped closer, lightly, like a cougar approaching a deer.

Hightower saw the cables of his muscles flex in his powerful thighs and calves.

She smiled.

'Something on your mind, Mr Hao?'

Hao stepped closer. 'My mind? Hardly.'

The men snickered and laughed. This was getting interesting.

The Ghanian grabbed the collar of Sorga's lab coat in a meaty fist.

'So, not your mind? Then it must be something smaller,' Hightower said. 'Much smaller.'

Hao cursed as he threw an open-handed slap at Hightower's face.

But Hightower's arm shot out like a bullwhip and slapped his face first. She struck him so hard the sound echoed on the steel bulkhead, and a hand-sized welt reddened the side of his face.

Half of the men laughed out loud; the others gasped with shock at the speed of her strike.

Hao did neither. He lunged at her with both hands out, reaching for her large white throat to break her neck.

But Hightower's heightened eyesight had detected Hao's microphysiological pre-assault indicators, which prompted her to lunge first.

She crouched down on her powerful legs, then thrust upward, her two hands close together in the shape of a triangle. She grunted as she drove the heels of her palms underneath his chin.

His shattered lower jaw smashed into his upper teeth with a horrific crack, and snapped his head backward like a Pez dispenser, severing his spine from the base of his skull, killing him instantly. His corpse flew into the air and landed with a dull thud on the rubber floor several feet away.

The nine surviving recruits stared at Hao's lifeless body in wide-eyed horror.

Hightower resumed her natural pose and straightened her lab coat as if nothing had happened.

The recruits turned toward her in stunned amazement. The Ghanian released Sorga apologetically and stepped away from him.

Hightower pointed at Hao's LCD monitor.

The recruits turned around and looked at it.

Hao's brain waves had zeroed out, and his heartbeat was fading rapidly toward a straight line.

'As I was saying before, your conditioning begins today. Technically, it has already begun. Any other questions, comments, or concerns?'

All heads shook.

'Then let's get to work.'

19

Dr Huxley couldn't wait to see her friend Dr Aline Izidoro. It had been more than two years since they'd had a chance to hug each other. Huxley tried to keep up on Aline's family news through social media, but it was no substitute for seeing her in person. There was always such joy in Aline's voice when she talked about her adopted twin girls and the adventures they got into. Aline led an amazing life as a medical doctor and public health professional, but clearly her passion was for her children. No doubt it was the alarming news that the infant mortality rate of the Indigenous Poison Arrow people had skyrocketed that had dragged Aline away from her own daughters and back into the bush. The infant mortality spike was also the reason why Aline was able to secure special permissions for them to enter into the highly restricted area designed to protect the lifestyles of the last remaining remote Indigenous tribes.

Huxley worried about the time. The detour around the illegal gold-mining camp had put them way behind schedule. There was even a chance the band of Indians had already pushed on. A flicker of concern kept buzzing around in Huxley's brain as she trudged the last hundred meters to the camp. After the storm abated and the satellite phone was back online and running, Huxley tried to contact Aline, but she didn't pick up.

In a way that made a lot of sense. Aline was probably operating under some kind of *Star Trek* 'Prime Directive' protocol – the noninterference with the natural progression of less-advanced cultures. The whole purpose of the protected zone was to allow the Poison Arrow people to remain in their natural state. If Aline suddenly started talking with an invisible person who was very far away on a 'magic box,' it would no doubt be as disruptive to them as an alien introducing some piece of mind-blowing technology to Amish dairy farmers. At least that's what she kept telling herself with the sound of heavy rain pelting the hood of her poncho beneath the latest cloudburst.

Linc turned around, his dark face and large white eyes framed in the hollow of his poncho hood. He had to shout above the noise of the raindrops pounding their rain gear.

'Just up ahead!'

Too exhausted to shout back, Huxley threw him two eager thumbs-up, despite the ache in her shoulders under the strain of the heavy pack. She couldn't wait to give Aline the two small necklaces of fine gold she'd brought along for the twins for their birthdays next week.

Dr Julia Huxley was an experienced combat surgeon and no stranger to death. She'd not only seen human carnage up close and personal, but had used her own skilled hands to repair wrecked and ruined flesh and bone, and by God's grace had even saved a few lives in the process. Over the course of her career she had conducted numerous autopsies, dissecting tissues, organs, and even brains to determine causes of death. Alive or dead, nothing fazed her on the operating table. In all of her years of medical experience she had never lost her cool, never turned away in disgust, never felt the least bit queasy.

But now, standing in front of the pile of charred Indian corpses, she had the overwhelming desire to cry – and puke her guts out.

'Must be thirty bodies in that pile,' Linc said grimly. 'Maybe more. It has to be the Poison Arrow people in there, don't you think?'

Without doing a thorough examination, it wasn't possible to positively identify the individual victims. But judging by the length of the few intact bones and skull fragments, her best guess was that these were the remains of local Indigenous people.

'Sure looks like it.'

Huxley's eyes scanned the human debris. Part of the pile had burned down to ash and the ash itself was a kind of slurry from the soaking rains that were falling even now. But there was also a large number of partial bones and skulls, and what flesh was still attached was brittle and dark like old parchment.

She forced herself to step closer. The unrelenting rain had quenched whatever embers may still have been burning hours ago. She held her hand close to the ash pile and felt no warmth whatsoever.

Huxley took a moment to stretch out the crick in her neck and the knots in her back after so many miles of hard walking with her heavy pack, which she had dropped against a nearby tree trunk. She knelt down close to the nearest skull fragment.

'You think the gold miners did this?' Huxley asked as she touched a bullet hole in the forehead fragment with a pencil from her kit.

'Not likely,' Linc said as his eyes searched the ground around the burn pile. He knelt down and picked up a brass shell casing and held it up for closer inspection.

'What'd you find?' Huxley saw another burnt skull with a bullet wound in the side of the head.

'It's a 9×21mm Gyurza.'

'Russian?' Huxley kept poking around the burn pile, looking for clues.

'Not just Russian. It's an armor-piercing bullet that the Russian Federal Protective Service uses.'

'Their version of the Secret Service. Specialized ordnance.'

'The FSB uses it, too,' Linc said. 'I don't think any of those guys are mining gold in the Amazon right now.'

Linc kept scanning the ground. 'I don't see any more shell casings. They must have policed the area. These are pros. Definitely not the gold miners.'

'Doesn't make any sense,' Huxley said as she pushed away a charred femur with her pencil, careful not to disturb the remains any more than was absolutely necessary. She made her way to the other side of the burn pile.

Linc saw another object gleaming in the tall grass. He dashed over and picked it up.

'Doc –'

But Huxley's heart fluttered as her eyes fell on a patch of lightly burned skin on a partially intact hand. Two small butterfly tattoos on the wrist had survived the fire. Huxley remembered that Aline had gotten the tattoos the day before she picked the girls up from the adoption agency.

'Doc?'

Huxley glanced up. A broken silver chain dangled from the tips of Linc's pinched fingers. A gold cross hung at the bottom of the loop.

Huxley nodded. 'Aline's.' She pointed at the charred hand. 'That's her, for sure.'

'Why kill all of these people?'

Huxley stood. 'I intend to find out.'

'Do you want to bury them?' Linc asked, thinking more about Huxley's friend than the other bodies.

'No. It's technically a crime scene. We should leave everything as it is and let the authorities take over. But we can try and figure out who did this. There's gotta be more clues in there somewhere.'

'There might be, but we should leave.' Linc held up his machete. 'Not exactly a great defensive weapon against guns.'

'I'm sure the bad guys are long gone.'

'Not necessarily. We really should get out of here.'

Linc glanced up into the trees. The sun was not only well hidden behind storm clouds, but setting somewhere beyond the tall canopy. It would be dark soon and Huxley was too exhausted to make it all the way back to the airstrip, especially in the black of night.

'We passed a clearing about five klicks back,' Linc said. 'We should set up camp there.'

Huxley glanced at the burn pile. Her heart sank. She hated the thought of leaving Aline here, exposed to the elements, unburied and unattended. The word *sacrilege* tore across her heart. But the thought of spending the night here in close proximity to her friend was too much to bear, and bringing out her remains might hamper any future investigation.

She marched over to her pack with renewed vigor. 'The best thing we can do is get back to civilization and report this.'

Linc held out Aline's chain and cross and lowered it into Hux's open palm.

'Thanks.' Huxley glanced at it, then shoved it into her shirt pocket, fighting back her emotions. Now was not the time to grieve.

'We can leave the medical supplies behind,' Linc offered as he nodded at her ruck, worried about his friend.

'I can't stand the idea of those thugs stealing Aline's meds.' Huxley grunted as she pulled the straps across her shoulders. 'I'll be fine. Let's go.'

Linc lifted his massive backpack harness with relative ease and slipped it across his broad back. He nodded at Huxley, then headed for the trail where they had first entered.

Huxley followed close behind him, but stopped. She turned and cast a final glance at her dear friend lying in the ashes. She wondered what she could possibly say to Aline's husband and daughters, but the tears came on fast. She wiped them away before turning on her heels and disappearing into the bush.

20

In the early-morning light, Samson, the large, muscular Nigerian mercenary, pushed his way through the foliage and into the camp where the Indians had been slaughtered. Risto had ordered both him and Mat, the Malaysian merc, to separate in order to expand the search area to find more Indians. They were all under orders from Dr Yanwen to collect more DNA samples from the other known bands of Poison Arrow people, but it was proving harder than they had anticipated.

Risto assumed they had successfully killed the one band of Indians without the knowledge of the other bands. But either the noise of the gunfire had carried or one of the Indians from the band they had killed managed to escape and warn the other bands. Whatever the reason, the elusive Poison Arrow people were living up to their reputation as ghosts in the jungle, the shadows of the forest.

Risto had established their search grid using the Indian camp as the primary reference point. Samson had covered the twenty-kilometer grid that Risto laid out for him and was returning to the reference point to begin the next one. He knew Mat was out there somewhere covering his first grid and Risto was conducting his own, smaller search with the two scientists in tow.

Samson dropped his pack against a tree trunk and

retrieved his canteen. He took a long pull of water to quench his raging thirst, his mind struggling like a drowning swimmer. So many questions had been flooding his brain for the last few hours, but he couldn't formulate the sentences or the words. It was as if a man with a muffled voice were crying out to him from a distant shore. Thoughts about his past were muddled. Even as he tried to form images of his father and mother, all he could conjure up were vague forms without faces. His clouded mind made him uneasy, and the rising drumbeat of a massive headache was telling him to push all of it away, and so he did, as easily as he reholstered his nearly empty canteen. Strangely, his headache subsided immediately.

The smell of the Hispanic woman came back to him. It was such a waste to kill a beauty like that without taking pleasure from her. But even this thought caused his temples to throb, and so he put that resentment away as well and enjoyed the immediate relief. His sharpened eyes glanced about the camp with no particular interest in mind; it was just easier to look than to think. But there were patterns in the grass that seemed unfamiliar.

He stepped closer to the firepit and knelt down. His thick index finger hovered above a massive boot print, tracing it without disturbing it. The print was almost as large as his own. He stood and lifted one heel so he could examine his own boot print. It definitely didn't match the one at his feet nor the prints of any others – the mercenaries and scientists all wore the same brand of boots.

Samson pulled the encrypted radio from his hip.

'Risto, Risto. Samson here. Over.'

The Nigerian waited for a moment. The handheld

radios only had a practical range of eight kilometers in the forest in the best of conditions. But with the intermittent storm and all of the trees, he found that often he couldn't reach Risto or Mat. But a moment later, Risto came online.

'Risto here. Did you find the Indians?'

'No. But we have company.'

'What kind of company?'

'The kind that wears size-sixteen combat boots.'

Risto crushed the radio in his hand, nearly cracking it. This was bad news all around. Samson was a great tracker, which was why he was chosen for this mission. He wouldn't be mistaken.

Risto keyed his mic. 'Gold miners?'

'I don't think so. I found another set of tracks. A woman. What do you want me to do?'

Risto hesitated. Samson was right. *Who would be out here?* His boss, Salan, had contacts in the Brazilian government. If the authorities had sent regional or federal troops into the area he'd know about it.

There was only one way to find out. Risto keyed his mic again.

'The only way in here is by plane. I want you to get to that airstrip as fast as you can. Don't let anybody take off. If you catch up with whoever it is on the trail, capture them – but don't kill them. I need to know what's going on. Contact me when you find them. Understood?'

'Loud and clear.'

'Then get moving.' Risto then radioed Mat and asked him, 'How far are you from the airstrip?'

'Twenty kilometers. What's the problem?'

'Samson thinks we have visitors. I've sent him to the airstrip. I need you to get there as well.' Risto gave Mat the same instructions he gave to Samson and rang off.

Dr Yanwen approached Risto. Her short hair was matted, and her skin blistered with bug bites. She was exhausted after the grueling all-night search.

'I just heard what you said. It's imperative we don't kill anybody else.'

'Leave security to me,' Risto said.

Yanwen summoned every fiber of courage left inside her exhausted body. She was tired of the intimidation, the insects, the heat. Mostly she was frustrated that the other bands of Poison Arrow people had eluded them. But the last thing she wanted was to get arrested for accessory to murder. She looked over to Dr Schweers for support. The large German woman nodded her encouragement.

'You're in charge of *my* security. Killing whoever else is out there doesn't protect me. It endangers all of us, and, more important, the project.'

Risto shot her a withering glance, his eyes narrowing like a striking great white shark. 'You heard my orders. Capture, not kill. I need to find out who they are.'

'And after you do? Do you plan to let them go?'

Risto grinned. 'What do you think?'

Yanwen started to protest, but stopped, her mind processing.

'Ah, now you're seeing the big picture,' Risto said. 'If they turn us in, there is no more project, at least not for you. You'll be in jail, or worse, once they finish with you.'

'Who? The Brazilian government?' Schweers asked.

'Not likely. I suspect it could be a far worse threat.

That's why we need to find out who it is, how they found out about us, and what's the risk to the entire project.'

'Perhaps we should just leave,' Schweers said.

'We're not finished with our mission,' Yanwen countered.

Risto slammed his radio into its holster. 'You two stay put and get some rest. Don't move an inch. My men will take care of business, and I'll keep searching for your precious Indians. Keep your radios on. And while I'm gone, make yourselves useful and set up a camp for us here.'

Before either scientist could protest, Risto disappeared into the bush to complete his search grid.

As soon as Risto left the clearing, Yanwen turned to Schweers. It was the first chance they'd had to talk since the slaughter the day before.

Schweers's primary responsibility was to keep the three mercenaries medicated at critical intervals during the operation. Their genetically altered bodies were pumped full of excess adrenaline, testosterone, and endorphins. Those genetic alterations, combined with other therapies designed by Dr Hightower, heightened nearly every aspect of human physical and cognitive performance, including vision, strength, energy, pain reduction, fearlessness, and euphoria.

The danger, however, was that if their genetically altered bodies were left entirely unchecked, the combination of enhancements became the functional equivalent of driving an automobile with the gas pedal permanently smashed into the floorboard. The consequences could be catastrophic to the subjects and anyone around them — exactly like what happened yesterday.

Yanwen marched over to Schweers. She kept her voice low just in case Risto was still somehow, incredibly, within earshot.

'This is all your fault. How could you have lost their med patches? You should have been more diligent.'

Schweers rubbed her face with frustration. The pharmaceutical patches were designed to counteract the surging adrenaline and its ancillary physiological and psychological effects by taking the foot off the gas pedal and allowing their minds and bodies to relax. The mercenaries knew the purpose of the patches was to protect their health. But they didn't care. In fact, they hated them and referred to them derisively as 'brake pads.' When the mercs were fully locked and loaded, they felt like invincible supermen. And what superman ever wanted his cape taken away from him?

'I don't know how I lost them. The more I think about it, I wonder if Risto or one of the others stole them.'

'That's ridiculous.'

'Is it? You know they hate their brake pads.'

'It doesn't matter,' Yanwen said. 'As soon as we collect the rest of our DNA samples we'll head back to base and get restocked.'

Schweers's eyes misted up at the thought of the Indian slaughter. 'I still think we should tell Dr Hightower what happened.'

'Dr Hightower's work is proving itself every day, and the two of us have the chance to help her change the course of human destiny. I don't want to lose the opportunity to be part of that. Do you?'

Hightower's clinic was on the bleeding edge of

transhumanist technology – the science of creating Humanity 2.0. The first step was to vastly improve the performance of the human organism through biotechnology. The next step would be to merge the advanced capabilities of that improved organism with artificial intelligence through wireless brain–computer interface implants. Those implants would not only link every mind to the power of a quantum internet, but also to each other for true telepathic communication. Ultimately, human biology would be done away with and immortality achieved by uploading human consciousness into a universal and immortal cloud.

This was the religion that an atheist like Schweers could believe in. Hightower was not only the high priestess of her faith, but the object of her worship and devotion.

Schweers shook her head. 'Of course not.'

'Then we keep our mouths shut and our heads down. We'll get through this.'

'But I keep thinking we could have been thrown onto that burn pile with the others if Risto had lost complete control.'

Yanwen knew Schweers was right, but there was nothing she could do about it. She had to keep the skittish German scientist from panicking.

'But he didn't lose complete control, did he? So stop worrying.'

'I hate the idea of being party to more killings.'

'It can't be helped. If the authorities find us, the project could die – and so could we.'

'I understand. It doesn't mean I have to like it.'

'You know as well as I do that science often advances on the suffering of others. Sometimes the few must be sacrificed for the benefit of the many. It's not a pleasant thought, but it's reality.'

Schweers sighed with resignation. 'Then I suppose we must stay put like Risto said.'

'Agreed. But I'll be damned if I'm going to be his housekeeper.'

Samson press-checked his pistol and reholstered it as soon as Risto cut the radio transmission. He drained the last of his water and ran the calculation through his head. At a straight shot, the airstrip was over thirty kilometers away. The rainfall distorted the boot prints. There was no telling how far the intruders had gotten. The only way he was going to catch up with them was to run like hell.

It could've been worse, Huxley thought. Last night's hard march through the rainforest in the dark was a hazard even with the LED headlamps and setting up the camp was a royal pain.

Thankfully, Linc had the presence of mind to pack hammocks for their sleeping bags that also featured full mosquito netting. Not only did it spare Huxley the savagery of the relentless bloodsucking aerial assault vehicles that swarmed around them all night, but it kept her tushy high and dry when the thunderclouds burst open and flash flooded their little camp at two in the morning.

A few hours later they woke with the rays of the morning sun filtering through the dark canopy. Skilled as the big ex-sniper was with a rifle, hand-to-hand combat, knife fighting, and land navigation, Linc deferred that morning to Huxley's food-prepping skills. Linc had saved their bacon – literally – by suspending all of their supplies in the air. This prevented scavenging animals from stealing their food and, as it turned out, from the rest of it being swept away by the torrent of water that spontaneously erupted during the night beneath their hammocks in the storm.

Huxley had used her trusty German Esbit pocket stove and lit up its tiny solid fuel tablets. Within minutes she had boiling water and put together two cups of instant coffee.

It wasn't as good as the fresh-ground joe they got on the *Oregon*, but the Starbucks VIA Italian dark roast was strong enough to satisfy the two Navy vets. While Linc finished his first cup she used the flameless heaters to warm up a couple of breakfast MREs stuffed with hash brown potatoes, peppers, onions, and bacon.

After they ate and downed a second cup of coffee, they took care of their personal hygiene, packed up the rest of their camp, and headed out early. Neither of them had slept well. Huxley was as sore as she had ever been after yesterday's hard marching under the heavy pack. But the desire to get back to civilization to report the brutal murder of Aline and the band of Poison Arrow people drove her on this morning.

'Won't be long now,' Linc said over his shoulder as a light rain began to fall.

'I'm right behind you.'

'You're a beast, Doc.'

The tall jungle canopy helped shield them from the rain above, but this part of the trail was muddy and puddled, with tangled roots that slowed them down.

The sudden burst of distant gunshots ripping the air far behind them stopped them in their tracks.

The rain had stopped a few minutes ago. The jungle was buzzing with insect noises again, along with the screech of colorful birds.

Thiago Cunha lit another cigarette, his battered, secondhand AK-47 slung over his thin shoulder. The teenager was glad for the responsibility of guarding the gold camp, though it didn't pay well at all. Technically, it paid well enough, but his uncle was skimming half of his salary as a 'finder's fee' for the position. No matter, he thought, as he took a long drag on the Marlboro. He was learning his trade as a gunman, getting three meals a day, and free access to the prostitutes the bosses brought in on Sundays back at the village. Even if he got paid nothing, it was still better than working like a slave slinging pay dirt and gravel into the sluice boxes like the poor devils he guarded.

Thiago opened his mouth like a carp and gently exhaled a ring of cigarette smoke, pretending to be like the pipe-smoking wizard in the *Lord of the Rings* movie, which he had seen many, many times. He smiled as he managed a circle of smoke and laughed as the circle drifted lazily away from his face.

But inside the circle, like a rifle scope, he suddenly saw the blurred image of a huge figure in the distance breaking through the tree line at a dead run. The man was black as coal, his muscled arms slicked with sweat. What shocked Thiago most was the speed with which the bearded man moved across the flat ground, legs pumping, arms pistoning, like someone running full tilt down a mountain slope.

Captivated by the sight, it suddenly occurred to Thiago that the man was an intruder. Before he could shout a warning and slip the AK off his shoulder, the large Black man pointed a pistol at him. It flashed a single shot.

Thiago's corpse hit the dirt as Samson sped past in a dead run.

That single gunshot was enough to alert the other guards, but that didn't bother the big mercenary. His eyesight keened, his tireless legs churning, Samson didn't slow his pace. The staccato roar of half a dozen AKs ripped the air as their wild shots tore chunks of bark out of the trees, scattered cawing birds and shrieking monkeys, and sent miners diving for cover. None of the guards managed to draw a bead on the speeding mercenary as he raced through the camp, his pistol cracking as fast as he could pull the trigger. By the time his big combat boots were splashing through the river bordering the camp, five guards lay dead and four wounded, their cries and curses a distant echo in the forest behind him as he raced down the trail toward his targets.

'That came from the gold camp,' Huxley said. 'Sounded like AKs.'

'And a pistol,' Linc said. 'Nine millimeter, or maybe bigger.' He pulled his machete from its scabbard. 'Either way, we're outgunned.'

'We need to keep moving.'

Linc cast a glance back up the dark, rain-soaked trail snaking its way toward the gold camp. He couldn't shake the feeling that something terrible was coming down the pike.

'Yeah, we do.'

22

A light rain began to fall as Samson cleared the river, but it turned into a drenching downpour moments later. He slowed his pace to match the unevenness of the trail beneath his boots, though he felt neither weakness nor fatigue. He was on the ultimate runner's high – times a thousand. Every nerve ending tingled with a rising sensory frenzy. He felt an inexpressible joy whenever he pushed his body to its ultimate limits, and any form of combat only heightened his sense of power and invulnerability. He could conceive of the concept of fear, but he hardly remembered what it must have felt like, as if it were a dream lost upon waking.

Samson's mind snapped back into focus as his eyes caught sight of the two big packs parked against the tree trunks up ahead. He stopped dead in his tracks and listened. Nothing. They must have heard him coming, dropped their gear, and ran ahead to get to the airstrip.

'It won't be long now,' he said to himself as his legs sprang into action. He launched himself down the trail, his brief respite and the nearness of battle completely replenishing his reserves. He thundered past the packs, his boots splashing in the water, his eyes searching the darkened trail ahead as he raced at full speed, risking the uneven roots writhing on the puddled path.

As he turned a slight bend in the narrowing trail, a rope

leaped up from the ground and stretched tautly across the path about neck high. Anyone else would have been clotheslined by the length of nylon rope that Linc and Hux had raised in a flash to catch their pursuer unawares and knock him to the ground.

But in the nanosecond between seeing the rope and colliding with it, Samson ducked.

Linc couldn't believe his eyes. For a second he wondered if the big man had simply run through the rope. *How could he have missed it?*

But the nylon was still in his hands and the shocked look on Huxley's face across the trail was a mirror image of his own mind-numbing confusion.

The only effect the rope had on the hulking monster was that his high-speed ducking motion threw him off balance and he tumbled with a splash onto the sloppy trail.

Linc snapped out of his temporary trance and charged at the mud-splattered Nigerian already climbing to his feet and reaching for his pistol. Linc leaped at him like a linebacker, wrapping his massive arms around the man's waist and pinning his arms to his sides. Linc's muscled frame was flying fast enough that the collision knocked the larger man down and the two of them hit the ground hard, putting the Nigerian on his back.

Linc reached for the pistol to tear it away from Samson's right hand before he could fire it, but the Nigerian threw a weak punch across Linc's wide back with his left fist. The shot was completely underpowered and only a glancing blow to the side of Linc's head, but it still rang his bell.

Huxley raced up with her machete raised over her head while Samson was still on his back and partially pinned by Linc.

'Let go of your gun or I'll gut you like a fish!'

But in the time it took for Huxley to bellow out her threat, Samson had managed to slip his left arm around Linc's neck and roll the two of them away from Huxley. Samson was now on top.

Huxley charged closer to get a clear shot at the Nigerian, but that was a mistake. Samson's long leg shot out and his boot crashed into her shin, throwing her backward with a cry of pain.

Linc twisted inside the larger man's grip, his hand still on the Nigerian's pistol. In the titanic struggle, Linc managed to slide his thumb onto the magazine release and pop the magazine out and into the mud.

Samson heard the mag release and relaxed his grip on Linc's neck to recover it.

That was the opening Linc was waiting for. He drove his bald skull like a bowling ball into the Nigerian's chin.

Stunned, Samson loosed his grip around the pistol just enough for Linc to pull the weapon out of his hand. Linc rolled out from beneath the larger man, and spun up onto his feet in a crouch, pointing the pistol at the Nigerian, who had also sprung to his feet.

'Time to settle down, man,' Linc said, aiming the pistol at the Nigerian's chest.

Samson grinned – and sprang at Linc like a bolt shot from a crossbow.

Linc pulled the trigger, but the mud-caked gun jammed on the single bullet still in the chamber.

Now it was Linc's turn to get hit with a flying tackle – only this time, the two men didn't go tumbling to the ground.

For the first time in his adult life, Linc felt like a child as the stronger Nigerian lifted him into the air with ease.

Huxley screamed as she lunged at Samson, swinging her machete. The Nigerian spun around, using Linc's long legs like baseball bats. Linc's boots crashed into her shoulder and knocked her down sideways into the mud, the machete flying from her hand.

Huxley drew a short camp knife and leaped to her feet just as Samson lifted Linc even higher, then threw him to the ground like a rag doll. Linc *oo*fed as the air was knocked out of his lungs and his head thudded into the soft mud.

Huxley thrust the three-inch blade at Samson's back to sever his spine, but the big man was faster than she was. The Nigerian backhanded her away with a flick of his tree trunk arm, knocking her out cold. He marched over to Linc, who was still gasping for air, and raised his boot to smash it down on Linc's skull. Just as he was about to drop the hammer, he heard a splash behind him.

He turned around just in time to see Tiny swinging a tree branch like a broadsword. The wood shattered across the Nigerian's face and opened up a wide gash in his forehead. With blood gushing down into his eyes, Samson lunged blindly at the big Swede with outstretched hands. But Tiny lowered his head and drove straight into him, planting the crown of his skull squarely against the Nigerian's jaw with a sickening crack.

Samson staggered backward, more surprised than hurt, his entire face a mask of blood streaming from his forehead wound.

Tiny charged forward on his wobbling leg, his own adrenaline surge masking the horrific pain in his ankle.

The Nigerian threw a devastating punch that only missed because he was blinded by the blood in his eyes.

Tiny countered with a throat punch that crushed the Nigerian's windpipe.

Samson stumbled away from him, clutching his broken larynx. Tiny pressed his attack, plowing into the Nigerian with his broad shoulders, his massive thighs churning beneath him, just the way he had been taught to tackle by his coaches at the University of Wisconsin years before.

The big Nigerian fell backward with a splash.

Tiny fell on him and raised his anvil of a hand to smash the man in the face.

But the gasping Nigerian threw a wild punch that rocked the Swede's jaw, making him see stars.

Tiny grunted with rage, then raked his rock-hard elbow across Samson's temple, stunning him. The Swede then clutched the man's skull and twisted it, shoving his face deep into the puddle of mud, submerging it. Samson's huge body thrashed and bucked, but Tiny held on until the last muddy bubbles finally gave way to death.

Tiny sighed deeply, exhausted. He turned to Linc, who was just able to crawl to his feet, and still trying to catch his breath.

'You okay, partner?' Tiny asked as he rose to his unsteady legs.

'You move pretty fast for a guy with a busted ankle.'

'Hardly. Took me four hours to get here. Get your med kit. I'm worried about Dr Huxley.'

23

Smelling salts woke Huxley up in a hurry.

'Tiny? How'd you get here?'

'My Uber driver never showed up, so I hiked in, one limp at a time.'

The doctor rubbed her aching jaw. 'Linc, grab me a couple of Tylenol, will you? This headache is something else.'

'Anything broken?' Linc asked.

'Just my pride. I need to spend more time on combatives when we get back to the *Oregon*.' She glanced over at the Nigerian's corpse in the middle of the trail. 'Who finally took out King Kong over there?'

Linc pointed at Tiny. 'The Swedish cavalry.' He had already fetched the packs with the medical gear and brought them closer to the injured doctor.

'How long was I out?' Huxley asked as she washed down a couple of Tylenols with a swig from her canteen.

'Just a few minutes,' Linc said.

Huxley held out her hands and the two big men helped her up. Tiny was obviously in pain. She pointed at a fallen log. 'Take a seat in my office. I'm going to splint you up – and get you some pain meds.'

'Who was that fella?' Tiny asked as he limped over to the log.

'Probably one of the killers,' Linc said, fetching more Tylenol as Huxley pulled out a splint roll and tape.

'Killers?'

Linc nodded grimly. 'We found the camp. Dr Izidoro and the Indians were all murdered. We hightailed it out of there so we could report it.' He threw a thumb at the Nigerian. 'He must have tracked us somehow.'

Huxley cut and wrapped as they talked.

'We should get out of here,' Tiny said. 'Did you get a look at that guy? There was something weird about him.'

'You mean the fact he picked me up like a Raggedy Ann doll and slam-dunked me into the dirt?'

'No. I mean, his eyes, his arms. His whole body. Look at him.'

Huxley finished taping up as Linc limped over to Samson's corpse. He grabbed Samson's shirt in his fist and pulled his face out of the mud, then splashed water on it to clean it off.

'Hey, Doc. Come look at this.'

Huxley squeezed the splint gently. Tiny winced. 'What happened to "rest, ice, compress, and elevate"?'

'Well, I did. Sort of. A little. Once.'

'Doc.'

'Coming.'

Huxley crossed over to the corpse and knelt down next to it.

'Tiny's right,' Linc said. 'See the acne on the side of his face? And his arms. I've seen ripped guys in the gym before, but he's beyond shredded. He's like a mini Hulk without the green.'

Huxley handled the corpse gently. Everything about him seemed larger, overly developed, even misshapen. The word that came to her mind was *disproportionate*. Even the veins running the length of his arms were the size of coiling snakes.

'His eyes are totally bloodshot,' Linc added.

'That could be from the drowning.' Huxley leaned in closer. 'But you're right. He's not normal. He has all the signs of endocrine overload. That accounts for his incredible strength.'

'But did you see the way he moved? Greased lightning. Hard to believe for a guy this bulked up.'

'Yeah. Something else is going on there.'

'Like what?'

'I'm not sure.' She pulled out her personal cell phone and powered it up. Fortunately, it was still working. It didn't have a tower signal, but she didn't need one. She opened the camera app and took several photos of the corpse.

'Any ID?' she asked as she headed over and grabbed her medical kit.

'Nothin' on him.' Linc's eyes shut with a flash of pain.

'You better let me take a look at you.'

Linc stood. 'We need to get out of here. No telling how many more of these bridge trolls are out there looking for us.'

Huxley glanced over at Tiny and back at Linc.

'We need to park here for a while. Give you both a chance to recover.'

'Linc's right,' Tiny said with a grunt as he stood. 'We need to skedaddle. Like my grandfather always said, "There's no rest for the wicked and the righteous don't need any."'

'Fine. Just give me a sec.' Huxley opened up her kit and

crossed back over to the corpse. Linc searched the trail for the jammed gun and dropped magazine.

'I think you're a little late for his annual physical,' Tiny said to Huxley.

'Just grabbing a couple of samples for my lab back on the *Oregon*.' She took small amounts of blood and tissue, swabbed his mouth, and stored everything away in secure containers to prevent contamination of the samples.

While she was collecting her specimens, Linc was busy taking down Samson's red dot polymer pistol and cleaning it out as best he could in a nearby puddle. He also cleaned the magazine loaded with eight 9mm bullets – smaller than the Gyurza shell casing he'd found at the murder scene. Stripping, cleaning, and reassembling the Glock-style gun, magazine, and bullets only took the trained operator a few minutes. He slammed home the mag and racked one into the chamber.

Huxley packed up her samples and gear and shouldered her pack. Linc began reaching for his.

'No way, buster. We leave it. And that's your doctor's orders.'

'But you said you didn't want the bad guys to get those supplies.'

'I need you to help Tiny with that ankle of his. With any luck, the good guys might find them out here on the trail. But if we don't get moving right now, the bad guys will definitely find *us*.'

With Tiny's massive arm draped across Linc's broad back, the two big men developed a kind of three-legged-race walking pace. Despite her own battered shin, Dr Huxley scouted up ahead for obstacles and cleared what she could, then circled back behind her two friends, just to be sure they weren't being followed.

She tried taking over for Linc for a spell, but her tiny frame could barely support Tiny's massive weight, let alone help him walk.

Finally, four hours after they'd begun their final journey, including frequent rest and rehydration stops, the three of them emerged onto the airstrip, where the Cessna Skyhawk stood, ready to roll. They stopped on the edge of the clearing to take a final breather.

'She looks pretty good,' Huxley said, seeing the nose strut fully extended. 'Weather's clear, too.'

'She's a little banged up, like me,' Tiny said. 'But she's a workhorse. I've already preflighted her, so we can get the heck out of here.'

The three *Oregon* crew members hobbled across the airstrip toward the plane. Tiny pulled open the pilot-side door and helped Huxley inside to her backseat with her kit as Linc made his way to the copilot door, but didn't get in.

A pistol shot cracked in the distance. A 9mm round plowed through the plexiglass windscreen.

All eyes turned toward the sound of the blast. A beefy Malaysian was over a hundred meters away, charging toward them at full speed and firing his pistol one-handed. More rounds spanged into the windscreen.

'The boy can shoot!' Tiny said.

Linc pulled his pistol and fired two shots. 'Tiny, get this plane fired up and let's get out of here!'

'On it.'

'We can't leave him here,' Huxley said as Tiny hit the starter. Linc fired two more shots.

'Can't stay put, either.' The engine coughed to life and the prop started spinning. 'Buckle up!'

The ex-SEAL sniper was a crack shot, but the Malaysian was moving fast and in a randomized pattern. Linc couldn't track him in his sights. His shots had missed, but they'd forced Mat to alter his course. When the Cessna's engine coughed into life, the Malaysian picked up speed and opened fire again. Bullets thudded into the soft aluminum engine cowling and sparked off the propellers.

Linc fired back, but still couldn't hit his target – or if he did, there wasn't any effect. He only had two bullets left in his mag and he let them fly. Suddenly they were gone.

Mat fired his last shot, landing a round square in the windscreen, where Tiny's head should have been, then threw his empty gun away.

Tiny slammed the throttle forward and the engine revved up.

The Malaysian closed the distance in a heartbeat, heading straight for the pilot's door. All Linc could do was charge him.

Big mistake.

The two men collided like rutting bighorn sheep. Linc thought he'd been hit by a Buick; the air was knocked out of him and he saw stars in his eyes, and for a second he thought he might have even broken his neck. Despite the fact that Mat had practically run through him, Linc managed to wrap his arms around the smaller man's waist and hold on for dear life. Linc couldn't believe the Malaysian could still be moving with his own massive weight now wrapped around his torso. Linc fought to trip him up by wrapping his legs around Mat's. Just as Mat was about to reach the plane, the Cessna began pulling away, and Linc's legs finally did their trick and toppled the Malaysian, tumbling him into the wet grass.

Mat howled with rage as the Cessna rumbled toward the other end of the field. He turned his fury onto Linc, whose massive hands were pawing at him, trying to get purchase on the Malaysian's wiry body to pin him to the ground.

But the Malaysian easily shrugged him off and leaped to his feet, the Cessna's engine roaring behind them. Linc jumped up as fast as he could, but as soon as he was erect Mat threw a kick into Linc's chest that tossed him onto his back. Mat jumped at Linc, but the big man managed to plant his boots in the Malaysian's gut, barely keeping the man's arms from reaching Linc's throat and strangling him. The mercenary's bulging eyes were red with blood and fury, his drooling mouth snarling murderous curses in a language Linc didn't speak, but fully understood.

Linc knew he was losing the battle, but the sound of the Cessna's roaring engine gave him hope. Tiny would be taking off any second, flying directly over them.

The propeller blades sliced through Mat's spine before decapitating him in a gory flash of blood. The force of the prop tossed Mat's corpse aside as the ground-skimming plane roared directly overhead, the front tire just inches above Linc's body.

Slathered in Mat's blood, Linc rolled over in time to see Tiny land the plane again with an ugly bounce as his nose gear struggled to stay taut with just bicycle-pump air in its piston.

A few minutes later, Linc squeezed into the cockpit and the plane was in the air. The three friends were all banged up and worn down, but glad to be alive and finally heading home to the *Oregon*.

24

Juan Cabrillo opted for an inconvenient forty-minute cab ride from Ben Gurion Airport to Ashdod, Israel's largest port city, located halfway between Tel Aviv and the Gaza Strip. He decided to make the best use of his time in the backseat of the white Mercedes taxi by catching up on emails.

The large Tel Aviv airport was the closest place for Gomez Adams to land the tilt-rotor. Juan considered renting a car, but instead hailed a taxi that would get him to Ashdod just as fast. Sarai Massala insisted he keep as low a profile as possible. He was happy to avoid having even his fake name entered into yet another database or getting his slightly altered features recorded on more CCTV cameras at a rental car counter.

'First time in Israel?' the driver asked in a Russian accent as thick as his bushy Brezhnev eyebrows. His wiry hair, like the stubble on his face, was salt-and-peppered. He met Juan's eyes in the rearview mirror.

'First time in Ashdod.'

'You know, Ashdod is one of the oldest cities in the world. Seventeenth century BCE.' He exaggerated the pronunciation of the last word, *Bee – See – Eee* for emphasis.

'Goliath. Philistines,' Juan grunted.

'You know your history. Unusual for an American.'

Juan rubbed his knuckles absentmindedly.

'Sister Barbara was an enthusiastic teacher of the Old Testament.'

'You are here on business?'

'Yes.' Cabrillo turned his attention back to his phone, hoping to avoid further conversation. A few moments passed.

'What kind of business?'

Juan didn't look up from his phone. 'Greeting cards.'

'Greeting cards?'

'You know, Happy Birthday, Happy Anniversary, Happy Bar Mitzvah.'

'Oh, sure. Interesting line of work?'

'Very. Lots of travel.'

The cabbie's eyes searched the back of the cab via the rearview mirror. 'Where's your sample case?'

Juan held up his phone. 'It's a new world. All virtual.'

The cabbie laughed. 'Yeah, of course. Well, Ashdod is good for business. Biggest port in Israel. My brother lives there. Many immigrants.'

'A lot of Russians there?'

'Russians, Moroccans, Argentinians, French, Ethiopians, Georgians, you name it. All Jews, of course.'

'Of course.'

Juan tried to hide his irritation. Most talkative cabdrivers were either bored or trying to talk up a tip. In this case, Juan thought, the gabby cabbie might be talking himself out of one.

Cabbies were also excellent sources of intel, pumping

unsuspecting passengers for information they passed on to legitimate or criminal intelligence operatives. In his fifteen years of fieldwork with the CIA, Juan had gleaned quite a bit of actionable intel from hack drivers he'd encountered. He knew Massala was former Mossad and she was deeply concerned about her security. It was distinctly possible the Russian was connected to the famous Israeli spy agency and somehow they had gotten wind of their meeting.

'Where do you live in America?'

'Pigeon Forge, Tennessee.'

Cabrillo was certain the obscure reference would shut the cabbie down. He only knew about it because he was the best man at Max Hanley's wedding to his second of three ex-wives. She had insisted on tying the knot at the little white chapel in the Dollywood theme park. Juan had fonder memories of the fresh fried pork rinds than of the bride.

'Dolly Parton?'

'The best.'

'You know her?'

'Smart lady, great music.'

'"I'm Workin' 9 to 5"!'

'I'm partial to "Jolene," myself.'

'My brother went to Dollywood last year. He sent pictures. Very nice.'

Suddenly Mr Brezhnev ran out of questions. Either he had exhausted his entire English vocabulary or he had completed his surreptitious inquiry. Mostly likely, the fact that Juan was neither carrying nor wearing anything of particular value must have made him less interesting to his inquisitive friend.

Juan glanced out the cab window. The original Ashdod was millennia old, but the modern city had only been incorporated since the 1960s. That made it both ancient and new. From what he saw from the back of the cab, it had few virtues of either. And where they were headed seemed to be the least virtuous part of the city altogether.

Juan paid the cabbie his fare, but threw him a few extra shekels for coffee as a goodwill gesture before shutting his door.

He stood in front of a run-down single-story building in a run-down part of town. Its yellow plastic awning was begrimed and its two rolling doors shut and padlocked. A billboard over the glass door entrance read *Massala Importers* in English; it said the same thing in Hebrew and Amharic, the lingua franca of Ethiopia. A bell tinkled as Juan pushed through the unlocked door and stepped inside.

In contrast to the urban depression outside, the showroom was well lit and inviting, the air filled with sweet aromas of spices and coffee. A coffee roaster stood idle on the far side of the floor. Displays of a wide variety of food, clothing, and other sundries from several African and Middle Eastern countries were on display. The incredible colors and patterns on the large bolts of African cloth dominated the room.

Juan made a beeline for the Ethiopian coffee display. He picked up a bag of fresh roasted Yirgacheffe beans. He could smell the rich floral aroma before he even raised it to his nose.

'Good choice,' a woman's voice said. 'Organic, fair trade, and kosher.'

Juan turned around. He tried to hide his astonishment. Sarai Massala was even more stunning than her photograph.

The smiling fortysomething woman emerging from the back room looked like she had just walked off a runway in Milan. Somehow she made her work shirt and slacks a Tom Ford fashion statement. She was very tall and athletically fit. But what jolted Juan was her natural beauty. She didn't wear any makeup because she didn't need to. Her flawless skin was the color of brewed cappuccino, and perfectly complemented her luminous brown eyes and the thick mane of flowing black hair that reached to the middle of her back.

'I'm a fan.'

'Of Ethiopian coffee?' The woman grinned mischievously. She knew the effect she had on men, even as an older woman.

'Of coffee generally. And Ethiopian coffee . . . particularly.'

Juan stuck out his hand even as he tried to extricate his one good foot from out of his mouth.

'Juan Cabrillo.'

'So I assumed.'

Their eyes met. She took in the measure of the broad-shouldered, handsome American as she shook his hand. The back of her neck tingled.

Now she was the one on her heels.

'Sarai Massala. Thank you for coming, Mr Cabrillo.'

'So, what can I do for you, Ms Massala?'

'Sarai, please.'

'Only if you call me Juan.'

'What did Mr Overholt tell you?'

'Only that you needed help.'
'And you came just on his word?'
'I trust Langston with my life.'
'He assures me I can trust you with mine.'
'Is your life at risk?'
'Not yet.'

25

Juan took his first sip of freshly brewed coffee sitting in Massala's kitchen. His favorite cup of joe was the Cuban dark roast pour-over his chefs prepared for his breakfasts, but he was really enjoying the Yirgacheffe.

'This is outstanding.'

Massala smiled. 'I'm glad you like it. My father takes great pride in his business and especially his coffee.' She took a sip from her own cup.

Juan needed the caffeine boost, but more important he needed background information from the beautiful woman whose life could soon be at risk.

'Is your family from Yirgacheffe?'

'No, that's in the south. We were from up north in the district of Gondar.'

'Isn't that where all of the castles are?'

'And Beta Israel – the Ethiopian Jews.' She smiled. 'I'm impressed. You've been to Ethiopia?'

'I've read a few books. Gondar is the "Camelot of Africa," right?'

'Not exactly a place of fairy tales, I can tell you that.'

'When did your family immigrate to Israel?'

'We were part of Operation Solomon, the 1991 airlift that rescued the Ethiopian Jews. I suppose you've read about that as well?'

'It was an amazing feat. In that one operation Israel

airlifted nearly fifteen thousand people in just thirty-six hours.'

'I was twelve years old at the time, but I remember it like it was yesterday. We were so excited and scared all at once. It was truly a miracle.'

'Where are your folks?'

'My mother died not long after we arrived. Breast cancer.'

'I'm sorry. And your father?'

'He's in hospice now. Stage four pancreatic cancer.'

'That's rough.'

A truck horn blared outside. Massala checked her watch.

'You'll have to excuse me. My delivery has come early. Make yourself comfortable. It will take me a little while. This driver doesn't unload. He just sits in the cab and smokes cigarettes.'

She stood.

So did Juan.

She frowned a question. 'What are you doing?'

'Langston said you needed help. Well, I'm here to help.'

'Don't say I didn't warn you.'

Juan toted the fifty-pound sacks of coffee beans like they were dorm room pillows and stacked them in the small warehouse space, while Sarai wheeled out boxes on a hand truck. They finished up in less than thirty minutes, but they were both drenched in sweat from the heat.

Massala signed off on the delivery invoice and dismissed the driver, then shut the rolling door and locked it. She turned to Juan.

'I'm sorry your coffee was interrupted. Can I make you a fresh cup?'

Juan watched the bead of sweat trickle off the end of her aquiline nose.

'A cold beer sounds better.'

'I was hoping you'd say that.'

Massala marched over to a refrigerator in the far corner. She pulled out two frosty cold Heinekens and handed one to Juan. They each took a long pull.

'You didn't finish your story,' Juan said. 'What happened after you arrived?'

'We were the fortunate ones, I think. My parents had some education and were able to better integrate into Israeli society than most. Sadly, many Ethiopians have struggled to make it here. My father was a businessman back home and was able to build a business here, too.' She gestured around the tiny warehouse. 'It's not quite as big as Amazon or Schwarz, but he always provided for us.'

'How did you get into Mossad?'

Massala looked Juan up and down as she took another sip of beer.

Juan shrugged. 'Not that it matters, but I used to be with the CIA, if you're worried about revealing any security secrets.'

'Sorry. Old habits. Langston said you were cleared top secret, though he didn't explain how that was possible, since you are no longer with the US government.'

'Let's just say I do an odd job for him every now and then.'

'Am I your current "odd job"?'

'Well, he's paying me, if that's what you're asking.'

'A mercenary.'

'The chairman of a corporation, technically. And an independent businessman, like your father.'

'Let's get out of this heat.'

Massala led them back into the air-conditioned kitchen, where they sat down.

'I was recruited by Mossad in my first year of college. I had just picked up my first modeling contract and they thought that might prove to be an interesting cover. It also didn't hurt my modeling career. I began walking some of the biggest runways in Europe and the United States long before I was expected to.'

'Sounds like an exciting adventure for a young woman.'

'It was, at first. Paris, Milan, New York. Beautiful cities, beautiful people, right? But it's a sordid business. Soul draining. Spying for Israel actually grounded me. It allowed me to give back to the nation that had saved my people. But it also cost my family dearly.'

'How?'

'My younger brother, Asher. He grew up without a mother, and Father was working insane hours just to keep the business afloat. I tried to be a mother to him when he was younger, but once I started modeling I was no longer around for him. He fell in with a gang and was eventually arrested – several times.'

'What was the name of the gang?' Juan already knew the answer, but he had to play dumb. Otherwise, Sarai would suspect he knew even more.

'The Sons of Jacob.'

'How did he get involved with them?'

'It started with marijuana possession, but then it

escalated to petty theft, then robbery, then aggravated assault. He was finally sentenced to prison. Last year while he was on parole he fled the country.'

'Where is he now?'

'The only lead I have is Kenya.'

'That's a lot of ground to cover. What about your friends back at Mossad? Someone there must want to help.'

'That's where I got the Kenya lead – but that's all my contact would tell me. Nobody is willing to risk their careers on my behalf. I can't blame them. I'm officially blacklisted. Worse, Mossad issued a burn notice on me. My spying career went out the window right along with my modeling gig. It was only because of Langston's interference with my government that I wasn't sent to prison.'

'Because of what you did for Langston?'

'Yes.'

Juan hoped she'd be more forthcoming about what actually transpired, since Overholt hadn't filled him in on the details, either. He'd have to be content with her answer for now.

'Maybe Asher's gang is our lead. We can reach out to them.'

'I considered that. But the Sons of Jacob are tough customers, as you Yanks like to say. Israeli-Russian mafia with international operations. My concern is that if we start making inquiries about Asher they might view him as a liability and kill him.'

'Yeah, they just might. Asher hasn't contacted you?'

'No.'

'Then how do you know your brother is still alive?'

'I don't.'

'If he is alive, he might not want to be found.'

'Possibly not. But there's a chance – a very good chance – that he's just in trouble and needs my help.'

'Why do you say that?'

'When we were younger, we were very close. He even sent me a few letters from prison. If he could reach out to me now, he would. I'm sure of that.'

'You said your father was in hospice. How long does he have?'

'A month, at most. Likely less.' Her eyes misted.

'And that's why you're in a hurry. Not for your brother's sake, but for his.'

'I owe my father at least that. But also my brother. I should have been there for him when he was younger. He wouldn't be in this situation now if I hadn't selfishly put my own desires ahead of my family's needs.'

'You were a kid doing your own thing, and you were serving your country. I bet your father was extremely proud of you – and still is.'

Massala blushed. 'Yes, I suppose so.'

'And you can't say your brother wouldn't have screwed up his life if you had been around.'

'I'll never know, will I?'

'You know, there's an old saying, "Character is destiny." He made his own choices. I suspect he would have made the same ones whether you were around or not.'

'I can't change the past. Maybe I can save his future.'

'You've got to find him first.'

'I know it's a long shot at best, and probably a fool's errand. But will you help me?'

Juan smiled.

She didn't have to ask.

Tel Aviv, Israel

The talkative Russian cabdriver pulled his Mercedes to a stop in the alley next to a late-model Hyundai sedan facing the opposite direction. He was face-to-face with the Hyundai's driver, a younger man in wraparound Oakley sunglasses.

The Russian rolled down his window and handed over a thumb drive to his handler. The Russian had a camera system inside his Mercedes that recorded every passenger and their conversations.

'Anything in particular?' the driver asked as he handed it to the woman sitting in the passenger seat.

'Greeting cards. Who knew?'

'What are you talking about?'

'You'll see.'

The cabbie rolled up his window and headed home.

26

Riyadh, Saudi Arabia

Prince Khalid wore his finest white *thobe* trimmed in gold, and the traditional Saudi headdress, the red-and-white *ghatra* with its black-corded *aqal* holding it in place on top of his graying head. His hand-tailored flowing robes and headwear were made from the world's finest cotton cloth and as expensive as a Francesco Smalto suit, but eminently more practical in the sweltering heat of the Saudi desert.

But today their function was merely symbolic. Khalid sat in an air-conditioned VIP suite above the crowded viewing stands, protected from the blistering heat punishing the tarmac outside.

The Royal Air Show was a new annual event initiated by the crown prince and designed specifically for the Saudi population. There were over a hundred and thirty thousand Saudi citizens in attendance today, nearly double from the year before.

Unlike the grander International and World Air Shows, which targeted a global audience of politicians and defense contractors, the Flying Royal, as it was locally known, was meant to increase the civilian population's personal connection to its rapidly expanding Air Force. First and foremost, it was a chance for the public to take selfies with its glorious pilots and officers, climb aboard multimillion-dollar fighter jets, touch the vast array of (dummy) missiles and bombs, and post all of their experiences on their social media. Building up such goodwill was an important step in heading off civil unrest.

And there was unrest. Despite the young crown prince's social reform campaigns – entirely conservative by Western standards, but breathtakingly shocking by Saudi norms – the fact remained that power and wealth still resided in the hands of the very few. Much of the government's money had gone into exponential increases in defense spending, particularly in air defense. The Flying Royal was a hands-on opportunity to experience what all of those petrodollars were purchasing. It was also designed to kindle patriotic pride in the Saudi Royal Air Force and help blunt the objection to the kingdom's brutal air war against poor Yemen.

With over three hundred and sixty combat aircraft, the Royal Saudi Air Force was one of the largest and most modern air fleets in the region. There was nothing more thrilling or terrifying than the sight of fast attack aircraft flying in perfect formation at low altitudes, their jet engines roaring like the voice of Allah himself.

And finally, the Flying Royal was sending the not-so-subtle message that all of that raw airpower at the disposal of the Saudi royal family could be deployed against the kingdom's enemies, foreign and domestic.

As the former head of the Saudi intelligence service, Prince Khalid was fully aware of the civil unrest brewing among the population. Raw demonstrations of overweening military power weren't the solution. The young crown prince's reckless reform programs were causing all the unrest. Culture and tradition were the bedrocks of Saudi society. Western-style modernization would only bring ruin, as new wine always ruined old wineskins, as the prophet Isa so wisely taught.

But no matter. Today was another celebration of Prince Muqrin's promotion to colonel. Khalid was surrounded by loyal friends who were enjoying the spectacular flying demonstrations just outside their shaded window. Wide-screen TVs inside the suite carried the live broadcast of the day's events. The simulcast was also going out on local television and radio networks, along with worldwide social media streaming.

The air show's master of ceremonies identified each aircraft, what units they belonged to, their pilots and crew, and their performance characteristics. His voice boomed over the loudspeakers outside and inside the VIP suites. The whole event was produced like a televised Formula One race.

The schedule of upcoming aircraft had already flashed on the suite's monitor. One of Khalid's oldest friends, Nayef, laid a soft hand on his arm.

'The deputy crown prince is next!'

The other royal princes surrounding Khalid clapped him on the shoulders and thighs, smiling and laughing with him.

The emcee announced the next aircraft, a Eurofighter Typhoon, and its famous pilot, 'His Royal Highness, Colonel Muqrin bin Khalid!'

The TV monitor displayed a stock image of the handsome pilot and his aircraft, still just a smoking speck in the distance. The highly unusual wing configuration stood out against nearly every other fixed-wing aircraft. The Eurofighter Typhoon had double delta wings, a smaller one fore – called a 'canard' – and the other aft, and larger.

The TV image cut to a live GoPro camera shot inside the cockpit. On cue, the helmeted Colonel Muqrin threw a thumbs-up from behind his blackened visor.

Khalid heard the muffled shouts and applause of the audience beyond the windows.

'You must be so proud!' Nayef said.

Khalid nodded, his eyes fixed on the distant speck roaring toward the airfield at nearly the speed of sound. He couldn't stop beaming.

He was proud, indeed.

The suite's thick glass hardly dampened the Eurofighter's twin turbofan engines screaming just thirty meters above the runway. The roar of the speeding plane drowned out the cheers of the audience and the blare of patriotic music as it shot past like a bullet – and suddenly rocketed into the sky.

Colonel Muqrin held a soft but steady grip on the stick as he pulled it close to his body.

The agile fighter, designed for dogfighting, responded brilliantly to his every touch of the stick and throttle. His G suit mitigated the familiar but still unpleasant effects of the high gravitational forces now exerting against his body in the steep climb toward the sky.

The high-tech heads-up display flashing in his custom-fitted HMSS helmet gave the pilot total informational awareness everywhere he looked around the cockpit and outside the canopy. The colonel's eyes scanned the virtual instrument panels projecting inside his visor, instantly taking in the data stream. All systems were functioning perfectly.

When he finally reached two thousand meters in altitude, he began his next maneuver. He knew that every eye below was on him now and he really wanted to impress them – particularly his father.

In a seamless dance of synchronizing hands and feet, the experienced pilot pushed the aircraft into a high-speed loop until the nose of his aircraft was pointed straight down at the dark gray tarmac far below.

'Fantastic, Colonel. Perfect execution,' the tower voice said in his helmet.

'Just wait for the next one.'

Muqrin smiled, imagining the looks on the faces of all the children down below when they saw what he was about to do.

But suddenly a sharp pain stabbed deep inside of his skull. He cried out.

'Colonel?'

'This will be an incredible maneuver,' Nayef said, completely mesmerized by the fighter's plunging dive. It seemed a stunning display of cold-blooded nerve and piloting skill.

Prince Khalid's smile faded with each accelerating heartbeat.

The Typhoon rocketed toward the earth like an angry star, its wings twisting erratically.

Khalid stood.

Moments later, the fighter arrowed into the desert sand.

Over a hundred thousand voices cried out at once as the fireball erupted in the distance, the emcee's panicked shouts breaking over the speakers.

Khalid's mouth quavered. 'My . . . son.'

Nayef wrapped his arms around his friend, shouting prayers to Allah.

Khalid cried out.

'My son!'

27

The Persian Gulf

'There she is,' Juan said in his headset as he pointed down below.

Even through the electronic buzz of her comms, Sarai Massala could hear the pride in Cabrillo's voice.

From this altitude, the *Oregon*'s white-painted hull and superstructure shone like a pearl against a blue velvet blanket of water as it lay at anchor in the northern end of the Persian Gulf. The ship had four tall cranes, two forward, and two aft, also gleaming white in the bright sunlight. The forward pair of cranes faced each other, as did the two aft. The five hatches were all painted white, but the middle one featured a black-circled *H* – the international symbol for a helipad.

'It's magnificent,' Sarai said. 'What kind of a ship is she?'

'The *Oregon* is a hundred-and-eighty-meter-long Handymax-class break-bulk carrier. Basically, a cargo ship – with a few modifications.'

'What kind of cargo do you carry?'

'Oh, you'd be surprised.'

Juan sat in the copilot's seat next to George 'Gomez' Adams, steady as a rock and calm as a napping cat, despite the flashing warning light.

Low fuel.

The AgustaWestland AW609 tilt-rotor was pushing its operational limits to the extreme by flying directly from Tel Aviv to the *Oregon*, anchored just beyond the territorial waters of Kuwait City. But the risk of running out of fuel was outweighed by the unfolding chaos of civil war on the ground in Iraq. Setting down for a refuel there might mean never getting off the ground again.

As a former Mossad agent, Sarai Massala had flown aboard many types of aircraft, but the two-and-a-half-hour flight on the otherworldly AW was a first. The cockpit featured six digital displays, along with all of the switches, dials, gauges, and toggles found on most modern aircraft. It was a highly complex informational environment. She had no idea how any pilot could master all of it.

But the most remarkable feature about the tilt-rotor was the two big Pratt & Whitney turboshaft engines on the ends of its wings. They could be rotated from the horizontal to the vertical – turning the forward-flying aircraft into a helicopter – by simply manipulating a thumb switch on the cyclic. The reverse was also true. It had been an amazing thing to see and experience firsthand.

Massala had read about the tilt-rotors used by American combat forces. But to actually fly aboard one when the machine converted from airplane mode back to helicopter mode was quite remarkable. Though assisted by automated systems and visual displays, the key to a successful conversion from helicopter to airplane and back again was the sure hand of a skilled pilot.

Massala was introduced to Gomez Adams when she

first boarded. The rakishly handsome aviator wore an easy smile beneath a gunfighter's mustache, and spoke with a Texas drawl as smooth and sweet as apple butter.

'It's a pleasure, ma'am.'

Massala had walked the world's fashion runways with some of the most beautiful men in the world. She had found nearly all of them to be relentlessly arrogant and painfully shallow. With his lean physique and dark shoulder-length hair, Adams was as attractive as any of them. But that was where the similarities ended. She saw no vanity in him, but rather a fierce intelligence behind the brown eyes. His self-assured confidence was born of actual achievement rather than the genetic accident of good looks. That confidence was a quality Sarai was certain many women found irresistibly attractive.

'Stole him from the Night Stalkers, the 160th Special Operations Aviation Regiment,' Juan said over the whining turboprops. 'My best drone pilot, too.'

As Juan and Sarai settled into their seats and buckled up, she asked him, 'The name "Gomez" is Hispanic, is it not?'

Juan chuckled. 'His real name is George Adams. We call him "Gomez" because of a dalliance he once had with a woman who bore an uncanny resemblance to Morticia Addams.'

'I'm not sure who that is.'

'Didn't you ever watch the old *Addams Family* TV show?'

Massala shrugged.

'Uncle Fester? Thing? Lurch?' Juan's voice rang with incredulity.

'I'm sorry, I don't know it.'

'It's a classic.'

Between the ship below and the remarkable aircraft she was flying in, Sarai began to think there was a lot more to this Juan Cabrillo than she had first imagined. She wondered what other surprises he might have in store for her.

'Ladies and gentlemen, secure your tray tables and stow your electronics because we're coming in for a landing,' Gomez said over the comms. 'And please, keep your hands inside the car at all times.'

Moments later, Gomez deftly handled the cyclic, throttle control lever, and rudder pedals to bring the tilt-rotor to a gentle touchdown in the center of the *Oregon*'s helipad. Once the AW was firmly planted, he killed the engines and began running through his postflight checklist.

'Thank you,' Massala said as she shook Adams's hand. 'That was a remarkable piece of flying.'

'It's a remarkable machine.'

'And don't blame him for the lousy in-flight service,' Gomez said, nodding at Juan. 'If I'd have known we were going to have a passenger I would have had something better for you than Gatorade and protein bars.'

'We'll make it up to you, I promise,' Juan said.

Sarai smiled. 'No worries.'

Juan and Sarai deplaned as one of Gomez's 'hangar apes' – an aircraft mechanic – climbed inside the cabin. Juan swore he heard Gomez mention a mechanical situation to the tech. He made a mental note to check with Gomez about it later.

As Massala and Cabrillo stepped away from the helipad, a monstrous hydraulic motor spooled up into an industrial whine as the helipad began descending to its hangar belowdecks.

Juan led Sarai aft toward the bridge superstructure on the stern of the ship. The hot and humid air was in sharp contrast to the air-conditioned aircraft cabin. A hard, high sun burned hot in a hazy blue sky, the heat absorbed and amplified by the steel decks.

'How old is the vessel? She seems brand-new.'

'She's two years old. But trust me, she doesn't always look this good, especially topside.'

'How did you acquire it?'

'We had it built according to our specifications. She's actually the third iteration of our original concept, and the best yet, if I do say so myself.'

'What happened to the other two?'

'The same thing that happens to all of us in the end.'

Juan pulled open the door at the base of the bridge superstructure and cautioned Sarai about the trip hazard the door coaming posed. He led her down a freshly painted, well-lit, linoleum-tiled corridor to the public mess hall. It featured ordinary picnic bench-style seating and a stainless steel serving station. Everything was clean and unoccupied.

It all seemed very normal to Massala, though she had yet to pass a single crew member. Each area had a security camera fixed on the ceiling, but that didn't strike her as an extraordinary precaution in these perilous times of ocean piracy.

Juan then led her down another unremarkable corridor

to a janitor's closet featuring two walls with shelved cleaning supplies and a sink with a whiteboard next to it. He saw the confused look on her face.

'What you're about to see is not exactly top secret because we're not technically part of any government agency. But I would consider it a personal favor if you never mentioned to anyone what you will experience aboard my vessel. I'm asking this only because secrecy and anonymity are the two defenses that best protect the lives of my people.'

'I understand. Your secrets are safe with me.'

'Thank you.'

Juan pressed his hand against the whiteboard and a second later an electronic lock clicked. Juan pushed on one of the shelved walls and it opened into a secret corridor.

'I wasn't expecting that,' Sarai said, nodding at the door. 'Or that,' pointing at the whiteboard. 'A hidden palm print scanner?'

'We take security seriously.'

'How seriously?'

Juan motioned toward the open door.

'You'll have to follow me down the rabbit hole to find out.'

28

In sharp contrast to the thin linoleum floors and harsh fluorescent lighting of the cramped janitor's closet, Sarai stepped into an opulent corridor featuring plush carpeting and fine art paintings lit by soft picture lights highlighting their beauty.

'I've seen this one before,' Massala said, stopping in front of an oil painting featuring cowboys around a campfire at night.

'That's a Remington,' Juan said.

'It's a beautiful copy.'

'Actually, it's a signed original.'

Sarai arched her eyebrows. 'Remarkable.'

He pointed at three more pieces hanging farther down the long corridor wall.

'We use an art consultant, Beth Anders, to invest a portion of our profits into fine art like these pieces. They appreciate even faster than real estate or other hard assets. They also make for a better work environment.'

'How many do you have?'

'Unfortunately, some of our best items went down when we lost our last vessel.'

'That's a tragedy for everyone who loves art.'

'And for our insurance company, who had to pay out a handsome fee. Fortunately, we still have many that we store in bank vaults onshore. We rotate them in and out to avoid a complete loss in the event of another shipboard catastrophe.'

'I'm no art expert, but I imagine there's quite a bit of money tied up in paintings like that.'

'And that's not counting the personal collections of many of my crew members. Paintings, sculptures, even period furniture. My people are a lot more artsy-fartsy than they like to let on.'

Sarai's lovely forehead wrinkled with confusion. 'I don't normally associate Michelangelos with your average band of mercenaries.'

'I'll take that as a compliment, though I'd say we're anything but average, judging by our corporate revenues – all tax free, by the way.'

'I apologize for the poor choice of words. So far, I've seen nothing "average" about your operation.'

'No offense taken. But just in case you need convincing – well, you ain't seen nothin' yet.'

Given Overholt's confidence in Massala and his own impression of her, Juan felt comfortable giving her a brief tour of the *Oregon*.

'Everything above decks is a working cargo vessel, but it's mostly for show. The real *Oregon* is a ship-within-a-ship belowdecks, which is where we're headed now.'

Juan led her down a glass and steel staircase more befitting a luxury cruise liner than a warship. He stopped at the doorway and motioned for her to step through.

Massala passed inside and instantly froze, her smoky eyes wide as dinner plates as they took in the scope of the room. Juan came in beside her. They were standing at the rear of the operations center.

The first thing that grabbed her attention was the seamless three-hundred-sixty-degree floor-to-ceiling wraparound displays. The 8K HDR LCD screens gave the impression that she was standing outside on the bridgewing high above the deck and able to view the entire world around her everywhere she looked.

The rest of the room was equally dramatic. The op center itself was a tiered semicircle of steel, glass, and metal touchscreen workstations. In the center of the top tier of workstations and nearest the entrance was the captain's chair, and seated in it was Linda Ross.

'This is . . . incredible. I feel as if I'm standing on the deck of a starship,' Sarai said. 'Like in *Star Trek*.'

'You're not far off the mark,' Juan said.

'And you must be Captain Picard,' Sarai joked.

Juan shuddered comically. 'No, no, no. James T. Kirk, all the way.'

Linda swiveled her chair around and flashed a smile as she stood. She rose to her full five-foot-eight stature, strong and lean, and extended her hand. Her bobbed haircut flashed alternating streaks of golden brown and deep maroon.

'My name's Linda Ross. You must be Sarai Massala. Juan briefed us about you.' Her high-pitched voice belied her command presence, and there was an edge in the soft green eyes.

They shook hands. 'Nice to meet you,' Massala said. 'Love your hair.'

'I call it Peanut Butter and Jelly. I change my hair color a lot. Kind of a weird habit.'

'Not so weird,' Juan said. 'Linda spent several years in the US Navy on an Aegis cruiser as an intelligence officer and on a staff assignment at the Pentagon. I'm no psychologist, but I think after so many years of Navy regulations, she decided she needed to cut loose a little bit.'

'Don't quit your day job, Chairman,' Linda said with a wink. 'You're a better captain than a pop psychologist.'

'The Navy was foolish enough to deny her a vessel to command, so we scooped her up,' Juan said. 'Now Linda is my Vice President of operations. If I'm not in command of the vessel, it's either Linda or Max Hanley that has the conn.'

'That's a great deal of responsibility,' Sarai said. 'You must be quite capable.'

'Juan gave me the chance of a lifetime. I wasn't about to give anything less than my best. Besides,' Linda said as she pointed at the command chair, 'this might just be the easiest ship in the world to captain. Anyone sitting here can run every single system, from navigation to weapons to comms to engineering.' Linda nodded at Juan. 'And he's the guy who designed it. In fact, the whole vessel.'

Sarai nodded. 'Very impressive.'

'It's getting warm in here,' Juan said. 'How about we finish the tour?'

Juan led Sarai down to the bowels of the *Oregon* to show her the vessel's high-tech magnetohydrodynamic engines, but Max Hanley was nowhere to be found to give her the nickel tour of his prized baby.

'Max is the President of the Corporation, but he would tell you he's just a glorified grease monkey.'

'Excuse me?'

'Max is my chief engineer. He takes care of these engines and just about anything else with a moving part. He's usually down here somewhere. I was hoping you could meet him.'

'I don't know much about naval architecture, but it seems to me this engine room is comparatively quiet.' Massala spoke without having to raise her voice above the low thrum of the ship's engines. 'Is this normal?'

'Anything but. We're like an oceangoing Tesla. Our magnetohydrodynamic engines are powered by seawater,' Juan explained. 'The engines strip away free electrons with supercooled magnets. The resulting electricity powers four pulse jets through vector-thrusting drive tubes. It's the fastest ship of its size in the world, and it runs on essentially free and limitless energy.'

'How fast?'

'Over sixty knots.'

Massala flashed an incredulous smile. At first she thought he was joking, but his gaze told her otherwise. 'Seriously?'

'Seriously.'

Juan took her down even farther to the lowest deck and over to the moon pool. He pointed out the two submersibles stored in their cradles suspended above the expanse.

'The big one is the *Nomad*, the smaller is the *Gator*.'

The larger sub was shaped like a blunt-nosed Tic Tac. The underwater workhorse had three bow portholes and powerful xenon lamps to help guide its two articulating mechanical arms, each sporting powerful gripper hands.

The smaller vessel was the polar opposite in design and function. The sleek and flat forty-foot-long deck and twin thousand-horsepower diesels shot the vessel across the surface like a cigarette boat at fifty knots. But with its low-profile cockpit and battery packs, it could be practically silent and invisible when near the surface – perfect for stealthy insertions.

'You have a shape-shifting cargo vessel with two submarines and a tilt-rotor. I imagine you also have combat capabilities?'

'The *Oregon* definitely has the capacity to reach out and touch someone by land, sea, and air.'

'So . . . is the *Oregon* an intelligence-gathering vessel or a warship?'

'Both.'

Juan then showed Sarai some of the crew's amenities, including the Olympic-size swimming pool that occupied one of the ship's ballast tanks, the fully equipped gym facilities, and jogging track. 'A healthy crew is a happy crew,' Juan explained.

Just as they were about to check out one of Juan's favorite rooms, the gun range, he received a text from Eric Stone.

Ready when you are.

29

Juan and Sarai made a beeline for the *Oregon*'s paneled conference room. Eric Stone and Mark Murphy were seated at the long mahogany table, totally engrossed in their laptops.

'Sarai Massala, I'd like to introduce you to two of the sharpest knives in our drawer, Eric Stone and Dr Mark Murphy.'

Murphy and Eric glanced up. Neither of the twenty-somethings had the emotional maturity to hide the obvious pleasure they took in Massala's stunning looks. Eric Stone shot up out of his chair. Murphy did, too, but banged his knees on the table as he did so.

Eric held out his hand. The young former Navy officer still wore his brown hair trimmed short and crisply parted, but had exchanged his military uniform for his customary oxford button-down shirt and khaki slacks. Of late, he'd replaced his normal reading glasses with stylish Warby Parkers to improve his odds in the internet dating game.

'My friends call me Stoney.'

'Nice to meet you, Stoney.'

'Besides being a world-class researcher, Stoney is my primary helmsman. Nobody can drive the *Oregon* better than he can.'

'Nobody except for you, boss,' Stone said.

Juan shrugged in agreement.

While Eric looked like a junior executive who'd been lab-grown in a corporate cubicle, Mark sported the urban camouflage of a punk rock skateboarder. Adidas skate shoes, black chinos, and a T-shirt featuring his new favorite synthpunk band, the Snide Fairies, that also listed the concert dates of their recent 'Don't Puck with Me' European tour. Murphy's wispy chin beard matched the mop of unkempt hair on top of his enormous head.

'Dr Murphy,' Massala said. She gripped his uncalloused gamer's hand.

'Oh, please. Murph is fine.'

'I won't tell you how many PhDs Murph has or how young he was when he earned his first one,' Juan said. 'But there's a good reason why he's our chief weapons officer – and another exceptional researcher.'

'Ah, boss. You're embarrassing me.'

Juan gestured toward the conference table.

'Gents, show us what you've found.'

Stone and Murphy raced back to their stations like two schoolboys trying to grab the seat next to the pretty girl on the bus. Juan held back a chuckle. He could tell they both thought they had a chance to impress the former runway model – but what they might actually do with her if they managed to capture her affection was anyone's guess.

Stone and Murphy were best friends and had been since they'd worked together as weapons designers in the private sector before joining the Corporation. But whenever they were competing for the same woman, the gloves came off.

Part of Juan's brief to both of them was to keep

Asher's Shin Bet relationship under wraps. He had also ordered them to stay clear of both the Mossad and Shin Bet databases, though any others were open season. If it was discovered that the *Oregon* was hacking into Israel's intelligence community systems, it would be Overholt who suffered the blowback. Besides, if either agency had any actionable intel on Asher Massala, they would have already scooped him up.

The *Oregon*'s two best researchers lit up two different LCD wall monitors with their desktop displays to show their findings. Maps, photos, mug shots, social media pages, and other data points flashed on the screens as they spoke.

Massala noted the speed with which their fingers – and brains – operated.

'Of course, we started with the information you sent us, Ms Massala,' Eric began.

'Sarai, please.'

Eric continued. 'We used that as our jump-off point to dig into his background.'

As he spoke, several of Asher's class photos appeared on the wall monitor, each one older than the next, along with various sports pictures, and school records – grades, standardized tests, teacher evaluations.

'Asher was a gifted athlete, excellent student – at least for a while. High IQ.'

Murphy jumped in. 'And then the wheels came off.' Asher's mug shot appeared.

'His first arrest came at age seventeen for shoplifting, suspended sentence; three months later, arrested for assault and battery, but it didn't go to trial. No witnesses.

Age eighteen, grand theft auto. Sentenced to sixteen months, paroled after twelve. Convicted at twenty-four for involuntary manslaughter. Paroled after three years of serving a four-year sentence. Broke his parole. Whereabouts officially unknown. Believed to have fled the country.'

'Excuse me,' Sarai interrupted. 'But these are Asher's private records. How did you come by them?'

Eric and Mark exchanged an awkward glance with each other, and then with Juan.

'Boss?' Mark asked.

'She's on our side.'

Eric smiled. 'We're the *Oregon*'s tiger team.'

'The phreaks,' Murphy said.

Massala gave a confused look.

'*Hackers,*' Juan said with an edge to his voice.

'Yes, sir,' Eric said. 'Hackers.'

'Impressive,' Massala said. 'I would think Israeli databases would be well secured.'

Murphy grinned. 'Yeah, you'd think.'

'Go on,' Juan said.

'We started out by narrowing our search parameters to Kenya, since that was his last presumed reported location,' Eric began.

'And just did a basic search of your brother's name, Asher Massala,' Murphy added. 'We started with Kenyan police records –'

'More hacking?' Massala asked.

Murphy nodded eagerly.

'Go on,' Juan said.

'Yeah, hurry up,' Eric added.

'Shut up,' Murphy whispered. He nodded at the wall monitor. Asher's last Israeli police photo was still displayed. 'There are quite a few Ethiopians in Kenya, but no one that matched your brother's name or age in the national databases. So we ran our own custom-built facial recognition AI program to see if we could match him there.'

Murphy hit a key on his laptop and within seconds over thirty thousand police mug shots of Kenyan and other African faces stacked like playing cards next to Asher's police photo.

Massala shot an astonished glance at Juan.

'Yeah, I know. A couple of geniuses,' he whispered.

Eric continued. 'Our preliminary conclusion is that Asher has either never been arrested –'

'– or that the Kenyans do a lousy job of photographing their prisoners, which is also a possibility,' Murphy said. 'Their records, generally, are a mess.'

'Besides, we figured he was running-and-gunning under an alias anyway, which makes sense, since he's a fugitive,' Eric said. 'So we pivoted our search and took a run at the gang he's affiliated with, the Sons of Jacob.'

'"*Synovya Iakova*," in Russian,' Murphy said. He pronounced it perfectly.

'Practice much, Doctor Zhivago?' Eric whispered under his breath. He turned toward Juan. 'Anyway, it turns out they really are an international operation.'

'What kind of outfit is it?'

'According to Interpol records, murder-for-hire, kidnapping, extortion, drugs, to name a few. Seriously bad hombres.'

Juan saw the despair washing over Massala's face. He

wished he could comfort her with the knowledge that her brother was actually working undercover for Shin Bet – or, at least, had been. Though, the more he thought about it, he was glad she didn't know. She was an Israeli patriot. It would cut her to the quick if she found out he'd become a traitor on top of everything else.

'And right now the Sons of Jacob are operating in Kenya,' Murphy said. 'That lines up with everything we have so far on Asher.'

'Why Kenya?' Sarai asked.

'Kenya is in the top half of per capita wealth in Africa. Of course, that wealth is highly concentrated,' Eric said.

'What are they up to in Kenya?' Juan asked.

'They're into all kinds of grift, but their primary activity is stealing luxury cars and selling them in Europe.'

'And that fits with Asher's criminal background,' Murphy said.

'When I think of Kenya, I don't think of Lamborghinis,' Massala said.

Murphy scratched his scraggly chin beard. 'You'd be surprised how many luxury whips they have – Lambos, Mercedes, BMWs, Bugattis –'

'It's not just that they have them but that the police do a bad job of arresting anybody, let alone stopping the crime ring.'

'Bribery?' Juan asked. 'Or just lousy cops?'

'Sadly, Kenya is one of the most corrupt countries in Africa, and that's really saying something,' Eric said. 'But I'd say it's a bit of both. The upside is that Kenya has a relatively low murder rate, though property crimes are through the roof.'

'All right, so we know Asher is connected to the Sons of Jacob and the Sons of Jacob are big-time car thieves. Where does that get us?' Juan asked.

Eric held up a finger. 'If Muhammad can't get to the mountain, you bring the mountain to Muhammad.'

'Super fail on the analogy, bro,' Murphy whispered.

Stone ignored him. 'Knowing that we don't have any record of his arrest, we decided to check out the private CCTV cameras that are located around Mombasa, the main port city, and the capital, Nairobi, Kenya's biggest city and the location of the highest number of luxury vehicles.'

'Searching for an actual car theft,' Juan said. 'Smart.'

'Car theft and, more specifically, carjackings,' Murphy said. 'Modern cars, especially the high-end ones, are well defended against conventional break-ins. They use all kinds of electronic means to stop a car in its tracks without a key fob –'

Eric finished his sentence. 'It's just a lot easier and efficient to yank someone out of their car at gunpoint and steal it.'

'The local news reports say that if you don't resist, the only thing that happens is your car gets stolen . . .' Murphy's gamer energy suddenly cooled.

Eric was equally solemn. 'We ran our AI facial recognition through the CCTV databases and we found this . . .'

He punched a key. A grainy video from an overhead camera played out in real time. It was all video signal, no audio.

A black Mercedes G-Wagen was stopped at the traffic light between a Toyota pickup and a Nissan sedan.

A moped with two young Black males raced up next to it. Because of the camera angle from high atop a bank building across the street, their faces couldn't be seen.

The bearded man on the back of the moped leaped off the bike and pulled a pistol, then shouted as he tapped on the driver's-side glass.

The other cars that could raced away, blowing through the red light. Pedestrians on the sidewalks scattered.

The Mercedes window didn't retract. The young man smashed the glass with the butt of his pistol. The driver reached through the shattered window and grabbed the weapon.

Two gunshots flashed on the grainy image.

Massala gasped. She didn't have to see the face to guess who the shooter was.

'Get on with it, Stoney,' Juan said.

'Sorry.' Eric sped up the video. The shooter reached inside, yanked the door open, and pulled the driver – a Black man – out by his collar, tossing him onto the pavement.

The female passenger leaped out of her door screaming as the shooter turned to jump inside the Mercedes.

Eric tapped a key.

The image froze.

Murph tapped another key.

The image enlarged until the shooter's bearded face filled the screen.

Eric tapped a few more keys. The CCTV facial image and Asher's clean-shaven Israeli mug shot were both suddenly outlined in wire frames, with key identification nodes highlighted. The two wire-frame images separated from their respective photos, then joined together above them, showing a near-perfect match of the two facial structures. The words *99.4% confidence* flashed on the screen.

'Asher,' Massala said, her voice trailing off.

'We did some digging around,' Murphy said. 'The driver wasn't wounded. Just some hearing damage from the close proximity of the gunshots.'

'Thank God,' Massala said. 'When did this occur?'

'Three months ago,' Murphy said.

'I take it no arrest was made,' Juan said.

'No. But we did find this.' Eric punched another key.

Asher's bearded face appeared in a social media post. He was standing in front of a two-story building constructed from corrugated metal.

'This was uploaded two days later,' Eric said, anticipating the question.

'Any idea where it was taken?' Juan asked.

Eric nodded. 'The photo was geotagged. He was still in Nairobi at the time.'

'Sort of,' Murphy said.

'What do you mean, "sort of"?' Juan asked.

'That photo was taken in Kibera,' Eric said.

'Kibera?' Massala asked.

Murphy pulled up another image on the screen. It was a syndicated news service drone photo taken high above the urban squalor, showing acres and acres of rusted corrugated metal sheeting crowded together.

'The largest slum in Africa. Depending on who you ask, there are anywhere from five hundred thousand to a million people crammed into less than two square miles.'

'So, where does that leave us?' Juan asked.

Massala stepped closer to the monitor, fixated on the image.

'My brother is a violent criminal, tied up with killers, and lost somewhere deep inside a human anthill. I don't see any hope of finding him, let alone saving him from himself.' She turned to Juan. 'This was all a fool's errand. I'm so sorry to have wasted your time.' Her voice cracked with emotion.

Murphy and Eric turned their attention back to their laptops.

'You let us worry about finding Asher. But it's not just him I'm thinking about.'

She nodded as she dabbed away a tear from the corner of her eye with a fingertip.

'You're absolutely right. This is also about my father. Thank you for reminding me.'

'Let's get you settled in your cabin, and then we'll start making plans for the next step.'

Juan turned toward his crewmen. 'You two need to get back to your stations. Put your search engines on auto-pilot or whatever it is you do. I want to know if Asher pings on any other cameras, and especially if he's moved on to some other place, or maybe even another country. Otherwise, Kibera is our next stop.'

'Aye, Chairman,' they both said. They put their heads together and began formulating a search plan in lowered voices as Juan pointed Massala toward the door.

There was a lot to do and not much time to get it done. Asher wasn't just a needle in a haystack; he was a grain of sand in the vast, swirling sands of the windswept Sahara.

Juan held little hope of actually finding him, but he had to try.

What worried him even more is what would happen if they actually did.

Juan checked the wall-mounted digital clock. They needed to get moving; time wasn't Asher's friend, nor theirs.

He had hoped to greet Huxley and Linc in person and get a firsthand account of their Amazon adventure. But according to the text she had sent to Hali Kasim, they weren't due to arrive in Dubai until the day after tomorrow. Cabrillo didn't like the fact that she texted their travel itinerary to Hali instead of calling him directly. That meant she was hiding something. Juan would just have to wait until after he got back from Nairobi to find out what it was.

30

Indian Naval Station Vajrakosh
Near Karwar in the State of Karnataka, India

Jean-Paul Salan sat in the foremost troop seat of the aircraft's cargo bay, kitted out with his rifle, bump helmet, night vision goggles, and parachute rig like the rest of his twelve restive mercenaries. The dimly lit cargo area stank of JP-8 fuel and the sloshing contents of the 'honey pot' pinned against the bulkhead.

The C-130 Hercules could hold up to sixty-five paratroopers. But Salan had war-gamed the mission for twelve men only – and six companions. He and his men were perched on one side of the aircraft and the kennels on the other. Right now, with the red cabin lights low and the engines thrumming, the dogs were calm. That would change shortly.

The four roaring turboprops driving the aircraft made normal conversation difficult, but they were all connected by comms, so it wasn't a problem. They weren't exactly a talkative bunch anyway. They had been trained to move and think as one, and on his command. Salan wasn't running a social club and the work he'd done with Hightower proved that a fighting esprit de corps was easily manufactured. Or, more accurately, unleashed.

Salan checked his watch. They would be near the jump

point soon. He pulled the tablet from its pouch on his chest rig and checked the live drone feed again. He'd had a woman stationed on the ground for the last week monitoring the compound, tracking movements, and keeping the drone aloft. Everything was as it should be on this moonless night.

He ran through the operational plan in his mind one more time out of habit. Every plan had at least one flaw, but so far he hadn't found it in tonight's mission, even after this final run-through of his mental checklist. He wasn't worried. Plans never survived first contact with the enemy, and his tactical specialty was improvisation under fire. One way or another, he would complete tonight's mission to the satisfaction of his Saudi employer, his biggest contract yet.

Salan's comms clicked in his ear. 'Signor, we are ten minutes from the drop.' The pilot's thick Milanese accent rang loud and clear.

'Excellent.'

Salan stood as he opened the comms channel to his troops. All eyes turned to him.

'Equipment check!'

The twelve soldiers immediately stood. Each fighter checked the man in front of him, tugging on straps and pulling on buckles. Thirty seconds later, they turned around and repeated the process with the man on the other side.

Just as the equipment check was completed, hydraulic motors began to whine, lowering the rear-facing loading ramp from which they would all jump. The noise and rush of wind immediately filled the cabin.

Salan pointed to the man standing next to him wearing a specialized harness. The five men behind him wore the same device.

'To the kennels. Prepare for the jump.'

Salan had undergone some of Hightower's conditioning regimen to improve his physical performance, but had nowhere near the strength or stamina of the twelve mercs landing in the open field next to him. It was that herculean strength that allowed six of them to carry the two-hundred-plus-pound Malinois monsters in their special harnesses for their HALO jump. It also gave his mercs the ability to control the muscular animals and their hyper-adrenalized bloodstreams – at least for the time being.

The parachute jump succeeded without incident and the mercenaries quietly gathered around their leader. Salan hadn't yet activated the huge dogs, but they were alert and anxious, ready to explode in fury as they had been trained to do. He called them his little velociraptors, though there was nothing little about them. Once activated by his electronic signal, they turned into perfect killing machines, driven by the frenzy of bloodlust and nearly uncontrollable rage. The only thing that kept Salan and the other men safe were the special electronic transmitters each mercenary wore, each unit beaming ultrasonic pulses that humans couldn't hear, but warned the dogs away from attack. Anyone not wearing such a device was vulnerable to assault.

As Salan and the others were pulling off their parachute harnesses, the drone operator dashed forward out of the woods and into the clearing. The short-cropped, flame-haired Irishwoman gave him a thumbs-up and whispered 'Still all clear' in her comms as she approached. She wore an ultrasonic transmitter as well.

Salan grinned. 'Good work. Drone battery?'

'Twenty-eight minutes left. Reserve battery sixty minutes.'

'Excellent. Stay alert on that thing, and stay back. But join us at my signal.'

'Will do.'

Salan led his twelve men and their six dogs through a thick stand of mahogany trees surrounding the rectangular naval depot. Minutes later, he and the others were crouched near the fence just inside the tree line. Their primary target was the newly constructed warehouse facility on the east side of the compound.

But first he needed to take out the overnight two-man security crew inside the headquarters building monitoring the warehouse sensors. The building was located a half kilometer south of the target warehouse at the southeast corner of the complex, right behind the front gate.

Salan checked his drone tablet and saw the base yet again from his god's-eye perspective. The guards were all at their usual stations and the chief petty officer was making his rounds in his vehicle on the far side of the compound.

'Go,' was all Salan needed to whisper and his three-man team tasked with the headquarters assignment bolted off, one of them carrying a telescopic ladder tall enough to scale the double-stranded razor wire on top of the cyclone fencing.

*

Flying insects seemingly the size of hummingbirds attacked the buzzing sodium lamps high above the compound, banging into the glass with relentless fury. The lamps threw enough light onto the compound for the remote cameras to pick up any kind of movement, including the sudden approach of the three mercs to the fence.

The sixteen-foot ladder was quickly extended and laid on top of the razor wire. Two of the men scrambled up the ladder with unimaginable speed and dexterity, then dropped to the other side, falling fifteen feet to the ground with hardly a break in their running strides as they dashed for the headquarters building.

As quickly as they had scaled the fence, the third man pulled the ladder away and tossed it into the woods, then waited for his signal.

Leading Seaman Chakravarthy yawned, fighting back the heavy lead weights tugging at his eyelids. Banks of video and signal monitors surrounded his small workstation. The technician's primary focus all evening and into the early-morning hours had been the lines of code he and a few friends were cobbling together for a video game they hoped to put up on Meta's Horizon Worlds metaverse. There was no way Chakravarthy or any other enlisted sailor would ever make enough money in India's Bharatiya Nau Sena to buy a house and start a family. The metaverse was the future, and the future is where the money was waiting for him.

He glanced at his watch and then over at his friend Bahadur, sound asleep in his chair, his boots up on the desk. There was still ten more minutes until it was his turn to take over the duty station and another hour before the chief petty officer would stop by on his way to grab his customary cup of tea.

Just the thought of the chief storming into the room unannounced made Chakravarthy's blood pressure rise. Singh was a screamer. The chief had once made Chakravarthy's life a living hell for a month when he caught him sleeping at his station. Out of nervous habit, he glanced at the perimeter camera monitors, searching for Singh's Polaris all-terrain vehicle.

Chakravarthy leaned in close to the lowest bank of camera screens to try and find him, pushing his government-issue glasses back up onto his nose just as the door burst open. He nearly jumped out of his skin, startled by the noise.

But before Chakravarthy could turn in his chair and explain to Singh what was going on, a silenced hollow-point 9mm bullet plowed through the back of his skull.

His friend Bahadur met the same fate, still asleep in his chair.

'Clear,' the mercenary said, after killing the two-man HQ monitoring team.

'Very good,' Salan said, still inside the tree line with the rest of his men. 'Hold your positions until my command.' The two mercs he'd sent there were native Hindi speakers. If anyone called in with an alert or a concern, they could bluff it away.

Salan checked his drone tablet again. The guards were still at their stations, the barracks remained quiet, and the chief petty officer was still making his slow rounds on his Polaris. Salan made a quick calculation.

Time to go.

The former paratrooper made a single hand gesture and the point man dashed forward, cutting a man-sized hole in the fence with a handheld vapor torch. Normally, cutting the fence would set off an alarm, but with the monitoring station taken out, there was no fear of detection.

Salan glanced at the six men holding their dogs by their collars.

'Group one, ready?'

'Ready,' they replied.

'Release,' Salan whispered in his comms.

The first Malinois charged up to Salan, but its eyes were fixed on the man at the fence. Five more animals stacked in behind the beast.

'*Allez!*' Salan commanded, and the dogs bolted for the fence hole. As soon as they cleared the fence, he punched the activation trigger on his wristwatch.

'The rest of you – follow me.'

31

Seaman First Class Agarwal had joined the Indian military to escape an arranged marriage to a cretinous lout her mother favored, and for that escape, she was grateful. With any luck, the lecherous fool would turn his gaze elsewhere before her term of service was completed.

But Agarwal, born and raised in landlocked New Delhi, chose the Indian Navy in particular so that she could see the world, or at least the ocean. The irony was not lost on her that her first duty station was a landlocked compound several miles from the sea.

The cloudy skies hid the pale shadow of a new moon, but didn't quench the heat rising up from the cement beneath her heavy combat boots that also blistered her feet. Her small frame barely filled the Navy's smallest blue digital camouflage uniform, and the heavy rifle slung over her shoulder seemed nearly as tall as she was. A trickle of sweat slithered down her spine in a continual rivulet beneath the heavy fabric of her shirt.

But Agarwal found the physical discomforts a welcome distraction from the mind-numbing boredom of her assignment at the Navy's missile and ammunition storage complex. Night after night, absolutely nothing happened, save the regular passing of the chief petty officer's Polaris all-terrain vehicle – essentially, a 4×4 golf cart – on its endless rounds circumnavigating the one-kilometer-long, half-kilometer-wide perimeter. Invariably, the turbaned Sikh stopped at her post and made small talk. Though he feigned concern as her immediate commanding officer, Agarwal knew his intentions toward her weren't of a supervisory nature.

The only other distraction for the eighteen-year-old was to catch glimpses of the other guards walking at their respective corners, equally as bored as her. They threw each other furtive hand waves when the CPO wasn't around to chew them out for unprofessional conduct.

Tonight she stood her ground on the far northwest corner of the complex, desperately fighting the temptation to check her wristwatch every thirty seconds. The only thing keeping her from resigning from the Navy was the knowledge that her return home assured an immediate wedding to her betrothed, an oily-skinned junior banker with breath like rotted meat.

She felt the drop of sweat forming on the end of her nose and decided to play a game with it, trying not to do anything that might cause it to drop. Nearly crossing her eyes with effort to see it, she was suddenly startled by a man's sudden whimper in the far distance. She turned in the direction of the noise in time to see his flailing legs on the ground being dragged out of her sight without a scream.

Agarwal's heart raced as panic seized her. She reached for the radio mic clipped to her lapel and turned to call it in, when she suddenly saw the snarling mouth and vicious fangs of the largest dog she'd ever seen charging silently toward her at incredible speed. The terrifying vision was so shocking she froze in place and before she could cry out it was on her. Its giant paws slammed into her chest and the momentum of its massive weight at full speed bowled her over. Her fabric cap offered her skull no protection as it slammed into the cement. The pain exploded in her brain as white spots flashed in her eyes.

She opened her mouth to scream, but the dog's sharp fangs sank into her neck. A single shake of its massive head tore her life away before it sped off in search of its next victim.

Chief Petty Officer Singh drove along at a leisurely pace as he made his next circuit. He was lost in carnal reveries of the young Agarwal standing duty tonight when he caught sight of one of his men in the distance lying in front of the new storage facility, his limbs painfully askew.

Singh stomped the throttle as he snatched his mic to call in a warning to the barracks, but three whisper-quiet .300 AAC Blackout subsonic rounds fired from a silenced rifle plowed into his chest before he uttered a word. He was dead before his face hit the steering wheel.

Twenty-four sailors were asleep in their bunks, unaware of the horror unfolding around them. The barracks stood near the middle of the compound surrounded by the same mahogany trees that encompassed the entire naval station. Either the engineers had been too lazy or the defense department too cheap to clear out the hardwoods. The ammunition storage depot was never envisioned to be a battlefield.

That was a mistake.

A single guard stood outside the barracks entrance, his line of sight to the rest of the compound blocked by the tall trees around him. His mind was wandering and his hands occupied with lighting another cigarette. He heard the faintest noise, like the crush of leaves beneath a distant shoe. He turned just in time to see the tall Senegalese race past him, so close he could smell his musky sweat. Ignoring the sting beneath his chin, the guard turned and reached for his holster, but his hand froze when he saw the blade in the mercenary's hand and the ribbon of blood trailing off its razored edge. The guard reached for the burn on his neck, but all his fingers found was the gusher of blood pouring from his opened throat.

The last thing the guard saw before his eyes blacked out was the smiling Senegalese standing within arm's reach, wiping the bloody blade on his trousers.

The Senegalese holstered his knife as the Indian's eyes rolled back into his head, but the wiry mercenary caught the dead man in his arms before he hit the ground. He quietly set the corpse in the dirt a few meters away from the door as the other five mercs stormed silently up to the barracks and stacked by the entrance, their silenced short-barreled rifles at the ready.

The lead soldier gave a hand signal, pulled the barracks door open, and charged in, the others hot on his heels.

The Senegalese ran back to the door to guard their six. Just as he arrived on station he heard the muffled stutter of silenced automatic weapons firing in controlled bursts inside the building. A few startled shouts were cut short.

A dozen heavy feet raced through the wet leaves in the forest beyond the barracks compound. The Senegalese turned. His enhanced eyesight caught a glimpse of three Malinois hunting in the woods, running at full tilt, chasing prey.

32

The burly Egyptian mercenary grabbed the dead chief petty officer out of the Polaris and hauled him by his pants belt like an old valise to Salan, who was standing by the large warehouse door. Another merc leaped into the Polaris and stashed it between two buildings to get it out of sight.

Salan tore off Singh's turban and grabbed a fistful of his long hair, lifting his face up. He pried open Singh's right eyelid and motioned for the Egyptian to move the corpse closer to the retinal reader. The red flashing light didn't change. Salan pressed his fingers around Singh's eyeball more firmly, causing it to bulge out.

The red flashing light switched to green and the giant rolling door rumbled open on its massive ball bearing tracks.

As soon as the door cleared a few feet, Salan knelt down and dashed into the warehouse, followed by three other mercs, including the Egyptian, who hauled the corpse inside with him and tossed it to the floor.

Salan found everything inside exactly as his scout had described it, and just as he remembered it from the secretive drone footage she had managed to capture.

Salan checked his watch as he opened his comms to his entire team.

'Departure in seven minutes, twenty-nine seconds. Confirm.'

Twelve voices responded. 'Confirmed.'

The bearded Bulgarian mercenary, a former dock-worker, scrambled up the ladder and into the cab of the big Toyota forklift and fired up the engine. Capable of lifting ninety-five thousand pounds, the heavy-duty Loaded Container Handler could stack standard forty-foot shipping containers up to six high. Normally used at ports, it was the perfect machine for this particular warehouse. There were twenty-four such containers inside the facility, neatly stacked in four rows, each six high.

And inside of each specialized forty-foot container was a hypersonic missile.

The reengineered weapons were loaded inside their own containerized launch systems, which meant they could be both transported and launched from any ship deck or truck bed, hidden in plain sight.

'That one,' Salan said as he pointed at the topmost container of the nearest row, the easiest to get. The Bulgarian acknowledged on his comms and hit the throttle. The giant tires squealed on the slick cement floor as it lurched forward, filling the air with the acrid stench of burnt diesel.

Salan's watch alarmed in his earpiece. The helicopter would be arriving in five minutes. While his warehouse team was securing their prize, the others around the compound would be hiding bodies and covering their tracks in preparation for departure.

The giant Toyota's gripping device latched onto the four top corner castings of the missile's container and lifted it with ease. The Bulgarian deftly maneuvered the massive vehicle and its heavy payload away from the stack, and gently set the container on the concrete with hardly a sound.

Salan raced over to the container with a mustachioed Turk, a former weapons officer in the Turkish Navy who lost his commission after killing a fellow officer in a vicious barroom brawl.

The Turk removed a pocket-sized device and held it up to the electronic door lock that bolted the container shut. The scanner broadcast a spectrum of impulses. When it landed on the correct one, the two container doors opened automatically, revealing the contents inside.

Salan grinned ear to ear. 'Exactly what we came for, gentlemen.'

He was staring at India's latest hypersonic missile, the BrahMos-NGv2. The latest joint Indian–Russian weapon was a one-shot ship killer, possessing virtually the same ballistic characteristics as Russia's battle-proven Zircon hypersonic missile. The primary difference between them was that the solid-fueled BrahMos was somewhat smaller and completely self-contained, including its launch platform. The BrahMos also deployed a wide variety of targeting options: optical, laser-guided, and satellite coordinates.

The Turk dashed inside the close confines of the missile container. He ran his hands over the weapon's smooth skin, quickly assessed the visible component parts, and checked the readiness tags. He used a small electric screwdriver to open up the main access panel and point his LED flashlight inside. Finally, he removed the portable launch station – essentially, a ruggedized laptop with dedicated software – bracketed to the wall and inspected it.

Salan heard the heavy chop of helicopter blades beating the air in the distance. Time was nearly up. 'Is the missile ready for launch?'

'Fueled, fully energized, and' – the Turk held up the launch station with a grin – 'ready for launch.'

'Close her up.'

The Bulgarian set a second container down on the floor near the first one. The Turk dashed over to repeat his procedure.

'You've got two minutes. Hurry!'

'Yes, sir.'

'Acknowledged,' the pilot said over the thundering roar of his heavy-lift Mi-26 'Halo' helicopter. Salan had just given the order to land.

He turned to his copilot. 'We're going in.'

'Yes, sir.'

'Anti-aircraft radar?'

'Still clear.'

Salan's Russian-built Halo was a helicopter model that was also in service with the Indian military, and the nearby Kadamba naval base – home to India's only aircraft carrier and one of the largest naval bases in the region – was a constant hub of activity. The rotor noise of yet another helicopter even at this hour of the early morning wouldn't capture anyone's attention.

Most important of all, the copilot had taken the extra precaution of broadcasting a fake international friend-or-foe (IFF) signal, falsely indicating that it was an aircraft in Indian military service. For such a large and ungainly piece of equipment, the Halo was operating in a virtual stealth mode.

The aircraft was designed for transporting heavy military vehicles up to twenty metric tons, including ballistic missiles. Today's lift of two containerized BrahMos anti-ship missiles was well within its lift capacity, and there was ample space in the large storage cabin for Salan's team and their equipment.

Timing was everything. Salan was confident in his plan, but any unnecessary delay only increased the possibility of detection and, ultimately, destruction.

'Allez! Allez! Allez!' he shouted in his comms as men and dogs raced from around the compound and toward the giant helicopter, now set down on the concrete perimeter road. The pilot kept the big engines warm and the eight-bladed heavy-lift rotor slowly turning.

Four of Salan's fighters scrambled to the top of the stacked BrahMos launch containers and affixed cables to the top corner castings of the uppermost one. The top container was attached to the bottom one with ultra-secure twist locks, lashing rods, and wires. The specialized mil-spec containers were now practically welded together.

While the four mercs attached the cables, the female drone scout and the other fighters leaped through the Halo's cabin door. The dogs with their bloodied muzzles and gore-spattered coats and feet became instantly calmer after they were deactivated by Salan. They were also far more compliant, and took to their kennels without protest.

Two minutes after it landed, Salan boarded the Russian-built helo and gave the thumbs-up. The turboshaft engines roared to life, shaking the airframe with each increasing revolution. Moments later, the giant rotor lifted the chopper into the air, the cables tightened, and the BrahMos containers rose steadily into the early-morning sky.

33

Juan knew it was a long shot, but it was the only shot they had to find Asher Massala. Still, trying to locate one man in a slum crowded with as many as a million people in an area just one and a half square miles was a daunting challenge. He had a better chance of picking up a winning lottery ticket accidentally dropped during a New York ticker tape parade. But his job wasn't to play it safe or kvetch about the difficulty.

Like the SAS motto says, he reminded himself: *Who dares wins.*

Cabrillo had been right to be concerned when he overheard Gomez Adams talking to one of his hangar apes about a problem with the AW tilt-rotor. There had been a loss of pressure in one of the hydraulic lines. A pilot with lesser skill would have shown concern while in flight, but Adams, a former spec ops pilot, was unflappable. The hydraulic problem meant the high-tech aircraft needed both an immediate repair and a comprehensive safety inspection. All of that added up to Juan chartering a private jet to fly them from Kuwait City to Nairobi, Kenya.

They touched down at Wilson Airport, a much smaller affair than the bustling Jomo Kenyatta International. It was the kind of airport where passengers still boarded from the tarmac, and the food service court was a couple of vending machines. The less-trafficked aerodrome was a favorite for safari charter flights, Christian missions, and even UN food relief. With its three-story, blue-roofed control tower and hand-painted hangar murals, Wilson was also far more charming than Jomo. It was also closer to Nairobi's city center.

Wilson Airport also lived up to its reputation of being less fussy about customs inspections and passport control, especially for expensive private jets. Juan and Sarai each checked through one piece of fashionable Tumi luggage, neither of which merited an inspection by the customs agent, an attractive young woman specifically assigned to the new private terminal. As Juan had experienced all over the world, the wealthy were often granted privileges that were neither merited nor wise. He had counted on as much today.

'How long will you be staying with us, sir?' the customs officer asked.

'A day or two,' Juan replied. 'Maybe three.' He was dressed in faded designer jeans, a rumpled polo shirt, and weathered New Balance running shoes – the unofficial uniform of millionaire playboys trying to camouflage their wealth. Sarai also wore a stylish top-label but dressed-down outfit, courtesy of Kevin Nixon's expansive wardrobe closet and his nimble tailor's fingers.

'Business or pleasure?'

'Pleasurable business,' Juan said with a jaunty wink. The customs agent shot a glance at beautiful Sarai.

'Indeed, sir.'

'And a safari.'

'Always a good idea when visiting Kenya.'

'Can you arrange for our luggage to be delivered to our hotel?' Juan asked as he slid the luxury resort's business card across the counter.

'Of course.' The attendant returned their passports and they made their way through the duty-free shop to the taxi station just beyond the departure gate and climbed into the next taxi van in the queue.

'Where to, sir?' the blue-vested cabbie asked in a richly resonant baritone voice so common among African men. He smiled broadly from the front seat.

'To Kibera.'

The cabbie's smile disappeared.

'Kibera is a *slum*.' The cabbie emphasized the last word with a finger pressed into his palm. 'Very bad.'

'Yes, I'm well aware. Take us there, please.'

'Are you certain?'

'Of course.'

The cabbie turned around. 'Sir?'

'Is there a problem?'

The cabbie looked Juan up and down, his face betraying his thoughts. *You're crazy.*

'Have you ever been to Kibera, sir?'

'No, can't say that I have.'

'Those people in Kibera, they are cursed by God – and devils!'

'I wouldn't know about that.'

But in fact, Juan did. In a way, they were cursed. On the flight over, Juan had read up on the plight of Kibera's slum dwellers. They were mostly poor rural folk escaping the collapsing economy of the hinterlands in search of sustainable work in the city. Like most of the undeveloped world, Kenya was rapidly urbanizing, and its capital city of Nairobi was bursting at the seams with desperate people trying to find a way to survive. Out of Nairobi's nearly five million residents, almost two-thirds lived in some kind of slum.

The problem was that unskilled, uneducated rural laborers could only find menial work in the city – salaried positions with benefits were nearly impossible to find – so migrants could only afford to live in slums like Kibera. But once they arrived in Kibera they couldn't escape. Every aspect of their lives cost them money, from the poor-quality water they drank to the public 'toilets' they used – hardly more than sheets of metal for a moment of relative privacy, for which they were charged handsomely. Even shower facilities – another sheet of tin – had to be rented, and hot water paid for with their hard-earned money.

Most families lived in single-room shacks of corrugated tin no more than three by three meters in size. These shacks were unheated, uncooled, and had no running water or bathroom facilities. Families froze in the winter and boiled in the summer, and each morning before dawn, hundreds of thousands of residents – mostly men – left their shantytown to tramp for miles into the city to clean and cook and serve the middle and upper classes, who largely pretended places like Kibera didn't exist at all.

The most maddening thing, Juan thought, was that technically no one owned anything in Kibera because it was all government land. And yet, rents were collected and evictions ruthlessly enforced. Though no official government building codes existed, no renter was allowed to build anything more, or fix or improve their rental properties. Low-level thugs collected fees, rents, and dues. And according to at least one study Juan had read, most of that money eventually found its way back into the pockets of the corrupt politicians, who perpetuated the endless cycle of poverty. *Not much different than some Western governments*, Juan had thought as he scrolled through a research paper.

Even well-meaning aid organizations that sent funds to help places like Kibera only served to line the pockets of the crooked bureaucrats, who skimmed the money and used whatever else was left to build housing for themselves or their cronies.

'Kibera is dangerous, especially for a white man,' the driver said. He glanced at Sarai, then back to Juan. 'And for pretty ladies. What is your business there?'

'I'm trying to find a friend.'

'If you want drugs, guns, a prostitute – these I can get you safely. No need for Kibera.'

'Nothing like that,' Juan insisted. 'Just looking for a friend. Seriously.'

'My brother, actually,' Sarai said. 'And he's not cursed.'

'Then call him, and have him come find you at your hotel. Where are you staying?'

Juan pulled out his wallet and handed the cabbie a wad of Kenyan shilling notes – ten thousand in total, less than ninety American dollars. It was far more than the cab ride would cost. The *Oregon* kept a wide variety of hard foreign currencies stored away for emergency trips like this one. He didn't want to do a currency exchange even for a small amount at the airport for fear of triggering some kind of alert with a government agency.

The cabbie took the money glumly, like a Judas, and stuffed it in his shirt pocket.

'As you wish.'

Nairobi's relatively clean and modern streets rapidly deteriorated into depressing urban decay within minutes of their departure from the airport.

The cabbie explained that he was not allowed by his company to drive into Kibera directly, but Juan suspected he wasn't telling the truth. Instead, the driver dropped them off at Kenyatta Market, which was just beyond Kibera. He gave them walking directions to reach the infamous slum, but Juan already had coordinates plugged into the map app on his phone.

Juan thanked the cabbie for his troubles with another thousand-shilling note and a wave of his hand. The cabbie shook his head forlornly, made the sign of the cross, and wished them both luck before he drove away.

Sarai and Juan made their way through the gate and into the sprawling Kenyatta Market, about a twenty-minute walk northeast of Kibera proper. The market was an endless series of vendor stalls, most of them open-air, but covered with plastic tarps or corrugated sheet metal. Everything was available for a price, from cheap Chinese-imported tools to knockoff designer watches. Colorful fruits and vegetables were common fare. Butcheries displayed fresh-caught fish and meats, but they were usually unrefrigerated and often covered in flies. At times Juan caught a whiff of fried sweet plantains or roasted chicken in between the clouds of engine exhaust and cigarette smoke. The cement pavers beneath their feet faded away to dirt paths the farther they got away from the main entrance.

It was like every other Third World outdoor market Juan had ever seen, and how markets had been organized all over the world for millennia. American-style grocery stores were far more sanitary, but hardly more convenient, and far too costly to either build or maintain for a nation with an average annual income of six hundred US dollars – and less than half of that in the slums. The deeper they got into the market, the shabbier it became, and its offerings bleaker.

The two of them finally passed through the crowded market and into the squalid, crowded streets beyond as they followed the GPS coordinates Murphy had forwarded to Juan's phone. They faced crumbling cement block buildings, corrugated shanties, handcarts laden with discarded junk, shoeless children with dirty faces. It was a clichéd Third World postcard addressed from the far side of Hell.

And this still wasn't Kibera.

They headed southwest on a circuitous route until they reached a rank of public housing units displaying a banner proudly proclaiming it was a joint effort by a local government entity and an international development agency. Despite recent construction, they were as grim and artless as a Soviet post office. According to Juan's map there was, incredibly, a golf course just a three-wood shot away.

The public housing stood as a kind of border wall against

what lay behind it – Kibera, an island of even deeper poverty and squalor. It seemed as if the wealthier residents of Nairobi were trying to protect themselves from whatever 'curse' lurked in Kibera by throwing a wall of lesser squalor and despair around it. And yet, the city of Nairobi was utterly dependent upon its slum dwellers, a cruel kind of colonization by the rich Kenyans of the poorer ones, a pattern repeated throughout the continent.

Juan and Sarai made their way past the public housing complex and through the Lainia Saba entrance of Kibera. Juan had been in some of the dirtiest and poorest cities on the planet. He had a feeling that none of those places held a candle to what he was about to experience.

34

The streets – unmarked and unnamed – were actually just well-trod paths of dirt meandering between acres of corrugated sheet metal buildings butted up against one another. Open ditches drained alongside the road and reeked of human sewage. Barefoot children clad in rags scuttled along the banks sifting through garbage for anything of value that could be traded or sold, which was precious little judging by the meager collections of flotsam in their small hands.

Juan noted Sarai's visceral reaction to the sights and smells. Apparently she had never witnessed anything as tragically grotesque in her childhood in Ethiopia, let alone on the fashion runways of the world.

But it wasn't all bad news. A natural optimist, Juan saw the thinnest of silver linings shimmering in the muck. Despite the squalid conditions, humanity was thriving in its own way. Without a social security net to sustain them, the hardworking residents built their own small businesses, very much like the more established Kenyatta Market.

They also met their own needs. The air was filled with the sounds of hammering, sawing, grinding. Kiosks – *dukas*, in Kiswahili – sold cell phones, cut hair, and tailored clothes. Pots were repaired, knives sharpened, shoes fixed, clothes mended. Even medical services could be had in some of these tiny tin shacks, though of what quality Juan was uncertain. And everywhere there were children and the women who cared for them. Yes, there was indeed life, even in the midst of grinding, relentless poverty.

And everywhere there were empty plastic shopping bags, the bane of modern civilization. The ones not caught on thornbushes or nail heads skittered along like tumbleweeds through the streets. Juan counted hundreds if not thousands of them. Most were empty, many were not. There was no public sanitation or trash service of any kind in Kibera. According to what he had read, the locals who couldn't afford to pay for the privilege of defecating behind a tin door used the 'flying toilets' as needed and tossed them aside. There were plenty of those along the roadside, too.

The other thing Juan noticed as he checked his phone was that he was the only white person around. There had been a couple of English tourists at the entrance to the Kenyatta Market, but here in Kibera he was a real unicorn. It didn't make him nervous to be in the minority, but the cabbie's warning about his outlier status came back to mind.

'Not much farther,' Juan told Sarai as they passed a *duka* where two men were repairing worn moped tires with patches and glue. What Juan didn't see was the third man in the shop, who pulled a cell phone from his pocket and sent a text as they moved past.

Up around the crooked bend in the meandering walking path, three young men shambled into view wearing dirty and faded concert T-shirts, ball caps, mirrored sunglasses, and ripped baggy pants. They were the slum dog version of thugs trying to look like American gangster-rapper types. The effect would have been almost comical save for the length of pipe one of them held behind his thin leg, barely attempting to conceal it. They stood their ground, daring Juan and Sarai to advance farther. The one with the pipe lowered his glasses so that Juan could catch a glimpse of his menacing eyes.

Cabrillo chided himself. On a regular op in a foreign city he would have been running a surveillance detection route, using shop windows and parked car mirrors to catch the reflections of potential assailants who might be tailing him. But here in the slum he wasn't able to do that sort of thing. These local thugs were taking advantage of that disadvantage whether they knew it or not.

Terrain always dictated tactics and Juan immediately changed his to fit the new environment as best he could.

Juan stopped at a *duka* selling used shop tools displayed on a wobbly card table. He casually glanced around and spotted another knot of four young hoodlums approaching them from the other direction.

This was getting interesting.

Cabrillo picked up a rusted Crescent wrench and examined it.

'If you're shopping for my birthday present you're a month too early,' Sarai whispered. 'Or is there something else on your mind?'

'We've made a few friends.'

Juan next picked up a well-used wrecking bar that was apparently forged sometime during the Bronze Age. It had been spray-painted in a garish canary yellow to hide the deep pits and corrosion. The weight felt good in his hands. He set it back down.

'How much?' Juan asked an ancient woman sitting on a rickety folding chair.

She held up four fingers that were as brown and gnarled as oak branches.

Juan wasn't sure if that meant four American dollars or four thousand Kenyan shillings or something in between. He pulled his wallet to yank out a wad of Kenyan paper money, when a man's deep, soft voice interrupted him.

'I could use a construction worker like you at my church.'

Juan turned around. The man stood five foot five at most, but his presence was much larger. His eyes were bright and mischievous and his smile infectious. The flecks of gray in his thinning hair suggested he was older, but he seemed ageless. Unlike anyone else Juan had seen so far, the man wore polyester slacks, a long-sleeve dress shirt, and a clip-on tie.

'Sorry, friend. I'm not a construction worker. Just a tourist.'

The man nodded at the wrecking bar. 'Then you won't be needing that, will you?' He smiled even more broadly and held out his hand. 'My name is Anthony Olunga.'

One of Juan's talents was the ability to judge a person's character in a flash. The minute he laid eyes on Anthony Olunga, he sensed he was dealing with a very special man. He instantly trusted the total stranger.

Juan shoved his wallet in his pocket and shook Olunga's hand. It had a workingman's firm, calloused grip. 'Juan Cabrillo. This is my friend, Sarai Massala.'

Anthony nodded toward her. 'A pleasure to meet you both.'

'Same,' Sarai said.

Juan's eyes fell to the man's clip-on tie.

Olunga caught the look. He smiled, embarrassed, as he fingered the tie. 'My good tie was soiled earlier. All I had was this to wear for tonight's church service.'

'Are you a minister?' Sarai asked.

Olunga shrugged. 'Aren't we all?'

'Well, Reverend, I have to admit, no one has ever accused me of being ecclesiastical,' Juan said. 'Not that that's a good thing necessarily.'

'Please, call me Anthony. And welcome to Kibera, such as it is. How may I be of service to you?'

Juan pulled out his cell phone and showed Olunga the GPS location they sought. Olunga pulled on an old pair of reading glasses from his shirt pocket to see it as Juan expanded the tiny map with his fingers.

'Yes, of course. I know it. That's just a few minutes away.' Olunga slipped the reading glasses to the end of his broad nose. 'But I saw that some young gentlemen outside were impeding your progress.'

'Your eyes are better than mine.'

'Not likely. If you don't mind, I'd be happy to escort you to your destination. But may I be so bold as to ask why you want to visit the Bar Royale? There are better drinking establishments in Kibera, and certainly in Nairobi proper.'

'We're looking for a man who uploaded a photo. This one,' Juan said, flipping to Asher Massala's photo on his phone. 'Would you happen to know him?'

'He's my brother,' Sarai said hopefully. 'His name is Asher Massala.'

'The good shepherd leaves the ninety-nine sheep to find the lost one,' Anthony said.

'My brother is a lost sheep for sure.'

Olunga pushed the readers back up to his eyes and examined the photo closely. 'No, I'm sorry to say I don't recognize him. Who uploaded the photo?'

'A man named Lawrence Abuya uploaded it while at the Bar Royale. I don't suppose there's any chance you know him?'

'No, I'm sorry. But the owner of the bar, Boniface Muguna, will know.' The diminutive African pastor carefully folded his cheap glasses and returned them to his shirt pocket. 'Let me take you to him.'

Juan glanced over at the old lady in the chair. Her face was flinty with frustration at the loss of a sale. Juan pulled his wallet back out and handed her a thousand-shilling note – about eight bucks. 'Sorry for the trouble, ma'am.'

The old lady's eyes sparkled as she flashed Juan a toothless smile.

Anthony Olunga led the way out of the small shaded *duka* and back into the harsh sunlight. Juan saw that the two knots of street thugs had formed into one large group at the end of the road, pacing back and forth like nervous hyenas, blocking their way.

'Nothing to worry about. You're with me,' Olunga assured them. 'But stay close.'

Juan scanned Olunga's slacks and shirt for some kind of holstered weapon, knife, or even a small club, but he saw nothing. Olunga's oversize hands suggested a life of hard labor, but maybe they were boxer's hands as well, Juan thought. There was no telling from where the short-statured African got his confidence, but if it came to blows he would be the shortest man in the melee.

Olunga marched straight up to the boy with the pipe, the tallest of the bunch. Juan and Sarai stood close by as instructed. The other boys immediately circled around them. Juan started picking targets, and tried to concoct a scenario whereby he could save both Anthony and Sarai from the beating that was about to commence.

The tall gangster looked down at the smaller man in front of him, trying to intimidate him. Juan saw the boy's hand tighten around the pipe.

Here we go.

'Is your mother feeling better today, Philemon?' Olunga asked. There was genuine concern in his voice.

'Better? Yes.'

'Then the medicine is working?'

Philemon let slip the smallest of smiles as he nodded. 'Yes, it is. Thank you for getting it for her.'

'I just thank God we found it.'

A walkie-talkie crackled in Philemon's pocket. A distorted voice spoke in Kiswahili. Juan didn't speak the lingo, but he understood the tone. Philemon ignored it.

Olunga turned to another boy. 'Matthew, I haven't heard from your father. Did he take the job?'

Matthew shrugged. 'He did. He said to say thank you if I saw you.'

Olunga smiled. 'I very much doubt that he did, but I thank you for your excellent manners.'

The boy nodded, embarrassed by the attention.

'Let Brother Anthony by,' Philemon finally said, shoving the nearest boys away.

'Please greet your mother for me,' Olunga said to Philemon as he led Juan and Sarai through the parted sea of trouble. The boys dispersed in their wake.

After they turned the corner, Olunga said, 'Don't judge them too harshly. I've known them all since they were small lads. They were good little boys who grew up in a very bad world. But until they return to God, they will remain the devil's servants.'

'They certainly respect you,' Sarai said.

'They know I love them, even if I hate their gang life.' Anthony touched the side of his head. 'Gangster music poisons their minds as badly as the drugs.'

35

An enormous sun was half submerged on the far horizon, casting burnt-orange embers on the breaking waves far below. Despite her stoic countenance, Captain Kim Dudash could hardly contain her existential joy as she stood high above the sea behind the slanted glass of the towering command bridge.

In her wildest dreams as a young naval aviation officer she never imagined herself as the commander of the world's largest and most technologically advanced aircraft carrier. The *Gerald R. Ford* was also America's newest carrier and the most formidable weapon in her naval arsenal. A mathematics graduate of MIT, she was one of the first female aviators to fly the E2-C Hawkeyes in the 1990s. A naturally gifted pilot and leader, she rose quickly through the command ranks, and earned multiple combat and unit citations along the way.

The Navy had allowed her to rise as fast as her enormous talents could take her. Now she stood on the command bridge watching an E2-D Advanced Hawkeye catapult off the deck and climb into the sky for a night patrol. She could practically feel the plane's yoke in her hands and the vibration of the twin Rolls-Royce turboprops as the plane clawed upward. The giant roto-dome above the airframe – she always thought it looked like her grandmother's coffee table – provided nearly god-like vision over the battlescape, providing early warning against enemy vessels, aircraft, and anti-ship missiles.

The Hawkeye was just one of dozens of offensive and defensive systems that made the *Gerald R. Ford* the most powerful naval vessel in history, and the *Ford* was the cen-terpiece of a carrier strike group – the epitome of American power projection. The *Ford* strike group was comprised of several escort vessels, including a Ticonderoga-class missile cruiser and two Arleigh Burke-class destroyers. Two of the Navy's latest Virginia-class fast attack submarines shad-owed the armada beneath the waves.

The *Ford*'s true power-projection capability lay with its nearly ninety manned and unmanned aircraft, including America's most advanced fighter, the F-35C Lightning II.

Captain Dudash knew full well the weight of responsi-bility she bore as commander of the vessel. The Iranian-backed Houthis had renewed their attacks on Red Sea shipping again by laying seaborne mines, firing mis-siles, and dispatching gunboats, all of which were of Iranian manufacture or procurement. The multinational task force had been unable to stop the Houthi attacks, and Washington finally decided to send a powerful message to all of the players in the region. It was one thing to take potshots at a Panamanian-flagged freighter, but something else altogether to take on an invincible nuclear-powered aircraft carrier.

Gerald R. Ford's power-projection capability didn't just lie within its vast weapons arsenal. The perception of invulnerability was as important as any missile or aircraft on board. Any regional threat to stability could be quickly smashed by the carrier's aircraft and cruise missiles, but the fact that no enemy could touch her meant she was always free to do so. So long as her ship remained invulnerable, Captain Dudash could bring power – and thus peace – to bear.

Dudash raised her binoculars to her eyes, tracking the Hawkeye as it banked away, the last orange rays of the sun painting her gray belly. The Hawkeye's sensors were already feeding into the ship's computers and its own vast array of surveillance radars and sensors. Nothing in the area posed a threat.

Nothing could touch them.

36

A few minutes later Juan, Sarai, and Anthony Olunga arrived at the Bar Royale.

To Juan it appeared as neither a traditional bar nor 'royale.' It was another shanty *duka* about double the size of the tool store where they had been. Faded silver and blue tarps hung from the tin walls as a kind of decoration, but they only served to make the cramped space even hotter and nastier than it was outside. A couple of cheap circular fans whirred and clanged on the long crude plywood tables, where several disheveled men drank clear liquid out of dirty glasses.

Three men glanced up, blinking with unfocused eyes, when Juan and company darkened the doorway. The others were lost in their cups. Juan had been in some pretty bad dive bars over the years, but this one was the most pathetic he'd ever seen.

'They're drinking *changaa*,' Anthony offered. 'A very potent local brew. It's all a poor man can afford.'

A barrel-bellied man came in from behind a thin curtain. A three-day growth of stubble framed his round, unsmiling face. His eyebrows knitted furiously when he saw Juan and Sarai, but he softened at the sight of Anthony.

The African holy man greeted the bartender in friendly Kiswahili and he smiled in return. Anthony switched to English, Kenya's official language.

'Boniface, my two friends here are looking for someone. Perhaps you can help them.'

The bartender shrugged as he pulled out two glasses. '*Changaa?*' he asked.

'No, but thanks. I'm driving,' Juan said. He threw a thumb at Sarai. 'And she's pregnant.'

Sarai stifled a laugh.

The bartender harrumphed his displeasure at the loss of a sale. 'Who are you looking for?'

'Lawrence Abuya,' Juan said.

The bartender scowled. 'What do you want with him?'

Juan stepped closer with his phone. 'Lawrence Abuya uploaded the photo of this man several weeks ago from this location. I'd like to talk to him about it.'

'Lawrence is dead.' He pointed at the street. 'Killed by the police not three meters from that door a month ago.'

'I'm sorry to hear that.'

'Don't be. He was a thief and a drunkard. A real gangster.'

'Then God have mercy on his soul,' Anthony said.

Sarai stepped closer. 'Do you know the man in the picture? He's my brother. His name is Asher Massala.'

The bartender took Juan's phone from his hand. He studied it for a long time.

Too long, Juan thought. He was trying to decide what to say.

'No. I don't know him, and I've never seen him.'

'Are you sure?' Juan asked.

'Are you calling me a liar?' The bartender's voice sharpened.

The barflies behind them suddenly perked up.

'No, sir,' Sarai said. 'We're just very worried about my brother.'

The bartender gave Sarai a lascivious look-over, then locked eyes with Juan.

'It's good that you are friends with Brother Anthony. Good luck on your search.'

Brother Anthony, Juan, and Sarai stood outside the Bar Royale. A stream of women and their children paraded by. Most of them cast a furtive glance at the tall white man and the elegant Ethiopian-born Israeli woman at his side.

'Any ideas where we can look for Asher?' Juan asked Anthony.

'He's been missing for some time,' Sarai added. 'My father is very worried.'

'If your brother was a friend of Lawrence Abuya, and if Abuya was a gangster, then it stands to reason your brother was involved in a gang, I'm sorry to say.'

Sarai nodded grimly.

'I know a dear brother who was saved out of that life. Perhaps he knows something. Let me take you to him.'

'We'd be grateful,' Juan said. 'Lead the way.'

The journey to the next stop took longer than Juan cared for, but he understood the reason why. It seemed that half of Kibera knew Brother Anthony, a revered figure. They asked him for prayers, advice, and ways to access food, medicine, and even fuel. He denied no one, and treated each as if they were Kenyan royalty. More than one person told Juan and Sarai that Anthony was 'a holy man, in word and deed,' which only confirmed Juan's initial impression of him.

They finally arrived at a two-story corrugated tin building. A giant yellow sign read *Bible Institute for Pastors & Ministry Leaders*. Inside, Juan saw a hard-packed dirt floor and dozens of student desks lined in neat rows.

Brother Anthony beamed with pride. 'I graduated from here myself. The school serves the poor working clergy in Kibera, teaching the true words of the gospel and how to live them out with integrity.'

'That's hard enough to do where I come from,' Juan said. 'It must be a greater challenge here.'

'You in the West have your own challenges. But with God, all things are possible.' Anthony beamed. 'We're changing Kibera, one soul at a time.' Suddenly he saw the man he was looking for in the distance, a janitor carrying a simple, rough-hewn toolbox with a dowel for a handle. Anthony gave him a shout in Kiswahili and a great smile. The janitor smiled back and hobbled over.

When the man got closer, Juan saw his silver-stubbled face was scarred with a puckered knife wound poorly sewn, and burn marks on both hands, one of which was missing two fingers. Despite his apparent infirmities, Juan could tell by the way he carried himself that he was still dangerous in a fight. Anthony embraced the older man warmly.

'Brother Patrick, these are my new friends, Juan and Sarai.'

Patrick set his toolbox down, bowed slightly, and smiled. 'It's always a pleasure to meet new friends.'

Juan nodded in deference. 'A pleasure, sir.'

Patrick turned to Anthony. 'How may I serve you, brother?'

'My friends are looking for Sarai's lost brother. We have just learned that he was in the company of a man named Lawrence Abuya, who was recently killed.'

Patrick nodded solemnly. 'I knew him. He ran with the Cool Boys. They were working for the Russians here in Kibera and in Nairobi proper. A very bad lot, those.'

'Perhaps you knew my brother?' Sarai pulled out her phone and showed him Asher's photo.

Patrick's sharp eyes narrowed. 'Yes, yes. I met that boy. His name is . . . Duke Matasi. I remember him because he had a Kenyan name, but a foreign accent in Kiswahili and English.'

'Is there anything else you can tell me about him?' Sarai asked.

Patrick smiled pityingly. He turned to Anthony for guidance.

'Tell her the truth, brother,' Anthony told him. 'The truth always sets us free.'

Patrick nodded. 'He was running with the Russians, too. There was a chop shop on the far side of Kibera – a place where the cops never came. Except about seven weeks ago they did. Arrested all of them, including your brother.'

'Where is he now?'

'Last I heard, he is serving time in Kamiti, a maximum-security prison.'

'That's both good news and bad,' Anthony said.
'What's the good news?' Juan asked.
'You can drive there from here in about forty minutes.'
'And the bad news?' Sarai asked.
'It's hell on earth.'

37

On Board the Cloud Fortune
The Arabian Sea

Jean-Paul Salan stood on the bridgewing of the container vessel, admiring the enormous full moon looming in the starry sky. The warm night air ran its fingers through his long hair and cooled his skin. The enormous deck below him was stacked high with colored steel containers. His eyes fell on one in particular.

Hidden among them in plain sight was the forty-foot-long BrahMos launch container with its ship-killing hypersonic missile inside. Salan had his men paint a verifiable corporate logo on it along with an alphanumeric container number, a check digit, an ISO code, and operational markings for weight and volume. He also had a *Convention of Safe Containers* plate affixed to the lower left-hand side of the left door. Even to trained eyes the container appeared to be official.

There was virtually no chance of any kind of inspector coming on board the Korean-designed, Romanian-built vessel. It was even less likely that long-range cameras or drones might be used to record container information.

But Salan had survived his dangerous life and kept his mercenary organization largely secret by anticipating unlikely and inconceivable probabilities.

As per his Saudi employer's instructions, the other missile and its container had been delivered to the *Avatar*, the vessel of a high-ranking Iranian government official. Whether or not the Iranians had been as cautious as he in its transport didn't concern him. Salan's only responsibility now was to deliver the missile in his possession to Yemen and launch it on command.

Salan cupped his hands against the breeze to light a cigarette with his favorite Zippo lighter. He was quite pleased with how well his twelve men and six dogs had performed during the Vajrakosh naval base operation. Both their physical and behavioral conditioning had proven to be exceptional. If he had been required to deploy ordinary mercenaries, he would have needed a force at least three times as large and would have suffered both heavy casualties and detection, resulting in a less than fifty percent chance of success.

He took a long drag on his oily Gauloises and held it deep in his lungs, thinking. His Saudi employer, Prince Khalid, was ecstatic with the news that both hypersonic missiles had been successfully stolen, and the first had already been delivered to the Iranians. He was especially pleased that the second missile was on track for delivery to Yemen.

Salan slowly released the smoke from his mouth and watched it whisk away in the sea breeze. His eyes returned to the BrahMos launch container. The remarkable Russian-designed weapon was the most effective hypersonic missile in the world and, in fact, the only combat-tested and proven design of its kind. The cost to produce the ship-killing missile was a fraction of the money Prince Khalid was paying Salan to carry out his plan, but the role it would play was priceless to the Saudi royal.

Salan took another drag. The one part of the plan he never cared for was the Iranian connection. To steal the missile was a feat unto itself. Despite the supposed international arms embargo, patrol ships, and even pirates operating in the region, Salan was confident he could transport his cargo to Yemen. The truly problematic part of the plan was transporting the missile *into* Yemen in the middle of a civil war.

Given the fact the missile could be launched from anywhere, including the deck of the *Cloud Fortune*, Salan had urged his employer to avoid the unnecessary risk of smuggling it into Yemen.

But according to the Saudi prince, the whole plan hinged on the firing location deep within Houthi territory. It was vital the Americans believed the missile had been a Houthi-sponsored attack. The Iranian-backed Houthis were happy to accept this arrangement; they viewed the Saudis as American puppets and relished the opportunity to strike out at the Great Satan.

Because they had been warring against them for years, nobody would ever suspect a Saudi would be behind a Houthi attack. A launch from Houthi territory would also give the Iranians an argument for plausible deniability in the international community. It was thin cover, for sure, but the arrangement had invariably served Iran's diplomatic purpose in previous missile attacks.

There was one other advantage to the Yemen strategy, according to Salan's employer. The Houthis had launched several devastating missile attacks into Saudi Arabia over the years, hitting air bases and oil infrastructure facilities. With any luck, the Americans would respond to the attack by blasting the miserable Houthi rebels off the peninsula.

This would solve an intractable Saudi problem. The Saudi war against the Houthis had gone on far too long and was far too expensive. The so-called civil war was actually a proxy war between the regional powers, but it was the Yemeni people who had suffered three hundred and seventy thousand deaths, more than half of those from hunger and disease. The war was now considered the world's worst humanitarian crisis. The only way to cleanse Saudi guilt was to end the war as quickly as possible – something the Saudis had been unable to achieve – and sweep the entire affair into the trash bin of forgotten history.

After all, who remembers the Armenians?

Unfortunately, smuggling the missile deep into war-torn Houthi territory meant working with an escort from the Iranian Quds Force. Salan had dealt with them before. They were extraordinarily motivated and talented, a rare combination among the fanatics. But they also had long memories, and Salan had dropped more than a few of them with his long-range rifle scope in previous jobs over the years. He was almost certain they knew that, though his trusted sources told him he was not under suspicion – at least for this mission.

The greater problem was the Quds organization itself. Salan believed Khalid erred by informing the Iranians of his plan. He simply couldn't imagine the Iranians not taking a shot at stealing it. But with the other hypersonic missile now safely in their possession the temptation to steal Khalid's would blunt their instincts. No doubt the Iranians would begin reverse engineering it as soon as they got it to port.

Did that mean he could fully trust them?

Hardly. But he absolutely needed the Iranians to guide him to his launch destination. He would need to brief his men one more time on the situation and to remind them to keep alert. But he also had one other means to protect the mission. A means the Iranians wouldn't care for. Salan inhaled the smoke deeply, drawing the cigarette down to a smoldering nub. He held his breath and flicked the butt into the wind, and watched it disappear into the night behind him. He finally exhaled his smoky breath through a smile.

The Iranians wouldn't know what hit them.

38

Nairobi, Kenya

Juan saw the shock on Sarai's face when she learned that her brother was in a prison described by Brother Anthony as 'hell on earth.' He wanted to get her out of the Kibera slum and back into some kind of semblance of normalcy. He also needed to find a way into the maximum-security prison. Anthony and Patrick insisted on escorting the two of them out of Kibera and to the nearest taxi station. Juan and Sarai both thanked the gentlemen. Cabrillo slipped a large wad of cash into Anthony's hands as they shook goodbye.

'You don't need to pay me anything,' Anthony insisted.

'I know you'll spend it on the people who need it,' Juan said. 'Please don't deny a sinner the chance to earn a little credit with the man upstairs, okay?'

Anthony smiled. 'I will pray for Sarai's brother, and for the two of you. Godspeed, Mr Cabrillo.'

'Thanks. We can use all the help we can get.'

Juan appreciated any divine intervention he might receive from Brother Anthony's prayers, but his Catholic grand-father had taught him that God helps those who help themselves. That had worked out pretty well in the past, considering the number of close calls he'd had over the years, a missing limb notwithstanding.

Cabrillo's work brought him into contact with all manner of killers, terrorists, and other violent threats he encountered in the air, on land, and at sea. He and his crew had a long history of overcoming those challenges with superior tactical skills and kinetic force.

But the most intractable obstacles he usually faced everywhere on the planet were the self-serving government bureaucrats and inviolate standard operating procedures of their sclerotic institutions. As much as he would like to take a bazooka or a chain saw to the inevitable bureaucratic stone walls and red tape he encountered, he found his best recourse was always to call in his secret weapon: Langston Overholt IV.

Juan formulated his plan on the walk out of Kibera and by the time he climbed into the taxi he was already texting Overholt. He briefed him on his plan and Overholt agreed to play his part.

Sarai's mood had grown increasingly morose over the last several minutes, no doubt because she was contemplating the fate of her brother imprisoned in one of the most horrific penitentiaries on the African continent. Her mood brightened somewhat when the taxi pulled into a treed compound comprised of luxury villas located near the American embassy. They checked in at the front desk without incident and were escorted to their villa.

The bellman informed them that their luggage had already been delivered and a basket of fruit and wine had been set out for them. This courtesy plus his assurance of absolute privacy secured the man a generous tip.

Juan pointed out Sarai's private en suite on the far side of the premium accommodation. He suggested she shower and change clothes, and that they could either order room service or go to the resort's five-star restaurant for a good meal. She nodded her thanks as she shut the door behind her.

The villa's sleek, ultra-modern aesthetic was perfectly blended with thoughtful Kenyan themes and high-tech appliances, but it was the giant, multi-headed tiled shower that interested Juan the most. The villa was the very antithesis of the corrugated shacks and open sewage of Kibera not twenty minutes away by car. Whatever guilt Juan felt about the hotel resort he compartmentalized away so that he could enjoy it. But there was still work to do.

Before his shower, Juan called the *Oregon*'s bogus documents department. He ordered up a set of journalists' credentials for them both. He also requested a couple of fake social media accounts and AI-manufactured posts with text histories validating their stellar journalistic careers as cheerleaders for African development and social reform. Several of their manufactured journal articles praised the current Kenyan government and its authoritarian President as role models for the rest of the continent.

Cabrillo knew that even at this moment, Overholt was reaching out to the CIA station chief, who owed her career to the guidance and protection of the octogenarian spymaster. The *Oregon* would email the bogus documents to the CIA chief who, in turn, would have everything printed out and ready for Juan and Sarai by tomorrow morning.

The chief of station would also contact the embassy's senior career diplomat, who had excellent relations with the Ministry of Interior and Coordination of National Government, which had ultimate authority over the Kenya Prisons Service. The embassy would assure safe passage for the two 'journalists' seeking updates on the 'magnificent reform work' underway at the Kamiti Maximum Security Prison, and would reference a potential grant to support continued upgrades to the facility.

After the wheels had all been set in motion, Juan stripped down to his birthday suit, pulled off his artificial leg, and cranked up the shower's hot-water spigots to full fire hydrant mode. Leaning on the handicap support bar screwed into the marble tiles, Juan soaped, scrubbed, and sprayed for what seemed like hours. His skin tingled when he was finished and his lungs were full of steamy, cleansing air. He felt completely refreshed and renewed. But even as he toweled off, his mind slipped back to the squalor of the slum and suddenly it felt as if all of that scrubbing hadn't quite gotten rid of Kibera's residue after all.

The next morning, refreshed with a full breakfast and a pot of stout Kenyan coffee, Sarai and Juan took the five-minute taxi ride to the US embassy, met with the chief of station for a short briefing on recent events relating to the Kenyan prison system, picked up their documents, and headed for the infamous Kamiti prison.

They were greeted at the front entrance by a smiling, green-uniformed prison sergeant. He cheerfully escorted them into the administrative center of the prison, where they found the officer in charge, a short, rotund man named Gathiru. Dressed in an olive drab prison officer's uniform and thick glasses, Gathiru had the affable, back-slapping demeanor of a Boston-Irish ward heeler instead of a tough prison administrator.

'Welcome, welcome!' Gathiru said, cranking Juan's arm like a pump handle. 'Please, be seated!'

Juan and Sarai sat in two plush leather chairs opposite Gathiru's expansive mahogany desk. Behind him were dozens of vanity photos of him posing with international sports and entertainment celebrities, Kenyan politicians, and even well-deserving prison trusties dressed in trademark vertical black-and-white prison stripes.

Gathiru offered coffee, tea, and cigarettes, all of which were declined. The prison warden waited for Juan to set up his phone as a recording device before launching into a twenty-minute soliloquy about the great humanitarian advances made in the Kenyan prison system in general and at Kamiti in particular.

After his rehearsed speech, Gathiru led them on a tour of the facility.

Juan took the lead and asked the most questions, giving Sarai ample opportunity to scan the faces of the hundreds of prisoners they encountered on the grounds. Each man was dressed in a clean and seemingly new prison uniform, and the ones who made eye contact smiled broadly and waved. Gathiru made a show of stopping several prisoners and asking how they were getting along, if they had enough food and medical care, recreational opportunities, and so forth. The answers were always gushingly positive.

Gathiru explained that almost all the able-bodied men were working on the prison farms, in the food processing facility, or at one of the prison factories manufacturing children's toys and furniture. He then led them to each of those facilities. Juan and Sarai exchanged several secretive glances; it was clearly all one big dog and pony show. It wasn't surprising, really. What administrator of any organization didn't put on their best for visiting dignitaries? Still, something seemed amiss.

The final leg of the tour was through G Block, where the most hardened criminals were sequestered. In the one rank of cells they visited, there were only as many prisoners in a cell as there were beds, and they also wore clean, new uniforms. Gathiru was as jovial and paternal with these violent felons as he'd been with the petty criminals short-timing outside.

Juan pretended to be deeply interested in Gathiru's theories of prisoner rehabilitation as Sarai scanned the faces of the damned. Some of the looks she received caused her to shudder, but most of the faces were depressed and forlorn, and only brightened when Gathiru came around. The CIA station chief had told them Kamiti was far too overcrowded to be medically or physically safe and that, in fact, they'd experienced a recent outbreak of cholera. Juan had been expecting ten or twenty men to a cell instead of two or four.

Gathiru was smart enough not to linger too long in G Block and ushered his two foreign guests to the cafeteria, where they were feted with fresh vegetables, beef, and chicken harvested from the prison farms.

'Maybe prison farm-to-table cuisine will become a thing,' Juan said, but neither Gathiru nor Sarai caught the joke. Smiling prisoner-waiters explained what the local dishes were in charming Kenyan accents while they served the meal with ice-cold bottles of local Kenyan beer.

Gathiru gave another speech in praise of Kenya's enlightened presidency, the health of the Kenyan economy, and Kenya's bright, crime-free future before walking the two journalists back to his office. He didn't sit down, nor did he gesture for them to take a seat. Instead, he made a show of checking his watch, a stunning Patek Philippe. Clearly, the tour had ended.

'Have I answered all of your questions satisfactorily?' Gathiru asked.

'And then some,' Juan said. 'Your transparency and depth of knowledge is quite refreshing. I believe you'll enjoy the article we'll be preparing.'

'Please be sure to send me a link,' Gathiru said.

'Of course,' Sarai said. 'And to the minister as well.'

'Excellent.'

Juan raised a finger. 'But actually, there is one more favor you could do for us.'

'Name it.'

'We always like to do a human interest angle in our reporting. It makes the story more relatable.'

'I agree,' Gathiru said.

'There is a Kenyan woman living in London who reached out to us. She said that her son is incarcerated here in Kamiti and that she has tried to reach him on several occasions. She's quite worried that something has happened to her boy. The prison has, as I'm sure you're well aware, a reputation for brutality and violence among the prisoners.'

Gathiru's permanent smile suddenly vanished.

'All in the past, as you yourselves have seen today.'

'Of course,' Juan said. 'And that's what will make this story so special. We would love the chance to visit with this prisoner, take a picture of him, and send it to his mother. It would be a beautiful gesture and a great way to summarize visually everything you and your team have accomplished here.'

'I don't see a problem with that,' Gathiru said. 'What is the prisoner's name?'

'Duke Matasi. He was arrested and convicted earlier this year.'

'I don't recognize the name,' Gathiru said without hesitation.

'I'm sorry, but you have over three thousand, four hundred prisoners here. How can you possibly know all of the names?' Sarai asked.

'I know my people. That's my job.'

'Perhaps you can double-check your files? Just to be sure?' Juan said.

Gathiru stiffened. Juan could see the wheels turning behind his eyes, calculating odds, weighing outcomes. He picked up a phone and punched a button. A voice answered on the other end and Gathiru barked a command in Kiswahili along with the name Duke Matasi. A few moments passed, and the voice returned on the other end. Gathiru practically threw the phone back into its cradle.

'As I said, there is no record of a Duke Matasi in our custody, nor has there ever been a Duke Matasi.'

Sarai had taken the opportunity to pull up a picture of Asher on her phone while Gathiru was on his. She showed him her brother's picture.

'Perhaps Duke Matasi was here under another name. Do you recognize this man?'

The warden's eyes narrowed. 'No, I do not. You'll both have to excuse me now, I have other duties to attend to.' He called to a guard standing outside his door. 'Please escort them to the front gate immediately.'

'Yes, sir!'

Juan fished a business card out of his shirt pocket and handed it to Gathiru. 'If you happen to run across him or if you have anything else you'd like to tell us, please don't hesitate to contact me.'

Gathiru glanced at the card and then pocketed it. 'Of course.'

'Thank you for the tour. It was most informative,' Sarai said as she followed Juan and the guard out of the office.

39

On Board the Sekhmet

Lab-coated Heather Hightower had her eyes pinned to a microscope. The mercy ship's big diesel engines thrummed throughout the steel hull like a heartbeat. Named after the Egyptian goddess for healing, the *Sekhmet* had proven to be the perfect cover for Hightower's surreptitious scientific endeavors, many of them illegal.

Operating a mercy ship provided several advantages, not the least of which was that foreign governments were loath to board and inspect a ship providing free health care to the sick and needy. That sort of thing could only lead to bad foreign press and the ire of the international humanitarian community.

On the single occasion when an Egyptian patrol boat insisted on such an inspection, Hightower fitted several of her crew members with surgical gowns and put them into hospital beds affixed with bandages, blood pressure monitors, saline drips, and other nonessential accoutrements. The patients might have been fake, but the high-tech medical equipment, clinical facilities, and highly educated personnel were completely authentic. The suspicious Egyptians fell for the *Sekhmet*'s ruse without question.

The *Sekhmet* also gave Hightower a legitimate reason

to pull into virtually any port in the less developed world. The ship was always enthusiastically received. In fact, the *Sekhmet* had accrued an incredible bank of goodwill over the last few years by visiting the same ports repeatedly.

She and her medical colleagues would dispense vaccines, provide infant wellness checkups, and supply basic vitamin supplements and antibiotics as needed. Smiling children in the arms of their grateful mothers made for excellent publicity photographs with local officials and *Sekhmet* staff. Those goodwill images were instantly uploaded to the *Sekhmet*'s social media account, providing Hightower's floating medical operation both irrefutable virtue signals and political legitimacy worldwide.

Never one to waste a valuable resource, Dr Hightower also used the humanitarian medical treatments to secretly collect DNA samples from interesting human specimens without their knowledge. Spinal deformities, bone torsions, cleft palates, abnormal musculature, and other genetic anomalies were all fascinating data points for her to collect.

She also took the opportunity to inject unsuspecting subjects with new experimental treatments and returned months later to see the results. From a science standpoint, it was always better to conduct clinical trials without the subjects' knowledge, especially if those trials went sideways. Hightower knew that nobody noticed the random deaths of poor people – particularly their own politicians – because they were always dropping like flies.

The ones who survived but developed serious conditions would invariably, and ironically, turn to the *Sekhmet*'s 'mercy angels' for treatment – and secret follow-up analysis of the results.

But useful as all of that was, the primary mission of the *Sekhmet* was to provide a steady stream of conditioned recruits for Jean-Paul Salan's mercenary organization. Poor countries had even poorer prison populations and it was from these she recruited new subjects for her HH+ conditioning program.

The *Sekhmet* selected its ports of call for its mercy medical missions to correspond with the best prison populations to draw from. She had already built a network of cooperative prison wardens she paid handsomely to identify prisoners for the Humane Justice Program (HJP). The nonprofit organization presumably rehabilitated prisoners off campus, helped commute harsh sentences, and acquired free legal representation for indigents. But all of that was really just a cover.

In reality, the HJP bribed wardens to identify prison candidates that fit Hightower's physical and mental criteria who had no known family relations who might inquire as to their whereabouts. After prisoners were transferred into Hightower's custody, wardens were required to destroy any record of them having existed.

The system had worked perfectly so far, and no one had been the wiser. No corrupt government cared about the welfare of its worst citizens. Wardens with crowded prisons were also happy to pocket the per diem stipend the state paid for prisoners they assumed were in jail but who now were no longer there. 'I'm running a prison full of ghosts!' one of them had joked with her.

Cash flow was the least of her problems. Jean-Paul

Salan was paying for all of it. Not only did he pay handsomely for each recruit she successfully conditioned for his mercenary army, he also paid her a percentage of his profits.

All of that money funded her visionary work in genetic research and, ultimately, the human revolution she was engineering, one DNA strand at a time.

Her late husband, Dr Jonathan Hightower, was an early pioneer of clustered regularly interspaced short palindromic repeats – CRISPRs, for short – a technology that made editing human genes as easy as fixing typos in a word processing program. He had taken young Heather, his best graduate student, under his wing and taught her everything he knew about 'hacking biology.' It wasn't long before she surpassed the brilliant researcher, fueled by her commitment to transhumanist philosophy and a vision of a new humanity.

She was utterly consumed with the blood sample in her electron microscope, when the overhead comms chimed with a message from the bridge.

'Dr Hightower, there's a call for you.'

'Who is it?'

'Mr Salan.'

Hightower stood. 'I'll take it in my office.'

'Aye, ma'am.'

Moments later, Hightower cracked open a bottle of Berg iceberg water, fell into her office chair, and punched the speaker button on her phone.

'Jean-Paul, *ça va*?'

'*Ça va mal.* I just got a call from that cretinous prison warden Gathiru.'

'Our man in Nairobi. What did he say?'

'A pair of journalists came around earlier today asking about Duke Matasi.'

'That's strange. What did they want to know?'

'They said they were doing a story about prison reform, and that Matasi's mother had been searching for him.'

'That's not possible. Matasi's file said his mother was dead.'

'Perhaps Matasi lied,' Salan said.

'Why would he lie about a thing like that?'

'Why does anybody lie? Or steal? Or play chess for that matter? People are random. They do what they do.'

'There's always a reason for why people do what they do.'

'You talk like a scientist.'

'And you talk like a nihilist.'

'I can't help it. I'm French.'

Hightower stifled her laugh. 'Either way, I'm sure Gathiru kept his mouth shut, of course. He's paid too well.'

'He said he kept quiet. I believe him. And he assured me they didn't inquire about the Humane Justice Program.'

'So what's the problem?'

'The problem is that they knew to ask about Matasi in the first place.'

'Mistaken identity? Someone else with the same name?'

'They showed Gathiru his picture. No mistake. It was him.'

Hightower's cheeks burned. She was as angry as she was concerned. They'd never even come close to being discovered before.

'Perhaps we should kill Matasi.'

'Why? I paid good money for him, and he's now a valuable asset in my organization.'

'Then he's not my problem, is he?'

'But you are the next stop on the line if those journalists keep snooping around.'

'I'm not concerned. My tracks are covered,' Hightower said.

'Your tracks were covered in Nairobi, too.'

'There's not much I can do then, is there?'

'I'm only calling to give you a heads-up. Have your security watch doubled, and stay alert.'

Hightower's jaw clenched. She didn't like taking orders from anyone, especially a man, and especially an inferior man like Salan.

'You sound paranoid. They're journalists, not special operators.'

'How do you know that?'

Good point, Hightower thought. She hadn't considered the possibility.

'I'll alert my security team.'

'Kamathi captured their images on a CCTV camera. I'll have those forwarded to you. Be sure to contact me if there are any problems.'

She stood, her finger hovering over the off button on the phone.

'Anything else?' Hightower asked.

'Is your next delivery of recruits still on schedule?'

'Of course it is. Why wouldn't it be?'

'Don't get your *culotte* in a wad. I'm just checking.'

'Don't you have better things to do? Aren't you on a mission?'

'I'm in transport at the moment, and I'm a . . . how do you say . . . a multitasker?'

'You sound more agitated than normal. Please tell me you haven't altered your conditioning regimen.'

Jean-Paul Salan lay on an examination table in the container ship's small infirmary. An IV-drip bag full of his own reconditioned blood hung from a stand beside the table, a tube snaking from the drip to a swollen vein in his forearm.

The Franco-Algerian's eyes gleamed with animal energy, and his body tingled all over from the surge of hormones coursing through his body from his enhanced endocrine system.

Hightower's CRISPR technology enabled his body to produce higher levels of testosterone and inhibit myostatin production, both of which contributed to increased muscle mass and aggression. It also increased epinephrine production, which sharpened his senses and oxygenated his blood. But it was the surging endorphins that blocked his pain receptors, elevated his confidence and mood, reduced stress, and made him unreasonably happy.

Salan also knew it was the endorphin rush that made him crave ever-increasing levels of it.

Hightower's voice crackled on his encrypted cell phone speaker.

'You sound more agitated than normal. Please tell me you haven't altered your conditioning regimen.'

'Of course not. You told me not to, and I always listen to my doctor.'

Salan had paid one of Hightower's technicians a great

deal of money to secretly smuggle the new supply to him. Not only was he battling an engineered addiction to both power and pleasure, he was also in an undeclared war against Hightower's monopoly. As soon as Salan's under-cover scientist on board the *Sekhmet* could acquire the technology and expertise, he would build his own labora-tory and cut Hightower out of the equation entirely. Until then, he had to be patient, something he found increas-ingly difficult.

'I don't like the sound of your voice. I'm warning you, Jean-Paul. I've taken you to the utmost limit without put-ting you at risk. If you step over that line, there will be physical consequences. I know it must bother you that you can't keep up with your super soldiers, but you've got to put your ego aside.'

'You don't have to remind me. I'm well aware.' Salan tried to mask the surging rage welling up inside of him. Hightower had only allowed him and his most trusted lieutenants ten percent of the conditioning his mercenary soldiers received. They needed it to stay competitive with the super mercs under their command. Salan also took the conditioning for his own ego. He wasn't getting any younger.

'Just one degree over the line I've set for you and you could be shortening your life by years, even decades. Your mercenaries might be able to outrun and outfight you now, but in two years you'll be standing over their graves.'

'Anything else on your mind?' Salan squeezed his fist and relaxed it, trying to get the IV drip to go faster.

'I know how good it all feels. Trust me. But you'd be

better off licking tabs of acid for a high than ramping up the protocols.'

'Just stay alert. And call me if there's any problem.'

Salan killed the call and closed his eyes, enjoying the rush.

He understood the risks. But all of his life he had pushed beyond the boundaries others set before him. He was well aware the conditioning was dangerous, even addictive. But who could resist being younger, faster, stronger?

Of course, she had agreed not to engage in any mental conditioning herself, despite the increase in focus and mental acuity. But could he trust her? He saw the control they were both able to exercise over his mercs; he harbored no illusions about this beautiful scientist. She would put him on a leash as quickly as he let her. But someday soon, she would be the one tethered to his will.

40

Juan and Sarai took an overnight first-class Qatar Airways flight from Nairobi to Dubai near where the *Oregon* was now anchored. There they would catch a ride from Gomez Adams and the AW back to the ship.

The flight was roomy and luxurious, and gave Juan and Sarai plenty of time both to catch up on some much-needed sleep, but also to review what little they had uncovered on the trip, especially at the Kamiti prison. The only real lead they had generated came from the business card Juan had handed the warden, Gathiru. The card itself had a micro-bug embedded in the fake newspaper logo affixed to it.

'Lucky he put that card in his shirt pocket,' Sarai had said as they both listened to the recording back at the villa. Despite the rustling of the shirt fabric against the microphone, the words were fairly clear, even from the other end of the call. Juan forwarded the recording to Murphy and Stone to clean up.

'I made the subliminal suggestion for him to do that by pulling the card out of my shirt pocket first. It's an old trick from Tradecraft 101. I'm just glad it worked.'

'How did you know he was dirty?'

'That Patek Philippe Calatrava on his wrist was the main giveaway. Also, his micro-expressions when we mentioned Duke Matasi's name and showed him Asher's photo.'

'I can't wait to see what your team comes up with.'

'We'll know soon enough. They should have something by the time we get back to the *Oregon*.'

Dubai, United Arab Emirates

The next morning, Juan and Sarai landed at the busy Dubai International Airport (DXB). As soon as they were processed through customs they grabbed a cab and headed south for a forty-minute ride to the Dubai World Central Airport (DWC), where most private and chartered flights were now directed.

The two of them made their way to the private chartered terminal pulling their luxury suitcases behind them. Juan caught sight of the only other two passengers in the waiting area.

'We'll pay for half the gas if you'll let us hitch a ride,' Huxley said in a weary voice, beaming as she stood.

Juan swallowed up the diminutive doctor in a bear hug. The rings under her eyes indicated fatigue, but her hazel irises only darkened when she was upset. She had every right to be. She had emailed her report about what happened back in Vale do Javari. Understandably, the death of her friend had wrecked her emotionally. But she and her team had also nearly been killed by a couple of physically superior brutes, who managed to inflict quite a beating on Linc and Tiny.

Juan had been shocked to learn of the massacre of the Poison Arrow tribe. He had relayed the details to Overholt and a contact he had in the Brazilian government, urging an immediate investigation. He privately promised Huxley that the *Oregon* team would devote its full resources to solving the murder of Dr Izidoro at the conclusion of Sarai's project.

'Glad you all made it back in one piece.'

Huxley nodded. 'Same here.' She glanced at Linc. 'Thanks to him.'

Juan grabbed Linc and the two of them hugged it out, pounding each other on their wide backs.

'Tiny deserves all the credit,' Linc said.

'How is he?'

'He twisted his ankle pretty good,' Huxley said. 'I got him braced and bandaged well enough for him to fly home to West Palm Beach. He sent a text saying he made it and he's squared away.'

Juan laid a hand on Linc's shoulder. 'You good?'

'Good enough for government work,' Linc said.

Juan thought his friend looked pretty worn-out as well.

'Long flight, I bet.'

'The longest. But I slept like a log,' Linc said, his eyes shifting to Sarai's lovely face.

'Oh, sorry. Franklin Lincoln, Dr Julia Huxley, this is Sarai Massala.'

Linc stuck out his big hand. 'Friends call me Linc.'

Massala took it. 'Sarai.' She turned to Huxley. 'Dr Huxley, it's a great pleasure to meet you. Juan has told me all about his crew. I understand you and Linc were in the Amazon?'

Huxley ducked her question. 'The only people on board who call me "Dr Huxley" are the lunkheads who forget to report for their annual physicals.' She shot Juan a look. 'We're not big on titles on the *Oregon*.'

'I'll brief you on Sarai's mission on the tilt-rotor,' Juan said to his crew members. 'Speaking of which . . .' He pulled his vibrating cell phone out of his pocket. 'Gomez says he's ready to go. Let's head for the barn.' He reached over and snatched up Linc's heavy ruck before the former SEAL could grab it.

Sarai did the same with Huxley's gear.

The two *Oregon* crew members protested, but neither Juan nor Sarai would hear of it.

Juan's admiration for Massala only went up as he led the way to the gate.

Juan briefed Linc and Huxley on Asher Massala, their trip to Kibera, and the dead end they'd hit. The two tired crew members were deeply interested, but both obviously still had the Amazon trip on their minds.

As soon as the AW landed back on the *Oregon*, Juan suggested breakfast, but Huxley and Linc waved him off.

'After a long flight I always need to clean up and change clothes,' Linc said.

Huxley nodded in agreement. 'We ate on the plane not too long ago. We'll catch up with you later after we freshen up.'

'Seriously,' Juan said. 'Both of you, take twenty-four hours off and get rested up. We've got you covered.'

'I've been on my butt for what seems like a week,' Linc said. 'The last thing I need is more rest.'

Huxley nodded at her small medical kit with the samples she took from the dead merc. 'And I've got some tests to run.'

Juan nodded.

Just one more reminder that he had the best crew in the world.

41

Sarai was thrilled to ride in the tilt-rotor again for the short hop from the DWC airport out to the *Oregon*. She had many questions for the large African American and the petite physician about their adventure into the wilds of the Amazon, a trip she had always dreamed of taking. But the looks on their faces told her now was not the time, despite their friendly welcome.

The aircraft had stayed in helicopter mode for the short trip. Sarai knew the changing sounds of the turbo engines meant the tilt-rotor had begun its descent. She looked outside her cabin window. There was only one ship within miles of their location and it was the one they were heading for, anchored in the dark blue waters below. Her nose crinkled up at the sight of the thick cloud of black smoke drifting out of the stack that painted an oily smudge across the pristine, cloudless sky.

It clearly wasn't the *Oregon*.

Instead of clean decks and a bright white-painted hull, Gomez Adams was angling the aircraft toward a dilapidated old rust bucket. Yes, it had a similar shape to the elegant *Oregon*, but this floating wreck had a faded black-painted hull that was streaked with long rivulets of rust. Her superstructure was the same color of green as a rancid avocado, and several of its windows were cracked and yellowed.

Sarai squinted through her window, but could only barely make out the name of the ship, *Norego Sunrise*, painted in faded yellow letters on her stern. As they descended she could see two of the cranes were out of service and parts of the rusted superstructure were patched with plywood. The decks were strewn with broken chains and hand tools, splotches of spilled swamp-green paint, and cigarette butts. A weathered and torn Iranian national flag hung limply on its crooked jack staff. She wondered if the ship was even seaworthy.

Massala turned toward Juan with a frown of confusion. She was greeted with Cabrillo's Cheshire cat grin.

'Beautiful, isn't she?' His electronically altered voice rang playfully in her headset.

'I don't understand. Why aren't we landing on the *Oregon*?'

'We are.'

She smiled as she shook her head incredulously. 'No. I don't believe it.'

'Our greatest strength is our ability to hide in plain sight. The *Oregon* has the capacity to change its name and paint scheme at the push of a button. The hull is coated with a special metamaterial that changes colors and textures with a simple electrical charge using pre-designed camouflage schemes stored in a designated computer.

'I also have a department that's tasked with making all of the other physical changes – like production assistants setting props on a film shoot. Our transformation routine also changes out our automated identification signals, cargo logbooks, passenger manifests, even the flag we sail under. My team has it down to a science now. They're faster than a Formula One pit crew at Silverstone.'

'You are full of surprises,' Sarai said. 'I suspect you have one or two more left up your sleeve.'

'Yeah. And I have a lot of sleeves.'

Juan was tempted to give Sarai the complete tour of the *Norego Sunrise*'s altered superstructure just so she could see how thorough the transformation really was – a total sensory overload. Automated misters stenched the passageways with stale cigarette smoke; the captain's cabin featured a filthy stained carpet, an unmade bed, and a clogged toilet. Simulated dead flies littered the windowsills and dead bugs clustered in the room's corners. All of it was designed to turn the stomachs, water the eyes, and drive any nosy harbor pilots and customs inspectors off the ship as quickly as possible.

But the last thing Juan wanted to do was to drive away the beautiful Israeli woman he now considered a friend. So instead he took a more appealing course of action and led Sarai to the *Oregon*'s fabled dining room belowdecks for an amazing breakfast.

Cabrillo's tastes always ran to the timeless and classic. It was no surprise to anyone that when the latest version of the *Oregon* had been built, he both reproduced and upgraded the previous dining room. The English gentleman's club decor featured dark walnut wall paneling, coffered ceilings, and polished brass. But Cabrillo added faux animal skins, handwoven Persian rugs, and Indian silks to soften and brighten the heavy ambience. In lieu of traditional stuffed animal heads hanging on the walls, original oil paintings of classic English, European, and American landscapes stood in their place.

Juan also added onboard phone apps for preordering and walnut cabinet digital stations at each table for menu updates and selections. Plush leather chairs, tables, and booths made for a sumptuous main dining experience. Along the far wall, chesterfield sofas and club chairs were arrayed near the floor-to-ceiling bookcase that featured first-edition hardcover classics, providing a venue for relaxed contemplation.

Juan and Sarai were promptly served a made-to-order breakfast prepared by a young woman, the *Oregon*'s newest gourmet chef. Juan went for American Wagyu steak and eggs, thick-diced home fries with Vidalia onions, and a pot of black pour-over Cuban coffee. Sarai opted for plain organic Greek yogurt topped with fresh-toasted muesli, purple Brandywine raspberries, and a pot of Earl Grey tea sweetened with honey. Anywhere else on the planet, the *Oregon*'s restaurant would have been Michelin star rated. But the only ratings Cabrillo's chefs required were the well-satisfied faces of the hungry crew, which they received on a daily basis.

Just as Juan wiped his mouth with a napkin woven with the finest Egyptian cotton, he received a text from Murphy. He and Eric were waiting for them.

'Time to see what the boys found,' Juan said as he stood, downing the last drops from his coffee cup.

Juan led Sarai straight to Eric's private quarters. He slammed the heavy iron ring knocker against its plate bolted to a door comprised of ancient crosshatched timbers studded with iron heads, all designed to blunt sword strikes and thwart battering rams.

'Unusual,' Sarai said.

'Are you referring to the door or to Eric?'

Just then, the door swung open. Eric stood in his stocking feet on a bare floor of rich red mahogany and ushered them into his expansive living room with a slight bow.

'Welcome to my humble abode.'

Taking their cues from sock-footed Stone, Juan and Sarai removed their shoes and set them on a tray near the doorway. Murphy's combat boots stood beside Eric's Italian brown oxfords. Juan noted that both pairs were polished to a high gloss.

Like every other crew member, Stone received a generous allowance to decorate his cabin any way he wanted. For most of the crew, including Eric, the *Oregon* was not just their home away from home, but their only home.

On the previous *Oregon*, Juan reminded himself, Eric's decor had gone for gamer chic, with wall-to-wall LCD monitors, and specialized chairs customized for Formula One racing, dogfighting, and tank combat competitions. But his new cabin reflected what Stone termed 'a more mature taste.'

The room exactly duplicated one of the opening scenes from Eric's favorite movie, *Inception*, set in a stylized Japanese castle. The room featured shoji sliding door panels painted in gold leaf and decorated with hand-drawn pastoral scenes. Eric even had a copy made of the famous oversize, black-stained willow chair with its remarkably tall and curved lattice back that gave it a throne-like appearance.

But the room's most striking element was a coffered ceiling crowded with over a hundred bright lantern-shaped LED lights that all reflected in the dark high gloss of a massive tabletop dominating the center of the spacious room, doubling the effect of the lanterns.

Sarai's eyes widened with wonder.

'This room is exquisite.'

Eric smiled. 'I think it has a dreamlike quality.'

'So would Christopher Nolan,' Murphy grunted as he glanced up from his laptop, referencing *Inception*'s writer-director. He was seated at the head of the table in the willow chair. Eric's laptop was next to his. A large wireless monitor had been brought in for the meeting and stood in the middle of the table.

Cabrillo fought back a chuckle. Both of his twenty-something researchers were particularly well groomed this morning.

Eric's oxford shirt and slacks had knife-edged creases and his hair was shiny and slick with pomade and parted with laser-like straightness.

Murphy's black jeans appeared to be brand-new. His black concert T-shirt still bore the fold marks from its plastic wrapper and featured a brightly colored group of felines playing electronic zithers.

Most notably, the air was clogged with the competing aromas of musky English Leather and Drakkar Noir too liberally applied.

'"The Stoic Kittens"?' Sarai asked, pointing at Murphy's shirt.

'You know them?' Murphy asked, smiling hopefully.

Sarai shook her head. 'Sorry. Just reading your T-shirt out loud.'

Murphy slumped with disappointment.

'Never mind all of that,' Juan said. 'What have you found?'

Eric pulled out a chair and motioned for Sarai to sit in it. 'Please, Ms Massala.'

'Thank you.'

While Eric was trying to score gentleman's points with the beautiful former model, Juan pulled out a chair for himself and sat down.

Max Hanley charged into Eric's cabin unannounced. He waved a meaty hand in front of his soured face.

'Good Lord! It smells like a couple of teenage skunks dry-humping each other at the perfume counter!'

The former swift boat captain was built like a barroom bouncer with a broken nose, thick forearms, and a high, hard belly that stretched his Columbia shirt to the limits. A thin patina of graying auburn hair dusted his weathered scalp.

Juan laughed as he shook his head. 'Sarai Massala, I'd like you to meet my second-in-command, Mr Maxwell Hanley. Max, this is our guest, Sarai Massala.'

Sarai stood and extended her hand. 'Nice to meet you, Mr Hanley.'

'Call me Max, please. Sorry about the colorful language.' Max sniffed the air like a bloodhound. 'I'm just not used to these kinds of aromatics.' He turned to Stone and Murphy. 'You testing some kind of new chemical weapon in here, boys?'

The two men shrugged innocently.

Max nodded with understanding.

Juan caught the glint in his best friend's eye. Despite three ex-wives, Max still had a thing for the ladies.

'I'm sorry we didn't meet last time you were aboard,' Max said. 'I was on the hangar deck overseeing a maintenance inspection on the hydraulic lift.'

'Juan told me you are the engineer responsible for keeping the *Oregon* in top shape. You obviously know what you're doing. It's an amazing vessel.'

'We try.' Max turned to Juan. 'Sorry I'm late to the briefing. We had an issue with one of the venturi nozzles.'

'Problem?'

'Not anymore.'

'Grab a seat. The Le Pew brothers were just about to get started on their brief.'

Max pulled up a chair next to Juan and Sarai.

'We managed to clean up the muffled audio recording of the Kenyan prison warden's phone call you sent us,' Eric said. 'We scrubbed out as many of the artifacts as we could. The warden's voice was clear enough, but the other one was digitally altered and we couldn't pull anything actionable from it. Bottom line, the warden mentioned this organization called the Humane Justice Program. Have either of you heard of it before?'

Juan and Sarai shook their heads.

'Yeah, us neither.'

Eric brought up the first picture on the LCD screen. It was a website titled *Humane Justice Program*. It featured an alternate title in French. He and Murphy had already put together a slideshow that flashed on the screen as they spoke.

Murphy pulled up several slides of HJP corporate documents and began his spiel.

'We did some digging around. It was founded several years ago by an attorney, F. Irwin Skinner.'

Max grunted. '"Skinner"? Perfect name for a *lawyer.*' He practically spat out the last word.

Sarai turned to Juan, frowning with curiosity. He tapped his ring finger and whispered, 'I'll explain later.'

Murphy continued. 'The organization is technically headquartered in the Cayman Islands.'

'There's your first red flag,' Max said. 'Probably operating out of a file cabinet drawer in Skinner's office.'

'No doubt there's a lot of shady stuff going on down there in the Caymans,' Murphy said. 'But there are also a number of legit operations, though they're often financed by the shady ones.'

'Which might be the case here,' Eric said. 'As you can see on the screen, we found several large donors from accounts that we couldn't further verify. We ran it by Russ and he hit a wall, too.'

Juan turned to Sarai. 'Russ Kefauver is a former CIA forensic accountant, and one of our intelligence analysts.'

'We agree with Russ that we're talking about some seriously well-designed shell companies,' Eric said.

'So where does that leave us?'

'Russ is still trying to untangle the legal knots, so we took a different tack. We ran the name "Duke Matasi" through every Kenyan government database we could find, paying special attention to law enforcement. We didn't find anything.'

'But we know he was at the Kamiti prison,' Sarai said.

'We don't doubt that,' Eric said. 'But if there was something illegal going on involving him, I wouldn't be surprised if his records were deleted so the bad guys could cover their tracks.'

'Red flag number two,' Max said.

'Hard to make a positive case from negative evidence,' Juan said. 'But your analysis makes a lot of sense. What else?'

'We went back to square one and pulled up the Humane Justice Program website,' Eric said.

Murphy clicked through a series of before-and-after photos featuring convicted men and women released to civilian halfway houses, job programs, and classrooms. Each photo featured a text asserting the virtues of restorative justice, sentence commutations, or alternative sentencing programs.

'We were able to track down the server where it's loaded,' Murphy said. 'There was one other website located there as well.'

He pulled up a second website called *The International Medical Justice Initiative (IMJI)*. Like the previous website, it also had a French title.

'You'll notice that both websites use the same fonts and layout styles. That tells us they were both created by the same unimaginative web designer.'

Stone clicked his wireless mouse and advanced the page. It featured the grateful, smiling faces of women and children from around the developing world served by compassionate, smiling IMJI staffers in scrubs and other medical garb.

'We did a little more digging around,' Murphy said.

'Both organizations were set up by Skinner under the umbrella of a nonprofit organization called the Micah Foundation.'

The lawyer's professional photograph was pulled up, along with two separate organizational charts, one for HJP and the other for IMJI. Skinner had a long, angular face topped with a head of curly salt-and-pepper hair and a neatly trimmed goatee to match. The top of each chart was headed by a box marked *CEO* and each box held his name.

'We tried reaching out to him through email and text, and left a voicemail,' Stone said. 'No response from him or the other officers listed on the organizational charts. Other than his official bio on both websites and a dated Wikipedia reference, he doesn't have any online or social media presence at all.'

'He might be dead for all we know,' Murphy added.

'Red flag number three,' Max said.

'Is he actually running those outfits?' Juan asked. 'Or is he just a figurehead?'

'Not sure. But we did find this.' Eric scrolled down the IMJI web page. It showed a photo of the mercy ship *Sekhmet*.

'According to the website, the *Sekhmet* is operated by the IMJI. And since both websites are on the same server, we figure the *Sekhmet* is connected to both organizations.'

'And this is interesting . . . why?' Max asked.

Murphy grinned. 'It's interesting because the *Sekhmet* is less than six hours away from our current position.'

Eric nodded. 'If we want to find out more about the Humane Justice Program, we need to board the *Sekhmet*.'

'Perhaps there is information about my brother on board her as well,' Sarai said.

'That's what I'm hoping.' Juan turned to Max. 'Who has the conn?'

'Linda,' Max said.

'Eric, send her the coordinates and set a course for the *Sekhmet*.'

'Aye, Chairman.'

42

Outside Riyadh, Saudi Arabia

It was customary in the Muslim faith to bury a believer within twenty-four hours of their death, though up to three days was permissible. In Colonel Muqrin's case the latter was necessary in order to cull the charred and scattered remains of the prince from the wreckage of his desert crash site.

Most of his body could not be ritually washed by his father because there wasn't enough of it to perform the ceremony. Under the watchful eye of the imam, Khalid did, however, bathe the relatively intact head, which had been miraculously preserved inside the four-hundred-thousand-dollar combat helmet Muqrin had worn on his last flight.

Muqrin's remains, such as they were, had been ritually shrouded with inexpensive linens, as dictated by the modesty of their religion, and transported to the King Khalid Grand Mosque by the crown prince's order, honoring his dead son. The funeral prayers were said over the body from a distance, the mourners segregated by sex, and each facing Mecca. Muqrin's mother wept like a lost child, and collapsed in a veil of tears, surrounded by her closest friends and relatives, each of them mothers who shared her grief.

Colonel Muqrin was then loaded into the bed of a freshly washed Toyota Hilux pickup truck and driven to the family cemetery. Only a few black-robed men were present, including Prince Khalid and Crown Prince Abdullah. Led by Khalid and Abdullah, Muqrin's body was carried on a pallet to an unmarked grave dug perpendicular to Mecca. The remains were gently rolled into position on the right side of the grave, where Muqrin would spend the rest of his days facing the holy Kaaba until the great Resurrection.

Khalid then recited the ritual burial prayer.

'Bismilllah wa ala millati rasulillah.' In the name of Allah and in the faith of the Messenger of Allah.

The other mourners – male cousins – tossed handfuls of dirt onto the corpse, kissed Khalid's hands, and departed in a separate vehicle.

Khalid shot a glance at Abdullah's armored SUV limousine parked in the distance. It was surrounded by armed bodyguards maintaining a respectful but watchful vigilance.

Why did the crown prince feel the need for bodyguards on his family estate? Khalid asked himself.

There was no chance of a foreign assassination out here. Khalid's own security forces were protecting them. There was only one explanation. Abdullah had finally come to realize that his life wasn't threatened only by forces outside the nation, but within. He had pushed too far, too fast. But the crown prince was too proud to change his course, Khalid knew, and would never bend his knee to either the will of God nor to any other man.

Abdullah lifted a handful of yellow dirt and tossed it onto his friend's shrouded remains. But the tall, barrel-chested royal stood frozen in place, unable to take his blurring eyes off of Muqrin's remains.

'You have done my family a great honor today,' Khalid offered. 'I am most grateful. I know how busy your schedule is.'

'He was like a brother to me. Closer than any brother I have. I could do no less for him.'

Khalid understood Abdullah's cruel subtlety. He was honoring Muqrin specifically and not Khalid or his family. And why should he? Hadn't Abdullah himself pushed Khalid out of his position as the head of the GIP and given it to someone else? Wasn't it Abdullah's so-called reforms that had stripped Khalid of his position as the deputy crown prince?

Granted, Abdullah had given that position to Khalid's son, Muqrin, but not as a token of respect to Khalid. His son was genuinely Abdullah's best friend, and shared all of the same terrible ideas of Westernization that the future king was even now implementing. To Khalid's shame, Muqrin was a co-conspirator with Abdullah in the plot to tear the kingdom away from its role as protector of the holy faith.

'My son was an eagle, fashioned with wings made by Allah himself,' Khalid said as he tossed three handfuls of dirt onto his son's body. 'The rest of my days will be filled with mourning.'

'Muqrin was a great pilot. The best we had.' Abdullah reached down and tossed in two more handfuls of dirt, as the ritual required. He brushed his hands against the fine black silk of his robe, staining it. 'My investigators are certain he was not at fault.'

'I have no doubt of that.'

Abdullah faced the smaller, elder prince. 'I promise to continue the investigation until his name is finally cleared.' Abdullah reached down and picked up two small stones in his hands.

Khalid did the same. 'I am most grateful.'

The two men proceeded to pile several small stones on the body.

The crown prince checked his watch. 'I'm afraid I must leave. There is a meeting I must attend.' He leaned in close and lowered his voice. 'In Jordan. Very top secret. I know you understand these things.'

'Yes, my prince,' Khalid said, feigning gratitude for Abdullah's trust. 'Allah's mercy on you as you travel.'

Abdullah nodded, then headed for his waiting limousine.

In fact, Khalid already knew all about the top secret meeting. After being forced out of his position as the head of Saudi intelligence, Khalid had created a shadow intelligence organization under the crown prince's haughty nose.

The plans Khalid had set in motion were proceeding perfectly, as Abdullah would himself soon discover.

43

Ahvaz, Iran
Headquarters, The Quds Force

Brigadier General Mehdi Sadeghi sat behind his desk, his belly spilling over the top of his green battle fatigues. He stared at the grim portraits of the aging and turbaned Supreme Leader and President glaring down at him from across the room.

Not much longer, he smiled to himself.

Sadeghi took a long drag on his e-cigarette, holding the mango-flavored vapor in his scarred lungs. He had first begun smoking in the trenches during the Iran–Iraq War in the 1980s, where he also suffered his first chemical warfare attack. The filthy Iraqis had deployed European chemical agents targeted with help from American satellite technology against his comrades in the trenches. *Thanks be to Allah*, the damage to his lungs had been minimal, but many of his friends had suffered agonizing deaths. The hatred in his heart for the infidels had long since kindled into an unquenchable flame.

Commended for his battlefield bravery against Hussein's murderous legions, young Sadeghi was quickly inducted into Iran's newly formed Quds Force, his country's version of special operations. He rose through the ranks by proving himself in difficult field commands, killing and wounding Iran's enemies in Lebanon, Bosnia, Syria, and Iraq, as well as on covert missions in Africa and even Latin America. Quds officers had been assassinated by CIA and Mossad agents for years, and he had escaped multiple attempts on his life. But he rested secure in the strong hands of Allah, who was the maker and shaper of his destiny.

And that destiny, he knew, was to lead Iran in a holy war against Israel.

The bald and bearded general was no longer a young killer slitting throats and assaulting rooms with sprays of machine-gun fire, but he was still handy with a blade and a rifle. Now he was playing the far more dangerous game of Iranian national politics. Over the last decade he had assembled a vast network of like-minded patriots who wanted to bring Iran into the twenty-first century and take its place as one of the world's great powers. The clerics themselves were causing massive social unrest, preventing the Iranian people from fully realizing their genius for war and business. A secular government founded in deep Islamic roots like Turkey was the model for Iran's future, and Sadeghi would be his country's Atatürk.

Sadeghi took another long drag on his e-cigarette as he read the encrypted text from his chief weapons engineer. The infidel mercenary Salan had delivered the hypersonic missile to an Iranian-flagged vessel captained by one of Sadeghi's loyal supporters. That ship was now proceeding to a naval port on the Persian Gulf, where it would soon be reverse engineered and eventually deployed by Iranian forces against Western navies and Israeli cities.

Sadeghi had known Prince Khalid for many years. The

Saudi had been an effective intelligence officer. Despite the fact Khalid practiced an idolatrous form of the Islamic faith, Sadeghi affirmed their shared hatred of the Israeli bandit state. Forced to live under the boot heel of the Great Satan, Khalid secretly had never wavered from his private commitment to wipe the Jewish invaders off the face of the map.

It was a great disappointment to learn Khalid had been sacked as the head of Saudi Arabia's General Intelligence Presidency. That boded ill for the direction of Saudi politics, and only confirmed Crown Prince Abdullah's desire to strengthen Saudi–Israeli defense commitments. Sadeghi was, however, delighted when Khalid arranged to meet with him secretly and was utterly stunned by his proposal.

Like Khalid, Sadeghi was alarmed at the direction his own country was taking. The imams that governed Iran made big noises about destroying the Zionists and waging war with the United States, but in fact they had been dragging their feet for years. Worse, the robed imbeciles were threatening war with Saudi Arabia, playing into the hands of the American neocon plotters, pitting Muslim against Muslim, as they had for decades.

Even Iran's vaunted nuclear weapons program was a sham, designed mostly as a propaganda tool, and only poorly operationalized as an energy program. Whereas Khalid wanted to put Saudi Arabia back under the authority of his conservative clerics, Sadeghi needed to wrest control from the feckless imams and return Iran to its rightful destiny as the destroyer of Israel and the leader of the Muslim world.

Khalid's plan seemed, at first, a fool's errand. But upon careful consideration, Sadeghi began to see the genius of it. First, Iran would gain a combat-proven hypersonic missile design that would neutralize any and all Western naval forces. Most important, it would mean the end of American naval dominance in the Persian Gulf.

Second, by launching Khalid's hypersonic missile from Yemen, the Americans would claim – without proof – that Iran was behind the attack. The current Iranian government would vehemently deny it, of course, because they would have had no knowledge of it.

What would the Americans then do? If the Americans decided to attack Iran, the Tehran government would likely fall and Sadeghi would be in position to take power. If the Americans decided to withdraw from the region for fear of Iran's hypersonic capabilities, then Sadeghi would step forward as the mastermind behind the plan that threw the Americans out – and still win the presidency, and put the mullahs to heel.

Even better, when Khalid became King of Saudi Arabia and Sadeghi became President of Iran, the first thing the new heads of state would do is announce a mutual defensive pact, proving their intentions as regional peacemakers.

Once this peace alliance was established between them, they would immediately prepare for war against Israel.

Sadeghi drew another lungful of mango-flavored vapor. He recently switched to vaping on his doctor's recommendation, but in truth he preferred vaping to smoking. The sweet, fruity flavors reminded him of his innocent youth growing up on his grandfather's apple orchard.

The general's encrypted phone vibrated. He picked it up and checked the message. His two hand-selected field operatives were in position. They would soon be meeting up with Salan and assist the *kafir* Frenchman on his mission to smuggle the hypersonic missile into Yemen.

His men would know what to do after that.

44

The Ad-Dahna Desert, Saudi Arabia

Prince Khalid shielded his eyes against the wind as he scanned the blistering blue vault of the desert sky. He stood atop a dune, a single wave in a turbulent sea of red sand stretching to the horizon. His white cotton *thobe* flapped in the breeze like a loose sail and turned his red-and-white headdress into a snapping battle flag.

His prized falcon was nowhere to be seen, hidden in the blinding sun high above his head, seeking its prey. Khalid's heart soared whenever the bird took flight. The razor-taloned angel of death was an extension of his own soul.

Khalid's left hand absentmindedly rubbed the Norwegian elk skin falconer's glove on his right like a talisman, willing the great bird to return to him.

He had just purchased the Altai Saker from a Canadian breeder for a hundred thousand dollars. Her purebred lines, her diving speeds of over three hundred kilometers per hour, and most of all her regal appearance made her worth every penny – and more. Khalid intended to breed his own new line of fearsome raptors on this particular family estate, his favorite in the kingdom.

The roar of a 4×4 Land Rover boomed on the far side of a nearby dune. Khalid turned toward the sandy track leading from his mansion in the desert and saw the cloud of dust racing in his direction. A moment later, the tall Rover crested the hill and slid to a halt. The driver's door popped open.

The combat boots of a uniformed officer stepped onto the scattering sands and marched unevenly toward Khalid. Lieutenant General Nawaf Faraj's sharp, lean frame was matched by his carefully trimmed gray mustache and short-cropped hair.

The two men exchanged the traditional salaam as the officer kissed Khalid on both cheeks.

'My dear Prince, my condolences for the loss of your son.'

'Thank you, my friend.'

The officer, the current head of Saudi Arabia's GIP, scanned the sky, shielding his eyes from both the swirling dust and the blinding rays of the merciless sun. Khalid's fame as a falconer was legendary in the kingdom. 'I don't see her.'

Khalid smiled. 'Which is what makes her so dangerous. What news do you have for me?'

'The autopsy results came back exactly as you predicted. Prince Muqrin died of a brain aneurysm.'

'And this was reported to Abdullah?'

'Just this morning. He is fully convinced it was a natural occurrence, as stated in the examiner's report. No one suspects a thing.'

Khalid nodded his approval. Salan's nanobots had done their work. Though everyone at his son's banquet had drunk the peach tea, the nanobots were programmed and targeted with Muqrin's DNA, which was why he alone was the victim. In this way, Khalid avoided all suspicion of his son's murder.

'Who conducted the examination? A credible source?'

'I flew in a German specialist. A Muslim, in fact.' The fearsome intelligence officer owed his position to Khalid, along with his family's fortune. But Faraj thought of Khalid more as a friend than a chief. He laid a gentle hand on Khalid's forearm. 'He treated the prince's head with utmost respect.'

'I'm grateful. The examination also proves there was no pilot error.'

'Exactly, my prince. Prince Muqrin lived and died a hero.'

'Our European friends will be glad to know their plane was also not at fault.'

'They will be informed shortly.'

'And what of the Allegiance Council?'

'The Allegiance Council has met and voted. As of this moment, you are the new deputy crown prince, taking the place of your beloved son.' Faraj couldn't hide his grinning admiration. 'Exactly according to your plan.'

'Abdullah has made too many mistakes and too many enemies too quickly.'

'Even as your many friends and allies remember all of your successes.'

'This will end any chance of Abdullah's proposed defense treaty with the Zionists,' Khalid said.

'It was an abomination from the beginning.'

'He won't care for my election.'

'Reelection, my prince. But he will accept it nonetheless.' Faraj's voice rang with finality. 'Or suffer the consequences.'

Khalid laid a hand to his chest and bowed his head slightly.

'I serve at the discretion of the Allegiance Council and submit to their wisdom.'

Suddenly, a shrill cry rang out high above them.

Without glancing up, Khalid extended his gloved hand just as the gray-and-white falcon landed deftly on it. The Saker clutched the elk leather glove in one sharp talon and a fat desert rat squirming in the other.

Khalid whispered a command to the stunning raptor. The Saker snapped the neck of the squealing rodent with its razor-sharp beak and began tearing it apart, consuming it piece by piece.

'You see? All is as it should be,' the general said.

Khalid nodded. 'According to the will of Allah.'

Khalid's main falconer ran up to fetch the nearly three-pound feathered predator just as Faraj's Land Rover pulled away and headed back to Riyadh.

Allah's will, indeed, Khalid told himself as he took in the wide horizon. His heart filled with pride. Everything was going exactly according to plan, just as Faraj had said.

Soon now, he would be king.

He tried to imagine what his father would think if he were still alive. He would have swelled with pride at the sight of his son sitting on the throne, but the knowledge that his grandson was killed by Khalid's hand would have put him in his grave.

The old fool wouldn't have understood. Perhaps that was why God took him early in life, sparing him much confusion. It was indeed the mercy of Allah.

In truth, Khalid had deep regret for murdering his own son, but it could not be helped. Muqrin was next in line to be king after Abdullah, who would soon be dealt with. But Muqrin had fallen under the same satanic spell that held Abdullah in its demonic grip. Muqrin was as committed to Westernization as Abdullah; in fact, more so. Not only would he have signed a mutual defense pact with Israel, he would have turned Saudi Arabia into a secular state.

God forbid.

Muqrin was his blood, but in Khalid's eyes, his son was also a traitor to his people and his God. It was necessary for him to die, as much as that grieved him. Had Muqrin been a faithful son, Khalid would have gladly seen him ascend to the throne. Did the holy Koran not say, 'Whoever among you abandons their faith, Allah will replace them'?

It was now Khalid's duty to carry on with God's divine mission.

Looking back over the last several days, Khalid realized his skills as an actor had not diminished since his days in London. He had played the servile subject to Abdullah and the grieving father to a nation.

But soon he would take on the greatest role of his life as the Custodian of the Two Holy Mosques, the Protector of the Two Holy Cities, the Servant of the Two Noble Sanctuaries. All he waited for now was the death of the crown prince and the launch of the hypersonic missile that would drive a stake through the heart of the Great Satan.

Inshallah.

45

The *Sekhmet* was just a few miles off the literal Horn of Africa, a great angular wedge of Somali coastline jutting into the Arabian Sea.

So was the *Gator*.

Linda Ross had turned the *Oregon*'s conn over to Max so she could pilot the stealthy submersible. After rocketing across the surface at breakneck speed, Linda took the *Gator* down and switched to its electric motors to approach the slow-moving mercy ship. There was no reason for the average person to think the converted passenger liner was anything more than she appeared to be.

But the crew of the stealthy *Oregon* knew better.

The *Oregon* was hardly the first ship to pretend to be a helpless vessel in the face of a dangerous enemy. As far back as the seventeenth century, the forty-six gun frigate HMS *Kingfisher* disguised herself as a merchant ship in order to lure Barbary corsairs to their unsuspecting doom. The Royal Navy extended the concept with Q-ships in World War I.

It was doubtful the *Sekhmet* possessed advanced sonar or radar capabilities, or worse, anti-ship weaponry, but Juan saw no advantage to bringing the *Oregon* potentially into harm's way when all he really needed was a taxi ride.

At two a.m., a brilliant full moon lit the eastern night sky, illuminating the starboard side of the northbound *Sekhmet* like a Hollywood searchlight. Linda had brought the *Gator* to the surface in the long dark shadow beneath the towering port side of the giant ship.

The submersible utilized a more advanced form of the AI-powered piloting software found on self-driving cars. The *Gator*'s sonar and laser sensors fed millions of speed and distance data points per second to the autopilot, allowing the vessel to track just centimeters away from the *Sekhmet*'s steel hull without colliding into it. With its flat twelve-meter deck just barely above water and its small, darkened cockpit, the *Gator* would have been practically invisible to the four men topside expected on graveyard watch. The rest of the civilian boat no doubt was sound asleep.

Juan stood near the *Gator*'s single open hatch. The submersible's interior lamps were off to hide the night insertion. The Gator gently rocked as it kept pace in the swell generated by the *Sekhmet*'s bow, which was making a loud but leisurely eight knots.

Cabrillo gazed up toward the railing looming some sixty feet above. He couldn't see it, given the upward sloping curvature of the hull. Despite the deep shadows, the churning white water coursing past the *Sekhmet*'s waterline was luminescent in the wine-dark sea. The noise of the churning prop and the rush of water muffled the *Gator*'s nearly silent progress.

Eric Stone was the first to find the blueprints for the original Greek passenger liner, but neither he nor Murphy could uncover the updated layout after the ship was converted to its current *Sekhmet* configuration. The location of the engine room and the bridge, the number of decks, and a few other structural details would be the same, but otherwise they were going in blind.

Juan glanced back down at the hatch. He saw the thick blond hair of one of his best Gundogs emerging from the shadows. Marion MacDougal 'MacD' Lawless was a former US Army Ranger. MacD had joined the Corporation after Juan rescued him from an Al Qaeda village in the mountains of Northern Waziristan a few years back while the model-handsome ex-Ranger was working for a private contractor.

A warm breeze kept the chill ocean temperature at bay. Like Juan, MacD wore blue hospital scrubs with name tags that read *Sekhmet* and *IMJI* with the Cross and Crescent logo blazoned beneath the words. The Magic Shop had created the costumes based on the *Sekhmet*'s social media photos Murph and Stoney had found on the web. All Juan could do was hope those pictures weren't terribly outdated.

'Nice night for a climb,' MacD said, standing on the deck and glancing up the side of the steel hull. His southern sweet-tea drawl was undiminished by the molar mic's bone conduction speaker. With the microphone custom-fitted to his back teeth, the Louisiana native hardly had to whisper to be heard, as his voice transmitted sound to Juan's inner ear via his jaw. Instead of sounding like earbuds, the bone conduction voice echoed inside of the skull with crystal – and unnerving – clarity.

'Shouldn't be too bad,' Juan agreed as he handed MacD his climbing gear – a pair of specially designed gloves and boots that fit around his athletic shoes. He glanced over the side at the passing sea. 'At least the fall won't kill you.'

'Maybe. I once seen a man drown in six inches of water.'

'Why didn't he just stand up?'

''Cuz I cut that *cochon's* string with a bullet to the back of his spine.'

The two men quickly kitted up, pulling on their specialized climbing gloves and boots. They did a comms check with Linda inside the *Gator* and press-checked their tranquilizer pistols. Bullets weren't an option; as far as they knew, the *Sekhmet* really was a mercy ship on a medical mission. Juan didn't want to get captured, but he didn't want to hurt innocent civilians, either.

The tranq pistols were carried in the appendix position inside their waistbands on PHLster Enigma concealment holsters. The unique thing about the Enigmas was that the holster was fixed to a belt strapped directly around the midsection independent of the wearer's clothing. Not only did this provide deep concealment for almost any size pistol, it also meant that even a heavy, all-steel gun could be easily carried wearing something with as little structure as hospital scrubs and not be seen at all.

Ideally, the same would be said of the two of them – not seen at all – then the tranq guns wouldn't be needed. But if they were, the small pellets delivered a heavy dose of sedative that dissolved instantly once it entered the body. Not only would this knock someone out without serious injury, but it would leave no evidence behind.

'Ready to rock and roll?'

'Like my bowlegged *tante* at a *fais do-do*.'

Juan spoke four languages fluently, but MacD's Cajun slang always threw him for a loop.

'Say again?'

'Like my drunken auntie at a bachelorette party.'

Juan and his entire complement of special operators had trained several times on the new climbing system by scaling the hull of the *Oregon* on the open sea. The concept was as simple as it was impossible. Like many of the most revolutionary DARPA technical advances, their engineers relied on Mother Nature for guidance. When faced with almost any seemingly insurmountable engineering problem regarding motion on land, at sea, or in the air, DARPA scientists turned to bio-mimicry – reproducing in mechanical form what God had already designed in his creations.

In this case, DARPA's Z-Man project was developing new ways for warfighters to scale vertical obstacles without the use of cumbersome ladders and ropes. They turned to the humble gecko, a lizard known to be able to climb virtually anything, including vertical glass walls, effortlessly. The gecko's toes contain millions of nanoscale hair structures that actually induce polarization of molecules, allowing it to 'stick' to just about any surface. DARPA geniuses found a way to nano-fabricate the same kinds of microstructures and 'Geckskin' was born.

Mark Murphy turned his weapons-designing genius to Geckskin, and with the help of the *Oregon*'s chief armorer, Mike Lavin, improved the Geckskin design, which they named GeckPads. The gloves and boots had worked well in testing, but tonight was their first operational deployment.

Juan placed his left hand against the hull and the glove stuck perfectly. With a practiced flexing of his palm and fingers, the glove instantly released – just like a magnet that could be switched on and off. While they had used climbing magnets in the past, the weight of the magnets and the battery packs made them too heavy and ponderous to use efficiently.

'Looking good, boss,' MacD whispered in his comms.

'Linda, prepare to disengage on my mark.'

'Aye, Chairman.'

Juan reattached his left hand to the hull, followed by his left boot. He lifted himself off the deck and proceeded up, alternating left to right.

MacD was ten feet below him and to his left – just in case Juan happened to fall. The biggest risk they took with the GeckPads was filth. A surface that was slick with grease or oil could clog the hair-like structures. But so far the climb was going well.

'Linda, disengage. Take up your position as we briefed.'

'Good hunting, boys,' Linda said.

On the superstitious *Oregon*, saying *Good luck* was a bad idea.

46

As a result of a weight-lifting injury, Dr Eric Littleton, director of the *Oregon*'s biophysical laboratory, had turned his attention to rock climbing and donated a portion of his annual bonus to install a climbing wall in one of the ship's gyms. Most of the *Oregon* crew were physical fitness enthusiasts, and Littleton's wall became increasingly popular, even as he made it more difficult to climb over the following months.

Juan had been just as caught up in the craze as the rest of the crew. Their weekly wall climbing tournaments were a unique blend of strength and problem-solving at speed, both great disciplines for a fighting crew. Littleton would have been a natural on this mission, but the former WMD inspector was one of the few crew members with neither combat nor undercover experience.

All those hours Juan and MacD had spent on the climbing wall were paying off handsomely tonight, especially when they reached the most curvaceous point of the hull, causing them to feel as if they were almost falling backward, even as they were climbing forward. They both knew that the soft water below could feel as hard as cement from an uncontrolled fall from this height. They took their time picking their routes up the steel hull, careful to avoid the rows of darkened portholes on each deck, just in case someone inside was looking out.

The ocean breeze had picked up considerably in the last two minutes, battering both of them with a sudden burst of cold gale-force winds. Cabrillo pressed himself close to the hull to keep the air from passing beneath him and lifting him up like an airfoil. At the same time he stiffened his body to brace against the windstorm, while keeping his hands and toes firmly planted against the steel.

'You okay down there?' Juan asked in his comms. The bone conduction was a godsend. The rushing wind in his ears roared like a passing freight train, making normal hearing nearly impossible.

'This ain't nothing compared to bein' in a bass boat in a hurricane.'

'And how'd that work out for ya?'

'The climb down the cypress was fine, but we never did find that boat.'

Juan started to laugh, but his stomach dropped as the ship rolled away from beneath him. He looked down to check on MacD, but just as he caught sight of the former Ranger, Juan saw the rogue wave slam into MacD's body, crushing him against the steel hull with a dull thud that Juan could hear even up this high. Worse, MacD's painful groan echoed in his skull as the Gundog's head cracked into the hull.

'Mac!' Juan cried out as MacD's grip gave way and he fell into the churn of the receding wave that had only missed Cabrillo's position by a few feet.

'Sitrep,' Linda called into Juan's comms.

Juan hesitated. He caught sight of MacD, who suddenly appeared on the surface, floating on his back, his face out of the water. He couldn't tell if MacD was conscious or not.

'MacD just got hit by a rogue wave and washed off. I think he's pretty banged up. I'm gonna drop down and get him.' Juan felt the wind suddenly drop and the air calm, as if nothing had happened. He began to loosen his grip to drop back into the water and swim over to his friend.

'Negative, boss,' MacD grunted into his mic. 'Gimme a sec and I'll be right back up with you.' He raised a weak arm and threw a thumbs-up.

'You stay put,' Juan ordered.

'I'm close,' Linda said. 'I can have him on board in less than two minutes. You good with that, MacD?'

'Sounds . . . lovely.'

Juan strained his eyes. He could barely make out the *Gator*'s flat deck emerging from the surface just a hundred yards from MacD.

'Get him back to the *Oregon*. I want Hux to give him a once-over. Keep me posted on his condition.'

'What about you?'

'I'll be fine. When I need you, I'll call you.'

'Aye, aye.'

Juan scanned the top deck one last time before throwing a leg over the railing and hauling himself on board. He quickly pulled the GeckPad gloves and boots off and stashed them in a fire hose box fixed to the bulkhead, then dashed through the doorway leading into the bridge's superstructure.

Without detailed blueprints of the vessel, all Juan could do was imagine how he would lay out a hospital ship. He didn't need to climb the stairs to reach the bridge high above. Not only would it be occupied, but what he needed would be belowdecks anyway. He had to figure out who was actually behind the *Sekhmet* and the mysterious organizations it was connected to. And with any luck he'd find Asher Massala in the search.

He pulled a SureFire Aviator pocket light and flashed thirty-nine lumens of red light into the darkened passageways so as not to draw attention to himself. Over the course of the next thirty minutes, Cabrillo made his way around three decks, each floor covered in well-maintained hospital-grade linoleum.

On the first deck he passed by patient, exam, and treatment rooms and a well-equipped surgery. He noted additional departments of dentistry, radiology, and audiology, and counted two X-ray machines and one open MRI unit. It all fit the images of the oceangoing medical support facility he'd seen on the web. What struck him as odd, though, was that all of the patient beds were completely empty, which accounted for the fact that no nurses or clinicians were on duty.

Where are the patients?

'Juan, do you read me?' Linda Ross asked in his comms.

'Five by five,' Juan whispered.

'Just wanted you to know I gave MacD the once-over. He's got a nasty bump on his forehead, but otherwise I think he's fine. No dilation of the eyes, no headache he'll admit to, and no broken bones, as near as I can tell.'

'That's good to hear. Tell him to take it easy.'

'He wants me to turn the *Gator* around so he can rejoin you.'

'Negative. Unless you have a CAT scan on board I don't know about, you can't be sure if he has any internal injuries.'

'Roger that. He won't be happy.'

'Happy isn't in his job description.'

Juan passed by another room with an electronic lock and peered through the glass window. He pulled gently on the door, but it wouldn't budge.

The lights inside were completely off and Juan's pocket light reflected off the glass, so he couldn't get a good view. As near as he could tell there were treadmills and other gym equipment inside, which seemed oddly out of place on a ship that serviced children with cleft palates and deformed limbs. In all likelihood, it was a recreational facility for the crew, just like on the *Oregon*.

Still uncertain as to what he should be looking for, Juan probed deeper into the belly of the ship. On the second level he had to dodge one average-sized fellow padding sleepily down the hallway toward a public restroom. Juan took the opportunity to stick his head into the man's open office door.

An LCD monitor stood on a disorderly desk. It displayed the *Sekhmet*'s navigational chart. Juan stepped in closer, his ear attuned for the sound of a flushing toilet. The ship was set on a northerly course toward the distant port of Mitsiwa, Eritrea.

Not wanting to press his luck, Juan dashed back out the open door and headed for the stairwell and the next level down. He scanned the locked doors down the hallway, checking the handles to see if any were left open. Each office door sign listed surnames from all over the world, along with academic degrees and job titles.

A shaft of light from a door window illuminated the corridor at the far end of the passageway and soft voices murmured behind it.

Cabrillo began to make his way in that direction when another door suddenly opened behind him. Instinctively, Juan sprinted swift-footed down the nearby staircase and wended his way to the lowest deck. He paused on the landing to see if he'd been discovered, but the female clinician in a lab coat was focused on the tablet in her hand.

Now that he was on the lower level, Juan decided to check it out. The stern area would be the engineering compartments, in which he had no interest. That left mid-ships and the bow to explore. He passed through an unlocked door into what seemed like another clinical area, but an empty cage in one of the exam rooms told him this was a veterinary facility, which was odder still.

His instincts led him farther toward the bow, until he reached a cavernous space. He didn't need to turn on the overheads because the smell told him all that he needed to know. He flashed his red light in the direction where the strongest odor came from and suddenly several pairs of eyes began popping open, some reflecting red, others green or blue. A chorus of low-intensity growling began and Juan killed the light. He backed silently out of the room before one of them barked, his heart racing in his chest.

Unless the *Sekhmet* had converted to a mercy veterinary clinic, these animals were being used for some kind of medical experimentation. He needed to find out what kind of experimentation it was. He suspected the room with the activity on the second level would give him the answer.

Cabrillo worked his way back up the staircase as quiet as a cat and paused at the stairwell, listening for any further activity. The last thing he wanted to do was get caught; he was technically trespassing and could well be arrested for his uninvited intrusion.

Certain the hallway was clear, Juan darted over to the heavy door. He counted three muffled voices. They sounded as if they were on the far side of the room and not approaching the doorway, so he took a chance, crept in close, and peeked through the thick glass.

Inside the well-lit room was a bank of nine raised hospital beds, and in each bed was a fighting-age male attached to an IV and a bag of blood. They all appeared to be in excellent health, some exceptionally so, and all of them were sleeping – or at least had their eyes closed. Several of them were of African descent. He scanned their faces in search of Asher Massala but came up short.

Juan reached for his waterproof digital camera to snap a few photos. The skin on the back of his neck began to tingle, but before he could turn around a heavy hand slammed his skull into the steel door and knocked him out cold.

47

Juan's eyes fluttered open, but his vision was blurred and unfocused. It only took a moment for him to realize that the railroad spike driven through his skull was just a thundering headache. He started to reach up with his hands to wipe the film from his eyes, but his arms were bound tightly to the bed. So were his feet and legs. Trapped.

A jolt of adrenaline surged through his veins as his heart began to race.

'Who are you?' a woman asked.

Juan turned to the sound of the deep feminine voice standing beside him.

Dr Hightower loomed over the hospital bed, risen to her full stature. The late hour and long working day hadn't diminished her striking Nordic good looks, a buxom Valkyrie in a lab coat.

Juan glanced at his bound hands and then back at her with a strained grin.

'Reminds me of my first sorority rush. Good memories. Any chance you're a Tri-Delt?'

'Either your cognitive abilities have been permanently damaged or you're attempting some form of sexualized humor. Let's try this again. Who are you?'

'The name's O'Reilly. Bernardo O'Reilly.' Still groggy, it was the only name Juan could think of on the fly. It was the name of the Charles Bronson character in *The Magnificent*

Seven, which Max had just shown in the *Oregon*'s surround-sound theater a week ago.

'He's lying,' a man's gravelly voice said. He stood behind Juan, completely out of his sight.

'Why do you say he's lying?' Hightower asked.

'Before he answered you, he folded in his lips and his eyes shifted around.'

Juan cursed himself. Those were rookie mistakes. He chalked it up to being knocked unconscious and half groggy. He needed to get on his A-game pronto. He spotted the examination mirror attached to the low ceiling and the image of the man standing behind him framed in the glass – a shaved head and a silver pencil mustache. Juan's nose even caught a whiff of stale cigarette smoke exhaling from the man's putrid lungs.

'Or maybe I folded my lips to wet them because I'm a little dehydrated and I was blinking because I can't see with all of this light blasting into my eyes.'

'His name doesn't matter,' Hightower said to the man beyond Juan's peripheral vision. She looked back at her captive. 'Okay, *Bernardo* . . . What are you doing on my ship?'

Juan's tongue slid along his back teeth, searching for the molar mic, hoping to activate it for a transmission, but it wasn't there.

'Looking for this?' The man stepped into view. He was short and powerfully built, though judging by the deep crow's-feet around his eyes and face, Juan guessed his age at around seventy. He held Juan's molar mic in his nicotine-stained fingers.

'I can't place the accent,' Juan said. '*Ossi*, if I had to

guess, which probably makes you former Stasi. You're built like an infantry *Feldwebel*, but you have the arrogance of an intelligence officer. Your need to show off tells me you never made flag rank. Probably a *Major*, or *Oberst*, at best.'

'*Ganz genau*. You have an excellent ear for language. My specialty was interrogation and counterespionage. You are most fortunate you are not in my custody, Mr Funny Man.'

The former East German security agent named Karl Krasner flashed an oily smile, then turned to Hightower.

'He's very clever. Do you see how he avoids answering any direct question? That alone tells me he has training. CIA most likely, perhaps DIA. His bone-conducting microphone confirms it.' He dropped the molar mic to the linoleum and crushed it beneath his shoe.

'You have a penchant for the dramatic – and the obvious. Leave us, Karl.'

'Yes, Karl. Do leave us,' Juan said.

Karl pointed a stubby finger at Juan. 'Be careful with this one.'

'Thank you for your concern.'

'I'll be just outside if you need me.' Hightower's security man nodded curtly, turned on his heel, and marched away, shutting the door behind him.

'Now, where were we?' Hightower asked. 'Oh, yes. You had just invented a name and no doubt were in the process of concocting some other lie about why you're here. But there's really no point in that, is there?'

'Is this when you threaten to torture me, and so forth, and so on?'

'Why bother? I already know you're a spy, that you have the means to infiltrate my ship without detection, that you carry advanced communication equipment – oh, and that you have a location tracker implanted in your thigh.'

Juan's eyes shifted around the room. He was in one of the clinical exam rooms he'd passed by earlier. He remembered the X-ray machine. Every *Oregon* crew member had a tracing transmitter implanted on them so they could always be found if they became separated or lost.

'Don't worry, the bug is still there.' She held up a wand and ran it over his left leg. It beeped when it found the transmitter. She then raised another handheld device.

'But I zapped your bug with this. It's no longer functioning.' She tossed both instruments onto the empty bed next to Juan. If he still had his tranq pistol in its holster, it would have registered on her metal-detecting wand.

Juan suddenly felt outwitted and out of resources. He strained against his bonds.

Hightower leaned in close, examining him. Her stark green eyes bore into his and her full mouth pursed.

'Nothing witty to say?'

'I'll come up with something.'

'No doubt. Until you do, how about answering my questions?'

'I'll answer your questions if you'll answer mine.'

'You do realize you're putting yourself at great risk, don't you?'

'Why? Because if I learn too much you'll have to kill me?'

'Something like that.'

'You'll probably kill me anyway. But until you do, I'd like my curiosity satisfied.'

'A game of "Show me yours and I'll show you mine"?'

Juan flashed a grin. 'So you *are* a Tri-Delt.'

'What do you want to know?'

'What's your name?'

'Dr Heather Hightower. What's yours?'

'John Sturges,' Juan said without hesitation this time – the director of *The Magnificent Seven*. 'What is the purpose of this ship?'

'The *Sekhmet* is a mercy ship. I run it. We provide medical services to underserved communities.'

'Underserved communities like dogs?'

'I didn't say that was *all* we did.'

'So why experiment on dogs?'

'The short answer is human benefit.'

'And the long one?'

'What we learn from the dogs we can apply safely to humans.'

'"Hightower,"' Juan said. 'I know that name. Are you related to Dr Jonathan Hightower, the famous geneticist?' Years ago Juan had heard the man give a lecture at Caltech. He was old even then.

Hightower's green eyes narrowed as she stiffened.

'Yes.'

Juan had hit a sore spot. He pushed on it.

'His daughter?'

All that was desirable in the stunningly attractive researcher suddenly blanched away in a wash of rage.

'His *wife*, thank you.'

'And all of this' – Juan motioned with his chin – 'is his legacy?'

'It most certainly is not. It's mine. I've created all of it.'

'We're all midgets standing on the shoulders of giants,' Juan said, pressing his advantage.

'I am the giant, Mr Sturges.' Hightower suddenly regained her composure. 'I stood for a brief time on the shoulders of a weak and unimaginative grocery clerk.'

'He was a genius.'

'He was an excellent technician. A brilliant researcher. But he couldn't see beyond his microscope.'

'How so?'

'Jonathan helped pioneer the process for gene editing – CRISPR. Have you heard of it?'

'Of course.'

'But he was afraid to use it. I'm not. He could have been Moses and brought humanity to the promised land, but instead he died in the desert of faithless cowardice.'

'"Faithless" is an interesting choice of words.'

'Nature provided Jonathan the key to controlling human destiny, but his trembling hand refused to take it, so I did. Humans are little more than germs with opposable thumbs and neocortexes. We are the product of millions of years of random mutations, the result of mindless evolution. Yes, a few of us have reached a point of enlightened self-consciousness, but the human race is largely vulgar, broken, and diseased. Rape, murder, war, poverty, pollution, drug abuse, morbid obesity, cancer – the list of self-inflicted wounds is nearly endless. And now we're on the verge of destroying ourselves and the planet.'

Hightower stepped closer.

'It's time to snatch evolution out of the hand of blind and pitiless Nature and take control of our own destiny through science.'

'You mean, transhumanism.'

'Exactly correct, Mr Sturges, or whatever your name is. I see the future and I know how to get there and I have the courage to do whatever needs to be done to bring humanity to its ultimate state of perfection. We won't survive the millions of years it might take to breed out our worst inclinations toward death and destruction. We certainly won't survive overpopulation. I will engineer a new form of human that will not only be physically superior, disease free, and brilliant, but also kinder, connected, and cooperative. It will happen through genetic engineering and the fusion of the human with the technological.'

Hightower stood tall again. 'I'm bringing a revolution to evolution.'

'That explains what you were doing with those men in that clinic with the IV drips. Are they volunteers or unwilling guinea pigs?'

'Does it matter?'

'It does to them.'

'Not anymore. I've seized their minds, wiped their unnecessary memories, and put them under my control.'

'You sound like my friend Max's first ex-wife.'

'Then I condition their bodies according to their genetic potentialities.'

'Who are you working for?'

'For all of humanity, Mr Sturges. And for Nature herself.'

'Aren't your guinea pigs human, too?'

'Of course. But it's upon their sacrifice that I'll build Humanity 2.0, a world of post-humans that will merge with artificial intelligence. A world where every man and woman will be a genius, living in perfected bodies without disease that never age in harmonious communities free of crime and war. Hate and fear will be abolished; love and art will prevail. We'll do away with religion because we will have faith in ourselves and our own abilities to change the world, explore the universe, and transcend death. We will no longer need gods because we will become gods.'

Her eyes had widened, the whites glistening in the glow of the overhead LED lights.

To Juan, she looked insane.

Hightower saw his skepticism.

'It's not your fault that you can't see it, any more than the deaf can't hear the symphony, or the blind see the colors of the sunrise. Nature has not endowed you with the same gifts she has given me – but thanks to me, someday you will be able to see and hear everything beautiful, and you will sing and dance for joy.'

'I hate karaoke and I'm a lousy dancer.'

She pointed at his right leg. 'Especially with that. Why is it missing? Genetic deformity?'

Juan shook his head. 'A Chinese gunboat.'

Hightower glared at him. 'Always joking.'

'What can I say? I'm a frustrated stand-up comedian.' He wiggled his prosthetic. 'Get it? One leg? Stand up? Frustrated? That's quality stuff. Work with me here.'

'So tell me, who sent you?'

'I've been hired to find a man who may be on this ship.'

'Duke Matasi.'

'How did you know?'

Hightower showed Juan a photo of him and Sarai in the Kamiti prison. Juan examined it. He didn't remember seeing a camera.

'Who's the woman?' Hightower asked.

'His sister. She was worried about him. Is Duke on board?'

'No.'

'Where is he?'

'You should worry more about yourself.'

'I would, but it doesn't pay as well. Is he on board?'

'Not anymore.'

Hightower ran a strong hand over the hard ridges of Juan's six-pack abdomen, then traced the length of his well-developed arms. Her touch seemed both clinical and sexual.

'You are an amazing specimen of a man. It's a shame to kill you.'

'It won't hurt my feelings if you let me live.'

'You know too much.'

'To be fair, you volunteered most of it.'

'What should I do with you?'

'Why do I get the feeling you only ask questions you already know the answers to?'

'You're smarter than you look. Another point in your favor.'

'How many points do I need to get out of this bed?'

'More than you have, unfortunately.'

'Can I use a lifeline, Regis?'

Hightower stepped back, as if examining him from a new perspective.

'Frankly, I want your genetic material.'

'Well, I'm kinda shy on my first date. Can we cuddle first?'

She ignored him. He could see that she saw him only as a lab animal now.

'I can harvest your DNA from your corpse, no question about that. You're more valuable dead than alive, at least scientifically speaking. But it would be more interesting to see how I might change the totality of you.'

Juan knew his life was dangling by the last thin thread of Hightower's sanity.

'I'll take door number two.'

'On the other hand, you might not be worth the trouble.'

'You're not the first woman who ever told me that.'

She ignored him again, thinking.

'I recently lost a man. I need a replacement. But he was a fighter. Are you a fighter, Mr Sturges?'

'I can throw a punch.'

'Have you ever killed a man?'

Juan's eyes narrowed. He wouldn't dignify the question with an answer.

Hightower smiled. 'Of course you have.'

'What do you want from me?'

'You'll see.'

48

Hightower led Juan down to the gymnasium that he had seen earlier but didn't enter. Karl followed closely behind with a pistol pointed at Juan's back, just far enough away that Cabrillo couldn't spin around and knock it out of the way before the German could get a shot off. The former Stasi officer was a pro.

Hightower tapped her key card against the electronic lock and it clicked open. As she stepped through the door the automated lights popped on. Juan was close on her heels.

The room was full of fitness equipment including a row of treadmills near a wall of LCD panels. This was the equipment that Cabrillo had barely been able to make out in the dark earlier. What he didn't see before was the six-by-six-meter cage near the back bulkhead. As soon as the lights popped on, a man rose from a cross-legged posture inside the cage to his full height of five feet, eleven inches – two inches shorter than Cabrillo.

He wore only gym shorts.

The man was lean without an ounce of fat on him. Every muscle and sinew flexed as he moved his ropy arms and long, sturdy legs. His shaved, sloping head seemed disproportionately large compared to the width of his narrow shoulders, and his ears stuck out from the side of his skull like school bus stop signs. He began cracking the knuckles on his oversize hands that were the size of rolled quarters.

To Juan he looked like a cross between Nikita Khrushchev and Gollum – with tats. They were primitive prison tattoos as near as Cabrillo could tell, but not Russian ink. He bore no images of the onion-domed Kremlin anywhere, stars on his knees, or epaulets on his shoulders. The largest one was a double-headed eagle clutching semi-auto pistols in its claws atop a shield emblazoned with four Cyrillic C's stretching across his chest. It was the national symbol of Serbia, which identified him as a member of the Serbian mafia.

If Hightower was planning on some sort of a cage fight, Juan wasn't concerned. He had at least thirty pounds of muscle mass over the Slav, along with the strength and aerobic conditioning of a world-class swimmer. Cabrillo was an accomplished martial artist and had years of experience in hand-to-hand fighting. The Slav didn't look like the kind of physical threat that Huxley and Linc had described in their Amazon report.

The Serb's clear gray eyes blinked furiously against the harsh LED lights as Hightower marched toward the cage. Juan and Karl followed.

'Hello, Vlastimir,' Hightower said.

'Hello,' Vlastimir said in a thick Slavic accent. He yawned violently.

'I'm sorry we woke you from your sleep.'

Vlastimir shrugged his narrow shoulders.

'How are you feeling this morning?'

Vlastimir nodded as he rocked from side to side.

'Do you know why you're here?'

The Serb shrugged again.

'Does it matter to you?'

'*Ne.*'

Hightower pointed at Cabrillo. 'I'm going to put this man in the cage with you. I want you to kill him as quickly as you can.'

Vlastimir nodded furiously.

'Good. Any questions?'

Vlastimir shook his head back and forth like he was trying to shake water out of his ears.

Hightower turned toward Juan. She smiled at his discomfort.

'No jokes, Mr Sturges?'

'Did you hear the one about the shark that bit a clown but decided not to eat him because he tasted a little funny?'

'The more scared you are, the worse your jokes become.'

Juan nodded at the cage. 'He doesn't exactly look like humanity perfected to me.'

'Vlastimir possesses a unique genomic sequence that has produced a highly unusual trait that I've managed to both isolate and enhance.'

'I'm assuming the trait you're talking about isn't long division. Or big words.'

'Vlastimir suffers from both speech and cognitive impediments. And yet, has a tested IQ of 147. I'm curious. What's yours?'

'Questionable at the moment.'

Wheels clattered as they crossed the doorway threshold behind them. Juan turned around. A young technician in scrubs pushed a hospital gurney toward them. A body bag lay on top of it, already unzipped. The gurney came to a stop just a few meters away from where Juan was standing.

'That cadaver duffel looks too big for your boy Slim.'

'You're right, it is. Any questions?'

'Suppose I manage to survive this ordeal. What happens next?'

'Then my assumptions about your genetic potential will have proven correct. You will then be folded into my conditioning program, beginning with stripping your mind.'

'In other words, "Heads I win, tails you lose."'

'More like, heads I win, tails you won't remember.'

'Touché.' Juan glanced over at Karl standing a discreet distance away, his pistol pointed at Juan's chest.

Cabrillo shrugged. The digital clock on the wall read 4:32 a.m. Sunrise would be in less than ninety minutes.

'Well, like my grandfather always said, if you eat a cat first thing in the morning, that'll probably be the worst thing you'll do all day. So let's do this.'

Hightower reached for the cage door, but stopped.

Vlastimir stomped over to the rear of the cage, his gray eyes darkening as they lasered on Cabrillo.

'Not the face, Vlastimir,' Hightower said. 'It's too pretty to break. And don't blind him.'

Karl pointed his gun at Cabrillo's prosthetic. 'In case you were wondering, I removed the small caliber pistol, plastic explosive, lock picks, and other devices stored inside of your leg. Very clever, I must say.'

Hightower opened the cage door.

'Mr Sturges, it's time to meet your destiny.'

*

Before the cage door could shut, Vlastimir was on Cabrillo. He shot across the distance so quickly Juan could scarcely believe it. The Slav's flying jump kick slammed into Juan like a runaway truck, crashing him against the cage.

Juan's thundering headache exploded into the red zone as his skull crashed into the steel bars. Hot white light exploded in his eyes. He sensed more than saw Vlastimir stepping back before unleashing a furious assault with his hands in a blur of blinding speed.

Shocked by the assault, Cabrillo's addled brain recalled an old formula from his engineering days. *Force equals mass times velocity.* The Slav's oversize knuckles jackhammered into his rib cage with the crushing energy of a pair of reciprocating five-pound mauls.

Juan covered up as best he could, twisting to blunt the speeding fists with his arms. It hardly did any good. Twist and cover as he might, Vlastimir's flashing punches found their marks as he picked his shots seemingly at the speed of light.

Suddenly, Juan felt one of his ribs crack. The pain shot through him like an electric shock. A second blow followed right after it, and then a third. The Slav knew he'd found his target and pressed home his attack.

Juan's lizard brain kicked into high gear. If he didn't do something quickly, he was going to die.

Cabrillo charged forward into the flurry of punches, his arms spread wide and his hands crossed in front of his face like the bow of a warship. The speed and pain of the still pummeling fists felt like he was pushing his way through a wood chipper. The only good thing about already being beaten half to death by Vlastimir's meat-tenderizing paws was that the adrenaline dump into his bloodstream and damaged nerves blunted the agony. Bulling forward into the punches took away the Slav's mechanical advantage, and the blows began glancing off of Juan's forearms and elbows.

Juan pressed in deeper, throwing Vlastimir off guard. The smaller man began bicycling backward and suddenly found himself off balance. He took his eyes off Juan long enough that Juan saw his chance. One of the Slav's long bare feet was suddenly forward and Juan stomped on the high pyramid of delicate bones in his midfoot. Cabrillo heard them snap under his heel like a pile of brittle twigs crunching beneath a heavy boot on an autumn hiking trail.

Vlastimir didn't even notice.

But as Juan lunged, Vlastimir stepped farther back, and when he put his weight on the crushed foot it gave way and he went down.

Juan dove headfirst, aiming his skull at the soft tissues of the man's face. A sickening crack and a gout of blood told Juan he'd hit his mark as the cartilage in Vlastimir's nose exploded.

But Juan didn't stop. He kept hammering the Slav with his forehead, battering the man's skull into the steel floor, while pinning his stunned arms. Seized by a berserker's mad fury, Juan kept bashing Vlastimir's face with his skull until the Slav stopped moving.

Cabrillo glanced at the man beneath him. With the fight suddenly over, his rage instantly abated. He put a hand on the broken man's throat to feel for his pulse.

'He's still alive,' Juan said.

'Finish him,' Karl said. 'It's a fight to the death.'

Juan rolled off of the tattooed fighter, took a deep breath, and climbed to his feet. He had to hold on to the cage bars to keep from doubling over and his headache was now a migraine inside of a supernova of intracranial misery.

But at least he was alive.

'Better get your man a doctor,' Juan said.

'You need to kill him – or I'll kill you!' Karl said, pointing the pistol through the bars.

'I won't hit a man after he's out.'

Karl raised his weapon to fire.

'Put that away,' Hightower ordered. She turned to the orderly. 'After we take Mr Sturges to the infirmary, come back and take Vlastimir down to the kennels for the morning feeding. The dogs will be hungry.'

'Yes, Doctor.'

Karl laughed. 'They love fresh meat.' He waved his pistol at Cabrillo. 'Come on, Mr Funny Man. Time to take a ride.'

49

Juan was grateful for the ride on the gurney. The LED lights in the passageway passed overhead as they made their way down the corridor. Juan didn't think he could've walked ten feet in his current condition and his brains felt like bruised cottage cheese inside of a cracked mason jar.

Dr Hightower walked beside him, Karl was in front, and the orderly was pushing the gurney from behind.

Juan thought he heard three short *pffft*s spit in the air. He knew he hadn't imagined it when he saw Hightower and Karl crumble to the deck, and felt the orderly behind him fall away, crashing the gurney into the bulkhead.

A smiling upside-down face suddenly loomed just above Juan's.

'Did ya miss me?' MacD asked.

'Like my *abuelita*'s chile rellenos.'

'We need to skedaddle, *vite-vite*.'

'Gotta grab the security camera footage first.' Juan tried raising himself up on one elbow with a groan. 'The office is on the deck just above us.'

MacD pulled a flash drive out of his pocket. 'Already snagged it.'

Cabrillo stood unsteadily by the gurney, his bruised and broken ribs burning like fire, his skull gripped in a hydraulic press on full crush.

MacD stepped close to Juan, who threw an arm around the Cajun's shoulders for support.

'Did I ever tell you why I lost the three-legged race at the Breaux Bridge Crawfish Festival?'

'I'm betting it involved a pretty girl and bottle of hooch.'

'Twins, actually, and a pitcher of Hurricanes. *Allons!*'

Juan winced as he laughed as the two men hobbled for the main deck. They needed to get clear of the ship before sunrise. The two of them passed three more crew members splayed out on the deck, put down earlier by MacD's tranq pistol.

'So much for stealth,' Juan whispered. 'No style points for you.'

'I was in a hurry.'

As they exited the final door for the main deck they nearly crashed into one of the lookouts walking a circuit. Before the guard could shout, MacD fired his last sleeper pellet into the man's throat, dropping him to the steel deck with a thud.

MacD delivered Juan to the railing. 'You have your GeckPads?'

Juan nodded toward the fire hose box where he had stashed them. 'Just over there – but there's no way I can make the climb.'

'Then we only have one option.' MacD called over to Linda. 'We're here.'

Juan was already lifting his good leg over the steel wire when he saw the *Gator* rise to the surface forty meters away.

'If you suddenly hear a splash and the agonizing scream

of an eleven-year-old girl, that's just me,' Cabrillo said. 'Here goes nothin'.'

He took a deep breath, clenched his teeth against the pain, and jumped.

Dr Hightower startled awake with the pungent stab of ammonia in her nostrils.

'Get that away from me,' she barked as she swatted away the nurse's hand holding the smelling salts. The tall Nigerian woman had just come on duty moments earlier and discovered the three of them knocked out. A quick examination showed they were not injured, only unconscious. She called for medical assistance immediately.

Hightower's eyes watered and her head was still foggy. Two other medical technicians had just applied the smelling salts to Krasner and the orderly.

'What happened?' Hightower asked.

'Some kind of tranquilizer,' the former Stasi operative said, climbing to his feet. 'Very fast acting. Impressive.' He snatched the radio off his hip and barked orders in German.

Off Hightower's look he explained, 'I've ordered a security sweep of the entire ship. First, for Sturges – and whoever helped him. Second, for bugs they undoubtedly dropped along the way.'

The nurse who administered the salts helped Hightower to her feet.

'Sturges is long gone, you can bet on it,' Hightower said. She rubbed a large bump on the side of her head where she struck the deck in her fall.

'We should get you checked out,' the nurse offered.

Hightower ignored her. She told Krasner, 'Be sure to check the security cameras to see who else we're dealing with.'

'I was just about to order it.'

Hightower looked at her watch. They'd been out for twenty minutes or so. She swore bitterly to herself.

'I'll be in my office. Report back to me what you find.' She yanked her arm out of the nurse's supportive grip. 'I'm fine. Thank you. Report to your station for duty.' She turned to the others. 'All of you.'

'Yes, Dr Hightower.'

Moments later, Hightower stormed into her office. She grabbed a bottled water out of her mini fridge and washed a couple of aspirin down before she snagged up the intercom phone. She called the bridge. The officer of the day, a Japanese national, answered.

'Murakami.'

'Initiate emergency plan Alpha. Inform Captain Hansson immediately.'

'Aye, ma'am.'

Hightower punched another button and rang up the galley. 'A pot of black coffee to my office, ASAP.' She added, 'Please,' without emotion. She had learned that such inane social conventions were important to lesser people. No matter. She fed her lab rats cheese, too.

What Hightower really wanted to do was scream. She was always in control, always in charge. No one dared question her competencies because her achievements were patently obvious for all to see. But now this Sturges intruder had upended everything. His rescuer even had the gall to put her down like a stray cat.

Her face reddened with shame at the thought of the Nigerian nurse discovering her helpless body splayed out on the deck, exposed and vulnerable. Her intercom rang.

'Captain Hansson here. Why was Alpha initiated?'

Hightower didn't care for his gruff manner. She excused it because he had just been woken up.

'We've had a security breach. Emergency plan Alpha is the protocol. Is there a problem on your end?'

'No, no problem. Murakami is about to initiate the course change and my chief engineer will take care of the rest.' Hansson was referring to all of the measures the *Sekhmet* would use to conceal her identity and location, beginning with stopping the broadcast of the ship's automatic identification system (AIS) signal. According to international maritime law, every vessel over three hundred gross tons was required to issue an AIS broadcast for the primary purpose of collision avoidance and maritime safety.

They would also stay far away from Eritrea, at least for now.

'Very good,' Hightower said. 'I want a review of the tactical situation in my office in fifteen minutes, including a summary of the radar records for the last twenty-four hours.'

'I heard you were attacked. How badly are you injured?'

Hightower felt her face flush again. Gossip traveled faster than the speed of light on the boat. She wondered if she was now the subject of ridicule among the crew. She tamped it down.

'No injuries. Just a short nap.'

'See you in fifteen.'

Hightower added, 'Thank you for asking,' but Hansson had already hung up. With the phone still in her hand, the intercom rang again.

'Sat call for you on line three, Dr Hightower.'

Hightower punched the button. Had Salan already gotten word?

'Hightower.'

'Hello, Dr Hightower. It's Dr Jing Yanwen.' Her voice reverberated through the static of a bad connection.

'Jing, yes, of course. How are things in the Amazon?'

'Not well, I'm afraid.' She went on to explain the casualties, including the death of the two mercenary guardians, Samson and Mat. Yanwen's reverberating voice was nearly impossible to fully understand. Another annoyance.

'Are you and Schweers okay?'

'Yes, we're fine. We're about to hike out out out out out . . .' Yanwen's transmission ended on that last echoing word. Hightower cursed the technology as she slammed the phone back into its cradle. It rang again almost immediately.

'Sorry, Dr Hightower. Satellite problems, I suppose,' Yanwen said. Her voice was clearer now and no longer distorted.

'Did you get our samples?'

'Yes, absolutely.'

'And they are secured and ready for transport?'

'One hundred percent. And I should tell you . . .'

'Tell me what?'

'There was an intruder, a doctor named Izidoro. She claimed to be treating the Aboriginals.'

'Treating them? How do you mean?' Hightower fought

to choke down the twin emotions of rage and terror. Rage at Yanwen's incompetent leadership, fear that the pristine DNA samples she had hoped for had been contaminated.

'According to her, she hadn't administered any pharmaceuticals or other gene-altering interventions. Bandages, sutures, tooth extractions – that sort of thing. I firmly believe the Poison Arrow specimens remain one hundred percent pure. It's all in my notes.'

'Where is Dr Izidoro now?'

Yanwen paused, her voice cracking. 'Risto dealt with her.'

'Put Risto on the line.'

Hightower heard Yanwen say, 'She wants to talk to you,' in a faint voice away from the phone. A few moments later, Risto answered. He had to step away from his female charges.

'Risto.'

'What happened?'

'Ambushed. Must have been several men, probably Brazilian Army.'

'Including the doctor?'

'No. That was a fluke. I've taken care of her.'

'How are Yanwen and Schweers holding up?'

'Skittish, tired. Complaining.'

'They're weak.'

'I won't be surprised if the German quits on you. Yanwen, too.'

'The samples are safe?'

'Yes.'

'Can you transport them?'

'The women?'

'The samples.' *You idiot*, she wanted to add.

'Of course.'

'Then kill the women, and take the samples to your safe house. We can't leave any loose ends – and certainly no evidence.'

'Understood.'

'Call me when you reach Brisbane.'

'Will do.'

Hightower ended the call as a soft knock tapped on her door.

'Enter.'

A server from the galley brought in a pot of coffee and a tray with a thick ceramic mug, along with a keto-friendly plate of scrambled eggs and bacon.

Hightower's mouth watered as the tray was set on her desk. She dismissed the server with a curt nod and a cursory thank-you and dug in, not realizing how hungry she was. For her, food was merely fuel.

She would need every calorie if she hoped to prevail in her call to Salan.

50

On Board the Oregon

Juan's eyesight was partially blocked by the cage cradling his head. Not that there was anything to look at except the smooth curved surface immediately above him. The cramped space echoed with the whirring, pulsing, and thunking noises of the magnetic resonance imaging machine as electronic currents alternated through its powerful coil-wired magnet.

'Almost done. You're doing great.' Dr Huxley's voice echoed in the overhead speaker inside the MRI chamber. 'Remember to hold still.'

Cabrillo wanted to crack a joke, but that required moving his jaw and he really didn't want to have to repeat the scan, so he kept his mouth shut. His undercover scrubs had been cut away and now he wore a hospital gown. His carbon-fiber combat leg contained a few ferrous components, so it had been removed back in the examination room. Otherwise his leg would have gone shooting through the air like a hurled spear when it got too close to the MRI's powerful magnet.

'Done,' she said. A moment later the table Cabrillo lay upon slid out from the MRI.

Huxley stepped from the glass booth and approached Juan's side. He could smell the bright scent of her freshly

337

laundered lab coat and her dark hair was pulled into its customary ponytail. But it was Huxley's 'concerned doctor' face that most caught his attention.

'What's the verdict, Doc?' Juan asked with labored breath.

'You *look* like you fell down the elevator shaft at the Burj Khalifa. Twice. But the MRI tells a different story. You're definitely suffering a mild concussion. I was expecting a subdural hematoma or some other intracranial hemorrhage, but your scan is clear. How is that even possible?'

'Clean living.'

Huxley cocked an eyebrow. 'Hardly. Remember, I'm the one who sutures up all of your wounds.'

'Which is why I send you a spiral-cut honey ham every Easter.'

'The MRI has confirmed my initial examination. No serious damage to the brain, no internal bleeding, no significant injuries to organs or tissues. That's all good news. But besides the concussion, you've sustained two clearly fractured ribs, three more cracked ribs, multiple contusions and edemas. In my professional opinion, it looks like you decided to pick a fight with a silverback gorilla and lost.'

'Sounds like I'm good to go then. I need to get to the bridge –'

Juan started to raise himself up, but winced with pain. Huxley gently pushed him back down.

'Take it easy there, fella. You're not going anywhere. Those cracked ribs are going to give you fits for the next six weeks or so.'

'I can't be offline for six weeks. Not even six hours,' Juan insisted. 'What can you do to fix me up?'

'Not much. What you require most is rest – and a lot of ice. We need to get your swelling down and the rest will help your brain and give you the energy you need for those ribs to heal on their own.'

'Time isn't a luxury I can afford right now. We've got to find the *Sekhmet* and board her.'

Juan began sitting up again, but Huxley pressed against his shoulders. Though he was far stronger than she was, the sharp pain in his side gave her the advantage. He lay back down.

'I get it, I really do,' Huxley said. 'But you're in no shape to do much of anything. I can give you some injections for long-lasting pain relief for the nerves around your ribs – but I'll only do it if you promise to limit your activities to an absolute minimum.'

'What about compression bandages?'

'No longer the standard protocol. The biggest danger you face is not breathing fully and that can lead to a bad case of pneumonia. Breathing's gonna hurt like the Denver loss to San Francisco at Super Bowl XXIV. But you've got to do it.'

'I promise to not stop breathing.'

'You know what I mean, smarty-pants. How's the headache?'

'What headache?' Juan said. Technically, he still had one. It was much better since Huxley gave him some hard-core pain meds, but his head still throbbed. At least the discomfort was manageable now.

'Didn't your mama ever tell you that lying is a sin, Mr Cabrillo?'

'How's MacD?'

'Bruised, mostly. No internal injuries. He's already up and moving. I've cleared him for duty starting tomorrow.'

'I ordered Linda to return him to the *Oregon* after that rogue wave took him out.'

'MacD decided to, eh, *modify* your order based on his improved medical condition and a "dynamic tactical environment."'

'That's just Ranger-talk for disobeying my command.'

'But Linda agreed with him. And I say good on them.'

'They'll be lucky if I don't keelhaul them.'

'How about sending them a couple of Christmas fruit-cakes and calling it even?'

Juan's face soured. 'Same punishment, as far as I'm concerned.'

'Before I forget, I'm going to have to replace your tracking device sometime soon. It got fried after I ran you through the MRI. Sorry about that.'

'No worries. It's already dead. Hightower found it and zapped it.'

'Let's get you rested up before we do the swap.'

Juan reached out and took Hux's hand.

'I'm truly sorry about your friend Dr Izidoro.'

Huxley nodded, fighting back tears. She took a deep breath and shook it off.

'Yeah. That was rough.'

'I promise we'll get to the bottom of it.'

Huxley nodded again. She knew Juan always kept his word. But it was time to change the subject. She would discuss her findings from the blood and other samples she took from the goon that Tiny had killed in the Amazon when Cabrillo was feeling better.

'Let's get you to the training room and into some ice. My tyrant of a boss says I've got to get you back in the game ASAP. Stay put while I get you a wheelchair.'

'Will do.'

Juan was glad to lie still and just breathe, painful as it was. He watched her sprint out the door and down the hallway.

In all the years he'd known Julia Huxley, he'd never seen her get even close to crying. His jaw clenched. He'd find a way to get justice for Hux and her murdered friend no matter what it took.

'Tell me more about this fight you got into,' Huxley said. She stood next to a large stainless steel tub full of ice and Cabrillo sat in the middle of it. It was the same kind of ice bath setup that pro athletes used for cryogenic therapy. The ice bath motor hummed as it circulated the near-freezing water.

'It would have made a lousy pay-per-view.' Cabrillo's teeth chattered from the cold. 'The guy was fast – supernaturally quick. Like his fast-twitch muscles were on hyperdrive.'

'Any unusual features?'

'Besides his Serbian mafia tats? He was sinewy, not an ounce of fat. His hands, maybe? They seemed a little oversize – they certainly hit like they were – and his knuckles were as hard as cinder block. He got his fight on as soon as I stepped into the cage. I don't remember a whole lot after that. Why?'

'The lab analysis I had performed on blood and tissue samples from the goon Tiny killed in the Amazon came back. It showed exceptionally high levels of testosterone, adrenaline, and endorphins. I suspect he'd undergone some kind of gene therapy, probably by manipulating stem cells.'

'You're dead on target, Doc. That's exactly the same domain Hightower told me she was dabbling in.'

'Pillow talk, Chairman?' Hux asked with a wink. Cabrillo was famously irresistible to most women. She was hardly the only female on board the *Oregon* who had considered a dalliance with the dashing ship's captain. But in Hux's case, she valued his friendship and their working relationship more than any momentary bedroom pleasures she might experience with him.

'The only reason that woman would come at me with a pillow would be to smother me,' Cabrillo said. 'She assumed I would either be killed or put under her mind control regimen, so she felt comfortable bragging about her achievements.'

'Can you describe what she's doing, exactly?'

'She told me she's using CRISPR to alter her subjects genetically. The only ones I saw were fighting-age males, including the one who clocked me good. She's a fully committed transhumanist – a Dr Mengele birthing the Age of Aquarius. Her ship is an entire laboratory for her experiments.'

'Your description fits with the subjects we encountered in the Amazon. Super strong, super fast, hyper focused, fearless. They must have been part of Hightower's program as well. We've got to find that ship and stop her.'

'That's the plan, soon as you let me out of this ice cream maker.'

Huxley checked her watch. 'Ten more minutes should do it.'

'I'm not sure if this is good therapeutic practice or an experiment in cryogenics.'

'Maybe this will alleviate your discomfort,' Maurice said in his cultured English accent.

Juan nearly leaped out of the tub, startled by his sudden appearance.

'Jumpin' Jehoshaphat, man. How do you do that? Are you part ghost?'

Maurice flashed a patient smile. The *Oregon*'s chief steward lifted the lid of the filigreed silver serving tray in his hand, displaying a thick oven mitt that stood on end. It seemed to wave at Cabrillo.

'Odd, that,' Juan said through bluing lips.

'It's a tea cozy of the ad hoc variety, lamentably.'

Maurice raised the oven mitt and revealed a double-walled glass espresso mug holding a steaming reddish beverage.

'*Vruca rakija,*' Maurice said. 'Hot Serbian brandy to warm your innards, Captain.'

Juan began reaching for the mug. He didn't bother asking Maurice how he knew he would be down here shivering in an ice tub or how he managed to time his arrival perfectly. The chief steward was better at hoovering up information out of thin air than a Stanley shop vac.

'Plum?' Juan asked as he lifted the hot glass with both trembling hands.

'Naturally. An excellent slivovitz home-brewed by one of our gifted sous-chefs.'

Juan downed the high-octane alcohol in a single throw, like a thirsty Yugoslavian *partizanski* on the run from Nazi partisan hunters. His eyes shut with rapture as the warm booze washed down his throat and flushed his guts with tingling heat.

'You're a lifesaver, Maurice.'

'Hardly, sir. Shall I get you another?'

'If it's not too much trouble.'

'Not at all, sir. Another will be arriving momentarily.'

'Too bad one of us is still on the clock,' Hux said with a playful pout.

She and Maurice had long shared a special affection for each other. The elderly Englishman treated her with the utmost respect tinged with the concern of a wise and kindly grandfather. She, in turn, held him in the highest regard for his old-world manners and superlative professionalism. He was practically the only crewman who never complained about his annual physical and kept himself in top condition – better, in fact, than most men half his age.

Maurice grinned. 'Not to worry, my dear doctor. Your medical license is safe with me. A delightfully warm "not toddy" is coming your way as well.'

51

On Board the Cloud Fortune

Salan stood on the bridgewing watching the burnt-orange sun rising in the slate-gray east. A chill wind rippled through his beard and mussed his hair.

'Red sky at morning . . .' he whispered to himself before taking another sip of tea. The call from Hightower was deeply disturbing. He had rightly discerned that the man sniffing around the Kamiti prison would follow the bread crumbs Hightower had carelessly left in her wake. He had also demanded she increase her security. He would deal with that incompetent *teuton* Krasner later.

There was no doubt in his mind that the man who identified himself as John Sturges – an alias, certainly – was an operator and connected with a technologically sophisticated organization. That idiot prison warden claimed Sturges was an American. He was probably right. Salan had sent Sturges's photo through his intelligence network of underworld contacts. His Israeli associates, the Sons of Jacob, came back with a photo that roughly matched Sturges sitting in the back of a cab. The cabbie described him as an American on a business trip to Ashdod.

Those two pieces of information alone confirmed

Salan's belief that Sturges was CIA or some other intelligence asset, as was the woman with him.

Lucky for Hightower, Sturges wasn't leading an assassination squad onto the *Sekhmet*, but next time he could be. Stealing the *Sekhmet*'s security drive was a standard operating procedure for a professional; so was leaving behind several military-grade listening devices. At least Krasner's team was capable of detecting and destroying those.

Salan tugged on his beard, thinking. Hightower was smart to initiate the emergency plan; they had to assume Sturges knew where she was headed. The *Sekhmet* had begun broadcasting a fake automatic identification signal and initiated other electronic countersurveillance measures. Unless Sturges was extremely lucky, the *Sekhmet* would soon be well hidden in a half million square kilometers of desolate ocean far from the Eritrean coastline.

Hightower was even smarter to plant a tracking device on Sturges. After she removed the tracker she found in the man's thigh, she replaced it with one of her own, a nearly identical model.

Hightower's technician couldn't explain why the signal didn't pick up until an hour later and shortly thereafter began moving at over five hundred kilometers per hour.

But Salan had seen it all quite clearly in his mind.

The Americans must have used a submarine to get close to the *Sekhmet* and also to get away, which explained why Hightower's radar hadn't picked up any kind of vessel within close proximity before and after the attack.

They must also have deployed a helicopter. According to Hightower, the American had been badly beaten by her latest genetic experiment, which might have necessitated a medical airlift. The only aircraft capable of an airlift at sea was a helicopter, hence the high rate of speed.

A brilliant operation by the Americans, Salan concluded. He checked his watch. Time to make a decision.

Was it possible that Sturges had been able to determine the location of the *Cloud Fortune*? His possession of the hypersonic missile?

No, it wasn't possible, or at least highly unlikely. There was nothing to directly connect his operation with Hightower's. The Americans claimed they had been looking for Duke Matasi, the lost son of an English mother.

Were they lying about that as well? No, why would they? What else would Sturges and his partner have been looking for at the Kamiti prison? Or for that matter, what was their interest in the man? He'd been a low-level street thug. Of what possible value would he be to them?

Whatever the reason for their search for Duke Matasi, it had led Sturges to Hightower. But nothing on Hightower's ship pointed at Salan.

True, Matasi was at Nine Saints now, fully into his next training cycle. But Matasi had no connection with the hypersonic missile operation. Therefore, Salan concluded, Sturges had nothing to do with it, either.

Hightower's IT expert reported that the *Sekhmet*'s mainframe had not been compromised, not that any information about his operation would have been contained on it. This was another confirmation that the *Cloud Fortune* and its invaluable cargo was safe.

But Salan's mission was stalled. His blood pressure ticked up a couple of beats thinking about the worst-case scenarios. He still hadn't received the go-ahead signal from the Iranian Quds Force operatives in Yemen, so he was stuck at sea for the time being. He felt like a fat duck on a still pond and somewhere out there was an unknown hunter with a loaded rifle aimed in his direction.

Salan knew he could play it safe and trust the *Sekhmet*'s emergency plans. He also put his faith in the extreme unlikelihood that the Americans knew anything about his operation. And even if they did, it would be nearly impossible for them to find the missile in time to prevent the sinking of the American aircraft carrier.

But Salan had never played defense in his entire career. If Sturges was hell-bent on finding Duke Matasi, he might track him all the way to Nine Saints – a catastrophic possibility that was now hanging over his head like the sword of Damocles.

'*L'audace, l'audace, toujours l'audace!*' was Salan's life's motto and the only tattoo on his body. No, he had to go on offense. He would find the Americans, identify their operation, and destroy them all.

An hour later, Salan stormed onto the bridge, barking '*Ford* – status' as he marched over to the radar station. He leaned on the operator's chair, looking over his shoulder at the screen.

The *Cloud Fortune*'s AIS transponder was integrated into the operator's radar display. Every six minutes, every AIS-equipped civilian vessel broadcast its self-identified name, call sign, type of cargo, destination, and ETA, among other stats.

But military vessels like the *Ford* broadcast a specialized

Warship AIS with minimized information that could be altered or turned off according to operational requirements. In this case, the *Ford*'s W-AIS was switched on because it was traversing a heavily trafficked sea-lane.

'Still holding a steady Red Sea course some eight hundred kilometers from the launch site,' the technician said.

'From now on I want updates on the *Ford* every thirty minutes. Contact me immediately if there are course changes.'

'Yes, sir.'

'And the *Norego Sunrise*?'

'Also holding steady.'

Besides its GPS location, the *Norego Sunrise*'s civilian AIS transponder self-reported the vessel as a one-hundred-eighty-meter break-bulk carrier freighting machine tools and industrial equipment to Jeddah, Saudi Arabia.

'And Sturges?' Salan asked. Hightower's tracker on Sturges had stopped transmitting for some unknown reason.

'Target Sturges is still presumed on board.'

'How far out is our helicopter?' Salan asked.

'ETA twenty-eight minutes.'

'Very good. Call me immediately if anything changes.'

'Yes, sir.'

Salan bolted for the door, heading for the lower decks.

No telling how long Sturges would remain on board that vessel. He wouldn't be surprised if the *Norego Sunrise* served as his mobile base of operations. There had been rumors for years of such a vessel. He'd always written them off as the fantasies of armchair sailors and drunken wharf rats. Soon he would know the truth, one way or the other.

He pulled out his radio and called his squad's number two as he descended the stairs.

'Find Diallo and bring him to the aft deck.'

'Yes, sir.'

'And bring your medical kit.'

Salan stood toe-to-toe with Diallo and stared into his unblinking eyes. The Senegalese was the youngest of the men on this mission, but well trained and perfectly conditioned both physically and mentally. He had performed as expected in the mission to steal the hypersonic missile. Salan had no doubt the young mercenary would serve his next purpose equally well.

The Senegalese was dressed as Salan had commanded, wearing only a pair of worn sneakers, boxer shorts, and a ragged T-shirt, along with a broken-down, oil-stained life vest that fit him poorly.

The wiry man wore a patchy beard that perpetually looked like it was just a few days old. Unfortunately for Diallo, his inability to grow a proper beard was what made him especially valuable for today's assignment.

'Do you understand the mission as I have explained it to you?'

'Yes, sir.'

'It will be extraordinarily difficult and excruciating. Are you prepared for this?'

'Yes, sir. Gladly and with pride.'

Salan studied Diallo's eyes. He was telling the truth. Hightower's mental conditioning had proven flawless. 'Excellent. Don't fail me.'

'No, sir.'

Salan stepped back and turned to his number two, a man named Moulin, an old comrade from the 1st Marine Infantry Parachute Regiment. Like all of Salan's trusted subordinates, Moulin had only been partly physically conditioned by Hightower so that he could keep up with the super mercs under his command. But Moulin had not been mentally conditioned at all. Salan didn't trust Hightower to not implant some kind of programming into his men that would subvert their loyalty to him.

Salan had gathered all of the necessary equipment and Moulin had already been briefed and came prepared as well. Salan nodded toward Moulin, indicating that his subordinate should begin his work.

The former combat medic pulled out a vial and a syringe, filling the needle with the proper amount of medication. He cleaned the crook of Diallo's arm with an alcohol wipe, rubbed a large vein until it became even larger, then administered the drug.

Within moments Diallo's eyes rolled into the back of his head and his legs buckled. Salan and Moulin let him fall to the deck. Cracking his skull on the steel plate broke the skin on Diallo's skull, initiating bleeding and raising a huge welt. This only added to the effect they were after. Moulin fetched two more vials out of his medical kit and filled the syringes with their contents.

Salan crossed over to a small propane tank and the attached flamethrower. His radio crackled with the radarman's voice.

'The helicopter is six minutes out.'

'Inform them we will be ready.'

Moulin inserted the second needle into Diallo's arm. 'A

diuretic, along with cortisone,' he explained as he drained the syringe. Within minutes, the Senegalese would be completely dehydrated.

Moulin pulled out the third vial and repeated the action. 'For pain.'

'Of course. We're not animals,' Salan said. More important, he didn't want the pain to rouse Diallo from his enforced slumber.

After Moulin finished he stood and stepped away from the prone body.

Salan turned the valve on the propane tank and punched the igniter button on the torch. A blue flame burst into life. He picked up the tank and the torch and marched over to Diallo's helpless form.

Salan heard the helicopter blades thundering in the distance. The clock was ticking. He pulled the torch's trigger and flames roared out of the cylindrical mouth. He walked the flames up and down the left side of Diallo's body, burning the skin until it blistered and bled, then blackened and burst like a wiener held over a campfire too long.

Diallo's underwear caught fire. Salan released the trigger grip and stepped back so Moulin could kneel down and pat the flames out. Salan thought about adding more burns to the Senegalese's body, but enough damage had been done. Diallo's mental training was such that he would have been able to override his pain response to the fire had he remained awake, but there was no point in making the damage any worse. If he burned him too badly he would die too soon. His body was likely already in shock. The Senegalese would never awaken from the comatose condition that Moulin's first injection had initiated.

Knocking him out wasn't a matter of mercy so much as operational security.

The helicopter roared overhead and its rescue sling lowered. Battered by the rotor wash, Moulin and Salan fitted the sling over Diallo's inert frame and signaled for the helicopter to lift him up. Moments later the chopper secured the unconscious Senegalese and flew to its destination.

52

On Board the Oregon

Juan shifted uneasily in the 'Kirk Chair,' his aching ribs giving him fits despite Hux's anesthetic injections. To hide his bruising and to maximize his comfort, Juan wore an orange and black Caltech sweatshirt and matching joggers featuring his beloved bucktoothed beaver mascot, along with cushy Saucony running shoes and a pair of Ray-Ban aviator sunglasses.

'Still no sign of the *Sekhmet*?' Cabrillo asked.

Linda Ross was at the radar station. 'No, sir. None.'

Juan couldn't believe it. He thought for sure they would have found her by now. He had seen the *Sekhmet*'s course and speed on her navigational display when he was on board her. The floating laboratory posing as a mercy ship was supposed to be headed for the port of Mitsiwa in Eritrea.

But on the medevac flight from the *Gator* to the *Oregon*, MacD had reported an intriguing bit of information he'd collected when searching the *Sekhmet*.

'I overheard two of the techs talking behind closed doors. One of them said in a very proper English accent, and I quote, "I can't wait until we get these muppets to Nine Saints."'

'I assume by "muppets" he meant the men Hightower

354

is conditioning,' Juan said over the roar of the AW's engines and his own blinding headache. 'But what is "Nine Saints"? A location? A facility?'

'Heck if I know.'

Before landing back on the *Oregon*, MacD radioed ahead with the intel he and Juan had collected. Thanks to their research wizardry, Stone and Murphy had managed to connect all of the dots just before Juan slid into the MRI machine. Over Hux's objection, Juan had a quick conference call with them on the ship's intercom while lying on the table.

'Nine Saints is the site of one of the oldest monasteries in all of Africa. It's located approximately 130 nautical miles southwest of Mitsiwa,' Murph had dutifully reported.

Stoney added, 'We assume *Sekhmet* will dock in Mitsiwa and transport their human cargo to the monastery either overland or by flight. We've checked commercially available satellite imagery over that area. It looks like the ruins of an ancient monastery.'

'Why would Hightower transfer her cyborgs there?' Juan asked.

'That satellite information is over four years old and right now that's our only source. It's a very remote region of a very remote country. The Eritrean government has locked that place down since it took over in '93, and our intelligence community has few assets on the ground —'

'— But we're working on a back door we have with the databanks at the National Reconnaissance Office,' Murph interrupted. 'The NRO will have something more up to date. My guess is that Nine Saints is more than what it now appears to be.'

But so far, they'd come up empty. No NRO satellites had been tasked specifically over the forlorn and empty corner of the impoverished authoritarian state. But at least one Keyhole-11 'Crystal' satellite was due to pass over the region within the next three hours.

The monastery angle might have been a miss, but the port of Mitsiwa was still a solid lead. Juan had ordered Eric Stone, the *Oregon*'s chief helmsman when he wasn't carrying out research duties, to set a course for Mitsiwa in hopes of picking up the *Sekhmet*'s trail. Mark Murphy occupied his customary seat at the weapons station.

But not only had the *Oregon* not picked up the *Sekhmet* on her mil-spec radar system, she also wasn't picking up any other live satellite navigational imagery or AIS transmission for Hightower's ship in the area. She'd obviously gone dark.

Was she still headed for Eritrea?

'Permission to enter?' Sarai asked as she stood in the doorway of the operations center.

Juan turned in his chair. 'Of course. No permission needed.'

Sarai entered, but her smile faded when she got closer to Cabrillo and saw the bruising on his head and face.

'You're hurt.'

'I'm spotted like a leopard. But I'll be fine. What can I do for you?'

'I heard you found prisoners on the *Sekhmet*. I assume you didn't see Asher?'

'I don't know if they were prisoners or not,' Juan said. He wasn't sure how much to tell her. He didn't have anything to report on her brother, but he might scare her with the possibilities. But then again, she was an adult and he wasn't her guardian.

'Some of the men I encountered were undergoing physical and mental conditioning – altering their bodies and minds through genetic engineering.'

Juan watched Massala's body stiffen.

'But I didn't see Asher. Hightower said he was no longer on board.'

'Are you trying to tell me he's dead?'

'It's more likely he may have been dropped off, especially if he's been conditioned.'

'Where would they take him?'

'The *Sekhmet* plotted a course for Eritrea, specifically to the port of Mitsiwa. But we have reason to believe she intends to transfer her guinea pigs to a place called Nine Saints in the interior.'

'For what purpose?'

'Unknown.'

'And you think Asher could be there?'

'That's our best guess, but we're waiting for further confirmation. Until then, we're headed for Mitsiwa.'

Cabrillo decided to stay on course for Mitsiwa. Even if the *Sekhmet* wasn't heading there they might still be able to get a line on the activity at Nine Saints – whatever that was.

'Excuse me, Chairman. I've been working on a theory,' Murphy said.

Juan turned toward the weapons station. 'Shoot. Pun intended.'

'I read your after-action report from the *Sekhmet*

operation. You said the man you fought was likely a member of the Serbian mafia — because of his prison tats, right?'

'Yup.'

'We know that Asher Massala was in prison, and we also know that the *Sekhmet* is conducting some form of genetic engineering.'

'I have a feeling you're leading up to something,' Juan said.

'I've been racking my brain about how all of this is connected — form follows function, right? Hightower might be using prisoners as her primary subjects for their genetic experiments.'

'For what reason?' Linda asked.

'Easy. Prisoners are castoffs,' Eric said. 'Who's going to miss them?' He suddenly blushed as he thought about Sarai and her brother. He turned to her. 'I'm sorry.'

'*Idiot,*' Murph whispered to his friend.

'No worries,' Sarai said. 'You're right. Generally speaking, most prisoners are social outcasts, especially after they have been incarcerated, if not before.'

'No, you're all missing my point,' Murph said.

'What *is* your point, Wepps?' Cabrillo asked. 'Wepps' was Cabrillo's nickname for whoever commanded the *Oregon*'s array of weaponry.

'Do you remember the Dirlewanger Brigade?'

Juan's eyebrows lifted above his sunglass lenses. If the glasses hadn't been so dark everyone would have seen the whites of his eyes pop open. He remembered it well.

'World War Two. Dirlewanger was a lunatic who formed the most vicious unit in the Nazi Waffen-SS. He recruited mostly criminals – and even the criminally insane. They called themselves the Black Hunters. They committed vile atrocities against unarmed civilians, murdering thousands.'

Murph nodded. 'They were so debauched that even members of the Waffen-SS wanted the unit disbanded, but Hitler and the other higher-ups saw them as useful. It's one of the ugliest chapters in the worst war in modern history.'

'So you're of the opinion that Hightower is building a "Black Hunter" outfit? Finding and genetically altering prisoners with a predisposition toward violence? Why?'

'I'm not so sure Hightower is behind it. You said she was a committed transhumanist. Sure, those people are nuts, but they aren't committed to warfare. I think she's just a tool in the hands of someone else. She's Dr Frankenstein, but she's not Dirlewanger, if you catch my drift.'

Suddenly an alarm sounded. Hali Kasim called out.

'Chairman, we just picked up an emergency distress signal. Somebody's in trouble.'

53

As soon as the *Oregon*'s electronics suite picked up the distress signal, its high-powered digital telephoto cameras instantly triangulated the location and zoomed in on the target. The image was projected onto the wall-sized LCD monitor.

The entire op center reacted visibly to the sight of a lone sailor floating in an orange life vest. The man appeared unconscious – possibly even dead. The flashing device on his vest was broadcasting an automated emergency signal that chirped in the *Oregon*'s overhead speakers.

'Hali, kill that alarm. Wepps, send a bird.'

'Aye, Chairman.'

Murphy punched a virtual toggle on his computer screen.

All eyes instinctively turned to the port-side wall monitor, where the launch tube was located. A second later, the tube thumped as it launched a projectile.

The projectile reached an altitude of three hundred feet before slowing into an unpowered descent. Suddenly, a pair of wings covered in artificial feathers sprang open. The wings expanded to their full span of five feet, exposing the body and tail of the seagull drone. Its wings instantly began flapping in a perfect replication of natural flight, yet another example of the genius of bio-mimicry engineering at its best. No observer beyond a hundred feet could ever discern the high-tech mechanism was anything other than what it appeared to be – a living, natural seagull in flight.

Murphy pulled up a screen-within-a-screen on the main forward wall monitor. The smaller screen provided the bird's-eye point of view, along with the targeting reticle Murphy put on the man floating in the ocean. A few moments later, the bird was circling directly overhead of the sailor, its onboard camera lenses zoomed tight on his half-burned body.

'Is he alive?' Sarai asked.

'Hard to tell. Wepps, can we get a closer look?'

'I'm no Gomez Adams, but I'll give it a try.'

Cabrillo dismissed Murphy's false humility. His chief weapons officer was a world-class gamer whose fingers operated with the fine motor skills of an obsessive-compulsive orb weaver spider. Sure enough, a moment later the bird's-eye camera alighted on the sailor's oil-stained life vest and the man's half-burned face filled the screen. Despite the drone's onboard 3-axis gyro, accelerometer, and other stabilizing sensors, the camera image rocked with the motion of the waves. The man's partially opened mouth seemed to be drawing shallow breaths with trembling lips.

'Hux, are you seeing this?' Cabrillo asked. Monitors were located in all of the departments. Unless she was in surgery, Huxley always followed the live action on the bridge so she could be prepared to respond more quickly.

'That man is definitely alive, but critically injured,' Huxley said. 'Dehydration, probably blood loss, and shock. He needs our help now or he's not going to make it.'

Juan frowned, conflicted. Given Murphy's new macabre revelations about Hightower's operation and a possible handler controlling her, he was more determined than ever to track down the *Sekhmet*. He also needed to get to Eritrea in good order for Asher Massala's sake. If he was in that socialist hellhole, he was no doubt part of the same operation and there was no telling how far along Asher was in his genetic conditioning. Worse, his captors may have discovered he was an undercover Shin Bet operative. Time was their enemy.

But Cabrillo's own code of ethics, as well as the Law of the Sea, required any seaman to render assistance to another sailor or ship in distress. Every eye in the op center was focused on the injured, unconscious man floating alone in the ocean's vast expanse. It was an image of utter helplessness, and every sailor's worst nightmare.

'Helm, set a course.'

'Aye, Chairman,' Ross said. She had already laid one in before Cabrillo even spoke. She knew the value he put on human life.

Cabrillo punched a comms button on his chair. 'Eddie Seng, Raven Malloy, report to the boat garage immediately.'

The boat garage door rolled up and a rigid-hulled inflatable boat (RHIB) launched down a Teflon-coated ramp, its outboard motors roaring before it hit the water with a splash.

Eddie Seng, the *Oregon*'s director of shore operations, sat in the bow clutching the handles. Like Cabrillo, the wiry Chinese American was a former CIA operative. Seng had served several hazardous years working undercover behind China's Bamboo Curtain before joining the Corporation.

Raven Malloy stood in the console, piloting the RHIB. The Native American beauty was the newest Gundog on the team, but had already proven herself on multiple operations. Neither Seng nor Malloy carried weapons for the rescue mission.

Raven cranked the throttle hard, red-lining the Yamaha engines. There was no telling how long the shipwrecked sailor had been in the water or how close to death he was. The rubber-sided boat rooster-tailed across the water with bone-jarring speed, its fiberglass V-hull shredding the choppy Arabian waters with ease.

Malloy, the adopted daughter of career military parents, was a West Point graduate and a decorated former military police investigator. After two tours in Afghanistan, she separated from the Army and worked security for an art dealer until she met Juan Cabrillo. Until that time she had never imagined herself as part of a mercenary organization. Now she was a fully trained and experienced special warfare operator, and quite a boat handler to boot.

Malloy deftly worked the throttles, maneuvering the small craft to within inches of the half-drowned sailor, throttling down in time to kill the wake. Eddie and Raven leaned over the tube and carefully lifted the injured man out of the water and set him on the deck before Raven smashed the throttles and the engines roared back to life.

Two burly *Oregon* deckhands balanced precariously near the garage's bay door as they gently lifted the semiconscious sailor from the RHIB's gunwale, then set him on a waiting stretcher held aloft by two more *Oregon* sailors.

Amy Forrester, Huxley's physician's assistant, unbuckled the man's life vest as Huxley prepped an IV cannula. As soon as Forrester tossed the filthy vest onto the deck, Huxley deftly inserted the needle into the thickest vein she could find on the back of the man's unburnt hand, while Forrester held the saline drip bag aloft. Another medical technician pulled off the man's ragged deck shoes and wrapped his water-soaked body in a blanket for warmth.

As soon as Huxley secured the needle in place with a Tegaderm film dressing, she called out, 'Sick bay, stat.' The two stretcher men bolted away with their fragile cargo with Forrester jogging along beside them.

'Good work,' Huxley called over her shoulder to Seng and Malloy as they secured the lift chains to the RHIB, but she didn't wait around for their response.

She had a dying patient to attend to.

Juan stood by the Kirk Chair in the operations center. He had watched the entire rescue effort on the big LCD monitors from the moment the RHIB launched out of the garage to Hux calling out 'stat,' thanks to the *Oregon*'s onboard CCTV cameras. He had no idea if the sailor would survive, but he knew the man's best and only chance was Dr Julia Huxley. In addition to the many lives she had saved over the years and the many more injuries and wounds she had attended to, Huxley had helped Juan through the trauma of losing his leg and later in his rehabilitation efforts. He always thought the Navy was crazy to let her get away, but he was happy to take advantage of their mistake.

'Hali, any news from the Sniffer?' Cabrillo was referring to the *Oregon*'s surveillance array that automatically monitored nearly all forms of commercial and military electronic communication, including emergency radio broadcasts. Every half second, the ship's Cray supercomputer sorted through a thousand frequencies, harvesting billions of bits of data out of the atmosphere. The Sniffer's neural network language translation program even allowed someone as linguistically challenged as Kasim to hold real-time written conversations with foreign-language speakers.

The *Oregon*'s comms director pulled his headphones off his head and onto his neck, mussing his already messy mop of dark curly hair.

'Nothing yet. No SOS, no government alerts, no sightings by passing ships. If a ship was sunk, nobody knows about it.'

'Not surprising,' Murphy said, turning in his chair. 'Some of the fishing trawlers in this area aren't exactly Coast Guard certified, and many of them operate illegally.'

'Must have been a heck of a fire or a nasty explosion,' Max said, 'judging by the burns on that poor guy.'

'He's the only survivor?' Linda asked.

'So it seems,' Juan said, his eyes narrowing. He turned back to Kasim. 'Keep your ears on, just in case something pops.'

'Aye, Chairman.'

'Do you want to dispatch Gomez in the AW for an area search?' Max asked.

It was a tough call. An area search would take precious time that Asher might not have. But Cabrillo couldn't ignore the possibility that other sailors were out there.

'We'll hold on Gomez,' Cabrillo said. 'Hali, put in a call to the nearest authorities. Tell them a ship of unknown size and crew has been sunk, possible survivors adrift at sea. Don't identify us – we don't want the hassle right now. Make sure your call can't be traced either.'

Hali pulled the cans over his ears. 'On it.'

Malloy and Seng helped the two deckhands secure the RHIB in its cradle before heading for the locker room to change out of their wet suits. A maintenance call pulled one tech away to another duty, leaving the second crewman behind to run a hose over the RHIB to wash away the corrosive salt water.

In the flurry of activity to get the wounded sailor to the sick bay and secure the RHIB for transport, nobody remembered to clear away the discarded life vest lying in the shadows just beyond the garage door, now shut.

A common housefly emerged from beneath the vest's large and puffy collar. It rubbed its forelegs together like a hungry gourmand before a sumptuous feast, its multi-lensed eyes adjusting to the light. It was followed by a second fly, then a third, until all twelve had activated. Each repeated the same mechanical movements as the first.

A moment later, they each took flight, traveling in multiple directions at unnaturally high rates of speed. In just over seventy minutes they would all be dead, their miniature lithium batteries totally expended, but their missions completed.

54

Jean-Paul Salan's eyes widened with each passing minute. He was reviewing the 3D schematic of the *Norego Sunrise* that his AI-driven video software program had stitched together from the encrypted microburst transmissions of his drone flies.

The 3D image was a nearly complete rendering of the interior of the *Norego Sunrise*. The lack of total completion was due, in part, to one of the drones being swatted by a crewman with a bedroom slipper, mistaking the drone for an actual housefly that had buzzed into her cabin.

Besides the 3D schematic, Salan's drone flies produced over one thousand photographs that his software put together like a movie that corresponded with the schematic. Salan could hardly believe what he saw. The *Norego Sunrise* was an incredibly sophisticated vessel.

The engine room was particularly fascinating. Even though he was no marine engineer, he had read about the magnetohydrodynamic propulsion system the *Norego Sunrise* appeared to possess. According to the most respected technical journals, they had yet to be successfully deployed. The *Norego Sunrise* clearly proved them wrong.

What astounded Salan, though, were the incredible contrasts the drone flies discovered. The top deck was a total wreck of rust and ruin. The topside bridge was a monument to decay and neglect and was even abandoned.

But belowdecks he discovered five-star crew accommodations that were beyond superlative, tasteful artwork decorating the common areas, and the recreational facilities of a cruise ship. If he didn't know better, he'd have sworn this was an oceangoing luxury liner.

His drones had also found a moon pool, two submarines and other watercraft, along with a cutting-edge tilt-rotor aircraft, stacks of torpedos, and crates of anti-aircraft missiles. The cargo ship appeared to be as heavily armed as a World War I dreadnought.

From the number of equipment bays, shooting lanes, and other ancillary indicators, he estimated there were at least six dedicated combat operators and perhaps as many as ten on board the mystery vessel. No doubt there were even more support personnel to pilot the various crafts and deploy the weapons systems, along with the crew needed to operate and maintain the vessel.

But it was the technological wonder of the blue-lit command center that most impressed Salan, particularly the weapons station. Apparently the *Norego Sunrise* possessed a 120mm cannon, a Kashtan 30mm Gatling gun combat module, and even a laser cannon.

It was all something straight out of a science fiction novel, Salan told himself.

Merde. He had never seen such a collection of magnificent contradictions. His mind swam with possibilities.

These and other discoveries only deepened Salan's suspicion that the *Norego Sunrise* was a highly advanced US government vessel, confirming his fear that the CIA or some other intelligence agency was snooping around Hightower's organization. The discovery of the ship's extraordinary capabilities changed his previous calculation. Before, he assumed he was only dealing with a couple of low-level investigators. Now Salan feared that Sturges and his incredible vessel possessed sufficient resources that could destroy him.

Salan's first temptation was to cancel his mission and flee the area. Hightower was well clear of the *Norego Sunrise*, making even greater distance by the minute. She was likely out of harm's way for the time being. But given the technical abilities of the *Norego Sunrise*, it was painfully clear that he had completely underestimated his opponent. Sturges might turn his attention Salan's way even if only by accident or coincidence. And for all he knew, Sturges really had discovered something on board the *Sekhmet* that put the *Cloud Fortune* at risk.

But running from a fight was something Salan had never done in his life. Even when ambushed in the field, he had always turned the tables on his attackers by advancing toward enemy fire, invariably disrupting the surprise assault. Today would be no different.

It was time to attack.

And then it suddenly hit him. A well-executed surprise assault by his team would almost certainly result in the death of Sturges and his crew. But it might also yield an even greater prize – the *Norego Sunrise* herself. He coveted the vessel like a Lothario lusting after the unobtainable wife of a murderous warlord.

Though his priority was getting the hypersonic missile into position and launching it on time, he needed to find a way to capture the *Norego Sunrise*, killing Sturges and anyone trailing in his wake.

Salan turned back to the 3D map, a plan already forming in his mind. All he needed to do was find a way to lure the *Norego Sunrise* into his trap.

He'd once read about how the ancient Inuit peoples hunted the crafty polar wolf. The hunter would dip a razor-sharp knife in a pot of seal blood over and over until it formed a thick frozen layer like a popsicle. He would then plant the knife handle down in the ground and leave the area. When a hungry wolf encountered the surprise feast it would begin licking the gruesome popsicle furiously, warming the frozen blood with its hot tongue. In its licking frenzy, the wolf wouldn't realize the frozen concoction was numbing its tongue. By the time it reached the razor-sharp blade, the wolf had no idea that each new lick rendered a deep slice into the dorsal surface of its tongue. Tasting more hot blood, the wolf would feed even more ravenously, not realizing that each additional lick only hastened its hemorrhaging. The engorged wolf wouldn't stop feeding until it bled itself to death.

You are the crafty wolf, Mr Sturges, Salan told himself. *But I am the clever hunter.*

55

Cabrillo marched into Huxley's clinic.

'I came as quickly as I could. What's up?'

'Follow me.'

Huxley led Juan to an emergency treatment bay behind a curtain. She pulled back the sheer material and nodded toward the bed. A sheet was pulled over the body.

'When did it happen?'

'I called his TOD eleven minutes ago.'

'Cause?'

'I'd be tempted to say the third-degree burns are what did him in. He was obviously in shock. His cool skin and blue fingernails were dead giveaways, but those could have been caused by the exposure to the cold water, too. We treated his burns, pumped as much fluids into his system as we could, and kept him in warm blankets. But apparently it wasn't enough.'

'You said "tempted" to say. What else are you thinking?'

'Well, as you know, shock alone can kill you. A trauma like the massive injuries he had suffered would induce it, and shock shuts down blood flow and oxygen to the organs, which can ultimately lead to death. It also can induce vomiting.'

Juan's face soured as he took in the stench of the dead man's emptied stomach.

'Yeah, I can smell it.'

'But a lot of things can cause vomiting.'

Huxley pulled back the sheet just enough to reveal Diallo's face, twisted in agony. One eye was opened wide, but the other featured a drooping eyelid.

'He came in unconscious and mostly stayed that way, but all of a sudden he went into a seizure and that woke him up enough to puke his guts out. Then he cried out and he fell back dead. I called for the crash cart, but it was too late.'

'Your best guess?'

'I wouldn't be surprised if he suffered a cerebral aneurysm.'

'What causes that?'

'High blood pressure and clogged arteries are the usual culprits. But he was a fit male in his prime. It could also be hereditary. Most likely it was caused by the trauma of being nearly burnt alive. No way in knowing unless we run a CAT scan right away. But I don't see that it matters.'

'Find any ID on him?'

'None.'

'Tattoos?'

She shook her head. 'I'm way ahead of you. No indication from his clothing or appearance that he had been in a gang or in prison. He was probably just a sailor – a fisherman, deckhand, something like that. His luck just ran out.'

'He doesn't remind you of the goons you ran into in the Amazon?'

'I mean, you could see he was very physically fit despite his injuries. But if he was working a boat, that would make sense. He also wasn't quite as odd looking as the others.'

'Do me a favor. Go ahead and grab blood and tissue samples and run those through your lab. You found elevated levels of testosterone and whatnot in the Amazon goons. Let's check and see if he's in the 'roid rage club, too.'

'Already pulled them. I'll have the lab results by tomorrow morning at the latest.'

'I had no idea you were so suspicious.'

'I watch a lot of true crime dramas.'

'Well, since we're dotting our i's and crossing our t's, can you grab a set of fingerprints and a couple of headshots for Murph and Stoney? I'll have them check their databases. If nothing else, we might be able to pass something on to the authorities. If he really is just another sailor lost at sea, I'm sure his family is looking for him.'

'What do you want to do with the body?'

Juan scratched the side of his face, thinking. Huxley could keep the corpse in their small morgue. It was actually Huxley's suggestion to add one after the ship had been built, but it was hardly more than a refrigerated closet.

If they did put him in the meat locker, how long would they keep him? And what would they finally do with the corpse if no one came to collect it? Drop it off at a port? What would happen to the body then?

'Put him on ice until you get the lab results back. If he

really was just a sailor we'll bury him at sea with all of the honors due him.'

'I'll make the arrangements with Max.'

'But tell Max if it turns out this is one of Hightower's goons, we might toss him over the rail like a bucket of chum.'

56

'Chairman, I'm picking up a signal,' Hali Kasim said. 'It's coming from the Nine Saints area.'

Juan shifted uncomfortably in the Kirk Chair sipping a cup of hot coffee. Sarai stood by him.

'What does the Sniffer say?' Cabrillo asked.

'It's mil-spec level encryption. It will take a while to decode.'

'Did we ever get access to that satellite feed from the NRO?' Juan asked. They were still too far away to deploy the *Oregon*'s drones and he wasn't willing to risk Gomez and the tilt-rotor violating Eritrean airspace – at least, not yet.

'Aye, Chairman,' Eric Stone said. 'She'll be swinging overhead any moment now. I'm initiating the live stream.'

'Wepps, put it up on the forward monitor, please.'

'You got it,' Murphy said. He tapped a few virtual toggles on his computer screen. The live satellite image sped across the moonscape of the Eritrean plateau as the most advanced iteration of a KH-11 spy satellite traveled at over twenty-three thousand kilometers per hour. The image showed the Nine Saints monastery apparently rebuilt, along with faint lines across the area. Moving at six kilometers per second, it only took a few moments for the satellite to pass beyond the area.

'We'll get another usable pass in about ninety minutes,'

Stone said. 'And a third after another ninety. After that, she'll be out of usable range for twenty-four hours.'

'Wepps, can you put that thing on a loop?'

'Sure thing.' Murphy tapped more keys. He created a twenty-seven-second clip that would repeat itself continuously. He then enlarged the moving image on-screen and hit the play button.

Juan and Sarai crossed over to the forward monitor and stood just inches away from it.

'Please freeze the loop . . . now,' Cabrillo said as the camera centered over the monastery.

The video clip froze into a single image. The big 8K screen was lifelike in its clarity and resolution. Juan pointed at a couple of anomalies surrounding the building.

'Is it me or do these look like tire tracks?' He stabbed another area. 'And these look like possible footprints.'

Eric stood and squinted through his Warby Parkers. 'Yeah, I think you're right.' He crossed over to the wall display and stood next to Cabrillo. Linda and Hali came over, too.

Hali put his finger on the LCD screen. 'See here? I think that's the outline of a tent – nearly perfect camouflage to hide something beneath it. And those lines might be the ropes securing it. Super hard to see.'

'Someone knows what they're doing,' Linda said, drawing on her experience as a former naval intelligence officer. 'I think I see a few more of Hali's tents.'

'What are we looking at?' Max said as he reentered the op center after a quick trip to the head. He stood back by the Kirk Chair for perspective.

'That's what we're trying to figure out,' Juan said. 'So

far we're seeing tire tracks, footprints, and camouflage tents.'

'They're obviously hiding something. Buildings, probably,' Stone said.

'For what? Equipment? Weapons? Vehicles?' Sarai asked.

'If Hightower is sending her men here, it's designed to accommodate them,' Eric said. 'So at least one of those buildings is a barracks.'

'Unless there are men already there,' Max said. 'Then they could all be barracks – including the ones we still don't see.'

'Maybe not barracks,' Linda said. 'Hightower said she's engaged in genetic engineering. These could be medical facilities of some sort. Labs, exam rooms, surgical wards.'

'Too remote and too dirty for medical,' Juan said. 'That's what the *Sekhmet* is for.'

Max approached the screen. 'My gut tells me we're looking at either a military base or a training camp.'

'Eritrea is a heavily militarized state. It must be one of theirs,' Murphy said.

'Highly unlikely,' Hali said. 'I doubt the Eritreans have access to the military-grade encryption codes that the Cray is having a hard time pulling apart.'

'Then it could be a Russian or Chinese operation. Even Israeli,' Linda said.

'The Cray has a database of nearly every known military encryption code, including the players you just mentioned. It doesn't recognize the origin of this one.'

Linda pointed a finger at Murphy. 'Don't even think it.' The lanky weapons officer was the *Oregon*'s most avid ufologist.

'Hali, send a text to Overholt. Have him reach out to our friends at the Office of the Director of National Intelligence. See if they've ever identified this location as an area of Eritrean military or scientific activity.'

'Will do.' Kasim bolted over to his comms station.

'Do you want me to resume play?' Murphy asked.

'Sure, go ahead,' Juan said.

The loop advanced again. Suddenly, a man emerged from one of the tents. Behind him emerged a man on a stretcher and then a third man carrying the rear.

'Can you freeze and zoom?' Juan asked.

'Got it.' Murph did both.

The two stretcher-bearers were Caucasian and appeared to be wearing scrubs. The man on the stretcher was Black and appeared to be in gym clothes.

'Tighter, if you can,' Juan said. The image of the man on the stretcher enlarged but was somewhat distorted.

Sarai inched closer to the screen.

'Is that the best you've got? I thought these things could read license plates from outer space,' Max said.

'Not the KH-11s. But I can run the picture through my bespoke imaging processor,' Murphy said. 'It will extrapolate a cleaner image by comparative data analysis. Gimme a sec.' A moment later, the man's face pixelated.

'I think you smudged it,' Max said.

'That's just the software harvesting graphical data,' Eric said. 'It will resolve in a jiffy.'

'Chairman, the Sniffer cracked the first word on that encrypted message,' Hali said, reading from his computer screen.

'What is it?'

'It's two words, actually. "*Sekhmet*," "*Sekhmet*." Sounds like the beginning of a standard radio transmit.'

Juan and Linda exchanged a glance.

'That confirms the connection between Nine Saints and Hightower,' Ross said.

The Black man's face went from a pixelated blur to crystal clarity as the software finalized the image.

Sarai gasped.

'It's Asher!'

All eyes turned toward the screen.

'Eric, please confirm,' Juan ordered.

Stone dashed back to his station. 'Running a facial recognition software analysis,' he said as his fingers flew across his keyboard.

A moment later, Asher's photograph appeared on the screen next to the face on the stretcher. The software confirmed a ninety-four percent match.

'Thank God,' Sarai whispered. 'He's alive.'

She was right, Juan thought. If he were dead they would have put him in a body bag or covered him with a sheet. But he might also be injured. That started a clock in his brain. They had just lost the burned and injured castaway because they hadn't been able to reach him in time. Cabrillo was determined to not let that happen to Asher.

Juan didn't need to pull out his trusty slide rule to know that the shortest distance between two points was a straight line. The straightest and simplest line to Asher he could think of was to contact the Eritrean government directly and find out if they would be willing to help recover him. The problem was this might be an Eritrean government operation that was somehow connected to

Hightower. Just inquiring about it might set off an alarm that could result in Asher's destruction. Until he heard back from Overholt or the ODNI he wouldn't pursue that option.

That meant he and his team of Gundogs had to go in for a snatch-and-grab. They would need to traverse unfamiliar terrain against a heavily camouflaged facility with an unknown number of defenses occupied by an unspecified number of persons with exceptional physical abilities. But finding and rescuing Asher was only half the battle. They had to get in and out without being discovered; otherwise, they risked starting a shooting war with a hostile foreign government.

And he needed to do all of that without getting any of his people killed.

'Just another day at the job,' Juan said to himself.

'Chairman?' Max asked.

'Nothing.' He punched a button on the console of the Kirk Chair, a direct link to Eddie Seng.

'Eddie, assemble the gang in the team room in ten minutes. We've got a mission to plan.'

'Aye, Chairman.'

57

On Board the Cloud Fortune

Jean-Paul Salan eyed the Saudi warship knifing through the blue waters of the Gulf of Aden, its one-hundred-and-fifteen-meter-long hull casting a long, fast shadow in the last light of a setting sun.

The French-built Saudi frigate *Al Madinah* bristled with anti-ship missiles, torpedoes, and an automatic 100mm deck gun, any of which could sink the *Cloud Fortune* with ease. But it wasn't the patrolling Saudi warship he most feared. The Yemeni civil war had resumed despite the Saudi's best efforts to crush the Houthis by force of arms. Saudi assets were now enforcing a naval arms embargo against the rebels, who continued to hold a large portion of Yemeni territory including its historic capital city of Sana'a.

What worried Salan was a secondary vessel, an approaching pilot boat with armed Yemeni soldiers on deck. An overly zealous inspection for contraband could unravel everything. Should things go sideways, the *Cloud Fortune* stood no chance of escape with the *Al Madinah* close by.

Salan's vessel was anchored in the calm waters of the harbor formed by a volcanic peninsula near the Port of Aden, which also served as its temporary capital city. He had finally received confirmation from his Quds Force contacts that the route had been cleared to transport the BrahMos missile to its final prepared destination.

The Iranian commandos had also secured the necessary tractor trailer with lift capabilities to deliver and install the containerized anti-ship missile. They also confirmed that they would be waiting in the pickup area near Berth 2 at the Ma'alla Multipurpose Terminal, where nearly half of the *Cloud Fortune*'s containers would be unloaded by the port's Liebherr ship-to-shore gantry crane.

As the pilot vessel neared the *Cloud Fortune*, a voice in heavily accented English crackled over the ship's loudspeakers requesting permission to board. Salan lowered his binoculars.

The *Cloud Fortune*'s grizzled Greek captain shot a wary look at Salan. The Frenchman nodded and Captain Chatzidiakos radioed his permission to come aboard.

Twelve minutes later, Chatzidiakos and Salan greeted the chief inspector, a Saudi national, on the *Cloud Fortune*'s bridge along with the port pilot, a thin Yemeni man. As they exchanged pleasantries, a half dozen armed soldiers conducted a perfunctory visual inspection of the deck.

The Yemeni port pilot happily accepted the carton of premium American cigarettes from Chatzidiakos's hand, while Salan gifted the inspector, a Saudi naval intelligence officer, with a twelve-hundred-dollar bottle of Four Roses bourbon. The Saudi secreted the prized liquor into his leather shoulder bag.

'Papers, Captain?' the Saudi inspector asked.

Chatzidiakos produced a neatly organized faux-leather

folio containing his cargo manifests, crew logs, and a sealed envelope stuffed with five thousand euros in crisp notes.

The Saudi thumbed through a few pages of the cargo manifests with a cursory glance before pocketing the envelope and returning the folio to the ship's captain.

'All appears to be in order, Captain. Welcome to Aden,' the Saudi said. He approached Salan. In a low whisper he said, 'Please convey my congratulations to Prince Khalid on his election to deputy crown prince. The kingdom will be well served by his able hands.'

Salan nodded. 'Of course.'

The Saudi inspector turned for the door and stopped. 'Gentlemen, I'll meet you at the dock and personally oversee your unloading. There won't be any problems, I assure you.' He called into his shoulder mic and barked orders to the soldiers on deck.

Ten minutes later, Chatzidiakos watched the Saudi and his soldiers on his CCTV monitor boarding the pilot ship and heading back to the port. Once they had cleared away, he turned toward the Yemeni harbor pilot. 'The ship is yours.'

The Yemeni pilot smiled and nodded through a cloud of smoke from one of his new American cigarettes as he took charge of the freighter.

Salan estimated that by midnight the *Cloud Fortune* would be unloaded and on its way to its next port of call, while he, his mercenaries, and his payload would be well on their way into the interior of Yemen's hellscape.

Two hours after that, he expected to receive a report that Sturges had met his fate.

As satisfying as that would be, Salan had other concerns.

He checked his watch. His assassin had reported an hour ago that the first phase of her operation was completed. But the crucial next step wouldn't take place for another twenty-four hours, and without it, everything Prince Khalid had planned for would be for naught.

58

On Board the Oregon

The op center began clearing out as the appropriate warfighters headed for the team room belowdecks. Sarai stayed behind with Juan as he started to ease himself out of his command chair, his face grimacing from the pain.

'A word in private?' Sarai asked.

'Sure.' Juan was relieved to sit back down. 'What is it?'

'Please don't take this the wrong way, but I don't think we should go after Asher.'

Juan tried to hide his shock.

'Why would you say that?'

'You said it yourself. There are too many "unknown unknowns" and that's putting your crew at risk for a man who's really nothing more than a petty criminal.'

'But he's your brother. And what about your father?'

'I know my father would feel the same way. You don't trade a dozen good men for one failed life. I'm especially concerned about you.'

Juan saw the genuine anguish in her face.

'This mission isn't just about your brother,' Juan said. 'This whole Hightower operation is something we've got to put a stop to. Who knows how many of these people she's already managed to engineer. But if the Chinese or ISIS or any number of other bad guys ever got a hold of this technology there would be hell to pay.'

'Then make that your only mission.'

'No offense, but I don't take my orders from you.'

'I'm sorry, you're right.'

Cabrillo nodded. 'But I appreciate your concern.'

'I know I'm treading on thin ice here but I have a favor to ask.'

'Name it.'

'I'd like to join you in the operation.' She smiled winsomely. 'I think you could use an extra pair of hands.'

Juan studied her. The last thing he needed was an emotional civilian gumming up the works. His team was a finely tuned machine, with thousands of hours of training and practice drills under their collective belts. They moved and thought as one.

But Massala was a trained Mossad operative, even if she hadn't been in the field for a while. And she was right, under the extraordinary circumstances, another gun on the ground wouldn't hurt.

'What if I have to order you to shoot Asher?'

'I know you would only issue such an order because it was absolutely necessary.'

'You didn't answer my question.'

'I will obey your orders without hesitation.'

'Let's hope it doesn't come to that. Eddie will get you set up.'

'Thank you.' Sarai's eyes remained locked with his. Despite her grateful smile, she seemed to bear the sadness of the whole world on her shoulders. Her brother's fate clearly weighed on her heart.

Now Juan faced a dilemma. Since he had just promised to bring her along, he needed to make sure she was completely focused and committed to the mission. Overholt told him that Sarai couldn't know about her brother's status with Shin Bet. But her not knowing that fact put her, and Asher, at risk. Under normal circumstances Cabrillo obeyed Overholt's orders without question. But in Cabrillo's mind the safety of his team and the success of the mission outweighed Overholt's need for discretion. If their roles had been reversed, Juan knew Langston would make the same decision.

Cabrillo grabbed her by the arm. 'Your brother is an undercover operative for Shin Bet.'

Sarai darkened. 'No. That's impossible.'

'It's the truth.'

'Why wasn't I told?'

'Asher was obviously under orders not to tell you. So were your old friends at Mossad. So was I. But I believe you needed to know now.'

'This feels like some cruel joke.'

'It's anything but. You have Israeli and American friends who are trying to protect you and Asher. And my crew is willing to lay down their lives for you both.'

Sarai's eyes began welling up with tears.

'I'm so sorry . . . and happy . . . and grateful. It's just so much to take in all at once. I don't know what to say.'

Juan laid a hand on her shoulder.

'You don't have to say anything. In fact, make sure you don't breathe a word about this to anyone. Overholt has put his career at risk for you. If you say anything about Asher and Shin Bet, you'll get him in trouble.'

'Never. Not a word.'

'Good. Then let's head down to the team room and get this show on the road.'

59

The team room was part frat house den, part training facility. Overstuffed couches, a couple of school desks, gym lockers, a dartboard, unit and battle flags, a big-screen TV monitor, and a wall-sized whiteboard were some of the furnishings. It was meant to be a place where the Gundogs could hang out and debrief over a couple of beers after a mission or, as was the case today, plan for the next one.

Eddie Seng stood at the front of the room, a red dry-erase marker in hand. He would put together the tactical plan, equipment lists, and the rest of the nitty-gritty details that could make or break an operation. But today Juan wanted to give the mission brief so that they all knew what they were getting into – and what was expected of them.

Besides the official tactical team, Juan had brought in Linda, Max, Murphy, and Stone, along with Hali, who would be running the tactical net and making sure comms were running smoothly, while also keeping an eye on the radar. Gomez Adams was flopped out on a couch like a pile of yesterday's laundry.

Cabrillo knew that behind the small talk, easy laughs, and casual postures, his people were fired up on adrenaline and laser-focused on the task at hand. No one was more focused than Sarai, who sat at a school desk near the front.

'Sorry for the short notice, but the clock's ticking,' Juan began. 'I think you've all met Sarai Massala and you all know that we've been searching for her brother, Asher. He's still our primary target.'

Cabrillo clicked a remote control in his hand and a map appeared on the TV screen.

'Asher just popped up on our radar minutes ago at a location known as Nine Saints in the interior of Eritrea. No telling how long he's been there or, more important, how long he'll stay there. He also appears to be in some kind of physical distress. Our mission is a simple snatch-and-grab, though there's nothing simple about it.'

'Is it ever?' MacD asked. 'Mr Murphy has a nasty habit of showing his ugly mug at exactly the wrong moment.'

'You're referring to Edward A. Murphy Jr, the aeronautical engineer with all of the bad luck, right?' Murph asked.

MacD grinned. 'Him, too.'

'We plan, but the enemy has a say, and then we improvise, adapt, and overcome,' Eddie said. He turned to Juan. 'What makes this particular plan especially not simple?'

Juan snatched up a marker and began scratching out his bullet points.

'First, we don't know who we're up against exactly, or how many of them there are. I counted twenty treatment beds on the *Sekhmet*, but only nine were occupied. I assume that means Hightower conditions up to twenty at a time. But how long does that process take? How many has she already delivered? We just don't have a clue.

'Second, we don't know how they're armed or even if they're armed at all – though we should assume they are. We don't know where they're located on the compound, and we don't even really know what the compound looks like.'

'What do we know?' Max asked, his thick arms folded over his belly.

Juan nodded at Linc and Huxley, who sat next to Max on another couch. 'I'm sure you've all heard what happened in the Amazon. It pretty much matches my experience on the *Sekhmet*. If we do come across anybody, expect them to be stronger and faster than anyone you've ever encountered.'

'Those dudes are *jacked*,' Linc said.

'They've been genetically enhanced by Dr Hightower. Their hormone production alone is through the roof – unreal levels of testosterone, adrenaline, and endorphins.'

'Yeah, they feel no pain, but they sure can deliver it,' Linc said. 'My bruises have bruises.'

Juan winced as he took a deep breath and gestured at his wounded rib cage hidden beneath his Caltech sweatshirt.

'Tell me about it.'

'I did some digging around on Hightower,' Murph said. 'She's worked hard to keep her name out of the limelight, but she's definitely hardwired into the CRISPR-verse. Her husband held like a dozen early patents on the technology. After he assumed room temperature, she formed a company called HH+ based on those patents.'

'She's a certified genetics genius,' Eric added.

'She's also a genocidal, megalomaniacal sociopath with a messianic complex,' Juan said.

Mark whispered to Eddie, 'And she's something to look at.'

'Murph? Something to add?' Juan said.

Murphy's face reddened like a sunburnt lobster. 'No, sir.'

'What about Asher?' Hali asked.

'We have to assume he's gone through Hightower's program, since he was recruited out of the Kamiti prison and apparently spent time on the *Sekhmet*. That means he's been both physically and mentally conditioned.'

Hali frowned. 'What do you mean by "mentally"?'

'Past memories wiped, new memories implanted. All designed to turn these unfortunates into thralls.'

'Thralls of Hightower?' Max asked.

'I don't think so,' Juan said. 'The human buzz saw I ran into was under her thumb. But I agree with Murphy's analysis. These genetically enhanced men are meant to be deployed by someone else. Given the presumed criminal background of most or all of them, we have to assume they're not being funneled into the Mormon Tabernacle Choir.'

'Can you imagine two hundred million Chinese super soldiers?' Murph blurted out. He was already playing the video game in his head.

Suddenly, the gravity of the mission hit everyone. Gomez Adams sat up as heads nodded around the room.

'You said "men." Do you think any women are involved?' Raven Malloy asked.

'Great question. Right now, I can't tell you. But since most incarcerated people are men, I'd have to assume we're talking mostly about men.'

'So, back to Asher,' Stone said. 'We're assuming he won't come along willingly?'

'He might, if he sees me,' Sarai said.

Linda shifted in her chair. 'No offense, Sarai, but if your brother has been brainwashed, there's no guarantee he'll even recognize you, let alone respond to you.'

'Even if he doesn't, at the very least, I can provide visual confirmation of his identity.'

'Agreed.' Cabrillo turned to the rest of the room. 'You all know I don't believe in lethal force unless it's absolutely necessary. The same applies here. We're operating in a condition of some moral hazard. These men – and maybe women – have all been brainwashed. In my book, that means they aren't completely responsible for their actions.'

'But if they're all violent felons . . .' Hali said.

'Then they need to be held responsible for those crimes, whatever they are. But that's not our gig. I also need to stress that we're invading a sovereign country that is not at war with the United States. In technical terms, we'll be breaking the law. It would be best for all concerned if we got in and out without detection.'

'What about Eritrean air and ground defenses?'

Stoney spoke up. 'As far as we know, they have no night vision capabilities, and Soviet-era equipment. If we stay low and fast and in the dark, I don't anticipate any problems, especially where we're headed.'

'Are we going in heavy?' Eddie asked. His primary concern was for his team, not the well-being of the genetic mutants they were going up against.

'We have to. We have no idea what we're facing. And while I don't want to kill any of these guys or gals, the safety of each member of the team is my top priority. So, the way we're going to square the circle is like this.'

Juan had been thinking about this problem ever since his encounter with the super Slav back on the *Sekhmet*. Short of killing the genetically altered fighter, how could anyone stop someone with that kind of skill set and not get themselves badly injured or killed in the process?

Cabrillo knew the answer lay somewhere belowdecks in the armory department. After the *Oregon*'s encounters with several nonconventional weapons systems during their Libya operation, Juan had asked his team to develop their own cache of 'less lethal' weapons. Juan knew there was no such thing as a non-lethal weapon. Even rubber bullets and pepper spray could kill people, rare as that was.

Juan turned back to Eddie. 'First, let's you and I get on the horn with the armory and see what alternative weapons packages they can put together for us.'

'Aye, Chairman.'

'I've got a few ideas of my own along those lines,' Murph said.

'Me too,' Stoney added.

'Outstanding. We'll brainstorm it later.' Cabrillo stretched out a couple of kinks he was battling. He was having a hard time keeping a straight posture owing to his bruised and battered rib cage.

'Second, since we don't know exactly what we're going up against, we're going in with everyone we have. Only technical support personnel will be left behind.'

The mood shifted in the team room. Juan saw the steely determination etching each face.

'Gomez?'

'Sir?'

'We'll need to hitch a ride with you on the AW, and then I want you on overwatch. Murph will be your backseater.'

'Sounds like a plan. The bird's already being prepped.' Gomez winked at Murphy, who threw him a thumbs-up.

'Eddie, you're in charge of the Gundogs – MacD, Linc, Raven . . . and Linda.'

Ross beamed. She wasn't normally part of ground operations, but she handled a pistol and an MP5 like a pro. She also trained with Eddie and the team as often as she could.

'All right,' Raven said as she bumped fists with Linda.

'And of course me,' Cabrillo added.

Eddie Seng stood a little taller, and nodded at Juan's rib cage. He took his command seriously.

'Are you cleared for action, sir?'

'I will be by the time we're on the AW.'

'I'll need a verbal confirmation from the doc.'

'You'll have it.'

Max held up a beefy mitt. 'If you think you're cutting me out of this little Boy Scout jamboree, you've got another thing coming.'

Juan grinned. Max was his best friend. The former swift boat captain might have been a little long in the tooth and a few pounds overweight, but there was no one Juan would rather go into a fight with.

'You're in the DING – and Stoney will ride shotgun.'

Max beamed. 'Now you're talkin'.' He pointed a thick-knuckled finger at Murphy's LCD display. 'But if I'm reading that map correctly, Nine Saints is some two hundred kilometers inland. Might take awhile to get there.'

'Not if we hook you up to the AW for lift.'

'I can haul seven thousand pounds above my empty weight,' Gomez said. 'It worked okay on the Libya op.'

Max smiled. 'I just wish we could blast "Ride of the Valkyries" on the loudspeakers when we go in.'

Juan chuckled at the *Apocalypse Now* reference. 'Not your stealthiest option.' He turned to the rest of the room.

'After Eddie draws up the tactical assault plan, you'll draw your preferred load-outs from the armory. Pistols, PDWs, ammo. You know the drill.'

'What about medical?' Linda asked. 'Amy Forrester was a combat medic.'

'Good idea. We'll rope her into our little rodeo as well. Hux will be on standby in the ER. But if we plan this right, we shouldn't need anything more than back rubs and mai tais when we get back to the barn.'

'So, back to the opposition. What do we do with the X-Men we don't take down?' Murphy asked.

'For now, zip-tie them and leave them for someone else to deal with. We'll grab any intel we can lay our hands on.'

'Why not bring them back to the *Oregon*?'

Max turned around.

'We don't have a brig and I don't think Dr Huxley has the resources to do any kind of deprogramming or de-conditioning. She could even wind up causing more harm than good.'

'Agreed,' Juan said. 'As soon as we clear Eritrean airspace, we'll call in for outside help to pick them up or do whatever we need to do for them. But for now, our focus is on Asher Massala.'

Linda Ross spoke up. 'I hate to be the nattering nabob

of negativism, but is there any chance this is all just a trap designed to kill us?'

Juan shrugged. 'We should assume it is a trap. Hightower knows we're looking for Asher. No doubt she's communicated that with her people on the ground at Nine Saints.'

'Sounds like they're holding all the aces,' MacD said.

Juan shook his head. 'We have one advantage over them.'

'What's that?'

'They don't know that *we* know it's a trap.'

Cabrillo faced the rest of the room. 'But you all know the deal. We're not a military organization. You're all volunteers. We've lost people before on missions not nearly as hazardous as this one. Anyone who wants to step away can do so now. No harm, no foul.'

He scanned the room. No one moved to leave – not even close. He wasn't surprised. Sure, they were professionals. But more important, his people were utterly loyal to each other. And they all knew there were far worse things than dying.

Juan turned to Eddie Seng. 'You take it from here.'

60

Off the Coast of Eritrea

The four men had parachuted into the water some eight kilometers distant, shed their silks, and began their long, arduous swim against the Red Sea's relentless current, stronger than they had anticipated.

The two fully conditioned mercs were unfazed by the long crawl through the murky waters despite their burden of equipment. They were still twenty minutes away from the starboard side of the ship they knew as the *Norego Sunrise*. Despite the boat's lights-out attitude, they could hear the metallic clangs, shouting voices, and whining hydraulics of a mission prep well underway.

Their two commanders, both former SAS corporals, were five minutes behind them. Like their charges, the corporals were weighted down with dry bags containing their weapons and gear. Already in top physical condition, the corporals had also received Hightower's partial physical conditioning, but still hadn't been able to keep up with the others.

Suddenly, the rumble of turboprops spinning up echoed across the water.

The two corporals stopped paddling to assess the situation. They pulled off their goggles.

'Should've already been there,' the first corporal said, treading water.

'Won't be long now.'

'Them or us?'

As if on cue, the tilt-rotor's engines shrieked as its throttles were slammed forward and the thundering blades lifted the AW into the star-blanketed sky. The hybrid aircraft rose and arced toward the Eritrean coast twenty-five kilometers due west, some kind of cargo slung beneath its fuselage.

'Call Sergeant Fellowes,' the first corporal said. He cast a glance at the two mercs. They were pulling farther and farther ahead, two machines plowing through the dark waters.

The second corporal tabbed his waterproof microphone.

'They're on their way, Sergeant.'

'Where are you?' Fellowes asked.

'Close.'

'Then best make haste, my sons. Time and tide waits for no man.'

The two corporals nodded to each other, pulled their goggles back on, and chased after their men, a ticking clock driving them both forward like madmen.

Gash-Barka Region, Eritrea

After dropping its cargo, the AW tilt-rotor clawed back into the air, scattering stinging dust beneath its blasting turboprops. It arced away toward a waning gibbous moon hanging low and far in the starlit western sky.

Max fell into the driver's seat of the dune buggy-like DING and secured his harness as Stoney did the same in the passenger seat. Like the rest of tonight's team, they both wore specialized helmets with head-up displays, along with advanced eye protection and noise-canceling headsets.

Max had designed and built the all-electric desert insertion ground vehicle with the help of a senior armorer, Bill McDonald, a former CIA desert warfighter. It featured forward-looking LIDAR, lightweight Kevlar armor plating, and an electronics suite that would make an F-35 Lightning pilot jealous.

For this early morning's adventure, McDonald, along with Mike Lavin, had rigged an automated, pintle-mounted surprise on the support bar where the M60 machine gun was usually located.

Max gave a quick scan of the gauges as Stoney double-checked the Benelli M4 semi-auto tactical shotgun secured in its scabbard near his knee. Both men wore Walther PDP 9mm pistols and carried tranq pistols on their chest rigs.

'Ready?' Max asked in his comms.

Stoney punched the geo-marker on the console map. The same map appeared in a picture-in-picture window on both of their helmet visors.

'Good to go.'

'Hold on to your thong,' Max laughed as he punched the throttle.

The DING's four nearly silent electric motors were each slaved to their own big knobby tires cranking over eight hundred horsepower. The sleek carbon-fiber rig launched like a rocket across the barren landscape toward its destination, the Nine Saints monastery.

Former SAS sergeant Angus Fellowes stood on the table-top escarpment some sixty meters above the Nine Saints monastery, his eyes glued to a pair of high-powered night vision binoculars. In Salan's absence, he was in charge of tonight's operation.

Standing next to him was one of his mercenary boots. The swarthy Algerian held a loaded RPG gripped in his vise-like hands.

A grin spread across Fellowes's angular jaw as the hot engines of the shadowy AW came into view some five kilometers distant. He spoke into his comms.

'I see the bugger. Won't be long now. Everyone pull on your slippers. The dance is about to begin!'

Gomez piloted the AW, his hands and feet working the tilt-rotor's myriad controls with effortless speed and pre-cision. The aircraft had dropped the DING and its two-passenger crew five kilometers southeast of the Nine Saints monastery and was now racing toward it.

Mark Murphy sat in the copilot's chair working the weapons suite, while Juan and the rest of the team were strapped in jump seats back in the spartan passenger cabin. They all wore the same HUD helmets, and each saw the same map and targeting displays on their visors. Cabrillo's helmet was even plugged into the DING's onboard sensor array, which allowed him to operate the vehicle's weapons system remotely in an emergency.

The AW was fitted with long-range night vision, infrared,

and electro-optical sensors. Even at this distance, ghost-white figures began appearing with crystal clarity on their displays.

'I count seven tangos so far,' Murphy said in his comms, though everyone saw the same images. Two figures were huddled together fifty meters north of the monastery, and three more were ninety meters south, lying in ambush near the wide-open area Cabrillo assumed was the helipad – and where they were scheduled to drop.

'It's the two gomers on top of that ridge that got my attention,' Gomez said. 'Especially the one with the boom stick.'

'I feel you,' Juan said. A relic of the Cold War, the 'boom stick' in question – a Soviet-designed RPG – was still an effective combat weapon, and perfectly capable of killing the AW and every member on board if they got within its limited range. Juan tapped out a series of way-points for Gomez to follow on his map.

'I like your idea, boss,' Gomez said. He worked the collective and cyclic controls to chase the path.

'It all seems too easy,' MacD said over the comms.

Juan turned to him. 'What's wrong with easy?'

'Nothin's wrong with easy when it comes to bourbon and women. But this? My Spidey-sense is tingling.'

'Duly noted. Wepps?' he called to Murphy.

'Sir?'

'Stay frosty on your scope.'

Two minutes later, Gomez had swung west around and beyond the monastery complex and far beyond the range of where the RPG team stood. No telling what other anti-aircraft weapons might have been hidden below.

When they were fifteen hundred meters away from the RPG team, Juan called out to Murphy.

'Wepps, light 'em up!'

Murphy grinned behind his blacked-out visor glass.

'Aye, Chairman!'

Murphy worked the joystick controlling the portable Active Denial System (ADS) strapped beneath the AW. To the casual observer, it looked like a small satellite dish. But in reality, it was a directed energy device, blasting short millimeter waves at its intended target. The lower frequency waves only penetrated the top skin layers, heating the fat and water molecules like a low-powered microwave oven, in just two seconds.

One of the challenges Juan put to his armory department was Hux's report that the genetically altered mercs didn't feel much pain. But the beauty of the ADS, they assured him, was that the body's response to being cooked from the inside out was entirely involuntary and autonomic. It wasn't pain so much as survival instinct that drove recipients into instant retreat.

Murph launched the first two-second blast of ADS at the two figures. They visibly moved but didn't flee.

Juan was surprised. Had Hightower found a way to override even survival instincts?

'Try it again, Wepps.'

Murphy pulled the trigger one more time.

The two white-hot figures on the display suddenly bolted away, one of them dropping the RPG.

'I guess I Jiffy-Popped them pretty good,' Murphy said.

Nervous laughter broke the tension.

'Gotta finish the job,' Juan said.

'Targeting now.' Murph punched a button on his station, activating a new weapons system. He then tapped on each of the seven glowing white figures on his night vision display. A red targeting reticle attached itself to each figure, including the two that had fled and had now stopped running. The targeting computer assigned each figure a number, one through seven, and identified them as such on everyone's displays.

'Launching drones,' Murphy said.

The three-man squad leader on the south side of the monastery, a hulking Romanian, heard the thunderous hammering of the big helicopter blades high overhead, but he could never quite catch sight of the aircraft. By the waning sound of the rotors, the aircraft seemed to be departing. He hadn't heard any shots, but Fellowes's howling in his earpiece told the Romanian that something bad had happened to his commander.

The Romanian wasn't afraid.

He and his two mates were hidden behind a collection of rocks forming a low wall demarcating the helicopter landing area, the perfect position to ambush the aircraft when it arrived. They each carried AK-47 automatic rifles, combat blades, and rolls of duct tape. Their orders were to capture the intruders if possible and to kill them if not. The Romanian much preferred the latter.

Just as the big helicopter blades faded away, a cacophony of high-pitched whines pierced the night sky. He sensed more than saw the fast-approaching threats and ducked instinctively behind the nearest boulder. The accelerating noises buzzed like giant hornets racing directly toward him.

Suddenly the night's darkness gave way to a blinding flash of six million candela – brighter than an exploding sun to his dilated pupils.

In the same instant, the first earsplitting explosion burst overhead, louder than the roar of a screaming jet engine inside of his skull. Now blind and deaf, the concussive force of the 40mm flash-bang had hit him so hard it sucked the air out of his lungs and knocked him out cold before he hit the dirt next to his unconscious companions.

On Board the Oregon

Salan's assault team had planned on breaching the shipside pilot's door with their handheld thermite cutting torches that generated metal vapor at over twenty-eight hundred degrees Celsius.

But as fortune would have it, the crew of the *Norego Sunrise* had opened the boat garage door located near the waterline in preparation for an emergency landing or waterborne rescue.

'This way, lads,' the senior corporal ordered as he slipped through the unguarded entrance.

The assaulters scanned for guards, but all the crew was busy in support of the night's mission. Salan's 3D maps had located all of the ship's CCTV cameras for them to avoid, but it was highly unlikely they were being monitored.

They had laid out their plan of attack based on Salan's

maps. Both of the fully conditioned fighters had been picked for this mission because of their particular predilections for extreme violence. The wiry Sudanese had been a child soldier and later a convicted felon guilty of multiple assaults, while the cannonball-shouldered Brazilian had learned his murderous trade on the vicious streets of Rio's worst favela.

In turn, Salan chose the two corporals because he could count on their discipline and experience to seize control of the wonder vessel and to deliver it into his hands.

The four mercenaries had stripped down to the bare essentials – weapons, comms, and a small equipment pouch. All carried razor-sharp kukri knives, made famous by the indomitable Gurkhas. The long recurved blades were devastating in close combat, the next best thing to a short sword. Each man also carried a silenced pistol.

The senior corporal whispered in his comms.

'Fast, gentlemen, and quiet.' He turned around and looked each man in the eye. The two mercs were straining at their leashes, eager for blood.

'Our goal is the ship, not a high body count. Kill if you must, but only as needed to achieve our first objective. After we capture the ship, we'll slaughter all but the most necessary survivors.'

The genetically altered mercs grinned wolfishly.

The senior corporal nodded. 'Let's take her.'

61

Gomez held the AW rock-steady just twenty feet above the deck, his eyes locked on the threat assessment displays and his ears tuned for any alarms.

Eddie Seng and MacD kicked the fast ropes out the cabin door and were the first down, followed by the others, with Juan and Sarai taking up the rear on each line.

Pain stabbed through Cabrillo's rib cage when his boots hit the ground. He flinched as he sucked a sharp burst of air through clenched teeth before signaling Gomez to drop the ropes. They coiled to the ground as the AW clawed and thundered its way back into the sky in order to take up overwatch, while Juan and the team took care of business down on the ground.

Raven and Linda bolted for the goat path that led to the top of the escarpment to secure targets one and two with the RPG, who were still down from the drone flash-bang assault.

MacD, Linc, and Eddie hit the three downed mercs near the helipad rocks with their tranq pistols, then began zip-tying their ankles and wrists.

Juan kept a sharp eye out. He wore his favorite FN Five-seveN pistol on his chest rig, but it was the South African Milkor multiple grenade launcher he unslung from his back and held at high ready. It had a six-round cylinder like a gunfighter's pistol, but instead of .44 caliber bullets it fired 40mm grenades. Like the suicide drones that had targeted the mercs on the ground, each 40mm round in Juan's Milkor MGL was a flash-bang grenade.

He called into his comms.

'How's it hanging, Maxwell?'

Max and Stoney stood over targets six and seven, both knocked out, their mouths agape, trickles of blood oozing out of their ears and noses from the flash-bang concussions they received from the suicide drones that targeted them.

As per their pre-mission brief, Max and Stoney shot each man with a single pellet from their tranq guns and were in the process of zip-tying them when Juan called.

'Almost finished here,' Max said.

'Soon as you're done, take up your next waypoint.'

'Will do.'

Max and Stoney were now tasked with watching the proverbial back door against hidden reserve fighters they hadn't located yet. The DING was well suited for the protective cover mission. The 'surprise' device the armory department had come up with for the DING was an automated, pintle-mounted Howa Type 96, a Japanese-built 40mm grenade launcher that looked like a thick-barreled machine gun. Like Cabrillo's Milkor, the belt-fed Howa fired 40mm flash-bang grenades with a 'flash' of six million candela and a skull-cracking 'bang' of one hundred seventy-five decibels. The Japanese grenade launcher had an effective range of fifteen hundred meters and could fire up to three hundred and fifty rounds per minute.

Stoney and Max leaped back into the DING to head

for their next position, when Linda called in over the tactical net reporting they had secured targets one and two and were heading to the rally point. Max punched the throttle, throwing independent power to each of the four big tires. The left tires spun forward and the right rearward, throwing rooster tails of fine grit in opposite directions as the DING turned on its axis like a tank. The former swift boat captain bellowed like a Viking berserker as he rocketed across the compound.

The Nine Saints monastery stood three stories tall and was comprised of two rectangular floors topped by a dome. The first floor was ringed with a series of arches that created a shaded portico around the entire building and helped support the second story, which appeared to be a later addition.

Standing just inches from the wall, Juan saw that the ancient edifice had been built with hand-fired mud bricks covered in the local version of stucco. The building had been recently painted in a mil-spec dull desert brown without concern for either style or religious convention.

On their first pass in the AW, Juan counted three points of entry into the monastery: south, north, and east. With mercs six and seven taken out, Linda and Raven could safely cover the north entrance, and the south entrance had been secured with the takedown of the three mercs near the helipad. Stoney and Max put a lid on the east door.

It was time to go in.

The rest of the team was stacked near the south door, careful not to alert the tangos inside by scraping their uniforms or equipment against the wall. A shut door was the least preferred entry option, but there were no other open points of easy ingress.

Eddie Seng took the point and MacD was his slack man at number two. Both men carried tranq pistols as their primary weapons. But they also had suppressed Sig Sauer MCX 'Rattler' short-barreled rifles slung over their shoulders. The Rattlers were chambered in hard-hitting, subsonic .300 Blackout. There was no telling how amped up the mutant mercs might be and the team needed enough firepower to put them down if it came to that.

Linc was right behind MacD, his large body a human shield for Sarai, who would follow in right behind him. His primary weapon was a short-barreled shotgun loaded with less lethal anti-riot 'bean bag' shells, each one hitting hard like a sledgehammer. Three would knock even the biggest man among them back on his heels. He also carried a suppressed Rattler as a backup.

Sarai was issued a 9mm Walther PDP that she carried in her chest rig and held a tranq pistol in her hands.

Juan was rear security. Though cleared by Hux for the operation, Juan conceded he wasn't at one hundred percent and therefore wouldn't lead the charge. He carried his Milkor flash-bang grenade launcher as his primary.

Everyone held their weapons in low or high ready. It was go-time.

Linc laid a hand on a C4 breaching charge in his kit in anticipation of blasting open the door lock. He watched Eddie gently test the handle. The heavy door swung open noiselessly on greased hinges, revealing the black interior of the first room.

Everyone anticipated an eruption of gunfire shredding the entrance. All that greeted them was a deafening silence.

Either no one was inside or the crew lurking in ambush maintained incredible fire control discipline. There was no way to tell without entering the building.

The *Oregon* crew had cleared countless buildings over the years. They all knew what was waiting for them on the other side of the door. Neither experience nor body armor could stop a well-placed bullet.

The 'fatal funnel' was the meat grinder where most breachers got killed. It was the immediate space inside the breach point of a room and therefore the known point of entry where the enemy could lay down concentrated fire. If they were going to be slaughtered, it would be here – or in one of a dozen other fatal funnels in rooms yet to be cleared.

Fortunately, there was tech to overcome it.

Eddie pulled out a small aerial drone and activated it with the touchscreen controller Velcroed to his forearm. He tossed the miniature quadcopter through the door and checked his screen while the others stood security.

All eyes fixed on the first-person-view drone camera image that now flickered inside of their visors, each anticipating all hell to break loose.

The Algerian stood in the small, windowless pantry, its single electric bulb smashed with the wire butt of his Škorpion vz. 61 machine pistol. His back was wedged into the corner in the space between two steel shelves stacked with canned goods. His hidden position gave him a perfect line of sight to the closed door, where any intruder would have to pass. No one could possibly see him until they entered fully into the room, at which point he would mow them down in a spray of automatic gunfire.

The Algerian heard the high-pitched whine of an electric motor approaching, but it was the bright LED light scanning the hallway that raised his blood pressure. He suddenly realized that, while the door was shut, the transom above it was open.

Moments later, the light approached the hallway ceiling and lit up the transom glass like a sunrise until the light itself lifted over the transom and the quadcopter slipped into the room. It lowered itself in a smooth arc and turned on its axis, its bright camera light sweeping the far wall.

The Algerian's hands white-knuckled his weapon, waiting for the light to turn on him.

'Lost the signal,' Eddie whispered in his molar mic, tapping his forearm controller.

Suddenly, the broken carcass of his drone quadcopter crashed through the open doorway, like trash tossed from a passing car.

'Got any more of those things?' Linc asked.

'That was it.'

'We're gonna have to old-school it,' Juan said. 'Everyone stay frosty in there.'

'Good huntin', *mes amis*,' MacD said.

'On my mark,' Eddie said.

Everybody dialed it in. Grips tightened, legs flexed. In just a few heartbeats, they would all charge through the door into whatever fate awaited them on the other side of the darkness.

62

Eddie pulled the pin on his 9 Bang stun grenade and tossed it around the casing into the hard corner as MacD launched his toward the opposite wall.

Unlike a regular flash-bang, the 9 Bang contained nine separate charges. The two grenades erupted in a brutal staccato of eighteen rapid-fire explosions. Anyone inside would have been hammered into blind unconsciousness by the audio-visual beatdown.

After the last deafening flash, Eddie charged in opposite the door hinges, MacD on his heels peeling around in the reverse direction, both with tranq pistols in hand.

The Cajun ex-Ranger hated the tranq pistol. He felt like he was heading into a chain-saw fight armed only with a Nerf bat. But he had seen how effective the tranq guns were with a well-placed shot and he knew how debilitating the flash-bangs were, even on the juiced-up mercenaries they were up against.

The others raced in behind them, a synchronized, high-speed ballet of precision and speed.

Cabrillo called this kind of close-quarters combat '*Swan Lake* with guns.'

Everybody felt the tyranny of the ticking clock. No doubt as soon as the AW had roared into the compound, somebody had sent an alert to whoever was in charge.

There was no telling what kind of reserves might be on their way to reinforce the compound.

'Clear,' Eddie said. He made a visual check of his team. All good.

One room down.

Juan glanced back at the open south doorway. No one was approaching from outside. He couldn't help but feel his team was exposed from that direction. He put a laser-activated Claymore in the doorway and set it. If anyone came running through they'd be blown to kingdom come.

Eddie nodded at the next doorway in the corner. His drone had recorded this room before it had been disabled. It was a kitchen, with a pantry on the far-side wall.

A pantry with a transom.

Eddie gave a hand signal for Juan to come up with his Milkor launcher and indicated Juan's target on the HUD display as Cabrillo took Linc's position.

The team stacked up again. Eddie tossed two more 9 Bangs into the kitchen. When the last flash-bang erupted, the team poured through the kill box.

Juan stepped into the cleared kitchen doorway and launched three grenades through the transom, its glass already shattered by the 9 Bangs. Three deafening rounds cracked and flashed inside the tiny room.

Eddie gave the signal. Linc breached the pantry door and Sarai charged in. She saw the prone figure on the floor in the corner and dashed over.

'It's not Asher,' she said in her comms.

Linc put a tranq pellet in the man's neck, then zip-cuffed his wrists and ankles.

'Target down and secured,' Linc said.

'Roger that,' Eddie said. 'We're pushing on.'

But how many more rooms to go?

Max and Stoney sat in the DING watching the house clearing unfold on their HUD displays. They also kept a sharp eye on the eastern doorway some hundred and fifty meters away just in case more tangos tried to crash the party inside.

They saw the light from the starbursting flash-bangs stuttering high in the windows and heard the muffled blasts behind the old brick walls.

What they neither saw nor heard were the two mercs who crawled out from beneath the reflective tarps buried in the sandy dirt ten meters behind them. Thanks to the intel Salan had provided, Fellowes had correctly predicted the assault formation Cabrillo's team would assume and even anticipated the support position that Max and Stoney now occupied.

The two genetically modified fighters stormed the DING like bolts of lightning. They were under orders to capture, not kill, and so they limited their attacks to hard punches and swift kicks that rattled skulls inside the padded helmets. In moments they rendered the two men semiconscious, yanked them out of their seats, stripped them of helmets and weapons, and duct-taped them like broiled chickens before tossing them into the backseat.

The shorter merc, a bearded Bulgarian, took the wheel as the bleached-blond Egyptian fell into the passenger's seat.

The Bulgarian had no experience driving an electric vehicle. He smashed the throttle and nearly lost control, not realizing that electric engines powered up fully at the speed of light, like a lamp after a light switch is hit. His enhanced strength and gross motor skills barely enabled him to regain control and right the vehicle before it flipped over, finally managing to steer the DING out into the night, away from the monastery.

'What the –' Murph couldn't believe his eyes.

'Problem?' Gomez asked.

'I think Max and Stoney just got jacked.'

Gomez checked his display. The DING was rocketing away from the compound. Something was wrong.

'I'll call it in to Juan,' Murph said.

'He's got his hands full already,' Gomez said as he smashed the throttles to the firewall and banked the AW toward the DING. 'We've got this.'

The electric-motored DING zipped across the hardpan in near silence, the only noise coming from the chirring of its big knobby tires in the dirt.

The AW suddenly throttled up far behind them, its big blades chopping the air like a summer thunderstorm.

The Egyptian turned around in his seat.

'We can't outrun him.'

The Bulgarian laughed, flashing dirty gold teeth.

'We don't have to. Get on that machine gun and see what you can do.'

The Egyptian grinned as he punched the weapons' touchscreen and grabbed the Howa's joystick.

'It's not a machine gun – it's a grenade launcher!'

'Even better!'

The Egyptian manipulated the joystick to lay the targeting reticle squarely in the middle of the tilt-rotor rocketing toward them.

Murphy gripped the joystick controlling the ADS heat beam until the targeting reticle centered on the DING. He zoomed in on the image on his screen. The DING was running fast but not evasively, as he had expected.

'Max and Eddie are in back all right. Can't tell if they're alive or dead.'

'Let's hope for the best,' Gomez said.

'They're gonna be spittin' mad at me after I hit them with this thing.'

Gomez grinned. 'Better you than me.' He nosed the AW down and drove it at the escaping dune buggy.

Murphy saw the DING's grenade launcher suddenly spin on its pintle mount and aim directly at them.

'Uh-oh. One of those dudes just activated the Howa.'

'What are you waiting for? Hit the toaster!'

Murphy pulled the joystick trigger and bathed the vehicle in a two-second microwave blast. The DING wavered, then shot ahead full throttle. The Howa's barrel flashed as it fired. The shots went wide, missing the AW entirely.

'I think you got his attention,' Gomez said.

'I can do better than that.' Murphy turned to another control station. His fingers sped across the keyboard. 'I can override him.'

The Bulgarian driver was still cussing from the short burst of microwave energy crawling beneath his flesh. He knew instinctively it had come from the helicopter chasing them. It wasn't so much the pain he felt as the sickening feeling that he was being cooked alive from the inside out and it caused him to panic, an emotion he hadn't felt in a very long time. In fact, he couldn't remember the last time he felt any kind of fear.

He heard the Howa 96 thumping behind him as the Egyptian fired off rounds, but judging by the man's foul language he had failed to hit the giant rotary aircraft pursuing them.

Suddenly, all of the DING's lights shut off as the engines lost their power.

'What are you doing? Hurry up!' the Egyptian cried out. 'He's on us!'

'It's dead!' the Bulgarian shouted, but he doubted the Egyptian heard him as the monstrous tilt-rotor roared overhead.

The Egyptian swore when he saw the fire control station was dead as well. He leaped up and grabbed the Howa's firing handles to shoot it manually. He ducked low and aimed the Howa's barrel almost perpendicular to the sky, putting the big bird directly in his iron sights.

He pulled the trigger and cut loose a long string of grenades directly at the belly of the thundering machine.

Gomez saw the man below dropping almost to his knees and raising the Howa up to fire at him. He doubted the flash-bang grenades would have much effect, but he couldn't take the chance. He countered the grenade launcher assault by increasing the pitch of the turboprop blades, which blasted a hurricane of wind down at the vehicle below, blinding the two men with stinging dust.

The flash-bang grenades were 'dumb,' not guided munitions, shooting out of the Howa's barrel like bullets. But the velocity of wind that the AW's Pratt & Whitney engines generated, coupled with the tilt-rotor's sudden vertical rise, completely defeated the fusillade of heavy 40mm shells. They blew harmlessly aside like someone tossing ping-pong balls at a high-speed ceiling fan.

'Murph – light 'em up again!'

Murphy had been tossed around inside of his harness when Gomez verticaled the AW but had regained his seat. He mashed the trigger on the ADS joystick and sent another blast of searing millimeter waves at the men below. Seconds later, the two mercenaries leaped from the DING and ran screaming into the desert in opposite directions.

'Crap – a seven-ten split!' Murphy said as he swung around to his automated flash-bang grenade launcher. He turned his targeting reticle until he found the shorter man and laid it on his back and set it. Then he found the other runner squirting through the brush and painted him as well. Both crazed men ran in a serpentine pattern, sensing that they were being targeted from above.

Murph punched a virtual toggle on the automated gunnery system. Within two seconds the computer had swiveled the barrel to both targets and fired. Two sharp cracks later, both mercenaries were facedown in the dirt, knocked out cold.

'Let's bag 'em and tag 'em,' Gomez said.

'Better hurry. I got a bad feeling,' Murph said as he unlocked his harness and headed for the cabin door.

63

MacD zip-tied the ninth merc, who'd been hiding in the fifth and last room on the first floor. The goon had shoved his pistol barrel through a crack in the door and emptied a mag in their general direction, but Juan cut loose with his grenade launcher and put a round smack into his chest. When it blew, it knocked the super merc out and threw him backward. Sarai was through the door and on him with a tranq pistol almost before the merc hit the floor. A hit with a flash-bang at that range would have killed most people, but the genetic enhancements had saved the killer's life.

Juan heard the revving of the AW's turboprops outside, but since Gomez hadn't reported in he assumed they had everything under control.

Eddie called in to Raven asking for a sitrep, while MacD finished up. The two women were well undercover and keeping a sharp eye on the northern side of the building, making sure no one got inside from their direction.

'All clear,' she said.

'Second floor – let's go,' Eddie commanded as he signaled toward the stairwell. The team stacked up just like they were taking down a narrow hallway, which it was, only this one was closer to vertical. Eddie shot up the first rise of rough-hewn treads two at at time until he reached the first landing, then turned on his heel and pointed his weapon up the next staircase.

An automatic rifle opened up from above and sprayed the stairwell. Half a mag into the assault, Linc opened up with his Kalashnikov shotgun. He put three bean bag rounds square into the man's forehead. The 'less lethal' rounds – standard shotgun pellets stuffed into a material 'sock' – proved to be otherwise at this close range, striking the man's skull with enough force to shatter bone. His corpse tumbled down the stairs and stopped at Eddie's feet.

'Status!' Eddie called out as he stepped over the merc's body.

Everyone reported. Miraculously, no one had been hit.

MacD was next over the corpse, and Linc was right behind him.

'Grenade!' Eddie shouted. A hand grenade bounced down the steps.

Juan saw the deadly charge skitter to a halt just in front of him.

His first response was to pick it up and throw it. But if he did, he could only toss it forward. If it exploded in midair it would kill Eddie and MacD at the front of the line. If he did actually manage to get it all the way up the stairwell and through the doorway from which it came, the blast would kill whoever threw it – and the thrower could be Asher.

Bad idea. The point of this mission was to save Asher's life, not end it.

It only took a nanosecond for Cabrillo to process that thought, and another half nanosecond to come up with a different solution. He grabbed the corpse in his hands and tossed it like a wet blanket on top of the grenade, then fell on top of the corpse to weight it down against the explosion.

Before Juan had even lifted the corpse, Eddie tossed a 9 Bang through the open door and MacD shattered the casing with his Rattler machine gun to keep the tangos away from the entrance.

A moment later, Juan both felt and heard the muffled *whump* of the exploding grenade beneath the corpse. The dead body was ample protection from the blast, but Cabrillo was glad to have the body armor anyway.

'Are you okay?' Sarai asked as Juan climbed to his feet.

He nodded at the corpse, a pool of blood now forming around the dead man's upper torso.

'Doing better than this poor slob.'

'That's number ten,' Linc said.

'Eleven down,' Eddie called through their comms. He and MacD had already sped through the doorway and tranq'd the merc on the floor.

Linc grinned. 'I stand corrected.'

Sarai's eyes widened at Eddie's call. She charged past Linc and Juan, who followed on her heels. Juan still trailed the group, his broken ribs slowing his pace. When he got through the doorway he saw Sarai on her knees examining the downed man. She turned around toward Juan and shook her head.

Not Asher.

Where was he?

'Fellowes? Fellowes? *Scheisse*,' the mercenary swore as she holstered the radio.

The Berlin born Afro-German could no longer remember the details of her past life as a contract hitter for a Nigerian drug cartel. But she had retained both her superior tactical skills and vicious cunning thanks to Hightower's selective mental conditioning program.

She stood in the cramped darkness of the cellar with two other mercenaries, waiting for the sergeant's orders to attack. All three wore Level IIIA Kevlar armor vests and carried AKS-74U short-barreled automatic rifles, compact AK variants with folding stocks and smaller-caliber ammunition. Perfect weapons for close-quarters combat.

'Something must have happened to him,' the Irish woman said. Her hair was short, purple, and spiked.

A bearded Lebanese shook his head. 'Or he can't respond at the moment. Be patient.'

'Patient? Patient? I want to fight!' The German stared at the low ceiling with clenched fists, and swore again. She was in charge of this little unit and Fellowes was her immediate commander. He was also her lover. She didn't dare fail him.

How much longer should she wait?

The *Oregon* team split up into smaller squads to clear the next series of rooms, tossing flash-bangs as they went, charging to their points of domination, clearing sectors, scanning for threats. Each squad moved fast, taking the initiative to the enemy in the hopes of throwing them off-balance. As in every other form of battle, victory in close-quarters combat was achieved through speed, surprise, and violence of action.

They passed through rooms that had all been repurposed into working offices, training facilities, even a small infirmary. Juan didn't see any laptops or cell phones and the paperwork left behind on the desks appeared at first glance to hold little intel value. Now was not the time to go rifling through file cabinets and desk drawers. He hoped the others had better success than he had finding actionable intelligence. If they had the time, they'd come back and conduct a more thorough search. Right now their primary mission was grabbing Asher and not getting killed in the process.

They'd cleared almost the entire second floor when they came back together at the last hallway, leaving five more mercs zip-tied and tranquilized in their wake. The team stacked again, each person holding the same position, each bearing the same sector responsibility.

Eddie glanced at his team behind him. They were breathing hard, but eager to move. He knew behind the smoky glass of the helmet visors were at least a couple of smiling faces. It was hard, dangerous work, but they were pros – and the best in the business.

Seng turned back to face the hallway just in time to see an AK-47 barrel turn the corner of a doorway and flash as it opened fire in a wild spray of lead. Heavy 7.62×39mm rounds tore chunks out of the plastered walls and gouged long fingers of splinters from the floorboards.

Eddie pulled out another 9 Bang and tossed it down the corridor. The AK-47 stopped firing before the flashbang erupted in its ear-shattering staccato. The hallway was still ringing with the whine of the pyrotechnics when the AK opened up again and unleashed another thirty rounds of jacketed lead down the corridor.

Seng pulled out another flash-bang and waited for the AK mag to empty out. As soon as he heard the sound of the empty metal magazine hitting the floorboards, he stepped out into the hallway to get a better angle. He tossed the grenade against the wall near the doorway where the gun had fired from. It bounced off the wall and shot through the doorway, a perfect bank shot.

He turned and ducked back around the corner as the familiar sound of an AK mag swap clanked behind him.

A moment later, a chain of fast-firing flash-bang eruptions split the air. At the last blast, Eddie thought he heard a body thudding onto the planked floor.

'Hold fast,' Seng ordered as he charged forward. Maybe what he heard was wrong or maybe it was a feint by the merc. Either way, he wouldn't allow his team to risk the dash through the ten-meter-long kill box. He slammed into the door casing with his Rattler raised to his eye.

'Clear.'

The rest of the team thundered up and maneuvered into the room as Seng kept his weapon aimed at the unconscious mercenary on the floor.

Sarai dashed over to the body. She cradled his head in her arms. Blood seeped from his ears and mouth.

'Asher!'

'Raven, Linda. Take a position inside on the first floor and cover our six,' Juan ordered on his comms. 'We're coming down.'

'Aye, Chairman,' Raven said.

The two women gave the compound one last scan, then bolted for the north doorway, their heads on swivels.

With their prize in hand, the team needed to beat a hasty retreat to the AW. According to the countdown clock spinning in Juan's visor, the team had been on the ground for just eighteen minutes. There was no telling when the bad guy cavalry would be showing up – and he didn't want to wait around to find out.

'Gomez, we've picked up our package and are on our way. See you in two.'

'Roger that.'

They weren't room clearing now, but they still needed to take precautions in the exfil.

Eddie took the point as usual, but Sarai came behind him as MacD and Linc carried unconscious Asher in a foldable fabric MedSource Fast Stretcher – a polyester blanket with carry handles brought in for just this occasion. Juan took the rear.

'Status?' Eddie called.

All clear, everyone signaled.

'Let's go.'

The German girl – Frieda – lifted the cellar door open on noiseless hinges and slid through the tiny gap like a greased spider. She held it open for her two comrades, who sped through with equally silent agility.

Frieda carefully lowered the door and signaled for the staircase. The Irish woman took the treads three at a time on cat's feet, the Lebanese close on her heels. They stopped at the first landing and Frieda caught up, then took the lead, heading for the second floor.

The heavy footsteps of Raven and Linda storming through the north door below and behind them caught the killing team's attention.

Frieda hand-signaled for the other two to head back downstairs, while she advanced upward, her eyes widened with joyous bloodlust.

The heavy wooden door on the north end wouldn't budge, so Raven put a door-breaching charge on the ancient handle and blew it. Linda yanked the door open and Raven charged in, Linda on her elbow.

Raven's eyes caught the tail end of a fast-moving shadow heading up the staircase as the two of them charged into the building.

'What the crap was that?'

'I didn't see anything . . .'

Raven called it in. 'Chairman, I've got eyes on –'

A machine gun roared as bullets chainsawed the support column near Raven's head.

Juan heard 'I've got eyes on –' when the storm of bullets from an automatic weapon cut off her transmission.

'Raven!' Seng shouted as he charged out of the room to help his two teammates downstairs.

But three steps into the hallway he saw – too late – the wide-eyed Afro-German crouched just below the landing and the short-barreled carbine she held that suddenly erupted in fire.

There was nowhere to hide.

Bullets sprayed the hallway, tearing into the walls before stitching across Eddie's chest. He tumbled backward from the impact, blood spraying from a head wound.

'Fall back!' Sarai shouted as she pulled her weapon from her holster. She drew a bead, but not before a 5.45×39mm round tore through her thigh. She shouted as she went down, her three pistol shots wide of the mark.

As soon as the gunfire erupted, MacD and Linc dropped Asher and grabbed their kinetic weapons. Another dozen rounds from the merc's gun tore up the walls and ceiling. The mag emptied. The time it took for Frieda to reload was the perfect time to attack.

With one exception.

Frieda's ultra-fast fine motor skills combined with hundreds of hours of training allowed her to change her magazine insanely fast.

But the AK platform let her down. The Cold War-era design didn't lock the bolt after the last shot of an empty mag. By the time she loaded a new mag and racked a round into the chamber, Juan had raised his FN Five-seveN and ripped six blistering high-speed rounds at the half-hidden figure.

Three of those specialized rounds penetrated her Kevlar body armor – just as they were designed to do.

The other three found their mark in her frenzied face.

Downstairs, Linda ducked behind another column as she drew her pistol.

'Rave – you good?' she called in her comms. The Native American gunfighter had dived for the nearest wall, putting another column between her and her attacker.

'All good.' Raven pulled the trigger on her Rattler, throwing rounds forward, unable to see where the gunman was. Gunfire roared upstairs. She couldn't make out the chatter on the comms.

Suddenly, the Irish woman sped out of the shadows, flying like a bat out of hell, a knife gleaming in her hand.

Raven rolled away just as the blade thunked into the wooden floor where her skull had been. The spike-haired woman yanked the knife out of the plank just as Linda put three rounds into her upper torso. The 9mm rounds punched her hard, but didn't penetrate the body armor.

The adrenaline-fueled killer turned toward Ross and threw her knife with a grunt. The blade found its mark in her bicep. Linda screamed and dropped her pistol as Raven squeezed the trigger on her Rattler. The .300 Blackout rounds found their mark beneath the Irish woman's chin. Her nearly headless body hit the floor with a hard slap.

Raven leaped to her feet to rush over to Linda, but two steps later she was hit by a flying body. The Lebanese slammed into her like a cross-checking hockey forward, hitting her so hard it stole her breath away, and his collapsing weight on her felt like a bag of rocks on her chest. She stared in horror at the knife in the man's upraised hand, his face a mask of fury. But his body jerked and flopped like a spineless doll when bullets found their mark and his corpse tumbled beside her, the lifeless eyes opened just inches from hers.

MacD thundered up and secured his weapon as Linda pulled the knife blade from her arm. MacD yanked an

Israeli bandage from his kit to stop the bleeding as Raven scrambled to her feet.

'How are the others?' Linda asked through gritted teeth as the Cajun cinched the built-in cleat tight over her wound.

'Sarai's gunshot. Eddie got a high-velocity haircut, but he'll survive. Lincoln and Juanito are tending their wounds.' He had to raise his voice above the AW's turbos roaring just outside the building as Gomez set the tilt-rotor down.

Juan and Eddie scrambled down the staircase with the still unconscious Asher slung between them on the fabric stretcher. Eddie's white head bandage was seeping red blood from his scalp wound.

Linc was right behind them, cradling Sarai in his arms, a tourniquet torqued above her leg wound, her face ashen.

'It's time to blow this popsicle stand!' Juan shouted in his comms as he disabled the Claymore. 'Raven, watch our six!'

He didn't need to give the order. She was already in place, her Rattler sweeping back and forth as she stepped in reverse, her back to the others as they raced toward their escape.

Ninety seconds later, the team scrambled onto the tilt-rotor and lifted off with Gomez Adams coolly reporting in his comms, 'We have bogeys.'

The radar computer identified them as a pair of slow-moving Mi-24 Hinds coming up from the base outside the capital city. They would arrive on scene within fifteen minutes.

'What do you want to do with the DING?' Gomez asked. It would take at least that long to hook it back up to the AW for transport.

'Burn it.'

Juan pulled off his HUD helmet and scanned the cockpit.

Amy Forrester had already bandaged up Max and Stoney, who were both shaken up and badly bruised but otherwise uninjured after their ordeal. Now Forrester was working on Sarai's wound, which was more severe than Linda's. She threw a quick glance at Juan. Her eyes told him, *She'll be okay*.

Linc was unwrapping Eddie's bloody head bandage so he could close up the bullet graze that had opened up his scalp with butterfly bandages. Despite the chest-thumping he'd received, the Chinese-American operator threw a weary smile and a thumbs-up to Juan, who nodded in return.

Cabrillo gazed at Asher lying on the fabric stretcher where they had dumped him, still knocked out from the tranq pellet. His body bore the outward signs of High-tower's modification regimen. Despite the hard, sinewy limbs, enlarged hands, and swollen veins, his face was oddly peaceful in its fitful sleep.

His rescue was immensely satisfying to Cabrillo. He considered Asher a comrade in arms of a sort, since he was technically an undercover operative for an allied security agency. But he was even happier for Sarai, whom he considered a friend.

The rescue had come at a high price to his people.

Cabrillo whispered a prayer of thanks that none of them had been killed. He was relieved they were finally heading back to the *Oregon*. Time to call in a sitrep to Hali. He snatched up the radio mic on his console.

'*Oregon, Oregon*, this is Duesenberg 29. Do you read me? Over.'

No response.

'*Oregon, Oregon*. This is Duesenberg 29. We are inbound. Do you read me? Do you read me?'

Juan saw that every open eye, wounded or not, was turned to him.

'*Oregon? Oregon? Oregon!*'

64

On Board the Oregon

Maurice sucked in another lungful of steaming air as rivers of sweat poured down his bare back. He loved the sauna and had long enjoyed the Swedish practice of a hot steam followed by a cold plunge into icy waters and repeating the process for as long as time permitted. Its advantages to physical health were undisputed. But the mental benefits of embracing discomfort was a cherished habit he had acquired as a young British Marine in the Special Boat Section so many years ago.

As chief steward on the *Oregon*, his primary duty was to serve at the beck and call of the senior officers, particularly Cabrillo. With all of the senior staff deployed on the Nine Saints mission, he had little to do until they returned.

More to the point, he couldn't sleep knowing his friends were traveling in harm's way. Whenever his people were on a mission, his mind invariably wandered back to the catastrophe in Borneo so many years ago. The fear of ever letting another comrade down in the heat of combat drove him from the armed service – and the sting of that memory proved to him yet again his decision had been a sound one.

Tonight his greatest concern was disappointing his friends by failing to greet them upon their victorious return with the finest spirits and hors d'oeuvres he could provide. He smiled at the thought of what awaited them. He had personally prepared several trays of Mexican street corn and lobster canapés and paired them with frosty cold bottles of St Bernardus Tripel.

He swatted away a bead of sweat hanging on the end of his long patrician nose and checked his watch. In thirty seconds he would flee the sauna and dive into the frigid water of the ship's Olympic-size pool, then dash back into the sweltering confines of the cedar-lined sauna.

Salan's four-man assault team split up as soon as they entered the boat garage, each corporal in charge of a merc. Their primary goal was to seize control of the ship.

Despite their vastly superior physical abilities and tactical training, the reality was that the four killers were up against at least twenty able-bodied men and women who served aboard a combat vessel. These may all have been support personnel, but it would be foolish to assume they didn't possess the means to defend the ship. The paras had taught Salan the old adage that, when it comes to numbers, 'quantity *is* quality.'

Salan's plan to overcome the deficit in numbers was brilliantly conceived. The *Norego Sunrise* support crew would be completely distracted by Salan's trap that he had set for the inland operation at Nine Saints. The crew would be focused on mission support and wouldn't expect a sneak attack. It was no surprise their guard was down and the egress into the high-tech ship had been easy.

Seizing the ship was the first task; holding it was the second. The numbers problem persisted.

Salan had a plan for that, too. Now it was time to execute it.

The four men moved in utter silence through the dimly lit compartment, their suppressed pistols in one hand and their long kukri knives in the other as they raced for the engineering section.

The *Norego Sunrise* was alive and awake but operating in near darkness to avoid detection by passing ships or aircraft while their Eritrea mission was underway. Though the ship was at anchor, the engines were idling in order to provide electric power to the vessel.

The first target was the emergency control room located in the main engineering section, where the thrumming magnetohydrodynamic engines were located.

The senior corporal led the way through the shadowy compartment, Salan's blueprints etched in his mind, though he carried a paper copy in his shirt pocket. His men were similarly equipped. The main door to the engineering section suddenly opened and a brawny figure stepped into the dim light of the doorway.

The corporal signaled for his team to halt while he advanced. He didn't fully trust either the Sudanese or the Brazilian to keep fire discipline nor resist the siren call of their kukri blades, so he took matters into his own hands. He sped with leopard-like speed in a low crouch and cracked the crewman on the back of his head with the butt of his gun. The man never knew what hit him. The corporal caught the heavy sailor in his arms before he crashed to the steel deck and laid him down quietly. Silence was their best defense.

He signaled for his men to advance with a hand gesture, then sped through the door and into the engineering compartment. The Sudanese closed the door behind them and the Brazilian took up a defensive position next to him as the two corporals ran over to the emergency control room.

Once inside, the first corporal located the intruder alert system, just where Salan's map said it would be.

'Masks on,' he ordered.

All four men pulled gas masks out of their small equipment pouches and put them on.

The senior corporal saw an array of buttons. He picked the appropriate one and pushed it.

Klaxon alarms suddenly blared, compartment lights flashed, and a woman's computer-generated voice stated loudly and firmly over the ship's speaker system, *'Intruder alert, all decks. Intruder alert, all decks. All hands, man your stations.'*

But initiating the intruder alert system produced another, more important result. Beneath the flashing lights and the blaring Klaxon *ah-ooh-gahs*, the ship's intruder system began pumping a highly potent sleeping gas throughout the entire vessel.

The Op Center

Hali Kasim bolted upright as he sat in the Kirk Chair when the intruder alert Klaxon began wailing. His blood pressure spiked like an oil derrick's geyser.

The junior helmsman glanced over her shoulder at

Hali from her station, her startled eyes wide as dinner plates.

Kasim dashed over to the emergency alert station and saw the flashing red warning light. His legs wobbled and his vision blurred as he scanned the control panel, trying to assess the nature of the threat as his clouding mind struggled to focus. He turned when he heard the helmsman crash to the floor.

He suddenly remembered about the sleeping gas and he reached for the radio to call Cabrillo, but he collapsed to the deck before his hand touched the mic.

The Med Center

Dr Julia Huxley was famous for not sleeping. It wasn't that she was an insomniac. She was one of those rare individuals who thrived on just a few hours of sleep. It was one of the reasons she had excelled in her medical residency, while her classmates shuffled like mindless zombies through their sleep-deprived hospital rotations.

Tonight she had been up rechecking the emergency medical supplies in the *Oregon*'s clinic, just to be sure everything was ready in case her services were needed after Nine Saints. She prayed they weren't. But that was her job and she was darned good at it. She would be ready, as always.

Hux was about to go back to the lab to examine the biological data she had collected on the sailor who died, when the intruder alert erupted overhead.

Her training kicked in. She sped toward her personal

locker to fetch her favorite sidearm, a Glock 19 semi-automatic. But three steps short of the locker she suddenly felt woozy and her vision blurred.

She hit the sterilized floor hard, knocked out cold by the gas.

The senior corporal checked his watch. After sixty seconds had passed, he hit the alarm's kill switch. The woman's voice silenced along with the wailing Klaxon, and the flashing lights returned to their monotonous low-power setting. More important, the ship's ventilation system cleared away any excess gas.

He turned to his men.

'You can take off your masks now. Anyone who inhaled that sleeping gas will be out for at least an hour. However, there might be stragglers.' He pointed at the Brazilian. 'You sweep the first deck. Anyone you find awake, kill them. We'll do the same as we travel to the operations center. Are we all clear?'

Heads nodded.

'Any problems, use your radios.' He pointed at the Brazilian.

'Go!'

Maurice was sitting in the dark, nearly naked, his ice-cold skin just beginning to absorb the sauna's welcoming heat, when he suddenly realized the intruder alert was sounding.

How long had it been alarming?

At first he wasn't sure what the noise was. Inside of the heavily insulated cedar box, even the wailing Klaxon was muffled and he could barely make out the computer-generated voice. He listened closely.

'*All hands, man your stations,*' echoed on the pool tiles outside.

How could there possibly be an intruder? Surely it's a drill or perhaps even a computer glitch, he assured himself.

But what if it wasn't?

He took a couple of deep breaths, pulling the warm moisture deep into his lungs, thinking.

If this was a real intruder alert, why hadn't the system's sleeping gas knocked him out?

Either that proved this wasn't a real alert or that someone had overridden the gas release and kept the lowest deck from being inundated with it.

It was also possible that the contained environment of the sauna had protected him from the anesthetizing fumes.

Either way, he wasn't going to sit around and wait for an all clear. If there really was an intruder, his friends would be in danger.

If not, he could always crawl back into the sauna. Captain Cabrillo wasn't due to return for some time yet.

Just as he eased the sauna door open, the lights and alarms all ceased. Maurice sighed with relief.

A system test, no doubt. Crisis averted.

He glanced at the gleaming waters of the pool and then back into the steaming closet, unsure which to enjoy next. But something struck him as terribly odd. Old instincts welled up inside of him.

He dashed to his locker.

*

Moments later, Maurice stood at his locker, his sweats neatly folded on the first shelf. He reached to the back of the second shelf and wrapped his hands around a familiar object. He pulled the shoulder holster out, his Webley service pistol tucked neatly in the saddle-grade leather, supple and smooth after decades of careful nurture.

He pulled the pistol, broke it open carefully, and checked the cylinder. It was loaded, of course. He kept the gun in the gym locker because it was more convenient to store it there, near the shooting range, than back in his stateroom. He set the holster down and retrieved another object from the locker, a well-oiled and sturdy scabbard.

He freed the spear-pointed dagger from its leather. Long ago, the rib-piercing blade had proven itself a trusted friend. It still felt as much a part of his hand as any of the fingers now wrapping around the ringed handle.

At that moment, an ice-cold grip seized his heart, an ancient terror he had battled for years.

But no longer. Not now.

He knew what he must do.

The big Brazilian raced through the corridors of the first deck on his way to the crew's quarters. His eyes were constantly scanning for movement in case the sleeping gas hadn't found everybody. His heart raced at the thought of actually running across somebody and seeing what the razor-sharp kukri could really do to a human body. So far he had only practiced on stray dogs.

He decided to search the medical department first since it was on his way.

He stepped over a sleeping crewman lying in the

hallway, the third unconscious man he had encountered. This one was dressed in hospital scrubs, either a doctor or a nurse. He was half tempted to bury his knife in the man's chest just to do it, but he couldn't bring himself to violate the corporal's orders. Besides, he had been promised there would be plenty of opportunities to wet his blade later, so he pushed on.

He turned a corner and entered a locker room. Another body lay on the floor. He started to turn away but saw something different.

A woman.

The Brazilian's eyes fixed on the form. Her dark hair was plain and pulled into a ponytail, but revealed an attractive face, and her oversize scrubs couldn't hide the incredibly voluptuous figure beneath them.

A bolt of testosterone shot through him like an electric shock. His mind focused to a pinpoint. His body stirred.

He glanced around quickly, as if the corporal were nearby and watching him, but he clearly wasn't. The Brazilian sheathed his knife and holstered his pistol as he dashed over to the helpless beauty and knelt down next to her. Seeing her this close, she was even more desirable.

He began to tremble.

The corporal's voice began ringing in his head, but he pushed it aside as he gave way to the fire raging inside of him.

His big hands grabbed the woman's shirt and ripped it open like a wet paper towel. Her exposed torso poured more gasoline on the raging inferno welling up in his loins.

'Get your filthy hands off her, you brute!'

The Brazilian turned on his heels, still squatting, his hand slipping toward his sheathed knife. An elderly man in gray sweats and a leather shoulder holster stood in the doorway, his bright blue eyes raging beneath a mop of wet silver hair.

Where did he come from?

In the span of half a breath, the Brazilian leaped to his feet and charged.

His muscled frame slammed the smaller man hard against the bulkhead, knocking his breath away. The Brazilian's thick fingers wrapped around the old man's neck as he pinned him high against the wall, his sneakered feet dangling just above the floor.

'Who are you, old man?' the Brazilian asked. He relaxed his grip just enough to allow him enough air to speak.

Maurice paled as the blood drained from his face.

'Tell me! Or I will snap your scrawny neck like a chicken!'

Maurice's eyes narrowed.

'My friends . . . used to call me . . . *Wraith.*'

The Brazilian gasped as the dagger's hilt slammed into his rib cage. The terrible blade sliced through the ventricles of his now fluttering heart, cleaving muscle and valve with each deft twist of the old man's hand.

The shocked mercenary glanced down at the liver-spotted hand giving the steel handle one last turn. A flower of blood bloomed through his shirt. He stared incredulously at the horror as his strength fled him, his legs and arms giving way, like a marionette when its strings are cut.

The Brazilian was dead before he hit the floor.

Maurice fell on top of him, his throat still loosely grasped in the larger man's hands. He rolled off the corpse and pulled his trusted fighting knife from the Brazilian's ribs. He wiped the blade on the man's bloody shirt and put it back in its scabbard in the small of his back. He dashed over to Huxley and felt for her pulse and sighed with relief when he found it.

He picked up the diminutive doctor and carried her into one of the exam rooms and laid her down gently on the exam table. He yanked open a couple of drawers until he found a blanket, then carefully laid it over her to cover her.

He hoped she would forgive him for arriving too late.

Maurice stepped back over to the corpse, his mind racing.

Well, this proves there are intruders on board. But how many are there? What is their goal?

He hadn't heard any gunshots. Surely this man wasn't alone. But if he wasn't alone, there weren't enough of them to travel in pairs – not a good idea in close-quarters combat.

The former SBS warrior instantly accessed parts of his brain he hadn't used in decades.

An experienced warfighter wouldn't try to clear rooms by himself, so the dead man hadn't been trying to do that. There weren't many of them. What then would be the purpose of sending a small team aboard a large, crewed vessel?

Maurice's eyes landed on the small equipment bag on the man's belt. He knelt down and opened it. A gas mask.

It all made sense. He glanced over at Hux's sleeping form in the next room.

This man's assault team had activated the intruder alert system to use the gas to knock down the *Oregon*'s crew. That meant they were trying to take it over.

But how?

Of course.

Maurice stood.

And ran.

65

The Op Center

Hali's body ached from his uncontrolled fall to the deck when he'd been knocked out by the gas and his nose burned from the smelling salts used to wake him from his stupor.

It took him a moment to figure out how he wound up back in the Kirk Chair, when his eyes began fluttering open. The senior corporal's first hard, open-handed slap to his face revealed who had put him there.

It was the second slap that made Hali's ears ring and rattle his brain, but it was the third one that brought on a near-migraine headache.

The senior corporal stood inches from his face.

'I won't ask you again. How do we operate those bleeding engines?'

'I can't tell you that.'

Slap!

The senior corporal stood and pointed at the helmsman, who was propped up in her station chair. Her left eye was blackened after hitting her station desk when she collapsed from the sleeping gas earlier.

'Then maybe she will.'

The junior corporal twisted her arm hard by the wrist. She gasped in pain. Through gritted teeth she hissed, 'I won't tell you.'

The senior corporal nodded. The other soldier torqued her wrist violently, audibly snapping the bones in her arm. The woman screamed.

Hali wanted to vomit. His face broke out in a sweat.

The senior corporal pulled his kukri.

'I'm going to skin her alive, inch by inch, until you tell me everything I need to know.'

Hali blanched. He couldn't let these killers steal the *Oregon*, but he couldn't let them torture his friend, either.

Suddenly, a gunshot rang out from the hallway.

The two corporals glanced at each other.

The junior corporal snatched up his radio.

'Akram! Akram! What is your status? Over.'

No answer.

The senior corporal nodded in the direction of the door.

'Go check it out.'

The junior corporal pulled his pistol and sped for the exit.

The senior corporal slapped the knife blade under Hali's chin.

'Don't think I'm done with you yet —'

A scream echoed in the hallway.

And the lights shut off.

The high-tech op center was normally lit by LED accent lights and the blue glow of the computer screen monitors at each station. But the lights and the computer monitors fell dark. Only a red power indicator on Hali's backup communication system glowed dimly.

The senior corporal stood in utter darkness.

He heard the helmsman scrambling for cover somewhere beneath a desk on the far side of the room. As far as he knew, there weren't any gun lockers in the op center. The helmsman was simply trying to hide.

The corporal began to panic. The situation was spinning out of his control. It was time to re-seize the initiative. He formed a plan.

He pulled his pistol and cracked Hali over the head, knocking him out.

He dashed for the far corner and raised his weapon. He had a clear shot at whoever would come through that door. With any luck, his opponent would see the man in the chair and hesitate just long enough to get a bullet in his ear.

Just as his eyes began to adjust to the dark, the corporal heard heavy footfalls jogging toward the entrance. A figure suddenly flew through the door and hit the deck.

The senior corporal fired three shots at the prone figure. The gun blasts lit the room like strobe lights, half blinding him. But he had enough eyesight left to see he had just put three rounds into the junior corporal lying motionless on the floor.

In the half breath it took for his brain to register what he had done, another figure dashed through in a low crouch.

The two men traded shots.

Both were hit.

The first .38 caliber round from Maurice's Webley tore into the corporal's shoulder. The second and third found their marks in his throat and forehead.

Maurice crashed to the floor with two rounds in the gut.

He balled up, his teeth clenched against the searing pain clawing his guts out. He whispered a prayer. But not for his relief.

He prayed desperately that he hadn't failed his friends.

He drove his face into the rubberized deck to distract himself from the relentless misery. He knew his life was draining through his fingers. Through the mind-numbing torment, he dimly perceived a familiar voice calling in the overhead speakers. Turboprops roared in the background.

It was Cabrillo.

'*Oregon, Oregon.* This is Duesenberg 29. We are inbound. Do you read me? Do you read me?'

Maurice tried to raise himself up to his knees and crawl to the station to answer the call, but he fell back to the deck in utter agony, clutching his bleeding stomach as tightly as he could, his fingers slick with hot blood. He shut his eyes against the pain.

Fearing the worst, he whispered a final prayer, begging forgiveness for failing his friends.

'*Oregon? Oregon? Oregon!*'

66

In the Air Over Jordan

Crown Prince Abdullah sat in the luxurious grip of his plush calf-leather seat. He watched the live stream digital map tracking the icon of his Gulfstream IV as it crossed the digital border of Jordan, but his mind was on the Romanian prostitute he had enjoyed last night. It was the most exciting experience of his young licentious life. They had made plans to meet again after his return.

Abdullah pushed the debauched memory away and glanced out the small window on his right. Flying just fifty meters away was one of his two military escorts, a Royal Saudi Air Force F-15E Strike Eagle. He saw the helmeted pilot beneath his bubble canopy throw a salute at the Gulfstream, then peel away, arcing his way back to Saudi airspace.

A moment later, an F-16 Fighting Falcon took its place, its tail emblazoned with Royal Jordanian Air Force markings. A quick glance by the crown prince across the narrow aisle revealed that another Jordanian F-16 escort had assumed its station.

Abdullah smiled. Every possible precaution had been taken to protect him on this historic mission. A joint task force of Saudi and Jordanian military and intelligence agencies was providing ground and air security for the trip. Both the Saudis and the Jordanians were concerned for Abdullah's safety, though for different reasons.

Jordan was wracked by its own internal security concerns, particularly the restive majority Palestinian population. The rebellious Palestinians deeply resented the Jordanian government for a number of reasons, not the least of which was its peace treaty with Israel. They believed the treaty explained Jordan's failure to use its vast military resources to wrest a Palestinian homeland from the Zionists.

But in recent years, new threats had arisen to the Hashemite kingdom. The Syrian and Iranian governments, Al Qaeda, ISIS, and even homegrown revolutionaries posed a constant security threat to Jordan.

Against all of these threats, the Jordanians had strengthened their military and economic ties with the United States. They also needed large infusions of cash to subsidize their faltering economic development, defense infrastructure, and burgeoning Syrian refugee crisis. Saudi Arabia was flush with the cash they needed.

At the crown prince's urging, the Saudis, among America's staunchest allies in the Middle East, proposed a bilateral defense treaty. After intense secret negotiations conducted by the crown prince, an agreement had finally been reached.

Today that treaty would be signed. It represented Abdullah's single greatest foreign policy achievement so far. Signing a mutual defense pact with Jordan – which already had a peace treaty with Israel – moved Saudi Arabia that much closer to Abdullah's ultimate goal: a defense treaty with Israel.

Originally planned as a secret signing, word had

unfortunately leaked out in the last week, though such a possibility had been rumored for months. No matter. It was a foregone conclusion now.

Abdullah's conservative detractors back home fully understood the significance of today's event and considered the treaty an unforgivable betrayal of both their nation and their faith. Such zealots were dangerous.

Certain Saudi royals had a long history of financing radical organizations like Al Fatah, Al Qaeda, and ISIS. Osama bin Laden was a Saudi royal, and fifteen of the nineteen 9/11 hijackers were Saudi nationals. Abdullah's security people knew these same elements were capable of reaching out as far as Jordan to stop the treaty signing, and would kill the crown prince if the opportunity presented itself. So would the Syrians and Iranians. Hence the extraordinary efforts to protect him today.

Abdullah checked his diamond-studded Hermès wristwatch. The Gulfstream would be landing shortly at Jordan's Muwaffaq Salti Air Base, recently enlarged and expanded by the generosity of the American taxpayer.

There was a gentle knock on his cabin door.

'Enter.'

The pocket door slid open. Abdullah's personal assistant, his cousin from his mother's side, stood in the doorway with the crown prince's personal encrypted cell phone in his hand.

'Yes?'

'It's Prince Khalid, on FaceTime. He insists it's quite urgent.'

Abdullah frowned. He didn't realize he had given his private number to the former GIP director. But perhaps because Khalid was now – *again*, he reminded himself – the deputy crown prince, someone in the chain of command had passed it along to him. Abdullah made a mental note to change his number. Khalid may have been forced upon him by the old reactionaries on the Allegiance Council, but it didn't mean he actually had to like him, let alone work with him.

Abdullah gestured for the phone and dismissed his cousin with a flick of his hand. He raised the phone to eye level. Khalid's weathered face greeted him with an arrogant smile. Abdullah could taste the bile rising up in his throat.

'Prince Khalid, I understand you have something urgent to tell me. Please do so quickly. I'm rather pressed for time.'

'Trust me, I'm well aware of how much time you have left. So let me skip the formalities. You know that I oppose the signing of this treaty with Jordan, as do many others. Is there any chance I can persuade you to abandon this folly and return home?'

'Absolutely not. And I consider your request an act of total impertinence. Even treasonous. How dare you!'

'Nothing could be easier for me. I am a faithful follower of Allah, a lowly finger of his magnificent hand. And I am pointing at you in judgment.'

'You are insane, Khalid. I will have you arrested before sunset.'

'You are so arrogant, so full of pride! You have held my family in contempt these many years.'

'What are you talking about? Your son was my best friend.'

'My son was your puppet. And I slew him on the altar of your ego.'

Abdullah's mouth fell open. 'What are you saying?'

'You serve Satan and the Zionists and you will not be the death of our people the way you were the death of my son.'

Abdullah slid his free hand toward an emergency button on his chair, his fingers out of sight of the screen, inching forward.

'You live like a devil, so you shall die like one.'

The crown prince smiled as his finger finally found the emergency button. He pressed it. His security team would respond within moments.

'Whatever do you mean, Khalid?'

'The Romanian woman you enjoyed last night was an operative in my employ.'

A cold shock of terror ran down the length of Abdullah's spine.

Khalid smiled at the fear twisting Abdullah's face.

The woman was, in fact, Salan's assassin, who transferred a new kind of biological nanobot into the crown prince's body.

'Does not the Almighty Allah tell us that there is an abode in Hell for the proud, my prince?'

'You must be drunk, you old fool. Expect the secret police to be arriving at your door very soon. I'm ending this call.'

'You may end the call, but first hear this.'

Khalid flipped a toggle off camera. A high-pitched tone screeched over the phone speaker.

'What is that?'

'The sound of your doom.'

Abdullah cursed and killed the call as heavy footsteps sprinted down the narrow aisle toward his compartment.

The pocket door flew open. Abdullah's personal bodyguard stood in the doorway.

'Your Majesty!'

The crown prince sat in his chair with wide, unblinking eyes.

Dead.

67

Yemen

Salan's convoy passed without incident through Yemeni territory thanks to the Saudi intelligence officer who prepared the way. He had secured safe passage through both generous bribes and the installation of pro-Khalid security personnel along the route.

Crossing into Houthi-held territory was more problematic. The two Quds Force escorts who joined them at the border had also made prior arrangements for safe passage, but the deeply suspicious and highly brutalized Houthis operated in independent bands. More bribes offered along with a few threats backed up by satellite phone calls to local commanders finally cleared the way.

A crisis nearly ended the mission when they reached their location in the rugged mountainous region. This was when Salan's soldiers finally emerged from their transport. Until that moment, the Quds Force operatives had been highly professional, even friendly. Salan dismissed an offhand remark by the senior Iranian about the location of the missile's launch computer. He assured the Iranian that the ruggedized laptop was safely guarded, but it was clear the Iranian was more than interested.

If the Quds Force commandos harbored any thoughts about seizing control of the missile for their own government, they were quickly squelched when the Iranians caught sight of his genetically altered men piling out of the truck. The two Iranians blanched with obvious fear and trepidation.

What devils are these?

Salan had to stifle a laugh. He had been around his *mutantes* for over three years and had forgotten the effect their altered bodies had on normal people. It was perhaps akin to a band of ancient *Homo sapiens* encountering an encampment of brutish Neanderthals with their thicker limbs, larger hands, and heavier builds, who were far more dangerous than their weaker competitors.

But what caused the two Iranians to pull weapons was the sudden appearance of Salan's favorite Belgian Malinois, Brennus, named after the famed Gaulish chieftain who sacked ancient Rome. Salan saw no need for the extraordinarily large animals on this defensive mission. It would likely take several days to accomplish, so he left the other genetically modified attack dogs in their kennels on the *Cloud Fortune*. The giant beasts not only required a great deal of careful handling, but took up a great deal of space, and would require prodigious amounts of food and water just to survive in the harsh Yemeni wilderness.

But Brennus was his special dog, and rank had its privileges.

Salan held up a hand. 'Gentlemen, I suggest you holster your weapons immediately. Otherwise, my dear Brennus will tear your arms out of their sockets.'

The Iranians hesitated.

A low growl rumbled deep in the dog's chest. The dog

bared sharp teeth the length of human fingers and snarled like a foul-tempered grizzly bear on the verge of an attack.

The Iranians quickly complied. They kept their distance from both the dog and the mercs, but maintained their professional demeanor with Salan. The Frenchman couldn't shake the feeling they still harbored ulterior motives.

Upon arrival, Salan saw the genius of their choice of location, and of the decision to fire the missile from Yemen. The thin veneer of Iranian plausible deniability was no doubt a factor. But Salan could sense the uneasy alliance between the Iranians and Houthis. A few brief encounters told Salan that the Iranians wouldn't complain at all if the Americans decided to carpet-bomb Houthi-controlled territory. The junior Iranian even confided to Salan in an unguarded moment that the godforsaken Houthis were as much a nuisance to Tehran as they were to Riyadh.

But most important of all was the actual missile launch site. Salan had never understood how a poor, unsophisticated people group like the Houthis had managed to deploy missiles and drones against Saudi targets without detection or destruction by high-tech Western surveillance. Now he understood.

The Iranians had hired North Korean engineers to build secret tunnels deep inside the natural caves of the Yemeni mountains. The North Koreans were experts at both building missiles and hiding them from prying Western satellites. The plan all suddenly made sense.

The specialized truck that carried the missile easily unloaded the launch container via its hydraulic lift and powerful cable winches. The entire container was then lowered carefully onto a mobile platform that set the missile inside the concrete structure designed specifically for missile launches. Judging by the burn marks and other debris in the interior, it had been used quite successfully on more than one occasion.

Salan was informed by the Iranians that there were dozens of such caves in this region alone and that many of them featured some form of North Korean engineering. Neither the Americans nor the Saudis had ever been able to locate one of these caves, but even if they had, any kind of ground assault would have been met with stiff Houthi resistance. Many of the older Houthis fighting in these hills still wore tire-tread flip-flops and fought with guns their fathers had carried in the war a generation before. Skilled, determined, and fighting for their very existence, the half-starved Houthis were more than a match for the better-equipped Saudi ground forces – many of whom were actually Pakistani hirelings – in this mountainous terrain.

With the missile finally installed and his men set in their positions, Salan was ready to test the launch computer. He opened up the laptop and powered it on. Within moments it established a high-speed connection with an orbiting GLONASS satellite, and the software alerts all read green. The BrahMos was ready for launch. He shut the laptop.

All he waited for now was Khalid's order to fire the missile that would turn the thirteen-billion-dollar *Ford* into a flaming hulk. While most of the forty-five hundred Americans aboard would die instantly in the strike, the sinking wreckage would drag the survivors down to the seabed, entombing them forever in a cold steel grave.

Everything so far had gone exactly according to plan.

Khalid had called him moments ago to inform him of the crown prince's gruesome death caused by a swarm of sound-activated nanobots shredding the blood vessels in his brain. Khalid's operatives had already pushed fake news stories into social media blaming sudden adult death syndrome for taking Abdullah's life, as it had so many young healthy athletes and other notables in the last year.

The path was now clear for Khalid to assume the place of the crown prince and, soon, the throne itself.

Salan's heart raced at the thought of the untold wealth that would flow his way once Khalid became king. That had been their bargain from the beginning and Khalid was an honorable man. All Salan needed to do was carry out the missile launch and his future wealth was assured.

Any minute now he would receive word from his strike team that the *Norego Sunrise* had been captured and would be on its way to a secure port. He also expected a call from Sergeant Fellowes describing the number of prisoners he had captured. He was particularly eager to learn the fate of Sturges. It would be extremely pleasant to extract whatever information he could from him before feeding him to Brennus.

Salan's reverie was disturbed by the mercenary running his comms.

'Excuse me, sir. An urgent message from Sergeant Fellowes,' she said in a thick Polish accent. She handed him the encrypted satellite phone. He took it with a confident smile.

'Fellowes? Salan here. Tell me, how did it go?'

The Polish mercenary watched the sunrise of Salan's smile darken into a raging storm cloud, his neck reddening with each passing moment. She pretended not to listen.

Salan fumed. Somehow the mysterious Sturges had not only discovered the Kamiti prison and infiltrated the *Sekhmet*, but had also managed to escape his carefully laid trap, capturing Duke Matasi in the process.

Sturges was no CIA agent. He was a warlock, a *jinn*, a trickster god!

Had he ruined everything?

Salan's mind raced, calculating. Why the interest in Matasi? It made no sense. Matasi was a pawn, nothing more. He had no knowledge of the larger plots at play. Could he really have been just a missing son?

He searched for the pre-programmed call number of the *Norego Sunrise* strike team. Just as he was about to hit the button, he hesitated.

If Sturges had escaped the trap, he was no doubt back on his ship. If so, Salan's men were either killed or captured. Calling them now on the sat phone, though encrypted and distributed through his own virtual private network, opened up potential vulnerabilities.

He handed the phone back to the Pole. No matter. The capture of Sturges and the *Norego Sunrise* were personal matters and had no relation to the larger plan at work.

He chided himself for being so shortsighted. Why try and steal the *Norego Sunrise* when he could build his own with Khalid's petro billions?

Salan headed out to check on each man in his unit. He needed them undercover and in position, and ready for anything.

He had made two mistakes so far. There could not be a third.

68

Captain Kim Dudash stood on the outer bridgewing with the giant 9×63 binoculars held to her eyes. The ungainly optics were heavy as a New York City phone book, but they were one of her most prized possessions. The US Naval Gun Factory Mark 37 had been issued to her great-uncle, a decorated captain of a World War II heavy cruiser. He, in turn, had passed them on to her when she entered the US Naval Academy trailing in his storied wake. Despite their vintage, the precision lenses were as crisp as the day they had been ground, and the mechanical parts still turned smooth as butter.

The binos held more than sentimental value. Her uncle's pale gray eyes had scanned the broad horizons of the blue Pacific with these lenses, ranging curtains of fire and steel onto his hapless Japanese foes. When she looked through them, she felt as if she were seeing the world with the same crystal clarity as he had seen it.

It was that same keen vision that first glimpsed the greatness stirring in a determined young girl climbing an apple tree in his backyard so many years ago.

She adjusted the focus ring on an approaching cargo plane. The twin-engined C-2 Greyhound's distinctive four

462

vertical stabilizers sharpened in her view. The senator would be landing shortly.

Dudash lowered her binoculars. She was inclined to unleash a string of expletives that would have made her dearly departed great-uncle, a devout Presbyterian, blush with shame. Senator Robin Stansberry's visit would cause all manner of disruptions in ship routines and her own schedule in particular.

But she held her tongue. She was always 'on,' as they say; her every word and gesture scrutinized by her crew, for good or ill. Cursing the arrival of the head of the Senate Armed Services Committee might have earned her a few points with the old salts on the bridge, but if word got out, her intemperate remarks might jeopardize her promotion to admiral – a promotion that required Senate approval.

This was hardly the first dog and pony show that she had to put on since she took command of the *Ford*. Ostensibly, today's visit was part of a fact-finding mission in the region, but in reality it was merely an attempt to bolster the senator's weak foreign policy credentials. Senator Stansberry was rumored to be making a run for the presidency in the next election cycle. No doubt today's visit would wind up in her campaign commercials.

It would be a great visual, Dudash admitted to herself. Two of the most powerful women on the planet standing on the deck of the most powerful aircraft carrier in the world.

Girl power with nukes.

And if she were honest, Dudash saw the advantage for herself. If she ever wanted to become the first female chairman of the Joint Chiefs of Staff, she would need the senator and perhaps future President advocating on her behalf. The sad reality was that the highest levels of military commands were often little more than political billets.

Dudash raised her binoculars again as the Greyhound turned toward the flight deck on its final approach.

69

Bushehr, Iran

Brigadier General Sadeghi's car passed through the third and last armed gate of the Islamic Revolutionary Guard Corps Navy base. The Quds Force general had known the base commander for years. Like Sadeghi, the admiral feared the fecklessness of the mullahs, endlessly dragging their manicured feet, always promising but never pursuing a total war against the Zionists.

The admiral was one of Sadeghi's biggest supporters and one of his few intimates that was fully apprised of the hypersonic missile operation he had engineered with Prince Khalid. Once Sadeghi became President, the admiral would become the head of a unified Iranian naval command and preparations would begin to finally push the Americans out of the region and drive the hated Israelis into the sea.

The base was completely secured against all external threats and, equally important, any regime spies that were constantly sniffing around. If the mullahs in Tehran discovered Sadeghi's conspiracy with Khalid, he would suffer a traitor's tortured death.

Sadeghi had received the security briefing announcing the death of Crown Prince Abdullah from apparent natural causes. He knew, of course, this was far from the truth.

465

The Iranian spymaster's admiration for Khalid only grew. The Saudi intelligence and protective services were first rate. The Quds Force had failed to inflict significant casualties upon the Saudi royal house over the decades, despite numerous attempts. With the crown prince now dead, it would be only a matter of days before Khalid advanced to the Saudi throne.

Khalid's ultimate success depended on Sadeghi assuming the Iranian presidency, and Sadeghi's ultimate ability to dominate the region depended upon the acquisition of the hypersonic missile technology stored securely aboard the *Avatar*, the freighter he was about to board.

The naval facility was perfectly secure, but there was no point in bringing the hypersonic missile onshore. The fewer eyes that laid on the wonder weapon the better. Spies were everywhere, and the base was well known to Western and Israeli satellites.

The *Avatar* was one of the newest and most advanced vessels in Iran's state-owned merchant fleet, one of the largest in the world. Required by international sanctions to identify themselves with the prefix 'Iran,' the ship was commissioned as *Iran-Malmir*, named after a war martyr, as all Iranian freighters were. Sadeghi had, in fact, served with Malmir and personally named the ship in his honor. Iran-flagged ships often changed their names and identifications to avoid detection. The *Avatar* was no exception. He was certain his old friend would understand the slight.

Sadeghi descended into the specialized hold of the *Avatar*. The humid salt air outside was thick with the typical port smells of diesel fuel and rotted organics, but inside the vast hold of the ship was a cool clean room worthy of a NASA facility.

The nine-meter-long BrahMos missile had been removed from its launch container and was laid out on a massive steel table, already disassembled into its constituent parts like a frog on a dissecting board.

Sadeghi's heart raced. All of his dreams were coming to tangible fruition.

Two dozen engineers, all hand-selected and carefully screened for loyalty to Sadeghi, were feverishly examining, measuring, photographing, and cataloguing everything on the table to the minutest detail, down to the smallest screw. Other technicians were doing the same with the launch container.

Though none of the scientists had been advised of the impending launch of Salan's hypersonic missile, they had all been informed that time was critical. Most suspected an imminent American or Israeli assault on their facility, a suspicion wisely encouraged by his friend, the admiral.

Iranian engineers had proven themselves masters at reverse engineering over the last few decades. By remotely hijacking American drones during the war on terror, they had become one of the world's most important drone manufacturing and exporting nations, often improving on captured designs. The Russian military had come to rely heavily on Iranian drone and missile expertise in their recent conflicts.

The acquisition of the hypersonic missile was the intel coup of Sadeghi's lifetime – a strategic game changer.

Sinking the *Ford* would drive the Americans out of the region, and deter any challengers who would assume the Great Satan's mantle.

Better still, once the technology was fully acquired by his own scientists and domestic manufacturing began, Iran under Sadeghi's presidency would instantly become a first-ranked naval power, controlling the region's shipping lanes. Sadeghi could then lead Iran into its next glorious phase, initiating the apocalyptic war with Israel that would finally usher in the appearance of the Twelfth Imam, the blessed Mahdi – Iran's Messiah.

So far, everything was unfolding according to plan. The next step was for Khalid to inform him of the *Ford*'s sinking, which should happen shortly. But nothing was certain.

Sadeghi had risen through the ranks as an operations officer. There he learned the hard lesson that a mission's success or failure depended upon paying attention to every detail. It was a lesson he had learned well. He needed to get his own eyes on the missile and assess the progress of the work. Though it had taken a great deal of effort for him to escape Tehran's scrutiny to make this trip, he found it absolutely necessary.

He caught the attention of the chief engineer with a beckoning finger. The squat, bearded man raced over, his face a beaming smile. He carried a ruggedized portable computer in his hand, its handle handcuffed to his wrist.

'It is a magnificent weapon system, is it not?' the chief engineer asked. 'Such genius in its design and portability.'

'What of its manufacturing quality? Are the Indians capable?'

The engineer nodded. 'The Indians are first rate. There's no question of its operational capability.'

'And the launch controller? Have you examined it?'

The engineer lifted the laptop to eye level.

'It's simple and brilliant. I could train any enlisted man to use it in ten minutes.'

Sadeghi nodded and smiled as his eyes raked over the deconstructed missile.

'I want you to show me how it works.'

'Of course.'

'All of it.'

70

On Board the Oregon

Juan stood next to the Kirk Chair. He was in too much pain to sit in it. Juiced up on adrenaline during the Nine Saints operation, he had overexerted himself and now he was paying the price. The left side of his upper torso was purpled and blackened like an overripe eggplant. He had been ordered back to his cabin for much-needed rest, but lying down in his bed was torture. More important, he needed to be here.

He caught sight of a spot of blood on the chair's armrest the cleaning crew had missed – Hali's blood, no doubt. It was a painful reminder of his comms director's savage beating. With a concussion and stitches, Hali had been confined to quarters to recover. He did so under protest. Like Cabrillo, he felt personally responsible for what had happened.

Cabrillo snatched up a container of disinfectant wipes and cleaned up the blood, still chiding himself for his failure to anticipate the counterattack on his beloved *Oregon*. His foolishness had cost his crew dearly. Whoever was running the Eritrea operation was top drawer. Smart, aggressive, surprising. In a million years he wouldn't have anticipated that move. He was no doubt dealing with a former operator with exceptional tactical chops.

Cabrillo wouldn't underestimate him again.

He had already organized twenty-four-hour armed patrols on all decks, putting weapons in the hands of any able-bodied sailor regardless of their combat experience. Murphy engaged the *Oregon*'s automated security systems against external threats. There was no telling what aces his opponent had up his sleeve.

Everything was quiet in the op center, but Cabrillo's brain was firing on all cylinders. The pride the crew would have normally felt upon Asher's successful rescue was dulled by the bloody price his people had paid. More to the point, someone had brazenly assaulted their ship. The *Oregon* was their home, and it had been violated. The mood was angry and sullen, but vigilant. All of the principals involved were reassessing their role in the night's events, especially Juan.

Cabrillo made a mental note to drop a letter of commendation into the helmsman's personnel file. His heart had nearly stopped beating when he called the *Oregon* for a sitrep but got no response. The junior boat driver didn't pick up the mic until she had assessed Maurice's condition. By some miracle he hadn't yet died, though the wounds appeared to be mortal. She sounded an emergency alert to the medical department before trying to staunch the bleeding with her own hands, despite her savagely broken arm. By the time she finally answered Cabrillo's frenzied call, Huxley and two of her techs had similarly recovered and arrived on the scene.

Thank God for that medical alarm, Juan told himself. It had helped stir Huxley awake as she was emerging groggily from her whiff of knockout gas. Hux told him it wasn't until she had grabbed her medical kit that she realized her blouse had been ripped open. She had no idea how that had happened, but a moment later when she nearly stumbled over the corpse of a dead merc she suspected he'd had a hand in it. She arrived at the op center with an oversize lab coat buttoned up to cover up her exposed flesh.

Huxley had Maurice prepped for surgery and was wheeling him to the operating room just as Cabrillo set foot back on the *Oregon*'s hangar deck. But a quick glance at the blood stains on the op center floor told Cabrillo his faithful steward was in big trouble.

He glanced up at the clock. Maurice had been under Hux's knife for over six hours. When he called down to medical for a report on his condition, Amy Forrester told him, 'If the man upstairs owes you any chits, you better call them in.'

Juan's hand crushed the armrest as he thought about Maurice still fighting for his life on that operating table. His selfless sacrifice had saved the ship. A cursory review of the facts made it pretty clear the elderly steward was the one who had taken down the four trained super killers. How was that even possible? There was a story to be told. Cabrillo prayed he would get to hear it sometime soon.

Several other members of the *Oregon* team had taken it on the chin pretty hard as well.

Sarai's thigh wound was serious, but Forrester's triage on the tilt-rotor determined the bullet had passed clean through the muscle without hitting an artery or bone. While Huxley worked on Maurice in the operating room,

Forrester stitched up Sarai in the day clinic. Massala was in a great deal of pain and would have to wrestle through a difficult recovery, but otherwise her prognosis was strong. Linc hadn't left Sarai's side since he carried her off the tilt-rotor and down to the medical department.

Huxley had neither the time nor expertise to deal with Asher at the moment. What she did suspect was that if he was like the other mercs she had examined, his adrenaline production was turned up to volume eleven. That one fact alone was shortening his life. She recommended putting him under sedation until they could arrange for him to transfer to a facility that would begin to reverse the genetic engineering that was killing him.

One of the medical technicians dulled Eddie Seng's painful head wound with local anesthetics. Forrester then stitched him up and sent him back to his cabin with a bottle of heavy-duty acetaminophen to dull the thumping he'd taken to his chest. The body armor had saved his life.

Cabrillo was glad to see Murphy at his weapons station. One of the few crewmen who had no prior military experience, the gawky tech nerd had proven himself a brave and steady hand in combat. He might have looked like Shaggy from *Scooby-Doo*, but he fought with the technical precision of a Sugar Ray Leonard. He was one of the few who had escaped any injury.

Linda Ross hadn't fared so well. The knife wound to her bicep wasn't life-threatening, but would require some reconstructive surgery. Despite her protests, she wouldn't be cleared for full duty for several weeks.

Max and Stoney, on the other hand, had suffered relatively minor injuries to their bodies, but major injuries to their egos from the surprise beatings they had taken. Both had been put on concussion protocols, which meant no combat or other strenuous physical activity for several days. They both milled about the op center in quiet contrition, anxious to return to active duty.

One of Hali's comms techs turned in her chair.

'Call for you, Chairman, from Mr Langston Overholt. He says it's urgent.'

Cabrillo wasn't sure what the call could be about. He had sent Overholt an email reporting Asher's successful rescue and his need for specialized care his ship couldn't provide at the present time. He briefly mentioned Asher had undergone a radical gene-altering program that had significantly changed his physical performance.

He didn't provide his old CIA mentor with the specifics of the Eritrea mission or the subsequent attack on his vessel. He was frankly embarrassed, and was still trying to sort through the events before he provided Overholt with the gruesome details. Had Langston heard something through other channels? There was one way to find out.

'Put him on speaker, please.'

71

'Lang, you're on speakerphone in the op center,' Cabrillo said.

'I'll keep this short. But first, congratulations on the Asher Massala rescue. Job well done.'

There was an urgency in Overholt's voice as it boomed in the overhead speakers.

'I'll pass that along to my crew. What's up?'

'I've just left an emergency briefing over at the Pentagon. The Indian government has only just informed us of a theft that took place a week ago. They report that two BrahMos-NGv2 hypersonic missiles were taken by force from one of their naval storage facilities.'

Max let out a long whistle. 'Hypersonics? That's not good.'

Like synchronized swimmers, Murph and Stoney turned as one to their respective computers and attacked the keyboards.

'Why are they telling us this now?' Juan asked.

'New Delhi has failed to locate the missiles and are asking for our assistance.'

Murphy pulled up an image of the BrahMos missile on one of the bulkhead displays. The image also laid out all of the technical details. Murph read off the most important facts.

'It's designed as a ship-killing missile. Approximately

thirty feet long and twenty-four inches in diameter with a max warhead payload of around nine hundred pounds. Speed is Mach 9. Range over nine hundred miles.'

'That's a lot of nines,' Max said.

'Conventional? Nuclear?' Cabrillo asked.

'Can be either,' Stoney said.

'Fortunately, the Indians have only loaded conventional warheads,' Overholt said.

Stoney shot a laser pointer at the screen.

'Its launcher mimics the dimensions of a standard forty-foot shipping container. The idea is to turn any eighteen-wheeler or cargo vessel into a strategic weapons system. It's Russian-designed, but built by India.'

'The Russians have the most advanced and only combat-proven hypersonic missile program in the world,' Stoney added. 'And this Indian version is next generation – faster, greater range, and easier to operate.' He pulled up an image of the laptop launcher controller. 'If you can play a game of Tetris, you can probably fly one of these babies. All you have to do is establish communications with a targeting satellite, hit the launch button, and cover your ears.'

'I don't have to tell you the threat this represents to international shipping generally, and to Western naval forces specifically,' Overholt said. 'If the Iranians, the Syrians, or a terrorist organization gain possession of these, it would be a disaster.'

'Suspects?' Juan asked.

'None, though our Indian friends relayed an incredible story regarding the operators who attacked their facility.

They claim the operators exhibited superhuman strength and speed. In your after-action report, you mentioned that Asher's physical abilities had been altered by genetic manipulation. I was wondering if there could be a connection between Asher and the Indian attackers?'

'If there is, that connection is Dr Heather Hightower.' Juan gave Overholt the briefest of summaries of her operation and promised a full report when time allowed. 'Right now, we need to focus on finding those hypersonic missiles.'

'Agreed.'

Murph smacked himself in the forehead. 'I'm an idiot!'

'No arguments here,' Stoney said.

'GLONASS, dude! GLONASS!'

Stoney's eyes widened with recognition.

'You're so right. Why didn't I think of that?'

Murphy dashed over to Hali's station and dropped in front of his Sniffer keyboard.

'GLONASS?' Max asked.

'Russian GPS. The Chinese have their own as well,' Stoney said. 'Their militaries required it and we sure weren't going to provide it.'

'What are you looking for, Wepps?' Juan asked.

'GLONASS transmits on its own specific wavelengths. I can program the Sniffer to seek those out. If those missiles are currently connected to the system, we can triangulate their ground locations.'

'This is outstanding news, gentlemen,' Overholt said. 'I can reach out to the NSA and the NRO –'

'No need,' Murph called out over his shoulder. 'I've got this.'

'Besides, they'll take too long,' Stoney said. 'And Murph's the best there is.'

Murphy grinned. 'Thanks, bro.'

'What if the launch computers aren't connected to GLONASS?' Max asked. 'What then?'

'Good question. That gives me an idea.' Stoney opened up a new window on his computer.

'The Sniffer isn't finding anything,' Murphy said. 'Doesn't mean it won't. We'll just have to be patient.'

'Time is not our friend,' Overholt said. 'I'm sure you read the President's daily brief this morning.'

Among the many security items listed, Senator Robin Stansberry was scheduled to visit the *Gerald R. Ford*, currently stationed in the Red Sea.

'Sinking the *Ford* would be a real coup for the Iranians,' Cabrillo said. 'And anyone else who hates us in the region.'

Max scowled. 'It's hard to believe that a nine-hundred-pound warhead could sink a hundred-thousand-ton aircraft carrier with Kevlar armor plating.'

Murph turned around in his chair. 'Kinetic energy is a function of mass times velocity. A tennis ball weighs twenty times more than a .22 caliber bullet. But no matter how hard you throw a Wilson, it won't kill anybody. But a .22 bullet fired from a rifle will plow through a human skull. Speed kills.'

'But that's not the half of it,' Cabrillo said. 'The *Ford* is a massive ammo dump riding on top of a floating gas station. If it's anything like the smaller Nimitz class, it carries over twenty-five hundred tons of munitions and two-point-eight million gallons of jet fuel. If that hypersonic hits either of those, it's game over. And don't forget about the nuclear reactors. And if all that missile did was wreck the flight deck, you'd shut down air operations and destroy the myth of the invulnerability of American sea power. Mission accomplished.'

'What about air defenses?' Max asked. 'Radar? Missiles? Fighters on CAP?'

'The BrahMos will be traveling at over ten thousand kilometers per hour,' Murphy said. 'At that speed it's generating a plasma cloud that absorbs radio waves, making it nearly invisible to radar. But even if you could track it, the missile follows a low-ballistic trajectory, which means there won't be time to intercept it. Worse, it's also maneuverable. I'd daresay the *Oregon*'s air defenses are second to none and we wouldn't stand a chance against it. Neither would the *Ford*.'

'Boom!' Stoney threw two hands in the air. 'Found you, you son of a gun.'

'How?' Murph asked, completely flummoxed.

'I searched the Sniffer's logs over the last twenty-four hours. Approximately thirty-two minutes ago, a GLONASS signal was geolocated . . . here.' Stoney threw the image up on a different screen. 'Looks like one of the launch laptops might be located in Yemen. We'll forward the coordinates. I'm willing to bet there's a platoon of SEALs or Marines on the *Ford* that can take care of business.'

'I'm afraid not,' Overholt said. 'Our government is walking a narrow tightrope in the region these days. Sending in the Marines without legal warrant would be viewed as an illegal attack on a sovereign state. We can't do that on the basis of a hunch. Are we absolutely certain that signal we've discovered is actually the BrahMos missile launcher program?'

'With absolute metaphysical certainty? No, sir,' Murph said.

'What's your gut tell you?' Juan asked.

Murph nodded. 'Sure feels like it.'

'That's good enough for me, Lang,' Juan said.

'The President would never authorize such an action on the basis of Mr Murphy's abdominal intuitions alone. Besides, even if we knew for a certainty the laptop is there, do we know where the missile is? That's the primary target.'

'Chances are, it's close,' Juan said. 'But I get your point.'

'And even if the BrahMos is at the same location, we have no proof the *Ford* is the target.'

Juan scratched his head, thinking.

'Wepps, any chance you could hack into that launch computer if it went live again? Shut it down?'

'Yeah, I'm sure of it. It just depends on how good their encryption is.'

'How long would it take?'

'Ten seconds, ten hours, ten days. No telling.'

'So where does that leave us?' Max asked.

Juan glanced around the op center. All eyes were focused on him. Cabrillo was thinking about his crew that wasn't there – especially the ones in bandages and stitches. His assault team was torn up. He couldn't ask them to give any more. Gomez was exhausted and the AW was in the service bay for needed repairs and maintenance. Even the

DING had been left behind in Eritrea, burned to the ground with a couple of thermite grenades.

But there was an American aircraft carrier steaming in the Red Sea with forty-five hundred crewmen aboard whose lives were now at risk. He had to do something.

'I'm going in. Alone.'

72

Juan tapped the comms button on the armrest.

'Hangar, prep the AW. I'm taking her for a spin.'

'But Chairman –'

'See it done!' Juan killed the call.

'You can't fly the tilt-rotor,' Max said.

'Of course I can. Why do you think I've been riding shotgun with Gomez for the last six months? Easy peasy, as Linc would say.'

'Not if he were here,' Max grumbled.

'Have you soloed?' Stoney asked.

Juan tapped his wristwatch. 'Ask me that question again in ten minutes.'

'Gomez won't like you flying his bird,' Murph added.

'Mr Adams might drive it, but I own the pink slip, so technically, it's *my* bird.' Juan headed for the door.

'Juan, my dear boy, I don't like the sound of this,' Overholt said over the speakers.

Cabrillo forgot Langston was still on the call. He saw the concerned looks in everyone's eyes. He appreciated the sentiment. But he had a job to do. He turned around.

'Look, we're all out of options – and time. If we had a drone with that kind of range or enough speed I'd send it, but we don't. I'll do a flyover, see what I can see. If I do get lucky and spot the missile, I'll put a laser designator on it and Murph can toss one of our cruise missiles in that direction. If not, I'll head on back to the barn. It's no big deal. Maybe a flyover will even spook them enough to get them to stand down for a while.'

'Don't you have an EMP missile in your arsenal?' Overholt asked. 'Wouldn't that take the BrahMos out?'

'We do. But I'm willing to bet my oldest Bordeaux the BrahMos is EMP hardened. The Russians are electronic warfare experts and the Indians aren't stupid. They don't miss a trick. But you've given me an idea. Wepps, call the hangar. I'd like Miss Delilah to ride shotgun with me.'

'Great idea.' Murphy flashed a toothy grin. He turned to his comms to make the call as Cabrillo headed for the exit.

'Who is this Delilah?' Overholt asked.

'A short-legged girl with a lot of moxie,' Juan called out.

Max reached out and grabbed Juan by the elbow. Cabrillo winced with pain.

Max's eyebrows took an *I told you so* jump off his forehead.

'We might need to sit this one out, buddy.'

Cabrillo glanced at Max's meaty paw on his arm.

'Can't do that. We've already crashed this dance, and too many lives are at stake. Besides, you've seen how I Watusi. Bridesmaids dig it.'

'Only the drunk ones.' Max nodded, then released Cabrillo's arm reluctantly. 'I'm coming with you. An extra pair of eyes and hands won't hurt.'

'You're grounded, bucko. Doctor's orders. Besides, with Linda out, I need your steady hand on the conn.'

Murph and Stoney both started to stand, but Juan waved them back into their seats.

'Gents, I appreciate the gesture, but I need you here carrying the heavy weight. This is a technical operation and I'm just the analog guy. Understood?'

Both men nodded, but exchanged a whisper.

Juan smiled at his crew. 'You'll see, in and out. No big deal.'

'Juan, my boy,' Overholt said over the speakers.

'Yeah, Lang?'

'Good hunting.'

Juan limped along the deck, grateful the slight breeze wasn't stiffer. Anything to make his takeoff easier.

The tang of salt in his nose always lightened his spirits, an emotional callback to his idyllic youth surfing Southern California beaches. The whine of hydraulic-lift motors wafted out of the cavernous hole from which the AW was now ascending.

The upturned tilt-rotor blades appeared first as Cabrillo approached the rising helo deck. He rehearsed his mental preflight checklist, though he would rely on the printed flight manual, thick as a phone book and Velcroed to his leg once he belted in. Lost in the details of switches and gauges flashing through his mind, he did a double take at what he saw as the lift deck finally locked into place.

Linc, MacD, and Raven were kitted up in their tactical gear, including body armor and weapons. Murph wore a pair of bell-bottom jeans, and the remnants of one of his concert T-shirts, which peeked out from beneath a chest rig. He held the oversize binocular-shaped laser designator in one hand.

'Well, kids. I see someone didn't get the memo,' Juan

said. The turbos instantly fired up. Juan leaned over. Gomez sat in the pilot's chair. He flashed a big smile and threw the world's sloppiest salute.

'No offense, Chairman, but we're tagging along for the ride,' Linc said.

'There's no need for an armed escort. It's just a flyover,' Juan said.

'Always loved a joyride,' Raven said.

MacD grinned. 'They say Yemen from the sky is beautiful this time of year.'

Cabrillo pointed at Murph. 'Delilah needs you back here.'

'Stoney's got her just fine. But without the Rattler-G' – Murph held up the Israeli target designator – 'she's blind as a bat . . . like most of Stoney's dates. Besides, nobody runs this unit better than me. And if it breaks, I can fix it.'

The accelerating turboprops were kicking up a noisome wind.

Juan nodded, scanning the faces of his devoted crew. He knew when he was beaten.

'Then let's saddle up.'

73

The tilt-rotor cabin roared with the noise of the big engines on either side of the fuselage. The props were upturned in helicopter configuration after the long flight in airplane mode.

Everyone except Gomez on the stick and Murph at his station had binoculars to their faces. They scanned the ground below through the windows. Thermal imaging revealed nothing but the shimmering heat from the rocks below.

'You're sure we're on the mark?' Juan asked Murph in the AW's comms. He knew they were. The display showed it. But all they could see below them was the mountainous terrain with rock-strewn valleys riven by a few dusty paths. His frustration was through the roof. They'd been on station for twenty minutes now. Cabrillo couldn't explain it, but he couldn't shake the feeling that time was urgently slipping through his hands.

'No question, we're on the mark,' Murphy said.

'Stoney, any more blips?' Juan asked. Eric was still on the *Oregon* and monitoring for GLONASS targeting signals in Yemen – or anywhere else they might appear.

'No, Chairman. Still a ghost.'

Cabrillo fought the urge to curse. He was certain the

486

missile and its launch controller were down there in the rugged escarpment somewhere. It was a perfect defensive location. The far side of the moon might have been easier to reach. But there was no way to know if the laptop was still down there. For all he knew, the laptop was merely in transport with the missile to an entirely different location when someone tested it. They could both be long gone by now.

But where? And how to find them?

Juan lowered his binoculars. He was wasting precious time.

How much longer should we hang around?

Cabrillo's gloved hand touched the weapon strapped tightly to his chest, an old habit. The stubby FN Herstal P90 was a short-barreled, bullpup design firing the same armor-piercing rounds as his favorite Five-seveN pistol tucked into his leg holster. The rest of his crew were also armed to the teeth. Unlike Eritrea, Juan felt no compunction putting these bad guys down even if they were brainwashed mercenaries – and maybe they weren't. Juan had no idea what the mercs in Eritrea were up to, but here in Yemen the tangos intended to murder Americans. That changed the rules of the game. No more flash-bangs and zip ties.

'Want me to take her down for a closer look?' Gomez asked. They were fifteen hundred feet in the air, well clear of RPG and rifle fire.

Juan seriously considered it despite the grave misgiving in his pilot's voice. Closer to the ground was better, but it was also a lot more dangerous. Shooters with just small arms could do serious damage to the AW at low altitude.

It might make more sense to widen the search area instead of going lower. He just wasn't sure.

But he was here.

'Take her down to a thousand. For now.'

'Gotcha, Chairman.'

Juan raised the binoculars to his eyes. He couldn't see a thing, but something told him someone was down there, targeting his team in their crosshairs.

Salan stood in the shadow beneath the lip of a cave, his binoculars fixed on the tilt-rotor aircraft circling above. The timing was suspect. Khalid had notified him to prepare for missile launch within minutes.

And now this.

When Salan first heard the blades chopping from a distance on its approach, he assumed it was a helicopter, but he couldn't figure out from where. The Saudi pilots were cowards, ever fearful of Houthi anti-aircraft fire. They always dropped their munitions from high altitudes, indifferent as to their effectiveness or the collateral damage inflicted on civilians.

So who could it be?

Salan knew it wasn't Iranian. The Quds Force officers assured him their government wanted to steer clear of this operation to maintain credible deniability. Salan believed them. The Iranian operators were patriots, and he respected that. They also planned on stealing the laptop immediately after the launch, which he also respected. He would do the same thing if the roles were reversed.

It was out of such respect he had the two Iranians

killed quickly and cleanly, and why they now lay buried in a shallow grave facing Mecca, as was their religious custom. He would feed their superiors a palatable fiction and falsely report their deaths as casualties of war, praising them as heroes.

Salan finally got a visual on the highly unusual aircraft – part airplane, part helicopter. He knew instantly it was Sturges. Sergeant Fellowes had given him a complete description of the vehicle. They were deployed primarily in military and security applications. A mere handful of civilians owned them. He watched the aircraft circle for the next few minutes.

It had to be Sturges searching for the missile.

Rage surged through Salan yet again. His steel-banded muscles tensed, and his outsized veins pulsed at his temples. His whole body was taut as a bowstring, his arrow nocked and begging for release. He was as amped up as his men. They cheered him when he ordered them to strip off their pharmaceutical brake pads. He wanted everyone at full throttle today, himself included. His self-treatment had pushed him way beyond Hightower's ten percent improvement limit. He was glad he'd ignored her.

He felt like a god.

Sturges had humiliated him before – twice. He wouldn't allow the American to beat him again.

How had that magician managed to find him here?

The man was full of endless surprises, making him far more dangerous than most. The fact he was still circling above and not landing was proof that even this wizard wasn't omniscient. His men were well hidden and the BrahMos was safely tucked beneath a wall of rock.

'Sir, he appears to be lowering his altitude,' one of Salan's men reported on comms.

'Maintain radio silence,' Salan hissed. No telling what bag of electronic tricks Sturges carried with him today. But his man was right. Was Sturges landing? Or just taking a closer look? Salan's adrenaline-fueled eyes narrowed on the fat belly of the tilt-rotor. Something in him snapped.

To hell with this guy.

Salan lifted the Russian Igla-1 surface-to-air missile to his shoulder, stepped into the harsh light, took aim, and pulled the trigger. The rocket leaped out of its tube and a second later its solid-fueled engine engaged, tearing into the sky.

'Tango on the thermal!' Murph shouted as the ghost-white figure stepped into view.

Warning alarms blared in the cockpit.

'He's got a lock on us,' Gomez said without emotion. 'Buckle up, buttercups!'

The tilt-rotor's automated defensive flares and chaff fired off as Adams slammed the throttles and yoke. The low-flying AW took a sickening, sideways dive.

But the Igla anti-aircraft missile was flying at over two hundred and fifty meters per second.

The result was inevitable.

Salan's eye tracked the smoking trail arcing toward the tilt-rotor. In the space of a heartbeat, the thundering machine jerked away like a poleaxed boar just before the Igla's 2.6-pound HMX warhead ripped the sky in a cloud of shrapnel.

74

What ultimately saved the AW from total destruction wasn't its automated defense systems or even Adams's lightning-quick reflexes, though lacking either would have doomed it. The speed of the Igla was too great for these to overcome it at this altitude by themselves.

What ultimately saved the tilt-rotor was those precious few seconds from the time Salan stepped out into the light, laid his iron sights on the aircraft, and waited for the missile's seeker element to lock onto the target. The AW's defensive measures – puffs of aluminum chaff and pin-pricks of white hot phosphorescence – temporarily confused the decades-old but reliable Soviet design. But a few seconds later, the Igla's locking alarm finally shrieked and Salan pulled the trigger, launching the streaking missile.

The resulting explosion was a near miss, but close enough for the shrapnel to kill one of the AW's two Pratt & Whitney engines and partly disable the other one. The wobbling AW suddenly manifested the aerodynamic efficiency of a thrown brick. In the hands of a less talented pilot, that brick should have arrowed into a flaming crash on the side of a mountain, killing everyone on board.

But Gomez was the best in the business. With a grin plastered on his determined face, Adams guided the plunging aircraft into a bone-jarring landing.

*

Salan shouted with joy as he watched the twisting wreck plunge like a falling leaf behind the mountain. He half expected a Hollywood-style fireball to erupt when it finally hit, but was perfectly satisfied with the knowledge he had knocked it out of the sky. A crash like that probably meant no survivors, which was unfortunate. Salan relished the chance to see Sturges's dejected face blanch with terror before he put a bullet in the man's head.

Still, he needed to check out the crash site. No sense in taking any chances and, with any luck, he might find a few survivors. They might come in useful later as bargaining chips and human shields.

He tossed the Igla launcher aside, keeping his eyes fixed on the mountain.

What to do? He checked his watch. Surely Khalid would be calling him any minute to launch the BrahMos. He should keep his people in position, wait for the command, and launch the missile. Only after his mission was complete should he then search the wreckage.

But what if there were survivors? What if they were calling in support even now?

Better to send his men forward and secure the area. He didn't need any of them for the launch, so he could stay back with the laptop.

But something in him hesitated. He was a soldier and trained to obey commands. The mission always came first. Hadn't he already learned that lesson? Going after Sturges earlier had cost him dearly.

Sturges. The man's name was like ashes in Salan's mouth. This was the man who had broken into his organization, invaded the *Sekhmet*, and wrecked his camp.

Salan felt himself losing control. And he didn't care. He snatched up his radio.

'*Écoutez, mes enfants! Écoutez bien!* Get to that plane now! Kill them all – but not Sturges. He's mine!'

Juan yanked off his helmet and unbuckled his harness. He willed himself not to scream as he squirmed out of the rig. He had survived the landing, but his ribs decided to punish him for it with an excruciating vengeance.

'Status?' he grunted out as he glanced around the cabin.

The rest of his team was shrugging out of their harnesses and scrambling to snatch up their equipment. They called out in the round. Everybody was sore and shook up. But no broken bones, open wounds, or, thank God, fatalities.

Cabrillo sniffed. The air was pungent with jet fuel.

Not good.

'We gotta roll. Weapons, ammo, water. Now.'

'Guess we found 'em,' said Murph.

'More like they found us,' Raven countered.

'Wepps, glue your hands to that laser designator.'

Murphy held it up. 'Never let it go.'

Cabrillo winked. 'Good lad.'

Moments later they had all piled out of the aircraft and stood several feet from it. Gomez pouted like his best girl had dumped him for a rodeo clown. He wore a chest rig holster over his flight suit and a battered straw hat that looked like it had been through a hay baler a couple of times. On him, it looked good.

'Good flying, George,' Juan said. 'Like they say, any landing you can walk away from –'

Gomez held up a hand. 'Don't even go there, Chairman. It's a dang mess. Sorry about that.'

'You've got nothing to be sorry about. We're all alive thanks to you.'

Juan was grateful he hadn't been on the controls solo when they were hit, as he had originally planned. If he had been, the mountain jackals would have been pulling him out of the wreckage in bloody, bite-sized chunks.

Juan sized up the team. They were rubbing sore necks and stretching out kinks, but they all looked eager to go.

'What's the plan?' Linc asked with a nearly six-foot-long semi-auto .50 caliber Barrett rifle slung over his shoulder.

That was the question, wasn't it? Juan asked himself. Whoever took the shot saw them go down. No doubt they'd send a squad up here to check them out.

Juan scanned the hills and mountains around them. The smart play would be to beat a hasty retreat, hide in one of those caves, and wait for the *Oregon* to arrange an exfil.

But there was still a hypersonic missile hidden around here somewhere, almost certainly aimed at the *Ford*, and no doubt poised for immediate launch.

Juan nodded at the crest of the mountain high above them.

'The anti-aircraft missile came from over in that direction.'

'Our tango popped up on our thermal over there, too,' Murph added.

Juan grimaced as he tightened his gun sling.

'Then let's hump it to the top and see what we see.'

*

494

Juan, Murph, and Linc posted up just behind the tall rocky crest with a clear view to the valley floor below. MacD and Raven were on either flank.

The small valley floor was just several hundred meters of space laid out between the feet of a half dozen smaller mountains. Each rocky climb was tracked with ancient goat paths. One of those paths led from the valley floor and toward them.

Gomez kept watch on the back door, his eyes fixed on the plane wreckage a hundred meters below. Despite the stench of leaking jet fuel, no fire had broken out. Gomez sighed.

Too bad the old girl couldn't be salvaged.

Juan pointed at a long, winding road large enough to accommodate big transport vehicles that twisted south toward the horizon.

'If they brought the BrahMos in overland, that was the route they used.'

Murph twisted the focus knob on his binoculars.

'I count five caves.'

'Seven,' Juan said, his eyes glued to his own pair of binos. 'But we're not looking for caves. We're looking for that damn missile and we've got zip.'

'Showtime,' Linc said as he peered through his high-powered rifle scope. He cast his index finger like a fly rod in the direction he was pointing. 'I count eleven fighting-age males, heavily armed, and all heading our way.'

They were streaming out of several caves and melded into a loose fighting formation – and moving with speed.

'MacD, Raven, you seeing this?'

'That ain't no second-line parade, I can tell you that,' MacD said.

'Looks like a swarm of murder hornets,' Raven said.

'Too many of them for us to take on, don't you think?' Murph asked.

'No doubt. But we can't run from them, either,' Juan said. 'There's a missile down there somewhere, I'm sure of it. And we've got to stop it.'

'There's no way we're going to move past, through, or around those guys. Usain Bolt couldn't keep up with them,' Linc added.

Just then, the knot of mercs picked up speed.

'I got a funny feeling something as insignificant as a mountain won't slow these guys down much,' Murph said.

Juan didn't want to sacrifice his people needlessly. Outnumbered more than two to one against physically superior fighters would get them all slaughtered. They lost the night advantage they'd had in Eritrea, and now it was them – not the mercs – who were in a fixed position waiting to get picked off. They were out of options.

Except one. Plan C.

He turned to Murphy.

'Wepps, let's call our girl Delilah.'

75

'Delilah? I don't understand,' Murphy said. 'I thought we were saving her for the BrahMos.'

'We were. But if we get killed before Delilah shows up, we won't get that missile anyway.' Cabrillo pointed at a spot fifteen meters above the valley floor where the angle of the mountain steepened violently.

'See that boulder shaped like a giant potato?'

'You mean Mr Potato Head?'

'That's your target.'

Murphy frowned. 'I don't follow you, sir.'

Cabrillo explained his thinking. He then added, 'You'll have to time it perfectly.'

Murphy's frown turned *way* upside down.

'Will do.' He lifted the Rattler-G designator to his eyes and lasered the rock.

As Cabrillo had predicted, the leading edge of the merc swarm slowed considerably as the mountain steepened. The rest of the platoon caught up to them quickly as they moved from the flat terrain toward the rising slope. Soon they were a tightly packed knot climbing toe to heel as they scrambled up the hill.

*

The herd of mercenaries washed around the potato-shaped rock like a rushing river, unaware of the Israeli Delilah missile screaming toward them.

The loitering cruise missile was originally intended for the BrahMos. The Delilah didn't have the range to be launched all the way from the *Oregon* to this position, so Cabrillo had it attached to one of the AW's hard points and launched it a few kilometers back. The Delilah was designed to loiter for hours at low speed over an area, waiting for a laser-designated target – like Mr Potato Head – to appear on its acquisition screen.

Over two hundred pounds of high-explosive material erupted at the center of the pack when the Delilah struck. The genetically modified bodies that weren't immediately incinerated were torn apart like pieces of confetti. The few survivors ran blindly down the hill, burned and bleeding.

'Do those poor slobs a favor,' Juan whispered in his comms as he put his red dot on the back of an armless mercenary stumbling mindlessly down the hill.

Cabrillo's rifle opened up along with the others.

Within moments, Salan's mercenary army lay scattered on the mountainside, dead.

'Wepps, show me where you spotted that tango on your thermal,' Juan said from the top of the crest.

Murph pointed out the approximate location. There appeared to be a cave close by.

That was Cabrillo's target. He issued orders for the rest of the team to check out the other caves as they raced down the mountain from their rocky perches.

Without the Delilah, the only chance they had to stop that missile was to destroy it by hand or seize the laptop controller.

But to achieve either, they had to find them first.

Grunting with each wincing step, Cabrillo made his way toward the cave Murphy had pointed out on the far side of the valley floor, his hand wrapped around the P90's thumbhole stock.

Higher up on the mountain slope Juan thought the valley looked like a natural amphitheater, but once he was on the bottom and glanced up, it felt like he was standing on the killing floor of the Roman Colosseum. The only thing that was missing were the gladiators.

A scream from behind a rock turned Juan on his heels, but not quickly enough. The Polish woman who had been manning the launch control in one of the hidden caves leaped out of nowhere and put three pistol rounds into his chest just as Juan cut loose with the P90.

Her gunshots hit his armor plate, knocking the breath out of him as he lost his balance.

But somehow Cabrillo's aim was true, and he stitched a row of armor-piercing rounds from the woman's hip to her chin. She spun around in a spray of blood as she crashed into the rocks.

'Chairman!' MacD's voice rang in Juan's comms as he climbed to his feet.

'All good – keep searching,' Cabrillo replied, gasping for air. He took a few deep breaths and caught his bearings, then swapped mags. The cave where Murphy thought the tango was hiding was just a hundred meters ahead. It was as good a guess as any where the BrahMos or its laptop controller might be.

He glanced back up at the ring of hills around him. He saw Raven duck into one cave, Murph into a second, and MacD into a third.

'Once more unto the breach . . .' Juan told himself as he charged forward.

Several limp steps toward the cave, Cabrillo heard a low rumble like a tank engine coming from the dark interior still ninety meters away. The volume and pitch increased as the noise accelerated out of the shadows. What emerged from the cave was worse than any tank.

Cabrillo had never seen such a large dog before – it was the size of a lion, and almost the same color. But the long black snout and speeding gait was all dog. Its wide, crazed eyes were bloodshot and the long teeth in its slavering mouth glistened in the sunlight.

Utterly shocked by the sensory overload, Juan froze. The dog lowered itself as it accelerated. It slowed just enough to spring-load its rear legs to pounce –

And its massive head erupted.

A second .50 BMG round tore into its spine just above the exploded neck. By the time the second supersonic round had found its mark, the two slower-traveling sonic waves of the gunshot blasts from Linc's Barrett finally caught up.

'Good shooting,' Cabrillo said in his comms. Having Linc high above on overwatch with that sniper rifle was like having an angel on his shoulder.

Maybe better.

'Too bad about his head,' Linc said. 'Would have made a great trophy on my cabin wall.'

'You would have needed a bigger wall,' Juan said as he jogged toward the cave entrance. 'Stay frosty up there.'

'Always.'

The cave's shadow was noticeably cooler, but was dusty, not damp. His comms lit up again. It was Raven.

'Found the missile.'

Cabrillo stopped in his tracks. 'Outstanding.'

'You want me to C4 this thing?'

Juan hesitated. Capturing a Zircon-style hypersonic missile would be a real intelligence coup. It was an Indian device, but built on Russian technology, the masters of the science. He could figure out a way to retrieve it later. . . .

But there might not be a later. That missile could be launched any second.

'Wreck it!' Cabrillo ordered and charged deeper into the cave.

Cabrillo crouched low as he pushed forward, his ears and eyes alert to sound and movement, but he heard and saw nothing.

He passed an empty portable camp table that could have been used for the laptop. A dozen cigarette butts littered the gritty dirt beneath it.

Twenty meters ahead, the cave took a wicked dogleg bend. He posted behind the natural wall that formed it. No telling what was around the corner.

'Chair . . . found . . . do . . .' Stoney's voice was breaking up in his comms. Cabrillo turned around and jogged back toward the cave entrance. The transmission cleared.

'Say again?' Juan asked.

'Repeat, a GLONASS targeting signal has been detected on a vessel in the Iranian port of Bushehr. It matches the earlier signal frequency Murphy found at the Yemen site.'

'That's gotta be the other missile.'

'I concur, sir. What do you want to do?'

What could he do? Cabrillo couldn't order an attack on an Iranian vessel in an Iranian port – that would be a *casus belli* for sure. And the same dilemmas still applied. That signal might just be pointing at the laptop and not the missile, but Juan's gut told him they were together.

But even if it wasn't pointed at the carrier, he couldn't let the Iranians have the BrahMos system, either. That would change the game in the Middle East, and maybe all of Eurasia.

'C4 in place, Chairman,' Raven called in.

Something was nagging at Cabrillo, but he couldn't place it. One of his brain's subroutines was running on overtime, solving an unspecified problem with uncertain data sets.

'Good job, Rave. Do it.'

'Yes, sir.' There was a short pause in Raven's comms while she checked her perimeter to make sure her teammates were clear.

In that instant, Cabrillo's subroutine found its solution.

Raven called out, 'Fire in the hole!'

'Belay that order, Raven!' Cabrillo shouted. 'Belay, belay, belay!'

'Standing down, Chairman. What's the problem?'

Juan began to explain his change of orders, when a flash-bang thudded by his feet. Before he could react, his ears were crushed by a sonic blast and his eyes blinded in a searing flash.

76

Juan's blinded eyes cleared into a blur, his ears still ringing with the flash-bang blast and muffled comms from his crew burbling in his skull. A sharp pain cut into his wrists. He flexed his hands. They were zip-tied behind his back. His ankles were bound together as well.

Salan stood over him, a wide grin smearing his proud Gallic face.

'Well, Sturges. How do you like the taste of your own medicine?'

'Sturges?' Juan grunted, his mind clouded. *What is he talking about?*

The Frenchman nodded. 'I didn't think that was your real name. What are you? CIA? DIA?'

'S.O.L.,' Juan said, a vascular migraine crushing the folds of his brain.

Salan frowned. 'Never heard of it.'

'You will.'

Cabrillo's vision cleared. He took note of the man's body. With his bulging eyes and veins, flushed skin, and cabling arms, he looked like a man trapped beneath a five-hundred-pound bench press he couldn't escape.

'Who are you?'

Salan snorted. 'The better man, clearly.'

'You work for Hightower.'

'No.'

'Then who?'

'Why do you care? Your time is very short. You should pray, if you have a weakness for religion.'

'Humor me.'

'*Cui bono?* That's all I will say.' Salan checked his watch.

'Am I keeping you from something?'

'Not at all. There is nowhere I would rather be on all the earth than here with you at this moment in history.'

'I'm flattered.'

Juan tried to get his bearings. Where was he? And how long had he been out?

A small portable LED lit up the enclosed space. Was he in the same cave? Another cave? A room within a cave? He couldn't make heads or tails of it.

Cabrillo recognized the ruggedized laptop lying on a flat rock. He groaned, but not from pain. He'd overplayed his hand, too smart by half. He should've had Raven blow the BrahMos. She wouldn't destroy it now. She was too good of a soldier to defy his orders.

Salan knelt down next to Cabrillo, holding a combat knife in his hand. He scratched an itch on his bearded face with the drop point tip. He saw where Juan's eyes were tracking and turned around.

'Ah, yes. The object of your desire. You came so close! And yet, it remains so far out of your reach. A pity.'

Salan laid the flat of his blade beneath one of Juan's blue eyes.

'I should do you the favor and blind you so that you

can't watch what I'm about to do to your aircraft carrier. Would you like me to do that for you?'

'Is this your idea of room service?'

Salan's phone buzzed. He turned and stood as he snatched it off his belt.

Still getting a signal down here, Juan thought, his mind clearing. But how? He craned his sore neck around until he spotted the cell signal booster cable running the length of the cave ceiling. He hadn't seen that before. He must be in a different cave. Salan must have picked him up and carried him. Another genetic monster.

Cabrillo clicked his molar mic with his tongue five times, a signal to his team that he was in trouble and couldn't speak. He doubted they could find him before his captor got too friendly with that knife, but it was worth a try.

'Immediately, sir!' Salan shut his phone. He turned toward Juan, helpless as a carp at the bottom of a boat.

'Well, Sturges. My employer has just given me the signal to launch the missile.' Salan waved the blade playfully in the air. 'But first things first.'

Salan stepped toward Juan.

Cabrillo's legs were pinned together. He lifted them and pointed the heels of his combat boots directly at Salan.

The Frenchman shook his head.

'What a pitiful defense! How do you say . . . "Not with a bang, but a whimper"?'

'In your case, it's the other way around.'

Juan flexed his right calf muscle, activating the electronic trigger of the single-shot 12-gauge shotgun secreted in his combat leg. The resulting blast erupting from Juan's heel launched a rifled Brenneke Magnum Crush slug, the caliber equivalent of a 20mm round. The three-inch shell's devastating recoil hammered Cabrillo's spine – and spoiled his aim. The shot went high.

But it was close enough. The grazing slug shattered the top of Salan's skull in a spray of blood and bone. His corpse crashed against the rock wall.

Juan's nearly deafened ears barely heard the shotgun blast, but he smiled as the bone-inducted voices of his team shouted his name in his skull.

They were searching for him.

And they were close.

MacD cut away Juan's cuffs at his wrists, while Raven slashed the ankle ties.

'Why didn't you want me to blow the missile?'

'Doesn't matter now. We have the laptop,' Linc said as he snatched it up in his hands.

'Help me up,' Cabrillo said. MacD and Raven lifted him to his wobbly legs.

'Stoney, you still tracking that second missile?'

'Chairman – you okay?'

'Answer me!'

'Yes, it's still on my screen.'

'Send me the coordinates.'

'On the way.'

Linc frowned, curious. 'You're not thinking . . . ?'

'Open up that laptop – and let's get outside for a better signal.'

The chief engineer continued to patiently point out the various screens on the BrahMos targeting software to General Sadeghi. He didn't dare tell the Quds Force general what he could and couldn't do, but having the laptop open and connected to the GLONASS system was incredibly foolish – and dangerous.

'Ingenious!' Sadeghi shouted, mesmerized by the simplicity of the program. He was pretending to target various American cities.

'Sir, do you have any other questions? If not, we should close it up. I would hate to drain the battery unnecessarily,' the engineer said, hopeful he wouldn't be caught in the lie.

'Just one more minute,' he barked.

The engineer mopped the sweat off his forehead. 'Of course, sir.'

Sadeghi got his minute, or almost all of it, before the hypersonic missile launched from Yemen by Cabrillo tore into the *Avatar*'s hull at nearly ten times the speed of sound.

The ship erupted in a boiling cloud of shredded steel, throwing molten shards a thousand meters in all directions, leveling anything standing it is explosive wake.

Two nearby warships were also sunk, and seven others damaged. Five warehouses were flattened, and hundreds of naval personnel on shore were cut down like dry grass.

Sadeghi was instantly vaporized when the missile struck,

along with all of the rocket engineers and the *Avatar*'s entire crew.

The BrahMos missile and its launch controller, the primary targets of Cabrillo's attack, were utterly destroyed.

Everything else was collateral damage.

77

On Board the Oregon
Several weeks later

Juan Cabrillo stood at his temporary standing desk, a vintage wooden shotgun ammo crate converted for the task by the Machine Shop. Its velvet feet were perched carefully atop a hand-carved executive desk that once belonged to a general in the Free French Army in North Africa.

His quarters were modeled after his favorite movie, *Casablanca.* It featured a unique blend of Moorish and French art deco styles decorated with period European and arabesque furnishings. Kevin Nixon even secured replica Bakelite phones, crystal lamps, and, best of all, an exact copy of Sam's upright piano from the movie café La Belle Aurore in all its battered glory.

He was holed up in his cabin finalizing his after-action report for Overholt along with a fat bill to cover his customary fee and an itemized list of his expenses, including the destruction of the DING. Overholt was a stickler for such accounting details, clinging to every penny of Uncle Sam's purse like each were his own.

The damaged AW was not expensed to the government. In fact, Gomez Adams was on the *Ford* at this very moment waiting to retrieve his beloved bird. Out of gratitude for their heroic efforts to save her ship, Captain

Dudash arranged for a Sikorsky CH-53E Super Stallion to airlift the wounded AW back to the *Ford* for repair in the carrier's state-of-the-art facilities.

'Chairman, Max Hanley for you on your private line,' Hali said in the overhead speakers. Dr Huxley had just cleared the *Oregon*'s comms director for active duty, fully recovered from his injuries. The Corporation didn't hand out medals like the Purple Heart, but Cabrillo did toss a nice little bonus into Kasim's last paycheck along with an extra week of paid vacation for his troubles.

'Thanks, Hali. I'm picking up now.'

Juan snatched up the Bakelite handset and put it to his ear.

'Max, everything okay? I wasn't expecting you back for a few more days.' As soon as the *Oregon* docked in Tel Aviv to deliver Sarai and Asher to an Israeli hospital, Max had caught a plane for San Diego.

'Vacation cut short. Kyle got called up unexpectedly. I'm stuck here at Bozeman airport with a three-hour flight delay, so I thought I would give you a ring and catch up on the latest.' Max had been out of reach since he'd left the ship. The last two weeks he and his son had been camping and hunting in Big Sky Country far beyond the reach of any cell tower. It was the first time he'd spoken to Juan since he'd left the *Oregon*.

'I gotta know. How was Kyle's ceremony?' Cabrillo was referring to Kyle Hanley's graduation from the US Navy SEAL Qualification Training Class in Coronado, California.

'The moment I saw that golden Trident pinned to his whites I thought I was going to keel over. I'm so proud of that kid.' Max's voice trailed off. The younger Hanley had been rescued out of the recidivist cult a few years back, got his head screwed on straight, and enlisted in the Navy.

'You have every right to be. Kyle's come a long way, and if he's like his old man, he has an amazing future ahead of him. Heck, if he ever musters out of service, maybe we can find a bunk for him on our little boat.'

'Wouldn't that be something?' Max said. 'But never mind all of that, I'm dying to know the details. What happened after I left?'

'Well, pardner, buckle in. It's quite a tale.'

'I'm all ears.'

Cabrillo glanced up at the antique brass maritime clock on the wall ticking away mercilessly. Time was short. He needed to cut to the chase if he didn't want to be late.

Cabrillo began with Overholt's recounting of events from his side of the desk, including the roundup of dozens of Salan's genetically modified mercenaries. If there were other mercs out in the world, they wouldn't live for more than a year from the date of their first conditioning. Without restorative treatment their metabolisms would burn out their organs or shred their vascular systems. The monstrous dogs all had to be put down.

The mercenaries who were captured were repatriated to their countries of origin. It was up to their respective national governments to decide what they wanted to do with them. The American government generously offered them free medical care to reverse the effects of Hightower's conditioning program.

'But there was one exception,' Juan said. 'A merc named Risto.'

Cabrillo went on to explain that, true to his word, Linc – with the help of Stoney and Murph – tracked Dr Aline Izidoro's killer to a safe house in Brisbane, Australia. The boys had managed to lift a partial fingerprint from the unusual 9×21mm Gyurza brass casing Linc had found in the Amazon. That fingerprint matched Risto's military records. The discovery of the specialized Russian MP-443 Yarygin pistol in Risto's possession confirmed their suspicions that he was the man who had murdered Aline.

With that evidence in hand, Dr Huxley confronted Risto in Brisbane. He bragged about his brutal murder of the missionary doctor a moment before he lunged for Hux's throat, but Linc put a bullet in his brainpan before his third step.

'What about the *Sekhmet*?' Max asked.

'She's riding the seabed.'

Juan described how Hightower's ship had finally been found and its operating systems hacked by Eric Stone, who then tripped its fire and carbon monoxide alarms, and triggered its automated 'Abandon ship!' warnings. The *Sekhmet*'s scientists and crew immediately abandoned ship. Cabrillo recorded everything with one of the *Oregon*'s camera drones including the massive below-the-waterline explosions that broke the vessel in half and sent her to the bottom.

'Neat trick,' Max said. 'I've got a feeling there's more to that story.'

'Let's just say I sent Overholt a copy of that drone recording along with the written testimony of one soaking-wet veterinary technician who said Hightower ordered the ship scuttled.'

'And?'

'What I didn't tell Overholt was that I offered the vet tech a get-out-of-jail-free card along with a first-class airline ticket back to her home in the Philippines if she would sign the testimony. I also forgot to mention that the massive explosions were caused by two of our wire-guided torpedoes, not Hightower's scuttling charges.'

'I bet Langston was drooling over the prospect of getting his hands on all of that technology.'

'He knows that biotech is the new arms race. A few of the rescued scientists had snatched up random thumb drives and file folders, but the bulk of the breakthrough technologies were lost with the *Sekhmet*.'

'Just as you planned, you clever dog,' Max said. 'Knowing you, you didn't want that kind of knowledge in the hands of secret government scientists working in unaccountable institutions.'

'And sinking the boat kept it from the bad guys, too.'

'What about the rescued scientists? They must have been a treasure trove.'

'Actually, they weren't.' Juan explained that the rescued scientists and technicians provided valuable bits and bobs of limited information. But after a week of interrogations at a CIA safe house in Djibouti, it became clear they were merely well-educated functionaries. The real genius behind the program was Dr Heather Hightower and she was nowhere to be found.

'Any clues as to her whereabouts?' Max asked.

'All we know is that she left the *Sekhmet* at its last port of call in Mogadishu, Somalia, without explanation, and made arrangements with the ship's captain to rendezvous in the near future. That's the last anyone has seen of her. Western intelligence agencies are still scrambling all over the globe trying to find her. They're scared to death she's fallen into enemy hands, willingly or otherwise.'

'Is that what you think?'

'No. I think she's gone to ground. I can only imagine the kind of monsters she's going to show up with when she comes back.'

Juan paused to clear his mind of those troubling thoughts. There was nothing he could do about Hightower. She was Overholt's concern now.

'How is Asher Massala doing?' Max asked.

'Sarai says his reversal treatments for his physical conditioning are going well.'

'And his mental condition?'

'His doctors assured Shin Bet that similar progress would eventually be made. But for now, most of his memories are still wiped clean, including all the evidence he gathered as an undercover operative in the Sons of Jacob organization.'

'That's too bad.'

'Well, the good news on that front is the Sons of Jacob are already being rolled up, thanks to intel gathered from our raid on Salan's ship, the *Cloud Fortune*.'

Juan shared one of the interesting tidbits the analysts had uncovered. Salan had in his possession a photo sent to him by the Sons of Jacob showing Juan in the back of an Israeli taxicab, along with Salan's notation.

Max chuckled. 'Greeting card salesman? I'm surprised you didn't call me on your shoe phone.'

'What can I say? I'm a sucker for Mel Brooks comedies.'

'Tell me about Sarai.'

'Her wounds are healing nicely. So nicely, in fact, that Linc is flying to Ashdod next week to spend his annual vacation with her, traveling the Mediterranean.'

'I thought maybe you and she . . .'

'I'm happy for them both.'

'Glad to hear it. They're good people.'

'The best.'

'Hey, wait a sec. There's an announcement. Let me put you on hold.' Max muted the phone.

Juan checked the maritime clock again. He might have to finish up this conversation later. He started to send a text to that effect, but Max came back on the line.

'Good news?' Juan asked.

'They pushed my flight another thirty minutes. I hope they don't close the bar in this place. I'm going to saunter in that direction.'

'Put it on our tab,' Juan said. 'After all, this is a business call.'

'Thanks, boss. I've been in this game long enough to know there's gotta be a wizard behind a curtain somewhere.'

'Your instincts are spot-on.'

Cabrillo went on to explain that Prince Khalid was the real mastermind behind the plot to steal the two hypersonic missiles, giving one to the Iranians and using the other to sink the *Ford*. He also relayed the fact Khalid was dead.

'By whose hand?' Max asked.

'Well, that's a story unto itself.'

According to Overholt, the news of Prince Abdullah's sudden demise roused the debilitated Saudi king from his deathbed. But it was the intel Murph and Stoney had extracted from Salan's phone and a thumb drive from Nine Saints that condemned Khalid to his final doom.

'The Saudi government's official report was that Khalid had died unexpectedly from natural causes,' Juan said. 'But Overholt learned from his Saudi intelligence contacts the true cause of Khalid's death was, in fact, the natural consequence of separating the man's skull from his neck, beheaded under the king's vengeful eye in the privacy of His Majesty's palace.'

'I'm guessing what seemed a merciful execution for Khalid's heinous crimes was, in fact, just the king's way of protecting the royal family from shame,' Max said.

'Exactly.'

'And what about our dear friends, the Iranians? They've got to be madder than scalded cats.'

'The mullahs called the missile attack on its naval facility in Bushehr an act of war. Iranian intelligence variously blamed either the Americans or the Israelis or both, despite the fact the BrahMos originated from Yemen in the territory of its regional ally, the Houthis.'

'So, they must be gearing up for war,' Max said.

'Actually, no. We pulled a real twofer. We gave Mossad actionable intelligence and they fed it to their operatives in Tehran, proving to the mullahs that while the missile had originated from Houthi-controlled territory, it was in fact two rogue Quds Force operatives who carried out the mission. So not only was a regional war avoided, the mullahs are now waging an internal purge of the Quds Force.'

'Letting the bad guys take out the bad guys. That's a nice piece of work.'

'And I forgot to mention that Langston, ever the gentleman, put in a good word for Sarai with Mossad, and gave her all deserved credit for the role she played in the entire affair. As a result of his report, Mossad officially forgave Sarai for her past transgressions. In so doing, the old fox also cleared his name and his letter of reprimand was expunged from his personnel file.'

'He never misses a trick, does he?'

The maritime clock chimed the hour.

'Hey, Max, gotta run. We'll hoist a few when you get back.'

'Sounds like a plan. Stay frosty out there.'

'Always.' Cabrillo hung up the phone.

Now it was time to have some fun.

Maurice lay in his bed propped up on pillows, and though dressed in pajamas – tailored and pressed, of course – he exuded an elegant confidence.

Dr Huxley's surgical skills had proven more than a match to his grievous wounds and his recovery had been exemplary under her care. He rather admired the stitchery she had rendered on his taut but pale stomach, now growling with hunger. His only sustenance had been a liquid diet since his surgery.

'I heard that,' Dr Huxley said. 'Either you're hiding a howler monkey under those bedsheets or you're ready to eat something solid.'

Maurice smiled. 'I suppose I am rather peckish.'

'I've arranged for a special meal for you. It should be here shortly.'

'I can't wait.'

There was a soft knock at the door.

'Right on time,' Huxley said as she slid the hospital bed tray into position. 'Come in.'

The thick wooden door swung open. Its finely carved oak timbers fit the decorative theme of Maurice's cabin, modeled after a fifteenth-century Tudor country house. Everyone assumed the English steward's choice of decor was aspirational. In fact, it was autobiographical – a replication of his childhood home. He had even managed to acquire a few pieces of furniture from the grand estate without raising any suspicions from Juan or the crew.

The linen-covered serving cart inched through the doorway, its silver serving cover gleaming in the lights as Juan angled through the door.

Maurice leaned forward. 'Captain?'

Cabrillo was resplendent in Maurice's customary livery. He wore black slacks with a crease sharp enough to slice a country ham, a crisp white shirt starched and stiff, spit-polished wing tips, and a waiter's cloth draped over one forearm.

'Sir, this is completely untoward,' Maurice protested. 'You are the captain.' He threw off his bedsheets and began to rise. Huxley laid a firm hand on his chest and gently pushed him back down.

Juan snapped his waiter's cloth like a bullfighter's cape, then stepped over to the bed, leaned over, and gently tucked the napkin into Maurice's pajama shirt.

'I may be the captain, sir. But you are the man who saved my ship and the lives of my crew. I am forever grateful.'

'We all are,' Huxley said as she wiped away a tear. She

knew well that Maurice had risked his life to protect her honor as well as her life.

Maurice shrugged. 'I merely did my duty, as did we all.'

'No, sir,' Juan said. 'You went far and above your assigned responsibilities.'

Maurice sat up straighter. 'It has been the greatest honor of my life to serve under you, my captain, and to stand with this valiant crew through every hazard, storm, and strife. I could do no less.' He took Hux's fingers into his own. 'You both have saved me in more ways than you can possibly know.'

Juan stood. 'No greater love, my friend. No greater love.'

The old steward's face softened. 'Ah, yes. The words of the Great Captain.'

Juan rolled the cart up to his bed and lifted the serving cover with a flourish. He pointed out each item on the menu.

'Poached eggs on lightly toasted crumpets. Steel-cut oats with Finlandia butter and single-forest organic Canadian maple syrup. And finally, Earl Grey tea with a splash of milk and a dab of raw Manuka honey, just as you like it.'

'My compliments to the chef for the sumptuous feast.'

'You're welcome,' Juan said as he set the food on the bedside tray.

Maurice's eyes widened. 'My, you are full of surprises.'

'You're one to talk,' Huxley said.

Maurice cut into a poached egg and crumpet, spilling the gooey yolk.

Juan shot a look at Huxley. She nodded. *Now is the time.*

Cabrillo cleared his throat. 'Maurice, you always seem to know everything that's going on aboard this ship.'

Maurice took a bite of the yolk-soaked crumpet.

Juan smiled conspiratorially. 'Have you heard the latest scuttlebutt?'

The Englishman rolled his eyes with delight. 'This egg is done to perfection.'

'Everybody wants to know your story,' Hux said. 'There's obviously more to you than meets the eye. Much more.'

Maurice took another bite.

'You clearly have combat training and experience,' Juan said. 'Royal Marines?'

Maurice nodded at Juan's clothing. 'I commend your sartorial selection, Captain. Does this mean I should seek employment elsewhere?'

'British Army, then?' Huxley asked.

Maurice fought back a smile as he dabbed away a drip of egg from his chin.

Juan shook his head. 'You are a mystery wrapped in an enigma, my dear fellow.'

Maurice gestured at his breakfast. 'With your permission?'

'Of course,' Cabrillo said. 'Dig in while it's still hot. We can talk later.'

'As always, I am happy to obey your orders.'

Juan relished the sight of Maurice tucking into his food like a starving orphan. The man's courage, loyalty, and self-sacrifice had saved his crew and slain Hightower's monsters.

Hightower.

Cabrillo's blood ran cold at the thought of the deranged scientist reemerging from her hidden lair, wreaking havoc on the human race with her hellish technology.

And if not her, then some other devil who could soon rise up with the same hideous strength.

No matter, Juan thought, as a peace settled over him.

There was always hope while sturdy souls like Maurice stood ready for the fight, come what may.

He just wanted a decent book to read ...

Not too much to ask, is it? It was in 1935 when Allen Lane, Managing Director of Bodley Head Publishers, stood on a platform at Exeter railway station looking for something good to read on his journey back to London. His choice was limited to popular magazines and poor-quality paperbacks – the same choice faced every day by the vast majority of readers, few of whom could afford hardbacks. Lane's disappointment and subsequent anger at the range of books generally available led him to found a company – and change the world.

'We believed in the existence in this country of a vast reading public for intelligent books at a low price, and staked everything on it'
Sir Allen Lane, 1902–1970, founder of Penguin Books

The quality paperback had arrived – and not just in bookshops. Lane was adamant that his Penguins should appear in chain stores and tobacconists, and should cost no more than a packet of cigarettes.

Reading habits (and cigarette prices) have changed since 1935, but Penguin still believes in publishing the best books for everybody to enjoy. We still believe that good design costs no more than bad design, and we still believe that quality books published passionately and responsibly make the world a better place.

So wherever you see the little bird – whether it's on a piece of prize-winning literary fiction or a celebrity autobiography, political tour de force or historical masterpiece, a serial-killer thriller, reference book, world classic or a piece of pure escapism – you can bet that it represents the very best that the genre has to offer.

Whatever you like to read – trust Penguin.